Moonwish

Sundowners Book Two

R.L. Merrill

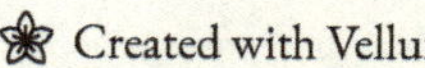
Created with Vellum

For those willing to fight til your last breath for the ones you love... I see you.

PROLOGUE

One week after the incident at Loch Lomond

Timothy Hicks

The employees squirmed before him, and he enjoyed every bit of their terror. He bathed in it, slathered it on like expensive skin products that promised to make you beautiful and didn't do shit. Once it soaked into his pores, it took mere seconds to light up his synapses like one of those high-speed films of cars on a freeway.

The power of fear. It made Timothy Hicks giddy. Made his dick hard, too.

He sat at the head of the table in a stark white conference room, underground in a bunker owned by BioBourne, the company his wife, Donna, had made wildly successful before she became a liability. Not only was Timothy now in charge of BioBourne's operations, but somehow, he'd managed to evade the police and take the reins of the western division of EVE: an amorphous entity called Elite Ventures Enterprises, which catered to the rich, powerful… and medically desperate. He glowered at his close circle of minions who had so far been less than helpful in cleaning up the fiasco left by his predecessor, Stephen Adams.

"With Adams out of the picture, my wife missing, and The Source out of our hands, we need to make a solid plan. We've got distributors lined up to carry the product to our clients, and I will not default on our agreements. So somebody better come up with a plan to get production back on track, or there will be consequences for all of you."

One of the things he'd learned over the past decade as CEO of his previous company was that the best way to get results from one's employees was to give them everything they could ever want, and then impress upon them the knowledge that it could all be taken away. Employees should like and respect those in charge, but above all, they should fear them. Just a little. Enough to keep them on their toes.

The employees sitting in this conference room in the BioBourne bunker were petrified.

"Mr. Hicks, sir? There is the possibility we don't need The Source to continue producing our, um, serum."

Courtney was one of the few women who'd been allowed to remain on the board at BioBourne when EVE took over the biomedical research company and put Hicks in charge. She was smart, hungry, and had plenty to lose if he needed leverage on her.

EVE had chosen wisely when they'd taken Timothy on in Stephen's absence. Yes, they had accumulated a lot of wealthy and influential people in the Bay Area, but those members were old. Timothy knew that old people usually wanted more time. They were in this game to find the fountain of youth or its equivalent. They believed that The Source was the answer to their prayers, that if they just waited long enough for technology to catch up, they could harness the power of this being who just might possess the gift of immortality.

In the meantime, the board members of EVE had expanded their research into other areas, including "health retreats," where clients who were members of EVE and their immediate family members were being treated for a plethora of ailments with trials of the synthetic serum created from The Source's blood. Through companies like BioBourne, EVE had the means to continue producing it.

That's where Timothy saw his opportunity. From adolescence, Timothy had known he was special. He had a little trick hidden up his sleeve that benefited him greatly, and it was just what was needed to overcome the current hiccup in EVE's plans.

With The Source out of reach, they either needed to find a way to work with the material they had already harvested to make the serum, or they needed to take their research in another direction and pray for success. There were an awful lot of ridiculously wealthy people waiting on this promised serum that would keep them young... indefinitely.

Hicks leaned back in his chair and linked his fingers over his chest. "And how would that be possible? We still haven't identified all of the particular elements necessary for the formula."

Courtney flicked her long, straight black hair over her shoulder and hesitated, as though debating whether or not she wanted to give Timothy the information she was holding on to.

She shouldn't tell him, and he figured she knew it. He had proven to be ruthless, often unscrupulous when it came to furthering EVE's mission.

"There are others who have been blessed by The Source and who practice The Way. They may not be as old or as potent, but it's worth analyzing their blood."

"Stephen told us the others in his cohort were slaughtered. He and Caleb are in police custody... Who else is there?"

She pulled up a file on her computer and asked to have access to the projector. He nodded at her and she connected. On screen popped three pictures.

"Mark Bullock. One who goes only by Cross; we don't have another name for him. And then there's Creed Lowell."

Timothy looked closely at the three men on screen. "And what do we know of these acolytes?"

"My source at the police department says that Stephen recruited Bullock and Cross to step in at the failed ceremony."

Stephen was in way over his head by the time Timothy joined EVE with his wife, Donna. He was short-tempered, prone to histrionics, and refused to let anyone get too near The Source. He'd kept his knowledge under wraps, so if he knew these men, knew they'd been in town, he'd kept it to himself for some reason. Was he trying to control them? Was he intimidated by them? The man preyed on people's fears, but for some reason, he appeared to have succumbed to his own. From what Timothy had learned of the night of the ritual, he'd basically surrendered and put up very little fight when the police arrived.

Timothy wasn't sorry he was gone.

"Interesting. And what about Lowell?"

The corner of her lip turned up, which stirred something in Timothy's groin. "According to my source, he's a nurse. He told law enforcement that he's been using what he learned from The Source for the past fifty years to heal the elderly in care homes around the country."

Hicks gazed closely at the pictures. All three images were taken outside at night, with only parking lot lights to illuminate their faces. But one fact was clear.

"You said he's been a nurse for fifty years? And these other men? They supposedly were in the commune with Stephen?"

"Yes, sir," she said.

None of the three men looked a day over thirty. Lowell, in fact, looked like a fresh-faced, straight-out-of-college kid. Stephen had mentioned there were others who had left The Source over the years, so if he knew these men existed—men who could have been useful test subjects—and he'd kept that information from EVE? They must be valuable, or he knew they wouldn't cooperate. That wouldn't be a problem for Timothy.

"Where can we find these three?"

She fidgeted slightly in her seat, the only acknowledgment that she was nervous about sharing this info.

"They were taken into federal custody at Loch Lomond and no one local has heard from them."

Hicks raised an eyebrow at her. "No one disappears completely, not in this day and age. Perhaps you could take a closer look, see what you can find out from your... source." It was good to have law enforcement in one's pocket. That fact was partly why Timothy had been able to find his wife when she'd run the first time. He'd caught her, but then after the debacle at the lake, she'd been taken back into protective custody, and no one seemed to know where they were keeping her. For all he knew, she was hanging out with The Source.

He vowed to get her back. She had a punishment coming to her. *I always get what I want.* But right now, he wanted to keep EVE on track. They had serum to deliver to their clients and they had some big promises to deliver upon. Nothing—not the lack of The Source, his missing wife, nor any law enforcement entity—would keep them from success.

"There might be a way to make them surface."

He turned his chair to face her. "And what would that be?" Courtney was trying her best to make herself useful. He appreciated her initiative.

"Lowell's boyfriend is in a convalescent hospital in town."

Hicks folded his hands under his chin. "And where one's true love lies... Excellent work, Courtney. Be sure to see me after the meeting."

She nodded and unplugged her computer from the projector.

Moments after he ended the meeting and gave the group their assignments, Courtney appeared in the doorway to his current office, ready to do battle for him and EVE.

She'd given him a lot of information that could be useful, and he intended to use it. He'd get what he needed from her. Maybe even more than she bargained for.

He always got what he wanted.

ONE

R oman

Three Weeks after the incident at Loch Lomond

The human body is a miraculous machine. Think about it. The liver can regenerate itself in as little as four weeks, the human brain can retain an amount of information equal to 20,000 dictionaries, and the circulatory system acts as a high-speed transportation system, moving 8,000 liters of the life-giving, life-sustaining elixir around our body every day that we all need to survive.

Blood.

I'd never given much thought to my blood until it was taken from me involuntarily. Not spilled, not withdrawn in a medical procedure... no. It had been *removed*. Pints of it. And I couldn't even be mad. Well, I could, but then I'd have to be mad at the man I'd fallen ridiculously in love with, and since he was the reason I got out of bed every day, and the reason I was currently strapped with wires all over my torso while running—walking, I mean—I had to let that shit go. I wouldn't be running for a long time to come, if ever.

I could be mad. Or at least perturbed, but I wasn't. Not really.

"Creed Lowell, I swear, when I get out of this place, I'm going to kick your ass—"

"Mmm, I can't wait."

The treadmill slowed to a stop. I grabbed for my water bottle while the nurses got the readings from my latest test, and I gasped like I'd just finished a marathon. Hopefully I'd done better this time and would be one step closer to getting released from the convalescent hospital. I felt better, stronger, but I still needed to use a cane, and I was nowhere near the shape I'd been in before. Hypovolemic shock is a bitch.

Creed's smile on the screen of the SAT phone made the pain lessen somewhat, though being kept away from him hurt more than I could stand.

"You're such a tease," I said, between gasps for air. "You're going to be in so much trouble when I get out of this place."

Creed sighed. "Promise? How much longer, have they said?"

The thing driving me through my rehab was that I knew Creed needed me as much, if not more, than I needed him, and I was desperate to be with him again. This FaceTime bullshit wasn't cutting it.

The door opened and my uncle—Santa Cruz PD Officer Reynaldo Cabral—entered with a laugh.

"Hey, Six Dollar Man, you almost done? I gotta get back." My uncle could be an asshole—my favorite nickname for him was Dicknaldo, after all—but he was just as anxious for me to get out of rehab and back to my life as I was. It wasn't only because he was sick and tired of being our go-between. He had possession of the super-secret bat phone that Creed and I had to use to communicate. Creed was being kept at a classified location by an FBI agent who was working with a non-governmental task force to deal with the events that put me here.

No. Uncle Rey wanted me out of here so we could all focus on finding the people who'd been wreaking havoc on our hometown, and who regularly took blood and energy from people without their permission.

The plan was that as soon as I was well enough to be released, I'd be secreted away in the dead of night to be reunited with my lover. It sounded like the plot of a romance novel, but in reality, it was much more serious than that.

"Six Dollar... fuck off. I'll be done in a minute." I used a towel to wipe my face, cringing at the thought that once upon a time, I could run a six-minute mile, and now walking for six minutes at two-point-five miles per hour had me sweating buckets and wrung out.

"Sorry, Rey. It's my fault we're taking so long. I love watching him sweat." Creed winked at me, but the absence of his multi-watt smile let me know that while this rehab was physically torturing me, it was torturing him by proxy.

"No problem, Nurse Creed. By the way, Vanessa wanted me to let you know that she's sitting in on Stephen's deposition tomorrow. Agent Barringer is going to be participating remotely as well, so I'm sure he'll keep you updated as much as he can."

"I'm aware," Creed said, his expression going dark. "Any word on Timothy Hicks?"

Rey shook his head. "Not yet. We've managed to get a few more names of folks involved, however, and it looks like what Stephen was saying about being a pawn may be sort of true."

"Bullshit," Creed said, but it was more of a summation than an interjection.

After my exsanguination at Loch Lomond in the Santa Cruz mountains, Stephen Adams had been captured by my intrepid aunt, Detective Vanessa Cabral. She'd barely kept herself from beating him to within an inch of his existence after he'd kidnapped her wife and son, and yours truly. But all Stephen would say was that everything he'd done was to care for The Source, that he had nothing to do with the attacks in town, nor the biomedical and financial organizations. We knew that wasn't true—at the very least, he would be charged with attempted murder, kidnapping, and the murders of the four young men who'd been leading the terror campaign in downtown Santa Cruz. Stephen Adams would never be a free man again.

It wasn't enough.

"I know," Rey said. "But I'm no detective, so what the fuck do I know? Anyway, I'll give you two a minute to wrap things up."

He stepped back out into the hallway, and I smiled down at Creed, who winced.

"As much as I love seeing you without a shirt, I'm not a fan of your current accessories."

I looked down at myself and poked at the monitors. "I don't mind it. Hopefully the doctor will like my results this time." I pulled the phone closer to my face. "How are you, though?"

Creed's smile didn't have the charm it used to, and the dark circles under his eyes worried me, though he always argued that he was fine.

"I'll be better when I can kiss you. Hold you. Who are you that you've turned me from a solitary man into one who *pines*? I may be the mythological creature of darkness in this relationship, but it's you who's put a spell on me."

If he'd been himself, if he'd smiled that flirty smile of his, I would have laughed out loud at his proclamation. But he was serious.

"There's nothing dark about you, and you know it. Babe, I'm sorry. I'm trying my hardest. If all my tests look good in the next few days, the doctors will start making discharge plans."

"I know you are, Roman. I'm just being morose. Ignore me. Please, take your time. You need to be well. I'm fine."

"You're not fine, though." I cocked my head to the side. "Have you, you know, been taking care of yourself?"

Creed smiled weakly. "Mr. Fletcher being here helps. I'm doing the best I can."

"What about... have you gone to *them*?"

The *them* I referred to was the center of this whole fucking debacle. The Source. If I were to believe everything I'd been told, they were an ancient being who had somehow figured out how to cheat death. I still wasn't too clear on the process, but there was no denying The Source was powerful.

"Cross and Mark have. I don't... I can't. I won't."

"But if it will help you—"

"I'm making do with what I have. Barringer and I are working on some additional, uh, energy resources."

"And I'll be there soon."

Creed's answering smile let me know what he wasn't able to say. He was struggling, and while he would never ask me to do anything that would set back my recovery, he *needed* from me. He needed *me*, and that was something that would continue to drive me until I was back in his arms.

"Soon," he breathed.

We could have said more, but we knew we were being monitored, and what we most wanted to say to each other was better left for the time we were truly alone.

"I promise. Stay well, okay? And hug Rhonda for me." I'd become awfully close with Creed's Doberman before the shit hit the fan. I missed her almost as much as I missed him.

Creed snorted. "Wherever she is. Traitor. She's enjoying herself way more than I am."

I gave him a sad smile and touched the screen with my index finger.

"Soon." And then the line disconnected. My eyes burned and I rested my weight on the treadmill bars, a wave of sadness threatening to buckle my pitiful knees.

I had to be strong for Creed during our infrequent calls, but returning to the status of a disabled person was infuriating and at times debilitating. I thought I'd hated it after my first near-death experience. I'd been surfing the often treacherous waves at Steamers Lane in Santa Cruz when I'd gotten caught by the undertow, and smacked my temple on a rock under the surface, giving me a concussion and rupturing my eardrum, along with the wonderful secondary lifetime afflictions of vertigo and tinnitus. Yay. Things had been much better in that department, actually, until Creed came along.

I wasn't complaining though.

See, for all intents and purposes, Creed was a vampire in that his survival depended on access to human-created energy and blood. He was no Dracula, although he *was* sexy as hell. He had this chemical he referred to as a pheromone that he released, which relaxed his... well, I don't want to call them *prey*, because that did make him sound like Dracula.

His "willing participant." The person relaxes, Creed says a blessing, he sinks his evolutionarily sharp teeth into a vein close to the surface, under thin skin, and he takes three pulls of blood. No more. He follows a very strict ritual that he was taught by acolytes of The Source decades ago. And that act, along with being a human energy recycling plant, has kept him from aging and gives him tremendous strength. He's spent his existence post-cult life taking care of elderly people in the evenings, when they need it most, feeding on their negative energy while providing healing energy in return. I'd seen him do it with my grandmother, and it was truly a miracle to behold.

Unfortunately, not all of the people who were instructed in the ways he was used their power for good.

And that, my friends, is how I came to be disabled once again. I fucking hated this shit.

"You and loverboy all done?" Rey called from the hallway. "The nurses want to unhook you from your wires and you need to get back to bed."

I groaned. "I don't want to go back to bed."

Yeah, I sounded like a whiny brat, but I was so tired of this.

"I know," Rey said quietly. He stood next to the treadmill, maybe to catch me, maybe for emotional support, as the nurses unhooked all of the wires and assured me I was continuing to make improvements. They handed me a second towel to mop up the ridiculous amount of sweat I'd conjured up.

"The doctor will see you this afternoon and go over the results."

I thanked them, and they left Rey to escort me back to my room. I pulled on my UCSC Banana Slugs sweatshirt and reached for my cane. *Jesus.* Twenty-five, almost twenty-six years old, and I needed a damn cane to get around.

"I really think you ought to revamp your wardrobe when you get out of here. Canes are rad, dude. You could start wearing tweed and shit like a real college professor."

I rolled my eyes. "I *am* a real college professor. Or I almost was. At this rate, I'll go straight from grad student to retiree. Fuck, Rey, how the hell am I supposed to finish my program? How the hell will I ever get a job if I can't even walk down the hall without running out of steam?" I knew better than to let myself wallow because it took energy I didn't have to waste.

"You're getting stronger all the time, pamangkin. You're going to be fine. What you need is patience, and I know that doesn't come easy for you."

I grunted in agreement. Rey knew me better than I knew myself. I think I reminded him of how he was as a teenager. He hadn't gotten in nearly as much trouble as I had, but then, he and my aunt Vanessa had survived a childhood marked with tragedy.

Their parents died at Jonestown.

"I know, I know. I'm trying. It's just—it's been almost a month."

"Yeah... since you *died*! You seem to forget that fun little fact. You're lucky to be out of bed at all. Now be a good patient. I've got a treat for you."

He said that like he was talking to a dog, and I wished I had it in me to deck him. Not really, though. I merely wanted the ability.

We entered my room, and I went straight to the bed "like a good patient." I carefully lowered myself onto the mattress, in case my arms or legs decided to take a vacation on me. My blood pressure was still prone to dangerously low levels, and I continued to suffer bouts of fatigue. I'd slept more since I'd died than in all of the years I'd been in higher educa-tion. The doctors couldn't tell me how long it would take for me to get back to my previous level of fitness. They wouldn't assure me I *could even* be that fit again. Thankfully the damage to my kidneys was moderate and not severe enough that I'd need dialysis. Yet. That's all we knew at the moment of my prognosis. It was a day-at-a-time scenario.

"Your roommate get liberated?" Rey asked.

"Let's get you reconnected here, Mr. San Angelo." My nurse, Wilhelmina, reconnected my heart monitor, the pulse ox finger thingie, and made sure my oxygen was within reach in case I needed it. Fucking old man shit up in here.

I looked to the empty bed next to mine and sighed. "Mr. Chu adequately recovered from his hip replacement surgery and his family picked him up yesterday." Yeah, Mr. Chu was like ninety years old, and even he healed faster than me. I'd been through two roommates already. "Apparently, I'm getting a new roommate sometime today."

"Hopefully they won't be put out by the sheer number of books you've managed to collect. Speaking of... Pliny the Elder, huh? A little light reading?"

"Yes! Thank you!"

Rey dug in his messenger bag and pulled out a large tome. "Ms. Beckett at the library wanted to make sure you had everything you needed and insisted that I bring these over right away." He tossed his nonexistent hair and slid pretend glasses down his nose to wink at me.

"Eh, she likes Creed more than me." I accepted the book from him and my weak-ass heart sped up just enough, but not too much to make my monitor start freaking out.

"You finding anything interesting in these books?"

I'd already cracked open the Pliny and was running my fingers over the page. "Yeah. Humans have been ingesting human blood for a long fucking time."

Rey cursed under his breath and hooked his thumbs in his utility belt. "Weird fucking shit. Didn't I tell you how tired I am of weird shit?"

"Uh-huh." I was already immersed in the book, ready to tune everything out.

"Yeah, yeah, I know you and your books. Hey, remember tomorrow I'm busting you out for evening bingo, so rest up, hear me? Lola wants to see you."

"Uh-huh."

My grandmother's move to an assisted-living facility was the catalyst for the events that led me here. Creed was her nurse at Puesta Del Sol. I'm not sure who she missed more, him or me. As far as she or anyone at the home knew, he'd had a family emergency out of state. The saddest part was that with him gone, Puesta Del Sol was a melancholy place. Sure, Lola and her sisters still watched their programs and played bingo, but she was deteriorating at a more rapid pace without his healing. Who knew how long we had with her, and here I was being an old man myself. Thankfully I was making progress. The sooner I could get out of there, the better for all involved.

I was pretty sure Rey said goodbye before he left, but I was deep into Pliny's description of peasants running into the ring toward fallen gladiators to drink from their open wounds, how they believed the vitality and strength these warriors possessed could be gleaned through their fresh blood.

There were so many instances of humans resorting to blood drinking, which they thought provided physical benefits... What if La Mente, or whatever the organization was calling itself these days, traced its practices back to these ancient times?

I couldn't wait to go over all of this with Creed. I had a mountain of examples to share with him, as soon as I was well enough.

A knock sounded on the doorjamb sometime later, jarring me from the text.

"Hello, Mr. San Angelo," Wilhelmina said. "I'd like for you to meet your new roommate, Dr. Alistair Gardner."

Two orderlies wheeled in a gurney with a silver-haired, gaunt old white man with piercing blue eyes. He may have been wheeled in, but he looked ready to do battle.

"Nice to meet you," I said, watching him curiously.

He gazed around the room with a raised eyebrow. "You as well," he said. I detected a faint accent.

"You two should have plenty to talk about, seeing as you're both in academia."

I smiled and steeled myself for the comments. Every older white male professor I'd met throughout my journey discounted me as a young blowhard with no substance to back it up.

"Splendid," he said. "What is your discipline?"

"Criminal Psychology. And you?"

The old man grinned. "Cultural Anthropology, with an emphasis on paganism in ancient and medieval times."

It was my turn to grin. I rubbed my hands together. "Emphasis on cults and criminal behavior. *Very* nice to meet you."

"Now, no getting excited, Mr. San Angelo. The doctor will be in shortly to discuss your test results and if he sees you getting riled up—"

"I know, I know, he'll take my books away."

Mr. Gardner raised both eyebrows this time. "Cruel and unusual punishment. What's next? Drawn and quartered? The Iron Maiden? I know all the best torture techniques, but taking books away from an academic is barbaric."

I laughed. "Good to know you have my back."

Wilhelmina did some work on Mr. Gardener's chart, and then checked my monitor.

"Your oxygen is kinda low. Let's get you hooked up for a bit, shall we?"

I grumbled, but my nurse laughed. She was used to this routine.

"I thought I'd be the grumpy old man in this scenario," Mr. Gardner said. "What's a young man like you doing hooked up to oxygen?"

I groaned and leaned my head back into the stack of pillows, my eyes falling closed. "How long you got?"

Transcripts from the Interview of Stephen Adams

My name is Eleanor LaBeau, Special Agent in Charge from the FBI Campbell Field Office, and today is November 20, 2022, and it is nine twenty-two a.m. Pacific Standard Time. I am recording this interview with subject Stephen Adams. We are in Conference Room B at the Santa Cruz Police Department for a follow-up interview about the events that occurred at Loch Lomond in Santa Cruz County, on the night of November 1, 2022. Joining us in person are Detective Vanessa Cabral and Captain Jaime Rojas, from the Santa Cruz Police Department, and via Zoom we have Special Agent Todd Barringer, and consultant Dr. Denny Verdell from the University of California San Francisco. Representing Mr. Adams is Alicia Plunkett, from Plunkett, Withers, and Soon Associates.

EL: Good morning, Mr. Adams. Before we start, can you please state your name, birthdate, and occupation.

SA: Stephen Adams, birthdate April 1, 1986, and until recently, I was the CEO of the financial firm Elite Ventures Enterprises.

EL: Thank you. And do you have any aliases? Any other names you've gone by?

AP: You don't have to answer that.

EL: Ms. Plunkett, Mr. Adams is not being compelled to testify, this is not a deposition, we're trying to get the facts straight about the crimes he's been accused of.

SA: Stephen Allman. Before I—

AP: Mr. Adams, you do not have to discuss any of this, and as your attorney, I advise you to not answer any of these questions.

SA: I just want it to be over.

EL: What do you want to be over?

SA: My service.

AP: Mr. Adams—

SA: I'm tired.

EL: Can I get you some coffee? Some water?

SA: Not that kind of tired. I want this to be over.

AP: May I confer with my client? Alone?

EL: This recording stopped at nine twenty-nine a.m. by request of defense attorney.

EL: The recording has been started again at nine fifty-three a.m. Defense council Alicia Plunkett has departed these proceedings at the request of her client, Mr. Stephen Adams.

EL: Thank you, Mr. Adams, for speaking with us. You are proceeding with this interview against your attorney's wishes?

SA: Yes. I just want this to be over.

EL: And you have been read your Miranda rights, and you understand that anything you say can be used against you in a court of law?

SA: Yes, ma'am.

EL: Thank you. You told us your name is Stephen Adams, and I asked if you had any aliases, any other names you have gone by?

SA: (clears throat) Stephen Allman.

EL: Thank you. And what is the birthdate of Stephen Allman?

SA: April 1, 1948.

EL: When did you first come to Santa Cruz County?

SA: 1968. I joined the Gateway of the Sun community.

EL: What can you tell me about the Gateway of the Sun community?

SA: They said they could teach us to heal people. I soon discovered we'd be doing this using energy we manipulated with our minds. I was looking for a roof over my head. Some food. I would have followed them anywhere food was involved at the time.

EL: And what happened once you joined the community? What, if anything, did you learn there?

SA: Mostly about what you'd call chakras, energy centers, and moving energy within our own bodies, some herbal remedies. Stuff like that. They were very strict, the teachers. I went along with whatever they said as long as they fed me. I'd been starving on the streets—I didn't want that life. I did whatever I had to do to survive. That's all I've ever done.

EL: What can you tell us about the one they call The Source?

SA: I don't want to talk about them.

EL: Can you at least tell us what your relationship was with them?

SA: I said I don't want— Look, shit went down, and The Source can't be left alone, understand? They needed someone to take care of them, and I got stuck with the job. It wasn't my fault.

EL: What wasn't your fault?

SA: What happened at Loch Lomond. The whole bullshit you arrested me for. I just want out; I want to be free of them.

EL: Let's back up. How long were you with the community?

SA: Three years.

EL: Was it there before you came or was it a new organization?

SA: I don't know what was there before I got there.

EL: You don't know whether the Gateway was a group before? What about The Source? Were they a teacher—

SA: I don't want to talk about them.

EL: Okay. What led you to leave the community after three years?

SA: There was a disagreement. Some of the teachers decided to break with the teachings, some of the students chose to leave. No one was willing to take on the care of The Source, so I took them with me.

EL: So it was an amicable separation?

SA: People chose to leave. No one forced us to be there and no one was keeping us there. Nothing about the community was forced. I don't care what you've heard.

EL: So you took The Source with you away from the property where you'd lived for three years. Did anyone else come with you?

SA: I'm only going to talk about myself.

EL: Fine. Where did you go with The Source?

SA: We traveled. For a while. I needed to keep them away from people. They... As I've said, I don't want to talk about them.

EL: Okay. How about telling me how you got by? Where did you get the means to survive?

SA: The others... they left money. I invested it. I had... connections. I invested the money in biomedical research, made a fortune, and then created Elite Ventures Enterprises to continue investing in this important work.

EL: And are you still the CEO of EVE?

SA: No. I was replaced. And now that I've fired the attorney provided by EVE, I have no further ties with them.

EL: Can I get you anything, Mr. Adams? Before we continue?

SA: I just want this over with.

EL: So the person called The Source has lived with you since 1971?

SA: I told you! Don't make me... You will *not* like what happens if you push me.

EL: Mr. Adams, I am merely asking questions relative to the situation that you've been arrested for taking part in. You can choose not to cooperate.

SA: I said... I do not want to talk about The Source. You can ask me anything else.

EL: Okay, then. Can you tell us where you've lived since 1971?

SA: I have always kept a permanent home in Santa Cruz County, but my work led me to travel abroad.

EL: And did you participate in any other communities like Gateway of the Sun?

SA: We... I visited some. In my role as caretaker and CEO. Some of the research our companies were focused on had similar goals.

EL: Goals?

SA: Goals. Overcoming human suffering, isn't that the point of all medical research? To end pain, illness?

EL: And the teachings of The Source were supposed to make that possible, is that right?

SA: Agent LaBeau, which terrifies you more? Living a long life in pain, or taking a bullet and having your life cut short?

EL: Mr. Adams, I'd like to know more about this medical research.

SA: I'm sure you would. Much of what we did is valuable proprietary information that I am not at liberty to discuss. I signed a thorough NDA when I left EVE. You understand, don't you?

EL: I understand that you would rather withhold information that would benefit this investigation than tell me what I want to know. We have witnesses who will testify that you held four innocent people hostage with the intention of using them for a ritualistic murder, that you attacked Detective Cabral and resisted arrest, and that you were present during the murders of four men in a house that was then torched to cover up the crime. It's your choice whether you cooperate in these interviews.

SA: Well, then. It seems you know everything.

Two

Creed

"You see what we're dealing with?"

Todd had played me the recording of the interview with Stephen, and we were both sulking on the back patio of the massive house on the secure compound where we'd resided since the events that occurred at Loch Lomond. There was a large expanse of green lawn bordered by redwood trees and a creek along one side of the property, and what was practically a moat on the other. There was a perimeter of electrified fence and cameras, which were being monitored by a crew of "security experts"—that's all Todd would tell me about them—and no one besides Todd's benefactor and his FBI supervisor knew where we were. Not Roman, not his family, not the Santa Cruz Police Department.

The men and women I'd occasionally run into outside and those who waited on us and kept the household fed were employed by Todd's mysterious benefactor. The property belonged to the man as well.

"He's so damned arrogant. Always was. I wish we could get someone on the inside at EVE."

"We have Donna Hicks," Todd said, "but she was only able to give us information about the blood research. Well, and the new method of indoctrinating members, I suppose." Todd tugged at the sleeve of his dress shirt and raised his eyebrows. "Sounds quite a bit different than what you went through."

"Exactly. Stephen didn't like doing without, so he made friends with rich folks to make sure that wouldn't happen again. Guess that didn't work out too well for him." Didn't matter. My whole existence had been about avenging my best friend Muse's death at the hands of those who mutinied against The Source and their disciples, and to find out that Stephen had been living fat and happy all this time, had expensive clothes, cars, and houses... Not that I wanted wealth and riches, but a little hardship on his part would have made things easier to swallow.

I folded my arms and rested my head on the table. It was getting more and more difficult to function and remain in a pleasant mood. I spent my days talking with Todd, looking over the evidence, giving him all the information I had and some I didn't even know was relevant, and evenings, I watched while he attempted to talk to The Source. Those conversations were exhausting.

When Todd demonstrated the kitchen appliances: "You mean that humans have discovered how power comes from the ley lines, and they use it to operate these contraptions?"

"No, there's a power grid that's fueled by wind, solar, hydroelectric dams, and some fossil fuels in this part of the country. Other parts of the world still rely on natural gas and coal."

"And these are channeled through the ley lines? This is so fascinating."

When Todd attempted to explain computers and the World Wide Web: "So humans have found a way to communicate via telepathy?"

"No, the internet is a collection of data, like a library without books. It's information is stored in the cloud... Not an actual cloud in the sky, but a system of servers... You know, it's really complicated to explain, and I don't think I have the expertise to do it justice. Let's circle back on this topic."

Todd remained calm, but I had to stifle groans each and every time. Mark and Cross did their best to explain all the ways Stephen had manipulated them, but The Source would turn each example back around on them as impossible, and try to make lessons out of them.

"Creed?"

I lifted my head at Todd's voice. "Sorry. Did I miss something?"

His expression was full of guilt and pity, like a parent taking a small child to the doctor for a vaccination. They know it's going to hurt but it's good for you in the long run.

"Are you able to sleep at all?" he asked.

I rested my chin in my hand. "I lay down. I close my eyes. But all I do is experience that night over and over. Seeing Roman drained of his blood."

"And you're not getting enough energy," he added.

I shook my head.

"But Mr. Jenkins—"

"Is one man. Puesta Del Sol, for example, had at least a hundred residents, thirty or so on my hall alone. Between the patients sundowning and the staff's exhaustion, I had a lot of energy to feed on. Here... it's peaceful."

He gave a crooked smile. "Which would recharge a person without your particular gifts—"

"They're not gifts, Todd." I had to fight to keep my eyes open. "And if I don't get an influx of energy soon, I'm going to be of no use to anyone."

The next day, Todd caught me in a particularly cantankerous mood. I'd spent the afternoon trying to meditate. The Source asked to join me, and then proceeded to provide narration and tell me my fucking flow was blocked and would I like them to assist me? Rather than tell them where they could shove their unsolicited assistance, I'd retreated to the gym and was taking out my anger on the rowing machine. As Todd came in to let me know dinner was ready, I snapped the pull cord and the machine clanged loudly in the cavernous space.

"Creed! Are you all right?"

The broken handle was still in my hand, and I was tempted to throw it through the plate-glass window, but the gentleman that still existed within me somewhere knew that wouldn't be the polite thing to do.

"I'm really not."

"I'm doing all I can, Creed."

"I know. But it's been three weeks. I'm running on fumes. Mr. Jenkins is benefitting from all four of us being here, but I can't take his blood more than once a month. That's what we were taught, how I have lived my life. If I don't get out of here, get somewhere I can replenish? You're going to witness the ugliest part of this whole supernatural existence." I fought dirty. "And you'll have to explain to Roman why you're in possession of a husk that used to be Creed."

He relented.

"Tell me what to do."

It took us nearly an hour to reach this particular den of iniquity, which simply had "Dancers Beer Wings" spelled out on the marquee.

"Full nudity and prostitution don't appear to be on the menu, so I'm guessing we're not in Nevada. Seems like every Podunk town on this highway has a biker bar or a strip joint, though. I'll take what I can get."

He rolled his eyes and sat back in his chair. "This place screams 'bad decisions.'"

I laughed heartily. We sat in the middle of a section filled with two-person tables. There were two stages in front of us, and booths along the back with dancers on platforms between them. The place was clean, in decent shape, and the dancers were of a higher caliber, I supposed you could say. They were of diverse ethnic backgrounds, healthy from what I could sense, and drug-free, unlike the clientele.

"I'm just asking you to pick one."

Todd huffed. I don't know why I was torturing the poor man. He did a good job of keeping details about himself tucked away while presenting a friendly and welcoming demeanor, but behind the eager feeb facade was a trained killer who knew how to handle himself. He could pretend to not be comfortable in a den of sin, but I knew better.

"How about two?" He gave me a knowing smirk, and I laughed. I followed his gaze to one of the back platforms, where the dancer was very obviously showing off for the bartender, who was watching her through a lustful haze as he made drinks.

"An established couple? Or workmates who've been flirting? Tell me, Mr. FBI Profiler, what do you think?"

Todd cocked his head to the side, and we watched as the female dancer licked two fingers and stared at the bartender as she dragged them down her left breast and to either side of her nipple.

The bartender clutched at his chest dramatically, as if he couldn't handle the tension.

"Alright," Todd said. "I'll proposition them to take us into a back room. I'll touch neither of them, I'm telling you that right now, but I want to see what you do."

I grinned. "You mean you want to observe how I feed in the wild? The creature in his natural habitat?"

"Right. Yes, I know you'll only do an Exchange with Mr. Fletcher or—"

"Roman. When he's well. If he'll have me."

I was fully prepared for Roman to tell me he never wanted to do that again. After what he'd been through… I wasn't sure I'd even be able to take his blood, any of it. I couldn't bear the thought of hurting him.

"Let's do this. I don't want to stay any longer than necessary."

I knew there were two parts to his statement. One, he was not like me. He didn't see a strip club as a place of nourishment, only as a place where people went to get off or to make money. Two, Todd seemed to be struggling with something, maybe… probably his sexuality. He'd asked a lot about how I fed off of energy, and anytime sex came up, he'd get flustered.

Well, he was about to get a lesson.

"That's the spirit."

We stood and went over to the bar. I leaned in and told him to let me handle it, and he slipped me a hefty wad of cash. It was lucky for him that I was not a flight risk. Where would I go? I was needed, and he was trying to help me with my task. I was tethered to him, to the compound we'd made our base of operations, to The Source.

No. I couldn't get distracted, couldn't let my anger over my situation drain me further. I needed to get totally blissed out and recharge in one of the only ways I knew to survive.

Todd and I ordered drinks from the lusty bartender, and I noticed he fucked up my whiskey sour while he was making eyes at the dancer. That was fine. I wouldn't be drinking it anyway. Not that I didn't drink alcohol, but I wanted to get as much energy out of this scenario as I could, and drugs or alcohol would impair my ability to take what I needed.

"Thanks, Riley," I said to him, handing him cash. He nodded and went back to watching. "She's gorgeous, your girl."

Riley nodded again... then looked to me, his smile slipping. "She's not mine. But yeah. She is."

I made eye contact with Todd, and then I let out a long breath. I triggered the pheromone that was about to take this proposition up a notch. "You want her, though."

Riley turned to gaze up at her once more, and the yearning hit me like a wet rag, slapping against my skin, begging to be addressed.

I held up some cash so only he could see. "How about a private room? You and her?"

He frowned. "I'm not... I'm just a bartender—"

"Who could stand an infusion of cash. What do you think she'd say? If we wanted to watch?"

Riley stared at me for a long moment, waiting for the punchline or maybe a hidden camera to pop out. "You're serious."

I nodded, releasing a bit more of the pheromone. "Absolutely. We'd be totally hands-off. She'd perform a lap dance, only instead of a client, she could feel safe and have fun with you. Don't you think she'd appreciate that? You guys take it as far as you're comfortable. I pay handsomely for the privilege of being a witness."

I gave him my most irresistible smile, the one that worked on gay and straight men alike.

"This could be your chance to show her you're not just flirting with her." I leaned a little closer. If my heart didn't belong to another, I'd probably have seduced this man and been a third in this arrangement.

"Uh, let me ask her. Hang on." Riley approached the other bartender, asked for and received a break, and then he smiled nervously at us as he approached the woman. Mirna was her name. She glanced up at us, smiled excitedly, and let him take her hand to guide her down the steps. They approached us, still holding hands.

"You want to follow me?"

She took the lead down a walkway behind the bank of booths. The floor slanted downward until we were below the bar floor. The hall turned dark before we emerged into a wider space with doors along one wall. Each had colored lightbulbs above them, all that we passed red, until we got to one with a blue light. Mirna opened the door and gestured for us to go inside.

The space was hardly big enough for four adults and three chairs. Todd and I took two chairs and sat with our shoulders touching.

The amount of sexual energy from the anticipation these two generated was enough to give me a nice buzz. Todd kept his expression blank, maybe with a slightly pensive look. His hands rested on his thighs and he looked between the dancer and bartender expectantly.

"So you just want to watch me give Riley a lap dance? You sure that's all I can do for you?"

She was sweet, but she was a businesswoman. I had no doubt she wouldn't do anything she wasn't comfortable with, but I could also tell that she liked Riley. A lot. And it would not put her out to be close to him.

Both of them were healthy, though she was on some prescription medications, I could tell. Birth control, antihistamine, and a prescription NSAID. Back pain. Hmmm.

"We'd just like to watch the two of you explore this chemistry you've got going on, if you don't mind. We'll keep our hands to ourselves, but by all means, touch each other however you'd like."

I leaned back in the chair and smiled, sending a flow of pheromones Mirna's way. Immediately, I saw her pupils expand and her expression soften. She turned to Riley and put her hands on his shoulders.

"You heard the man. Let's give them a show."

Riley put his hands on her hips and spoke softly. "You sure you're okay with this? I'll keep my hands to myself—"

"Don't be silly," she said, placing her hands over his and sliding them down to grip her bare ass. She wore wide-net stockings over a black thong, black sequined pasties, and she had on lace-up combat boots that hit below the knee.

Riley smiled and was already fully erect, the bulge pushing against the front of his jeans. Their excitement was palpable, and it began to slowly waft over my way, like a moist rain cloud moving through a thick sky.

Riley whispered to Mirna, though the room was so small even Todd could hear them.

"I've wanted to ask you out, but I didn't want you to think I had bad intentions, you know, like I'd expect something."

"I know you'd be the perfect gentleman. That's why I'm okay with this. I want this. I want to be here with you."

Todd shifted in his chair as the two began to breathe heavier, eyeing each other's lips and waiting to see who would move first. He leaned toward me and spoke next to my ear. "Are you... is it happening?"

"Like I've just done about two shots of whiskey. A slight buzz, belly feels warm, skin collecting a bit of moisture from the heavy air."

Todd looked me over, and then turned back to the couple.

"Mirna, I can't help it. I want you bad."

She laughed and ran her thumbs over his cheekbones. "I'm glad. I want you too." Her eyes flared and she licked her lips, her voice a little shaky. "Why don't we forget they're here and you can do whatever you want, whatever you've been thinking? 'Cause I can tell you right now, dancing for you earlier? Got me wet for you."

I glanced at Todd and saw his eyebrows shoot up. Yeah, this was going to be an excellent feeding. I'd be sated for quite some time after this.

Riley kissed Mirna lightly, and he moved a hand from her ass around her hip, to slide over her mound. "Really? Can I see?"

Mirna laughed and nodded.

Riley slid his hand between her legs, his middle finger gliding easily under her thong "Oh God. All that's for me?"

"It is. I love dancing in that spot, so I can watch you. I love watching your hands and your forearms when you mix drinks. I've wanted your hands on me for a long time."

"How 'bout my mouth?"

Mirna gasped as Riley lowered himself to his knees, keeping her hips in place.

"Yeah, oh *please*."

This was definitely a little closer to the action than I normally got, when usually I'd linger outside a window or a closed door. Being a few feet away? Especially with two people who've wanted each other for a while? Yeah, this was way more energy than I'd expected, and I sucked it all in, willing it into my skin, absorbing it into my pores, and letting it fill my lungs. Their innocent longing quickly combusted into a chemical reaction so heady, I became drunk off it. Maybe even a bit aroused.

Which made me think of Roman.

Gods, I missed him terribly, and while yes, I wished he were with me, I wouldn't be watching someone else have sex to nourish my energy stores. I'd want to be having sex with *him*.

What would he even think of this? We hadn't had a whole lot of time to really discuss what my energy feeding consisted of. Would he think I was a pervert? Or would he look at it from a clinical perspective? I wasn't sure which was worse.

And as much as I enjoyed ribbing Todd, I'd really pushed the bounds of decency making him bring me here.

I looked over to him, and I sensed his bewilderment. He was likely trying to override the WASPy/Puritanical upbringing so many people have about sex. He was engaged, curious, compelled to watch, although it made him feel... wrong.

Riley was single-handedly attempting to redeem all men as he paid complete attention to Mirna's lady bits, worshiping her with gusto. She'd draped a leg over his shoulder and was holding herself up against the back wall.

When she came, everyone in that room groaned. Her pleasure was tangible, and I siphoned off every bit of energy I could possibly glean from this encounter.

Riley sat back on his haunches and grinned at Mirna, his lips and chin glistening.

"That's what you've been keeping from me?" She smiled at him, and I was pleased to note that there was no acting on her part, no attempt to hide her true feelings of wonder toward the young man who'd proved he would slay for her.

Riley climbed to his feet and bent down to kiss her cheek. "Anytime you want more, I'd love to take you out on a date. A real date." He squeezed her hand and stepped out into the hall to wait for her, probably to make sure we didn't pull any funny business.

I stood and reached into my pocket for the thick wad of cash Todd had given me, and I held it out to Mirna.

"You were exquisite, my dear. A gift to a parched man." I bowed to her, and she laughed.

"Aw, sweetie, you didn't even give me a chance to do nothin'. I appreciate this," she said. "My tuition bill is due."

"A scholar," I said, pressing a hand to my chest. "How lovely. May we see you again? Do you have a regular schedule?"

Todd subtly elbowed me. Bullshit if he was going to tell me we couldn't come out again. I was a live wire after this infusion, and I'd be ready to put up a fight.

If I was expected to take care of *them* after everything that had happened...

"This here's my regular night. I'd love to perform for you again. Have any other requests?"

"No, ma'am. I prefer to remain an observer." I winked at her, and she gestured for us to walk out ahead of her. Smart. Never put her back to us. I had an intuition that she had experience with law enforcement, that she likely took self-defense courses regularly. I also sensed that she'd needed those skills once before and hadn't had them.

I'd be sure to bring her more cash next time.

Todd moved swiftly toward the exit, and I hustled to keep up with him.

"What, I put out for you and I don't even get a drink after?" I teased.

"I can't believe that just happened," he said, obviously shaken by the experience, but not quite as disturbed as he thought he'd be. "I can't believe we just... I can't believe they just... I can't."

I stepped down off the curb a little hard and stumbled, giggling as I reached for Todd. "It's a biological function, Agent Barringer. I suppose

I could have suggested MMA, but I've always been more of a lover than a fighter." I snorted and fell against him, finally getting a laugh from the uptight guy. We reached his undercover car and he hit the fob, causing the red lights to flicker. My gaze was caught by the bright lights as they flashed before fading to a more subdued red.

"Good thing you aren't driving. Wait, do you even drive?"

I shook my head. "Nope. Never got my license. Motorcycles, yes. But never a car."

Once we climbed in, I tried hard to get my laughter under control. I needed to hang on to this energy, not let it bubble over. Who knew when Todd would take me out again?

Speaking of, the agent flexed his hands against the steering wheel and grasped it hard enough to make his hands squeak. "Did you, um... does that arouse you?"

"What? Watching people have sex? Sure. But I try to focus on absorbing the energy, not the nature of the act. The energy is vital to my survival. I don't need sex to survive." Which was a lie, but I was trying to behave. "Besides an Exchange, sex is the act that creates the most energy in a quick period of time. Next is sundowning, then fighting, and in a pinch, a good sporting match will give me a minimal buzz."

He nodded. "I guess I can see that."

"Thankfully lots of folks have sex, and some even make a profession out of it. They understand it's a transaction. Sex workers are used to strange requests, and they're the most likely to protect their clients' identities. That's been helpful in the past."

Todd started the car, turned to back up, and then he paused.

"You can ask me anything, you know that," I said, giving him the in he needed. "I can see the wheels turning."

He sighed. "It's just... why not take *their* blood? The Source's? Why is it that you're opposed more than the others? I hate to see you struggle."

"I'd think after what you just saw, you'd know why. I don't *like* having to go to a strip club, Agent Barringer. I do it out of necessity."

"But the blood—"

"I don't want to be a leech. And because I never intended to live forever. I'm having a hard enough time accepting that if I want to survive... if I want to be with Roman... I have to keep up this way of life. That's how it feels now. Even after the mutiny, after I thought The Source was dead, Cross, Mark, and everyone I'd trained with, I'd had a purpose. Find Stephen and put an end to this shit. Then I could stop and live out the rest of my life naturally. No more energy, no more blood. That was my plan.

"Now it turns out that I not only *can't* stop or I'll die a painful death, but I can't bring down this whole entity by myself. And, if I don't want more people to get hurt, I have to try to heal The Source before they create mass destruction, and I need to help you folks sort this out on a legal level. So I'm sorry I dragged you into a strip club, Todd, but at least here, I got what I paid for. It was a transaction. When I take from Mr. Fletcher, it's a transaction, because I'm providing him something in return. I don't want to owe The Source, and I don't want to owe Cross and Mark. I just want a chance to be with Roman. It's the only selfish thing I've done, that I've ever wanted..."

I expended too much energy with that diatribe, and I was on the verge of blurting out some deeply personal shit.

It *was* selfish of me to continue existing, honestly. Knowing I needed to live off other people forever? I'd never get away from it unless I gave it up. I'd never been suicidal, though I had low moments where I wondered whether it was worth it to carry on. But here I was, contemplating giving up when I knew it would hurt Roman.

"I'm sorry, Creed. I'm sorry we've put you in this position. I'll take you to whatever house of sin you need. I'll do whatever I can for you. I just don't know that I can ever feel comfortable watching... that."

"Aw, Toddy, don't go getting prudish on me now." I waved away his instant protests. "I'm just fucking with you."

He shook his head and pulled out onto the highway, headed back toward the compound. Where I'd be existing. Waiting for Roman. For three weeks now, I'd had a handful of conversations with Roman, I'd spent time with Mr. Jenkins talking, listening to him sing, and he'd shared his blood with me to keep me functioning. The rest of my time, I spent talking to Todd, running with Rhonda, and avoiding the reason I'd been brought to the middle of nowhere.

Something needed to change.

Interview With Donna Hicks

TB: This is Special Agent Todd Barringer. The date is November 22, 2022, the location is classified. The subject of this interview is Donna Hicks. Thanks for speaking with me again, Mrs. Hicks.

DH: Please, call me Donna. The name Hicks makes my skin crawl. I'd file for divorce but I don't want to take any chances that Timothy could find me through the paperwork.

TB: I promise, when we capture him, I'll put you in touch with a good attorney.

DH: Thank you.

TB: Donna, I was wondering if you could enlighten me any more about the work EVE was doing. I know you've shared with me how you first came to be introduced to The Source and the ritual you were a part of.

DH: Yes. At the house off Highway 17. It was the most bizarre thing I'd ever experienced... and as I told you, Timothy and I had definitely done some interesting things together as a married couple. Sex clubs on

Molly, Burning Man on E, Joshua Tree on peyote... but this was something else. It felt like we were on drugs, but we didn't take anything. We walked into the house, were pushed into this room, which was sealed shut behind us, and there we were in this mass of bodies. A chamber of some sort was in the middle of the room, and it was illuminated, the rest of the room dark. The person... The Source... they were so beautiful. They were wrapped in red fabric that seemed to flow around them, like they were submerged in some sort of tank full of water. And when they spoke, their voice made my hair stand on end. People pressed in closer, they were touching me all over, like it was some sort of orgy rave but with no music going on, in an overcrowded elevator full of half-naked people. Old men and women, early middle-aged people like us, no kids, no teenagers...

TB: Was it explained to you what was happening at these events?

DH: Timothy said we were there as an offering to The Source, that they would judge whether or not our energy was a good fit for the program. We went monthly to these gatherings. The Source would speak sometimes, talk about the importance of maintaining balance in nature, in using the gifts we'd received to help those who needed them and only taking from others what we needed ourselves, but that wasn't the vibe I got. It reminded me a lot of those preachers in the multibillion-dollar churches who tell their congregation to be humble, you know? Meanwhile, their suits cost more than I made in a month at BioBourne.

But it seemed like The Source was one part of it, and the other was the handing over of our finances, and what we contributed would be put toward the mission of EVE, which was always a little nebulous. They mentioned that our sacrifices would mean we had access to the latest health technologies, that we would experience good health the rest of our time on this plane, we wouldn't suffer illness or the effects of aging. It sounded like bullshit, but they started to tell us they had uncovered the answers to stop cell degeneration. It was wild. And then they took over BioBourne. They put me in charge of the lab and brought in all these new scientists... It was bonkers, you know? Then they showed me the data. I had no idea at the time... I didn't know. It

was their blood. The Source's. And they were using it to make this...
serum.

TB: And what was the serum supposed to do?

DH: Make you young forever. Make you healthy, fit. Able to withstand
environmental pollution, catastrophic accidents, any type of cancer.

TB: Do you think that's possible?

DH: Before this? No way. Now? I saw things... data, live human trials...
I saw things I can't explain.

TB: Did you have any interactions with Stephen Adams?

DH: I did.

TB: Can you elaborate?

DH: He met with Timothy and I that first night at the mansion. I was
still in shock and kind of still high from seeing The Source. There was a
lot of *yes*. Yes, we will get you our tax returns. Yes, we will participate in
the work of EVE to improve the lives of all of the members. Yes, I would
be glad to introduce you to the CEO of BioBourne. I was so flattered
that he wanted to hear about my work, my lab, what I'd accomplished.
It wasn't often that the men Timothy brought into our circle were
confident enough in themselves to accept a woman into their midst who
was smarter and more successful than they were. But Stephen listened,
asked the right questions. Only, I felt like something was off about him.
He was interested, but not engaged. Polite, but not pleasant. And when
we left that night, I remember saying to Timothy that he'd better not
leave me alone with that guy again.

TB: Do you have any recollection, anything at all, about the leadership
of EVE? Any idea who else was involved, any other facilities you were in
contact with? Anything you can remember?

DH: I've given you everything I can remember, I think. I don't know. I've been running on adrenaline for so long. I still can't sleep. The only other thing... I heard some of the board meetings Timothy attended on Zoom. Yeah, he was on the board pretty quick. Quit his job without telling me, said he was all in with EVE, and I should be too. Anyway, I remember listening outside the door to his home office, trying to hear what they were talking about. There were a lot of foreign accents, so I think they're definitely multinational. There was a lot of talk about meeting benchmarks and supplying the serum to EVE's facilities.

TB: By benchmarks, they meant...

DH: They were trying to match as many markers as they could to The Source's blood, and they were supposed to meet deadlines, the benchmarks, how close they should be to total replication by a certain point, and there were benchmarks based on how much of the serum they could produce and how fast. They were building toward something bigger than their trials. They needed the formula to be finalized because they had distributors set up. I don't have more specifics than that. I never saw any of the documentation about the business side of it. I only had access to the lab docs, the research data...

TB: Thank you, Donna. That's all been very helpful. I want to ask you a few questions about your relationship with Timothy before you joined EVE, and what happened after. Can you describe how things were before?

DH: We were happily married in that we were partners in all we did. We had great sex, we liked the same level of activity versus down time. We were both driven. He deferred to me in major decisions. He wanted to please me.

TB: And how did things change?

DH: The first inkling I had that things were changing was when he agreed to everything EVE asked of us that first night. I'd told him in the car not to make any promises until we talked it through together. Be smart about it, is what I'd told him. But then I went along with it that night because I was riding the wave of euphoria that I know now was because of The Source.

TB: Sorry to interrupt, but can you talk a little more about that... feeling?

DH: Have you... You ever been under the influence of mind-altering substances, Agent Barringer?

TB: I'm not—

DH: Never mind. You wouldn't tell me anyway. It's hard to describe to someone who's never been high, but it's also *not* like drugs. There's nothing about it that makes your body feel sluggish or sick. It's like the high without the drugs, does that make sense? Like being turned on, like jumping out of an airplane, like accomplishing the greatest feat of your life, all at the same time. An orgasmic rush of elation. It's like fucking rapture. Sorry, I know that sounds unbelievable, but you *can't* believe it, not unless you experience it.

TB: But once it wore off...

DH: Yeah. Once it wore off, I started freaking out. What the fuck had we done? But Timothy, like, didn't come down. Something flipped in him that night, some sort of switch. He saw something, I think, and all of a sudden it was like "this is what's best for us, darling. Trust me. Leave it to me. All of our dreams are going to come true." And we'd never been like that. Dreams? No. Hard work, smart financial decisions, that was the philosophy we'd followed, and it served us well. Next thing I know, our fucking money was gone, there were strangers in our house, in our lives, strangers taking over my work!

I don't know how they did it but EVE—I guess Stephen Adams was behind it, as well as whatever bazillionaires he had behind him, I never met anyone else—bought up all the stock and took over the board, fired everyone in management, all the other researchers except me. They kept me, but I was under their control. It started out like a takeover, and then I was actually being escorted from home to work, supervised all the time. I couldn't take bathroom breaks alone, *nothing*. That's when I tried to run, and they ran me off the road. I met Detective Cabral, and she helped me get to my sister. But after a couple of days, my brother-in-law started acting weird, spouting some bullshit about how it was my place to be with my husband, that I was making a terrible mistake. Like he was brainwashed. He was *never* like that, he didn't even like Timothy!

TB: But he let Timothy take you.

DH: He sure as hell did, and if I ever see him again, I'm— Wow, sorry. I shouldn't make threats while being recorded by a law officer.

TB: I understand what you meant. How about your sister?

DH: I don't know that I can trust her after what happened. I've agreed to your witness protection program because I have... no one else. Why would I? I'm not the type to hang out with girlfriends at a resort or spa, go wine tasting. No, my life was my work and Timothy. That was all I needed. Guess that backfired.

TB: I apologize, Donna. You've lost a great deal. I hope that the program will be the fresh start that you need.

DH: Me too, but I tell you what, I will never stop looking over my shoulder. Those people have their fingers in everything. I don't even fully trust in *your* people, Agent Barringer. I'm sorry. But I know I don't have a choice.

TB: I understand. I'll do everything in my power to keep you safe.

DH: Let's hope it's enough.

THREE

R oman

Four Weeks After Loch Lomond

"They made *jelly*?"

Dr. Gardner and I had fallen into a series of daily conversations full of enlightening academic discourse. Okay, we argued every day. He had some outrageous stories to tell on the subject that had become a bit of an obsession for me. Blood.

I couldn't help it. When you nearly lost all of yours, when your boyfriend needed it to survive, it kind of became a big deal.

No, I hadn't told Dr. Gardner exactly why I was so interested. He knew I was studying La Mente, and that they had been practicing evil shit like using fear to control people, to torture them, and that blood research had been their endgame.

"Jam, my friend. That's right. Those Romans—ha! You're even

named after them—would go to great lengths to stay young. There are surviving records with the proper methods of collecting the blood, directions on leaving it out to congeal, and then boiling and separating, just as you would with fruit—"

"Oh, Dr. Gardner, not the blood stories again."

Our poor nurse, Wilhelmina, was used to walking in on our quite explicit and graphic discussions, and as much as she loved working with us, she did not enjoy the topic. She'd left our room with her fingers in her ears more than once.

"And what did they think eating this jam would actually do?"

"Out with the bad, in with the good. Quite a simple idea. They knew people died when they lost too much blood, so adding blood back in would theoretically heal you."

"Okay, but that's the Romans—har har, by the way. I'll have you know it was the colonizing Catholic missionaries who came to my parents' native Philippines who saddled me with this name."

"Really," Wilhelmina scoffed, as she took Dr. Gardner's blood pressure. "I have those same colonizers to thank for the name Wilhelmina?"

"You have a beautiful name, my dear. Wilhelmina, it means 'willing to protect' to the Germans."

She rolled her eyes. "Yeah, you can thank them for me for a lifetime of ridicule from American kids in school." She started checking my monitor. "Your oxygen levels and blood pressure have been leveling off." She leaned in closer and spoke in a stage whisper, "You two haven't been drinking blood, have you?" She winked, but I could only chuckle nervously.

Not yet, but someday? Perhaps?

Would I? I was undecided. How could I hate what happened to me when I knew that the existence of The Source, of the whole damned organization, was responsible for me having Creed in my life? That may be a selfish way of looking at things, but I couldn't help but be grateful for him. Have to have both, I guessed.

Once Wilhelmina was done with us, I continued my train of thought. "What about earlier than the Romans?

"You know the problem with that as well as I do. No surviving records. Say what you will about those colonizers, but they were quite efficient at wiping out all the history of their predecessors. They were a bit like the Chinese dynasties who came in and rewrote history after the fact to make themselves out to be heroes."

"I guess. Short-sighted of them, though. Perhaps those old records might have had useful information. Without the Christians insisting on burning down the place, we might not have spent hundreds of years in darkness. Maybe we wouldn't have had blood jam, but maybe we *would* have... answers?"

Dr. Gardner gave me a long appraising look. He did that a lot. He was still trying to figure out what a young kid like me was doing slaving away on a dissertation about a mysterious cult that we still didn't have a lot of answers about.

"Just what answers do you think we would have, Dr. San Angelo?" He liked to call me that. Said it would give me the motivation to finish. We'd had several conversations about how close I'd come to telling the university I wouldn't be finishing.

"Nonsense," he'd said. *"You will finish if I have to drag your ass across the finish line, and if I die before then, I'll come back and haunt you until you're done."*

I believed him. He was just as stubborn as me, if not more so.

"I don't know." My voice was barely above a whisper. I'd overdone it today with my walks, my reading... my arguing.

Dr. Gardner sat up in bed. He'd been here a week already, and I thought for sure he'd likely be out before me. That would mean being lapped by three senior citizens on my road to recovery, but Dr. Gardner was a machine. He just kept going, never complaining of pain no matter how tough his physical therapy went. For that reason, I tried not to grumble as much and I pushed myself even harder, even though Wilhelmina was on my ass.

I had someone who needed me to get better, and that was all the motivation I needed.

"My dear Dr. San Angelo, what has man coveted for all time? What drove those colonizers you loathe so much to come to the new world?"

"Money? Riches? Notoriety?"

"Immortality. Yes, true, in name they received it when they traveled the seas searching for those things you mentioned, although now chil-

dren are being taught in schools just what those conquistadors wrought upon the people they slaughtered. Perhaps their names will be lost to history eventually as well. Good riddance, you might say. But they were looking for true immortality. They believed there were not only riches, but the answers to eternal life beyond the ocean. There are still folks searching for it in the Amazon rainforest."

I rolled over on my side, barely able to keep my eyes open in the afternoons but desperate to keep our conversation going. For some reason, I had this feeling that Dr. Gardner was pushing me toward something, that his questions and topics were all leading me to the answers I was looking for, even though I'd been very, *very* careful not to tell him about the events that transpired, and nothing about Creed other than he was my boyfriend and he'd had to go away for work. I mentioned nothing about EVE.

"Aren't there still scientists who believe that they can cure most of the world's diseases using plants that are going extinct in the rainforest, or have they given up on that hypothesis?"

"There are scientists who still believe there are cures for a vast amount of ailments within the Amazon rainforest," he said. "But at the rate it's burning down and being destroyed by human encroachment, we lose that opportunity every day."

"Do you think there are uses for blood that haven't been explored?" I asked him. What if EVE or La Mente was actually onto something? What if what they were trying to do was actually possible? Would it be worth the sacrifices of the few? Like me? Thoughts kept floating around in my head, not fully developed, but with the promise of delivering the answers I sought. If only I could reach up and grab them from the aether, figure out the connection, why this was all happening.

"Roman, dear boy, you need your rest. It will come to you, the knowledge you seek. Before you know it, you'll be strutting out of here with that young man you're pining after on your arm. Then, the two of you should go far away from all of this nonsense. It's not safe for you to keep digging into the affairs of dangerous people."

"But how do you..."

I must have dozed off, because when I woke, Dr. Gardner was gone and a new nurse was checking my machines.

"Where's Wilhelmina?"

The woman turned around and smiled. "She had to leave early today. I'm Noreen. How are you feeling this afternoon?"

I pushed myself up to sitting, confused. The last thing I remembered was Dr. Gardner giving me some advice that sounded a bit like a warning.

"Where's Dr. Gardner?"

"Oh, he's had a visitor. Can I get you anything?"

I wasn't sure why she was poking around my monitors. I hadn't needed an IV in a week or so. I tried to shake off the sleep. Alarm bells were going off in my head.

"Is the doctor coming to see me today?"

"Uh-huh. Yep. She should be in shortly. We just need to get your IV going again."

What the hell was she doing? And my doctor was not a woman. I was about to put up a fuss when an unlikely savior arrived.

"Hey, what's up, Junior?"

Emmanuel stood in the doorway with his Nintendo Switch under his arm and two cups of boba.

"What's up? Why are you here?"

He wrinkled his nose. "Wow, nice to see you, too. Mama Ness brought me. She and Mama Bee are outside, talking to your doctor."

I glanced at the nurse, and she hurriedly packed up whatever she was doing on the counter next to my bed. "I'll be back after your visitors are gone."

I watched her walk out, and Emmanuel gave a nervous laugh. "I come at a bad time? Was she about to give you a sponge bath or something?"

"I take showers, dick. Can you get Tita to come in here?"

Emmanuel put the drinks down and set his Switch on the bed by my feet. Normally he would argue with me, but he must have sensed something in my tone, because he made a speedy exit.

I rubbed my hands over my face and wondered why I felt so disoriented. I'd been feeling better the past few days, and I didn't want to consider I'd had a setback. Every step backward, no matter how small, infuriated me. I needed to get the fuck out of this hospital bed and back to my life.

"Hey, Junior," Vanessa said. She wasn't smiling, but then she rarely did. Ever since her wife and son were nearly taken from her permanently, not to mention her nephew, she'd become even more serious. "You okay?"

"Were you just talking to my doctor?"

She looked to the doorway, likely to be sure Bernadette and Emmanuel were behind her. They were. Bernadette smiled big enough for both of them and came straight over to hug me and give me a kiss on my forehead.

"Your doctor is apparently out sick, so some other doctor is seeing his patients."

"Is she a woman?"

Vanessa frowned. "She is."

"New nurse, too. She seemed... off."

Vanessa pulled out her phone. "I'm getting your uncle over here."

"No, it's his day off, V. I'm just paranoid."

She raised an eyebrow and looked at me like I was ridiculous, before she stepped out into the hallway.

"Having a party and didn't invite me?"

No sooner had Vanessa left than Dr. Gardner came rolling in, pushed by yet another unfamiliar employee.

"What happened to you?"

"What a bunch of malarkey. They had me sitting outside the Physical Therapy room for half an hour and the bloody therapist never turned up."

That was an awful lot of changes for one day.

An alarm sounded on my monitor, the call bringing several folks inside my room, all of whom I recognized. The Noreen chick wasn't among them.

"Mr. San Angelo, your heart rate is too high. We need you to practice your breathing exercises, and we're going to give you some medicine to try to—"

"The nurse who was just in here, she... she was messing around, she said she was starting an IV, but I don't have one. She was going to give me something—"

"Relax, Mr. San Angelo. My apologies. I'm covering for Dr. Shahi. I'm Dr. Kaur," she said, squeezing my forearm. "Does that clear up the misunderstanding? I know we have security to be concerned about."

I nodded at her, trying to get my breathing back to normal. I had seen her around, but that nurse...

"There's a lot of chaos going around," Dr. Gardner said. "My physical therapist didn't show up for our appointment either."

"Ah, Mr. Gardner—"

"*Dr.* Gardner," I corrected her. I was being a dick and I didn't care. This all felt like too much discord to be coincidental.

"Of course," she said, smiling condescendingly at me. "Another misunderstanding. The physical therapists are all at training today. Dr. Shahi should have let you know, but since he didn't, let's see what we can do to get you back on track."

"Excuse me, Doctor," Vanessa said. "No offense, but I'd like for someone who's familiar with my nephew's treatment plan to take a look at him." She nodded at Bernadette, who held out her hand to the visiting doctor. "My wife is a nurse and familiar with the course of action Dr. Shahi has been taking with Roman."

The doctor looked as if she wanted to argue, but Vanessa was sporting that detective badge on her belt just daring someone to fuck with her.

The doctor used her ID card and logged onto the laptop in the room and, once she determined that Vanessa and Bernadette were both allowed to make medical decisions for me, let Bernadette view my records. While they conferred, Vanessa came to check on me. The alarms had thankfully been shut off, and my numbers were back in the fairly normal range. I was feeling less hazy, thank goodness.

"Rey will be here shortly, and he's bringing the bat phone. I want Creed and Barringer to know what happened. Barringer can find out if this was truly a mishap or if there's something suspect about it."

"Thanks, Auntie." I needed to touch base with Creed. He would talk me down or let me know I was right to be concerned.

I closed my eyes and tried to tune out the noise around me so I could focus on slowing my heart rate. I'd learned plenty about medita-tion as part of my degree, but only now that I'd been forced to use those techniques to save my own damn life was I finally a believer. The power of the mind was so vast, and we humans had never mastered the full capabilities. Dr. Gardner and I had been discussing this very topic. Guess it took me nearly dying to finally expand my mental capacity.

"Junior, what the hell kinda weird you got going on over here now?" Rey's voice helped calm me as well.

"Tiyuhin," I said. Invoking the Tagalog tended to happen when the shit hit the fan.

Vanessa pulled him aside and caught him up on everything, so I could continue my breathing. The two of them were talking in whispers by the door, and I was rolling my head around on my neck when I felt a hand on my arm.

In all of the chaos, no one had helped Dr. Gardner back into his bed, so he'd wheeled himself over to me.

"Trust your gut, son. You have a strong sense of intuition. You *must* trust it. This might have been a mistake, but if it feels like more, don't ignore it. I'm worried for you."

"You said something before," I said, pulling our earlier conversation out of the muddled mess in my head. "About digging into something dangerous."

He sighed and his brow furrowed. "I've been reading your paper on La Mente. Yes, I found it online. I do have tech skills, young man." He leaned in closer. "Organizations like those have a tendency to make innocent young academics disappear. Or wish they had. They can ruin your life, Roman, and you're just getting started."

I had no idea how to respond, or which part to respond to first, when Rey butted in.

"Hey, I've got loverboy on the line."

He handed me the bat phone, which I immediately cradled in both hands.

"Hi," I sighed, relieved to be seeing his face.

"What's wrong, baby? What happened?"

I didn't want to cry with so many people in the room, and I'd just gotten my heart rate back to a good place, so I went with diversionary tactics.

"Creed, I don't think you've met my roommate yet, Dr. Alistair Gardner. Cultural Anthropologist."

I turned the phone to face Dr. Gardner, whose eyebrows rose in surprise. "Hello, young man. You must be the charming nurse I've heard so much about."

Creed gave his most winningest smile. "Creed Lowell, R.N., Certified Respiratory Therapist, um, I think I have a few other specialties in there... How do you do?"

Dr. Gardner laughed heartily. "Oh, you are a charmer. No wonder you have my roommate twitterpated over here."

Creed's smile faded. "Hopefully not *too* twitterpated. Roman? Are you okay?"

"I am, it's just been a weird day." We couldn't go into it in front of Dr. Gardner, so I just smiled at my handsome boyfriend, maybe got a little mooney. "Tita and Tito are checking everything out, but I'm okay now that you're here."

Creed grinned back at me, and Dr. Gardner made a little grumble. I laughed. "Aw, what's the matter, old man? Jealous?"

He smiled kindly and shook his head. "Maybe a bit. It's been twenty years since I've had cause to make googly eyes. My partner passed a long time ago."

"I'm sorry you lost someone important to you." I looked directly into the phone. "I'd be lost."

"Roman."

Creed lost his smile completely. In all of our previous calls, he'd teased me, flirted with me, but he hadn't given me the "all hope is gone" look, and it was freaking me out.

Our playful conversation had turned dark.

Four

C reed

"I'm sorry," Roman said, and the weight of his words hit me like a boulder.

"Roman, listen to me—"

"Wait," he said, then I heard him ask Rey to help him with his chair. I watched helplessly while Roman, who had been the epitome of fitness, had to have his uncle get him situated in his wheelchair, and then push him out of his room and into a corner of the hallway.

"I'll be right here," Rey said, and I called out a thank you.

"He saluted you," Roman said. He had dark circles under his eyes and his skin was pale—too pale. "Now you listen to me. I'm doing better, just had a little hiccup today. Some new nurse came in—"

I started to interrupt him.

"No, please just let me finish, and then I want to hear from you. Please?"

"Whatever you need."

"Well, I need *you*. Okay? So whatever you were going to say, I want you to keep that piece of information front and center. Now, the doctor on call said there were some absences or staffing changes or whatever. It seems like it was a scheduling clusterfuck and not a security breach. Rey and Vanessa are going to get to the bottom of it, and they're going to have an officer outside my room until they figure it out. I should be out of here, though, I'm guessing in a week? Maybe two? I'm getting better, I swear. I walked up and down the hallway without using my cane today! Aren't you proud of me?"

"Roman..." I started, but then I just shook my head.

"Maybe I should be asking what's wrong with *you*."

"Do you ever wonder, while you're sitting in that hospital bed with wires and cords hooked up to you, just why it is that you're even speaking to me? How you can trust me after my dirty little secret nearly took your life?"

"I... *don't* wonder. It was a series of decisions, cause and effect. I make them all the time. I decided to trust you. I decided to love you. My choices. Creed, why are you even worried about this? We have bigger things to be concerned about. How are things going? Have you been able to make any headway with The Source? It's gotta be so weird to be spending time like this, all casual like."

"Yeah, you could say that. I've mostly been avoiding them, which hasn't gone over well. Cross and Mark seem to be taking back up their learning, and Todd is pushing me to talk to The Source, work with them. I'm just... I'm trying, but it's hard." I had to come clean, no matter what his reaction. I didn't want to hurt him, but the bitter part of me thought, well, maybe if I told him everything, he'd... end things. "I had to go out last night."

"What? What happened?"

I could be a total prick and just blurt out what a sick, twisted person I really was, or I could try to explain. It would likely hurt him either way. Maybe even telling him was further proof I was a narcissistic asshole.

"I needed energy. Since I don't have the patients' energy to... well, feed on, I've been getting..."

"Grumpy?" Roman's teasing smile made this even harder. Would he still smile at me like that after I told him what I'd done?

"You could say that, I guess. Look, I'm telling you this though you're going to hate it. I'm not really sure who I'm helping by telling you—"

"Creed? Just say it. Please."

Goddess. "Fine. I made Todd take me to a strip club last night, and I watched as a bartender ate out one of the dancers." It sounded even more deplorable coming out of my mouth. I was a disgusting—

"And did it work? Were you able to gain enough energy?"

"That's all you have to say? Jeez, Roman! I tell you I'm a perverted, voyeuristic piece of shit, and you ask if I'm *full*?"

I wanted to throw the phone. I was sick of feeling ashamed. I'd done this plenty of times before and it hadn't mattered because it was all a means to an end. Stay strong enough to destroy Stephen. But now that I actually cared what someone thought of me...

"Creed. You're not perverted, and who *isn't* a voyeur, huh? I fully admit I enjoy and get sexual gratification from watching pornography. My roommate in undergrad took me to a sex club once and I got off watching other people have sex, despite the fact I'd told myself I was only there for research. Creed, you have particular needs that are out of your control! You didn't choose this life—"

"Don't try to make me sound like a victim, Roman. I chose to continue, even knowing I'd have to live off of other people like a damned parasite—"

"Baby, please. Humans starve without affection, without touch, without love. There's a reason failure to thrive is a real thing. An adult inmate cannot survive long-term in solitary confinement because they need to be around other people. What you do is an amplified version of what *all* humans must do to survive."

I pinched the bridge of my nose and fought to keep tears at bay. Sobbing would undo everything I'd gained from last night's feeding. "You said once that I was an example of next-level evolution. But what if I'm actually a step back? My big brain can heal the sick and wounded, but it can't sustain my own life. Maybe instead of being an advanced form of humanity, I'm not fit to exist."

"Creed," Roman whispered. "I wish I could hold you right now."

"*Why*? To prolong a life not meant to be?"

"I can't accept that. First of all, I refuse to believe we weren't meant to find each other. And second, I want to hold you because obviously being away from my particular brand of sexual potency has got you all morose. You need a healthy dose of me, baby, that's all."

"Goddamn you." But I laughed. "For a smart-mouthed grad student, you sure talk like you know shit."

"That's right, I know shit. And I know *you*. I know when you're trying to run away from me, and dammit, Creed, we're not doing this again. I don't care if you had to fuck your way through a line of frat boys to get enough energy to last you. Well, as long as you wore condoms. And that you hated it."

That bullshit, along with his smirk, had me cracking up, which lifted my funk the tiniest bit.

"And as long as no one touched my ass?"

"Damn right," Roman growled. His dark eyes flared and he pursed his lips, that bottom one with the curve I loved so much. "That ass is mine. As soon as I can walk across the room without needing my oxygen tank, I'm going to have that ass again." His expression turned soft. "Baby, please don't talk like this." His tone went from cocky to pleading so quick. "You are so important, and you give so much more than you take. How can you even believe I would be upset? The only thing I'm upset about is that I couldn't go with you."

"Todd is probably upset too. I think he hated it, truly."

"He probably got all uptight about it, huh? I do think there's a freak in there somewhere," Roman whispered. I missed the little mischievous crinkle he'd get in his nose before giving me that wide smile full of large, straight white teeth, a shadow of dark hair on his upper lip that I knew was just as velvety soft as the hair on his belly.

"Maybe," I sighed. "I hate telling you this. And I hate you worrying about me when you're the one who needs the worry."

"Don't *not* tell me. There's nothing you can tell me that will tarnish my image of you. You're a good man, a generous and caring person who has dedicated his whole existence to making life better for others. And I can't wait until we're together and I can meet all of your needs once more. All of them."

"Roman, no. I can't. I won't hurt you."

He rolled his eyes. "I've got plenty of blood now, and it's pretty damn healthy too. I'll have Rey send you my records so you can see for yourself."

"I don't know what I did to deserve any of this, but I'll spend the rest of my existence trying to live up to this image you have of me."

"Hey Junior? I'm trying to pretend like I didn't hear any of that, but if you two get any mushier I'm gonna need a mop. And you need to get back to bed."

"Sorry, Rey," I called out. "Thank you for being our go-between. I promise I'll make it up to you."

"Shit. Next time take *me* to a strip club. I can't believe you got a private show like that."

Roman groaned and his facial expression made me laugh once more.

"Take care, Roman," I whispered. "I love you so much."

"I love you too. See you soon."

I had to believe he was right.

I returned to the compound and handed Barringer the SAT phone. He was in the middle of a call but he hung up and turned on me.

"I talked to Vanessa. It looks like it really was a series of mishaps at the facility. But we've got extra security—"

"I know." I rested my hands on my hips. "Please tell me these interviews are netting you something useful? That you have a lead on Hicks? Because I don't think I can take much more."

Barringer's eyes flared and he started to say something, but a flash of light and a crash from the other room sent us all running.

Mark and Cross stood on one end of the sectional, and Mr. Jenkins stood next to the chair on the other end of it.

The Source stood between a gaping black hole in what was previously the corner of the sectional, and broken glass where the coffee table used to be.

"It's okay, it's okay," Mark said. "They were just watching TV and they got a little agitated."

"Is anyone hurt? What the hell were you watching?" Barringer asked, surveying the damage.

"*Real Housewives of Salt Lake*." The Source turned their serene gaze toward us. "I thought it would be educational, that I might learn about the family unit and the role the female plays. But I fear for the future of society if this is what families are like. The amount of arguing these women partake in is upsetting. I've never known humans to disagree so much. Perhaps they simply need guidance, a being to bring balance."

I looked at the ceiling and counted to ten before I spoke.

"In case you weren't aware, despite the word 'real,' most shows on the television are sensationalist and absolutely unbelievable. Even programming that proclaims to be true is host to misleading information and outright fiction. Those women are more actresses than actual housewives. You can't watch this program and glean anything from it that's valuable. I can't even... who turned this on?"

The Source moved closer to me, and I prepared for punishment, but I honestly didn't give a shit anymore. Punish away.

"If you would only guide me... I am trying to understand the outside world so that I may fit in and become a contributing member—"

"The world isn't like TV! Shows like that present the worst of humanity. If you want to be a contributing member of society, you have to *listen* to people. Observe and ask questions, not assume you always have the answers."

They smiled brightly. "Then this is my first lesson."

I could fight this all I wanted, but I knew it was inevitable. I needed to instruct this ancient being in how to adapt and thrive in today's world. In order to be free of them someday, I would have to engage.

Damn, I hated having to do the right thing. I envied Mark and Cross and their freewheeling lifestyle of playing gigs and drinking blood. I was exhausted, all I wanted was Roman, and I was trapped here.

"Let's begin."

INTERVIEW WITH THE SOURCE

Special Agent Todd Barringer and The Source with Creed Lowell, Mark Bullock, and Cross present.

TB: Thank you for agreeing to speak with me.

TS: You are a kind man, Learner Todd.

TB: Thank you.

CL: Please refer to him as Agent Barringer. That is his title. He's here to learn *about* you, not *from* you.

TS: What does this mean? Agent?

TB: I work for the government of the United States of America as a federal law enforcement official. I am currently assigned to a special task force to investigate crimes with extraordinary circumstances.

TS: Law enforcement. Then you are a Guardian. Who was your Master?

TB: I... I studied at a facility called Quantico, and I learned from the behavioral specialists there. My master? I report to a Special Agent in Charge, the Director of the FBI, and the President of the United States. Special Agent in Charge Sandra Lopez is my direct supervisor. I'm also working with a civilian contractor who has a special interest in this case.

TS: I would like to know more about behavioral specialists... What does this mean?

TB: Well, a behavioral specialist is someone who has studied to become an expert in the field of understanding and predicting human behavior. In the FBI, we attempt to apprehend criminals by using knowledge about behavior patterns to predict their actions, rescue victims, stop further crimes from occurring. Whatever we can do, depending on the circumstances.

TS: When acolytes of The Way who are under my supervision break our rules and cause harm, it is my responsibility to enact punishment. Instructing acolytes in The Way is a huge responsibility. If I am to give them the power to heal, I cannot let them harm others. That would have devastating consequences.

TB: When you say enact punishment—

TS: When a person breaks your laws, what do you do?

TB: My job is to gather evidence that they've broken the law, for an attorney to present before a jury, who will then decide whether or not to sentence them to prison and for how long. That's a simplified way of describing it.

TS: In the case of acolytes who follow The Way under my supervision, it is my responsibility to show them how to walk the right path. If a Learner chooses not to adhere to the tenets of our faith, they are dealt with in a manner that is appropriate. Perhaps they are isolated, which for our kind is very painful and leaves us weakened. Or, if they continue to inflict harm, then they will experience the harm they have inflicted.

TB: An eye for an eye?

TS: I believe that is in the Christian Bible, is it not? We do not have a written text or scriptures. My brethren and I discovered The Way's benefits and rewards long before the Romans destroyed our civilization. Or attempted to, anyway. They were unable to destroy us completely. They may have forced us to practice in secret, to hold our gatherings away from their prying eyes, but they could not drive our faith from us. It was to their detriment that they slaughtered so many of us. Think of how advanced civilization would be at ending suffering if we'd had those centuries to perfect our practices.

CL: But you haven't taken steps to benefit from modern practices, either. Why remain removed from society when your teachings could improve the quality of life for so many?

TS: I dedicated my life to ensuring that only the worthy were taught The Way, and that those who learned our practices would in turn use their powers to improve the overall health of their brethren. By keeping the healing energy within our cohort, we would grow stronger, be closer to the Goddess, and be one with our Earth Mother.

CL: By remaining insulated, you selfishly decided who was worthy of peace and who would be forced to suffer. And you allowed The Way to be tainted by those who would use it for their own gain, hurting people along the way. What started as a noble pursuit turned into terror and pain for many. Who knows how many have been hurt because your teachings have fallen into the wrong hands?

TS: And this is why I want to make amends. But Guardian Creed, you have only seen the very surface of how our powers can be used for darkness. I pray you never see the true depths of the evil that men do.

CL: I came pretty close watching you nearly kill the man I love.

TB: This concludes our interview for today.

FIVE

R oman

Five Weeks After the events at Loch Lomond

Dr. Gardner and I fell into a routine of reading after breakfast, chatting after lunch until we both needed naps, and in the evenings, when we were restless but physically exhausted, we watched movies on my laptop. I usually let Alistair pick them out, as it brought him so much joy. This week, however, he'd been on a classic vampire movie kick.

"They're my favorite," he said, when I groaned. Not that I really minded. I was fascinated by the whole concept of the vampire in ways I'd never considered before. I'd seen *The Lost Boys*, or as we locals liked to call it, The Santa Cruz Vampire Movie, as had anyone who lived here, I assumed. But other than the *Underworld* franchise, and the *Dracula* with Keanu Reeves and his horrible accent, which I excused because Keanu Reeves, I had never really paid attention.

"What about those sparkly vampires?"

"Hard pass," I said. "Although, they are comedy gold. If you want contemporary, there's always *True Blood*, although those are pretty graphic."

Alistair wiggled his eyebrows as an orderly came in to help him to the bathroom. "I think we're both of a certain age. Why not?"

I barked out a laugh, grateful it no longer hurt to do so. I was feeling so much better than I had when I'd arrived at the rehab facility, to the point where I was starting to push myself a little more in my daily exercise. I wanted to get out of here and get to Creed before he blew a gasket.

Yes, my poor boyfriend was having to play teacher and babysitter to the being who'd made him what he was. It wasn't going smoothly.

"Aw, come on. It can't be much worse than teaching my freshman Intro to Psych courses. I practically have to potty train them," I'd said to him. I had seen so many new sides to my beloved over the past week since he'd decided to start imparting his life lessons to The Source.

"Okay, you try to explain the concept of consent to a being who's been worshiped by others for millennia. It's like trying to tell a lion not to eat the lamb."

"Perhaps you just need to model—"

"I tried that, Professor, with Mr. Jenkins, showing The Source how we... interact."

"And what happened?" I cringed, preparing for the worst.

"Well, I tried to let The Source try to do an Exchange with Mr. Jenkins while I supervised. First, The Source hit him with a huge whammy of pheromone and *then* asked him, which is like having sex with someone passed out drunk."

"That's an awful visual."

"You think?"

"How about you teach them about some of the most famous research conducted without consent? Tuskegee, Zimbardo's prison study, the Nazis. None of them had exact informed consent."

Creed sighed. "You're right. I will try, but it's been so long since they've been exposed to the evil that humanity inflicts... They're so sheltered, and even when Stephen kept them and fed them lies, he never showed them reality, just showed them false images, making them fear we were in the end of days. Real Mad Max shit. That's how he got them to remain in seclusion, believing that the work he was doing with EVE was to save lives. The Source didn't know. Stephen taught them that humans had become inherently violent toward each other."

"That's terrifying."

"Mr. San Angelo?" One of the front desk nurses popped her head in the door, pulling me out of that memory. "You have a visitor. He's not on your list."

The staff here knew that I'd been through an event and the place had good security, and they knew to call my aunt and uncle anytime someone not on the approved list came to see me. Before I could ask the woman, she nodded.

"The calls have been made. Your uncle is on his way."

"Thank you," I said, sitting up and pushing my hair back. I really needed to do something with this mess—it had grown out super long and I wasn't sure I was a fan. "Did the visitor identify himself?"

"Yes, sir. A Mr. Ken Ballard, from Longevity Health."

The name didn't ring any bells, but something in my gut told me it should.

"Remember what I said, Roman. Trust your gut."

It hit me. Alistair had said that before, the day of the clusterfuck.

He and I would be having a longer conversation about this when I returned, that was for sure. We'd grown so close that I hadn't really questioned his presence, but what if he hadn't been completely forthcoming about why he was here?

"Can I see him outside of my room? I'm not comfortable—"

"Yes, sir. We can wheel you out to the visiting area if you like."

"It's fine with me if you see him here, Roman," Alistair said as he returned to his bed. He had a crease in his forehead, as if he knew this was a concern.

"No, it's okay. I'd rather not do business in my sleep chamber," I said in a fake New Zealander accent that sounded like a terrible imitation of him.

He chuckled and rolled his eyes at me. "You're not improving, I'm afraid."

I slid out of bed, pulled my robe off the coat rack, and waited for the orderly to bring a wheelchair.

"Hey, when you learn to speak Tagalog, then we can talk."

Alistair proceeded to repeat what I'd just said in perfect Tagalog.

"Damn. You have to tell me how you know so many damn languages someday."

He tucked his hands behind his head. "It's a gift."

The nurse wheeled me out and I immediately spotted the guy. Gray slacks, embroidered polo, slicked-back hair, European trainers. He looked very Silicon Valley, too slick. He had a Scandinavian appearance that made me pause. Perhaps Mr. Ken Ballard was a longer way from home than I thought.

He approached me and shook my hand. "Pleasure to meet you, Mr. San Angelo." He had a slight accent that sounded Northern European, but I couldn't tell for sure.

"How can I help you?" I asked.

"First of all, I want to commend you on your miraculous recovery. Even for a young man your age, your body took quite a hit." He paused, and internal alarm bells grew louder than my tinnitus.

"I'm curious to know how you know anything about me *or* my health." I folded my hands in my lap and made like a blank slate. I tried to think of all the things Creed told me. I knew people like him could have psychic gifts, and though I had no idea if this guy was involved in anything unusual, I had to assume.

Ballard took a seat in a hard plastic chair next to my wheelchair, which I appreciated. Sketchy or not, looking up at him was hurting my neck, and it definitely put me in a submissive position that I didn't like one bit.

"Well, Mr. San Angelo, Longevity Health contracts with this facility to provide patients with options that go above and beyond what most hospitals and rehabilitation facilities are capable of. The doctors here screen patients, and if they seem to be good prospects for our clinical trials, we meet with them and give them the details. You would be transferred to our facility, and all of your treatment would be covered by our generous funding."

My pulse jumped, and I tried to keep my expression calm but the internal alarms were buzzing so loud I could barely make out his words.

"Interesting. My doctor did not discuss this with me."

He grinned. "And that's why I'm here."

Ballard was a picture of health, from his trim physique to the bleached white teeth and sophisticated haircut. He looked like he'd stepped out of a commercial for a fitness center, but it all seemed authentic. Natural. Like it did on Creed when I'd first met him.

"Clinical trials. What is your area of research?"

He smiled and leaned forward slightly as if to give a bit more oomph to his pitch.

"Our work is centered on giving our clients the most benefits possible to enable them to live long, happy, and healthy lives. We treat their conditions with the latest technologically advanced procedures and our state-of-the-art facilities provide a peaceful place in which our guests will thrive."

I shifted in my chair, acknowledging the part of me that wanted a quick fix, that wanted to be past all this weakness. *This is how they hook you*. Prey on your fears and manipulate you into believing that only through them will you achieve enlightenment.

"And what in particular do you think you can do for me? I'm getting excellent care here."

He leaned his elbows on his knees. "Mr. San Angelo, without significant intervention, you are facing a lifetime of care for the damage done to your kidneys, potentially even a transplant, and your heart is operating at about sixty to seventy percent despite the excellent treatment you're getting here. We can do more."

Fuck, he really had my records. He knew exactly what my fears were, how vanity would plague me for having to carry an oxygen tank and use a cane, potentially be on dialysis. All before I turned 30.

He continued in my silence. "We've developed techniques that use your own stem cells to heal your organs. We have developed a process by which we cleanse the bone marrow to remove impurities. And probably our most exciting program involves blood conditioning. We infuse your blood with receptors that beef up your existing platelets. It's very exciting work. Our elderly patients feel young again. Our younger patients feel... hope. It's that hope that I believe you carry in your heart, that you can eventually get back to your life, your work, your love."

Something nudged at my consciousness, and I pushed back at it. He was trying to get in my head. Already had... as he'd shown his hand at the end there. He wanted me to know that he knew everything.

"Thank you for your time, Mr. Ballard," I said, using the handrails on the wheelchair. *Fuck it*, I didn't care if it set me back, I was not staying close to this man a second longer.

He placed a hand on the arm of my chair, and his grin turned malevolent.

"Now, Mr. San Angelo, how about I wheel you back? We wouldn't want you to have an incident."

My heart started pounding in my chest and my vision got spotty. I couldn't hold up the ruse anymore. I was beyond freaked out.

Ballard walked around behind the chair, and when he pushed, it wasn't back toward my room.

Then the most blessed sight appeared in front of me.

"Tiyuhin." I was barely able to call out to my uncle before Rey was right in front of me.

"Can I see some identification?" His hand rested on his service weapon and his eyes held that "fuck around and find out" look that always made folks on the receiving end back down.

It didn't quite work that way with Ballard. I was too weak to look up, but I could feel the menace coming off of him.

"I was just taking Mr. San Angelo back to his room. We were discussing—"

"Step away from my nephew. ID. *Now*."

There was a long enough pause, and I prepared to dive out of the way if these two went at it.

Then Ballard stepped back.

"I'll see myself out. Mr. San Angelo, we'll be in touch."

He strolled out of the facility with his head held high as if he were untouchable. He knew Rey would stay with me. Rey called in the license plate as he watched the guy drive out of the parking lot, and then he lambasted the staff for leaving me unattended, without someone who was an employee or security.

"Rey," I said softly, tugging on his arm. It was all I could say, as I could barely keep my head up. He whisked me back to my room, where I was inundated with questions from Dr. Gardner. I couldn't answer him though. I allowed the orderly to hook up my oxygen, and I waited for the dark spots to go away.

"This was too close," Rey said into the bat phone. "It's time." He looked down at me and shook his head.

"We're very sorry, Officer Cabral."

"Where's the uniform assigned to his room?"

"He said he had a call, and he'd be right out front," the orderly said. "He went out to his car."

"Barringer. It's Rey. This place isn't safe. You need to get him out of here."

"But Rey," I interrupted, as I tried to remember what all he said. "He was talking about blood infusions and stem cells. You gotta tell Barringer."

"I will, but I'm getting you out of here," he said, only to me. "You'll have to do the rest of your recovery somewhere else."

"Rey, if they found me here, it's too late. They'll find me again."

Rey gave me a long, stern look, but then he winced. I knew how hard this was for him.

"This is my fault," he said. "Rest up. We're getting you out of here. Somehow." And then he was gone to harangue the nurses again, and I was left with Dr. Gardner.

"Who is it, Roman?" His voice was barely over a whisper. "Who came for you?"

"I can't tell you... or you'll be in just as much danger. I may be leaving though, and there's still so much I want to ask you."

He grinned. "Don't think you'll get rid of me that easily."

I tried to stay awake, but the situation exhausted me. I turned over to watch Rey arguing with people outside, but I couldn't keep my eyes open.

SIX

C reed

"Come at me again."

Cross and Mark were having a jolly good time sparring with the ex-military guys Todd had recruited for his task force. They loved testing their strength versus the skills the men had gained in training and combat.

"Fuck, okay," Cross said, tapping out when a tall, rangy guy named Gordon got him in some sort of full-body lock. "This would be a whole lot more fun naked."

Gordon laughed and released his hold a bit, but Cross remained trapped between Gordon's thighs. "You into that erotic asphyxiation stuff? Cause that's all the action you'd see, brother. A few more seconds in that hold and you'd be out like a light."

"A few more seconds and I'd have you right where I wanted you," Cross said... and suddenly I caught a whiff of him not playing fair.

Gordon's body relaxed, and with a few quick movements, Cross had extricated himself and flipped over to get an arm around Gordon's throat, causing him to tap out.

"What the fuck was that?" Gordon asked as they rolled away from each other, panting on the grass.

"That," I answered for Cross, "was cheating. Come on, Cross. Let's see what you can do without using your evolutionarily heightened senses."

I squared off against him, feeling restless today. Todd and I had snuck out to the bar again the previous evening, but instead of watching the lovely Mirna get off, I got high off of some seriously fucked-up bikers going at it during an initiation event that left a dozen men bloody but happily drinking by the time the cops showed up. That kind of energy left me itching for a fight, and Cross was giving me the perfect outlet.

"Oh, you want to go, Lowell? Doesn't seem fair, you being all honorable and shit. Even without chemical assistance, I can still whip your—"

I had him on his stomach with his arms yanked up behind his back, pinning his shoulder with a knee. "You were saying?"

He grunted and tapped out with a booted foot. I let him up and sprang to my feet, ready to take on someone else. Anyone else.

"What the fuck was that?" Cross said.

Mark chuckled from the bench where he sat tuning a guitar. "That was Nurse Creed kicking your ass, my friend."

Gordon and his brother Craig laughed. "He's quicker than you, Cross. Smaller guys can get the upper hand if they're quick and know how to leverage their weight."

Cross stroked his beard. "It's more than that, though. Isn't it? You're *way* fucking strong."

I shrugged. "Could be. Here," I said, approaching him with my hands out. I released some pheromone and his pupils dilated. I put my hands on his shoulders and breathed out slowly. "Sorry. I didn't mean to get carried away. Did I hurt you?"

"Yeah, man," he said, smiling at me kindly. "See? This is why you aren't a fighter, Creed. You aren't supposed to heal the boo boos of the ones who hurt you."

"You didn't hurt me," I whispered. "I'm sorry. I should have worked off this energy last night. I hate fighting."

Cross put his hands on my waist, and I rolled my eyes. "Always the hippie boy. A lover, not a fighter. Give me some sugar, baby."

He bent me backward and kissed me with a big ol' smack of his lips before I could shove him away.

We all laughed, and I felt a little better. That was, until Todd came to the door and waved for me follow, then hurried back inside.

The level of activity in the hub was more frantic than usual when I entered.

In the sunken living room of the compound, Todd and his two assistants, who were former law enforcement consultants, were arguing with someone on a laptop screen.

The Source was sitting about three feet from a large-screen television, blue eyes wide, furiously smashing buttons on a gaming controller, the rest of their body perfectly still. Rhonda walked over and collapsed next to them on the floor.

"Guardian Creed, have you ever driven a car?"

The singsong, lilting quality of their voice always caught me off guard. I was still angry with them, so therefore, I wasn't in the mood to be captivated, if that even made any sense.

"No, I haven't." I made to move past them to ask Todd what was going on, but The Source held up a hand, and their desire for me to stop and talk to them almost overrode my sense of urgency to reach Todd.

"Guardian Creed—"

Remembering my manners, I said, "Excuse me for a moment." The fact that the powerful being could crush me with their thoughts should have made me pause.

I felt their displeasure through the link we shared, but they let me go. Past Creed would have been unable to ignore someone's dissatisfaction or unhappiness and would have done whatever possible to bring them joy.

Present Creed was tired of doing without for the good of the order.

"What's going on?"

Todd turned to look at me without his usual smile in greeting.

"Roman is all right," he said by way of introduction, which did little to placate me.

"Something happened."

"He had an unauthorized visitor. Roman couldn't tell Rey much, but Rey called it. We're working on a plan."

"We need to get him out of there, Todd. Enough is enough."

He held up a hand and looked to me for permission before touching me, and when I nodded, he placed a hand on my shoulder and walked me out the back door.

"You know they can still hear you," I said to him, as he led me away from the compound toward the back of the property beyond the creek.

"We've been doing some experimenting, and it seems like running water might be a bit of an interference. But you're right, and that's why I need you away from them right now."

"What's happened?" Worry filled me with rage, and I felt it seeping out of me into the ground. I needed to remain on an even keel and that wouldn't happen as long as Roman was in danger.

"What do you know of Longevity Health?"

That name jarred me out of my fury. "I've heard of them before. I've applied to a couple of their facilities over the years, but I've always been denied. What about them?"

"A man claiming he was a representative from Longevity Health attempted to kidnap Roman today. Rey isn't sure what the guy said to Roman, but he was attempting to push his wheelchair out the door when Rey arrived."

My chest burned as if I'd swallowed an ice-cold drink too fast. "You have to get him out of there. *Now.*"

Todd held up his hands. "We are, Creed. We're working on a plan. We can't take the chance that we'll be followed—"

"You can't bring him here. If The Source is still in contact with any of the others—"

"I'm not, Guardian Creed."

I turned to find them standing ten feet away.

"I was not eavesdropping. I felt your pain, Guar—"

"Stop calling me that!"

Todd and The Source both flinched at the sharp tone of my voice. I should have been trembling in fear at the prospect of disrespecting this powerful being, but I was beyond that.

The Source lowered their head. "My presence makes you angry. I apologize. But you and I are bound, Gua— Creed. I cannot help that I feel your fluctuation of emotions, or that I sense what troubles you. I am not able to communicate with my followers across long distances, though I know you fear this."

"I fear a lot of things. Mostly I fear you'll hurt the people I love when you don't get what you want, Teacher."

They tilted their head. "You call me this, and yet you no longer consider me someone to learn from. You claim to follow The Way, but you no longer trust in me."

If I thought The Source was capable of making a joke, I'd think they were winding me up to get a laugh. But that was the thing. They were unpredictable, but I'd never known them to be duplicitous.

"I call you Teacher because we were never on a first-name basis, and despite the fact that you nearly killed my boyfriend, I have manners."

I'd pushed my luck, I knew it, and Todd's face had gone stark white. I saw his hand twitch above his sidearm as if he planned to defend... *someone*. It probably wouldn't be me and my big mouth.

"Creed, I feel terrible that your beloved was harmed during the cere-mony. I don't understand why Stephen misled me. I would never have taken from the unwilling. This is not The Way. If Stephen were here now, I would enact punishment."

They'd said that before, during Todd's initial questioning, but he'd tread carefully. None of us had known whether The Source would come willingly to this undisclosed location—which they'd done. But how long would they cooperate?

When I didn't answer them, The Source carried on. "I know you all fear me, but that is not how I would have it. I would have a family, as we did long ago. The Way has been my practice for several millennia, and is larger than me, and I have never intentionally harmed a soul—only punished those in my family who chose to harm others. That is not the path I chose to follow."

Tears formed in their eyes, and the trees above us began to sway with a wind that didn't affect any of the forest around us.

"I know I am responsible for letting Stephen grow so powerful. I should have been aware that he was manipulating me."

Before we ended up swept away by monsoon rains, I reached for The Source's hand, startling us both.

"Stephen's ability to show you what he wanted you to see was rooted in some skill or power he brought with him to Gateway of the Sun. It was your teachings that made him stronger. And then he made friends with people who had dubious intentions. He created a whole network of people who got rich off of studying your blood and the healing practices of The Way. *That's* what happened when you trusted the wrong person... and I can't believe this hasn't happened at other times during the millennia that you've been following The Way."

The Source sobbed and crumpled against me. I had no choice but to support their lithe figure... and to absorb their pain.

This wasn't like when I fed off of the negative energy of my patients, or off of Roman all the times I'd held him when he was sad. This was not something I chose to do, and yet I did it because it was in my nature. It made me feel... used.

"You are so strong," The Source spoke in my ear, feeding me waves upon waves of negative energy. "If only I could have spent the last fifty years with you, learning how you have taken my teachings and become such a powerful healer... As it is, the failure of the Samhain ritual has left me weak. I fear... the consequences for us all."

The consequences of their actions. Psychic power left unchecked? Their place in the order of nature? Since they'd been tapped into the ley lines in the area, could there be an effect on the ecosystem? The local environment? Or was it more vanity, the death of The Way? And what would happen to those of us who had been their initiates? How would it affect our existence, since we'd been taught that we were all connected?

"You may call me Amergin," they whispered. "Since I have failed you as your Teacher, we may go forward as equals, Creed." They stepped back and bowed their head. "I will not interfere in what you need to do. And Creed, I would heal your beloved, if he consents. While I am no longer your teacher, I do possess more power... for now. I would do this as an act of contrition, for you."

Never in all of the years that I'd thought they were gone, nor in the weeks since I'd known they'd survived, had I ever imagined they would take ownership for this fiasco. I wasn't ready to believe them.

"Thank you. I hope you'll understand if it takes more than this conversation for me to trust you won't hurt Roman again." I knew my words wounded them, but they had a lot of work to do before I could trust them. "Todd, please tell me there's a plan?"

His gaze darted between us, unsure if this situation would flare up again or not.

The Source—Amergin? Why did that name sound familiar?— bowed once more and backed away. "Forgive me for intruding. I would be willing to enter a sensory deprivation state if it would allow for you to trust me."

"But... that would deprive you of energy," I said, realizing what a sacrifice they were allegedly willing to make. Without the presence of others, the touch, smell, and sight of others, The Source would not be replenishing their energy. For a being such as myself, it would be detrimental. I likely wouldn't survive a prolonged experience like that.

They nodded. "It would. Stephen used to... I spent a considerable amount of time in that state while under his influence. He stated it was for my protection. I should have known, should have never given him such power."

"I'm sorry—"

"However, it would not harm me if it is for a short time. Long enough for you to rescue your beloved and take him elsewhere. I understand why you do not want the others to find me. I... appreciate what you are sacrificing to keep me from their possession."

I'd been so angry, I hadn't even thought about how they'd fared under Stephen's control, or how this current captivity was affecting them. They'd allowed themselves to be "captured" though you couldn't really call it that. They were a prisoner here as well.

"Do you sense them? The others? Do you know how many of them there are?"

The Source closed their eyes and breathed in. A breeze blew past me, ruffling my hair, though it was coming from them, not the atmosphere.

"The old ones are few. I don't feel them often. If they exist, they aren't close. Others like Stephen, like you and your cohort, there are more, but they feel different. You feel pure to me. Mark, Cross, Stephen... they are strong, but they seem... murky. Their energy is not like yours. I want to know why yours is different. I've been surrounded by Guardian Stephen and the others for a long time. I feel soiled. You can help me, Creed. But I must deserve you. I know you need time to trust me, but my offer stands. I will heal Roman. I will undo what I have done. Make it right. Then we will determine my place in this world."

I would have argued, asked more questions, but I needed to know Roman was safe.

The— *Amergin* left us. They walked slowly toward the massive house, and I watched until their red robes were merely a wisp.

"They grow weak," Todd said, and I spun around to face him.

"You can tell?" There really was something different about Todd, but it wasn't in my wheelhouse of different.

"It's like their glow grows dimmer. I see them improve when they're with you, but when they're sad..."

"I know. Fuck. As if I needed more guilt. Fine. Just get me to Roman, away from here. I need to know he's safe and he's okay. When he's strong enough, I'll come back and see to... them."

Todd nodded. "I've arranged for a safe place for us to meet him. He'll be guarded the entire time. I'll take you there."

"Thank you, Todd. You have no idea what this means to me. I'll do whatever you—"

"I know. You already have."

Seven

Roman

I'd never experienced anything like the special operation enacted to evacuate me from the rehab hospital, and to be honest, I didn't remember a whole lot of it.

I wasn't sure how long I slept before Rey woke me.

"Hang tight, Junior. I'll be with you the whole time, all right? But you keep quiet. No running your mouth, got it?"

I barely remembered saying goodbye to a sleepy Alistair, but I know I promised him we'd finish our conversation, whatever that meant.

The nursing assistants loaded me onto a gurney, and with Rey at my side, they wheeled me out the back bay to a weirdly marked ambulance.

"Does that say 'Corrections'? What the fuck?"

"Shut up, Junior," Rey warned. They loaded my gurney into the van and two men in prison guard uniforms shut the back doors.

I gave Rey a pleading look, and he grabbed my forearm and squeezed, shaking his head.

It was not a pleasant ride. It was dark out. The van needed its shocks replaced, but within a few miles, I fell asleep as the van took the windy road out of Santa Cruz. I had a fleeting thought about Lola, worried about her, when I would see her, how I hoped Emmanuel would fucking play bingo with her...

"We're here," Rey whispered. "Don't say a fucking word."

I stayed motionless on the gurney as the guys in uniform unloaded me and wheeled me into a hallway.

"We gotta get up now. You're gonna have to walk, hear me? Then it's a short drive."

I did what Rey asked and tried to breathe normally. I wasn't hooked up to monitors so I hoped my heart would behave while I was trying not to be scared to death.

Rey and the deputies loaded me into the back of a Town Car, and Rey climbed in next to me. A Filipina woman in a white coat and her hair in a bun got behind the wheel, said something to Rey in Tagalog, and he answered. My tinnitus kept me from making out anything they said. My Tagalog must have been getting rusty. She drove away from what looked like the back of a jail and navigated the city streets until she got on Highway 101, headed toward San Francisco.

"You two need any water?" the woman asked. She held up two water bottles in one slender hand, and Rey reached forward to grab them.

"Thank you," he said. "And thank you for coming, Dr. Santos. Roman, this is Dr. Carmen Santos."

"Hi," I said. I was woozy. I hoped that earned my forgiveness for my lack of conversation.

"Please call me Carmen. It's so great to meet you, Roman. I've read your paper on La Mente, and I'm so glad we'll have a chance to talk."

I frowned at Rey, and he patted my knee.

"Dr. Santos is a parapsychologist from the University of Edinburgh, and she's been recruited by Barringer's task force to help out with our situation."

Ah. So she was on a semi-need-to-know basis.

"What about Creed?" I whispered to Rey.

"He's meeting us there," he said with a smirk. "Don't worry, once we get you settled, we'll give you two plenty of time to catch up."

"Finally."

I dozed until I felt the car descend what felt like a fairly steep off-ramp and come to a stop. A couple more turns, a checkpoint, and then the sound of tires on gravel.

"Wake up, Junior."

"But it's the middle of the night?"

Besides the sounds of cars going by overhead, it was relatively quiet, wherever we were. Tall trees blocked part of the view and there were no lights outside.

The car door opened and Dr. Santos reached in to help me to my feet. Footsteps approached on the gravel and strong arms caught me around the middle.

"Roman."

Like a dream, the scent of warm cookies filled my nose, and I was swept up into an embrace. I tangled my fingers into familiar curls and inhaled deeply.

"I can't see anything. I'm dreaming."

I heard chuckles and more talking, but I just wanted to lay back down. It had been such a long day. Didn't these people realize I needed my rest?

"Of course, darling, just a few more steps."

I stumbled in my dream, that whole-body jerk thing that sometimes happens, and then I was floating. It smelled like cookies and... damp? Like water was all around, but not fresh water. Not the beach, either. I liked this particular dream. I liked it even better when I was set down on a comfy bed, no more of the crinkly plastic mattress like at the rehab hospital. Alistair thought it was horribly rude to give us the pee-pee pad treatment. I wonder what Alistair would think. Would he be jealous if he knew I was in a real bed?

My eyes shot open and I sat up quicker than I probably should have, setting my tinnitus off. The sky was gray like the dawn, from what I could see through the thin white sheers over the large windows.

I was in a regular bedroom—not at the facility—but it wasn't *my* bedroom, nor my house or a house I was familiar with. My heart started to thrum faster than was good for me—

"Shhhh, Roman. You're safe." The pressure of a hand on my chest turned my head to the side and—

"Creed!" I grabbed his face and kissed him, though he laughed and continued to shush me.

"Roman, shhh, it's okay."

I wrapped my arms around him tightly and squeezed my eyes shut, praying that if this was truly a dream, it wouldn't be over anytime soon.

Creed stroked my hair and continued to whisper sweet things to me. He kissed my forehead, my temples, my eyebrows.

"Is it really you?" I cried in the darkness.

"If it's not, we've got to have a conversation. Just whose bed have you been sleeping in? And what are pee-pee pads? And who's Alistair? Do I need to be worried?"

"No! But... where? How?"

"Shhh, we've got to get your heart slowed down." He moved his hand to my chest, and I tried to concentrate on the heat coming from him.

"My heart always beats fast for you, baby." I laughed, but I knew I needed to calm the fuck down or I was going to need my oxygen. Or worse.

And then, it was like I was floating on a cloud of the sweetest euphoria and every inch of my skin tingled happily. My heart settled into a perfect sinus rhythm, and I could breathe unencumbered for the first time since this whole disaster happened. He rolled me onto my back and adjusted my pillow.

"Did you do it? Is that what I'm feeling?"

"Yes, Roman," he said, his voice a quiet singsong melody in the dimly lit room. "Just a little bit of energy coming your way, working on healing those cilia and tissues in your lungs so they can get you enough oxygen. Starting off easy."

I closed my eyes and snuggled down into the bed. "Is this how my lola feels, I wonder, when you heal her? I miss her."

"I know you do," he said. "I'm sorry. We'll get to her soon."

"I've missed you, you know that, but *God* have I missed sleeping in a real bed."

Creed chuckled. "I can imagine. You can spread out all you want—"

"Where's Rhonda?"

"She's safe. She's with Cross. Can I get you anything?" Creed asked softly. He continued to stroke my hair as he leaned over me. "Water? Food?"

"Just you. I have a million questions—"

"We'll have plenty of time to talk. All you need to know right now is that we're here with protection, we'll have some conversations, and then when it's time for me to go back, you can decide whether or not you want to come with me."

"What do you mean? Of course I'm coming with you!"

"Roman, there are a lot of things to consider. Please, just be with me now. We can talk after you get some more sleep."

He kissed me, knowing I would submit to his wishes. We'd talked several times over the weeks we were separated, about how much we missed being close, the intimacy of touch, the brush of skin on skin... Being away from him was a form of starvation, even though we'd only been together briefly before our bullshit situation tore us apart.

"All right. Just know you won't be shushing me later when I'm going down on you—"

"None of that. Not until you're healed."

"Uh-huh. We'll see." I rolled over and wrapped myself around him once more. "Let me hold you. If that's all I'm allowed to do," I said, trying not to sound like a petulant child, though I tended to get that way. "I need my energy if I'm going to yell at you."

Creed chuckled. "That's what you want to do with your energy?"

"You're in so much trouble, Nurse Creed."

"That's my man. Go to sleep."

I put a hand over his mouth and shushed him this time.

EIGHT

C reed

"It's not fair. You're an old man in a young man's body, and now I'm an old man, wearing old man's pajamas, in a young man's body."

"Does that mean I get to call you my old man?" We were joking with each other, but it was time for a serious conversation.

"Don't go getting all heavy on me," Roman said, as he nudged me with his foot. "I can see you getting up in your head, so stop it."

It was a brisk but sunny morning on Yerba Buena Island in the middle of the San Francisco Bay, and we were sitting on a private terrace of the Nimitz House. Barringer's benefactor, whom he hadn't named yet, had very high-up connections, and they'd arranged for us to have the run of this fabulous historic mansion. Once owned by the Navy, it was the home of Admiral Nimitz, commander of the Pacific fleet during WWII. He lived in this home from 1946 to 1966. The island was the meeting point of the Bay Bridge spans and was home to the Navy for many years. Treasure Island was adjacent and was going through a massive reconstruction effort, while a lot of the military complex stood abandoned.

"I can't help it, I'm sorry. I'm glad you're here." I tried smiling, but one look at Roman's poor body and I wanted to cry.

Hypovolemic shock—the body's response to massive blood loss—had run amok. After getting him settled in the bed the night before, I'd scanned his body as I'd been taught by the Teachers at Gateway of the Sun fifty years ago. It was one thing to read of his injuries on the medical reports from the rehab facility doctor, but to see the total sum of them in front of me? Broke my damn heart.

Roman flicked his hair out of his eyes. It was the longest I'd ever seen it, and after his shower this morning, it was shiny black, gleaming in the sunlight. The pieces on top, which he'd always left a little bit longer, were now nearly to his chin. I loved it, but what I didn't love was how pronounced his cheekbones were, or how pale his skin was. It was nearly winter—we were two weeks from the winter solstice—so I'd insisted he take every opportunity to absorb Vitamin D into his skin.

He sat in the chair across from me with his feet in my lap for me to tend to and his head tossed back, his face to the sun. His cane leaned against his chair, but thankfully we hadn't needed to bring his oxygen tank out with us, as he'd been doing just fine without it.

I couldn't fully curse my powers or my life situation, knowing that I had the ability to supplement his medication and physical therapy with some healing of my own.

"I'm glad too, but you need to quit staring at me like I'm going to blow away. I'm much better, especially now."

I kept my gaze down at my hands as they worked his arches, the balls of his feet, his toes. His circulation looked good, which pleased me. Hopefully, with a few more months of physical therapy and my healing touch, he'd be back to nearly normal. The doctors had been worried about his kidneys, and I'd been ready to donate one of mine—hell, both of them—but they were back to functioning at 70% and improving. He might never have the endurance or energy level he once had, no matter what I did, but I'd give my everything to get him as close to healthy as possible.

That brought the burning tears of shame back to my eyes.

"I'm sorry, Roman. I can't forgive myself for this, for bringing you into this."

He frowned at me. "What makes you think this was all about you? Creed, my aunt and uncle would have been involved with or without you. My getting hired as a consultant? None of that had anything to do with you. But finding these guys? Putting a stop to the ceremony? That was you. You gave us what we needed, and what you told us saved my aunt and cousin. Saved *me*. So while you're over there beating yourself up, you need to add that to your mental stew."

"Why do you always let me off the hook?" My throat was so full, I could barely get the words out. "It would help if you would yell at me or something."

He snorted. "I'll spank you, if you want." He cleared his throat, and I looked up, making sure he was okay. His gaze was definitely accusatory now. "I *am* angry, though. I want to know why you haven't taken care of yourself, why you've waited. I know you were avoiding The Source, but Creed... you need their energy, at least until we sort this out and you can get back to being around people."

I took his feet off my lap and stood, moving away him before I began to breathe fire. I moved to the railing and stared out over the tree-tops to the calm, midnight-blue waters of the Bay. "You don't know what you're asking."

I heard his chair scrape, and I cursed.

"Don't get up."

"Don't tell me what to do," he grumbled.

My tears fell on the railing as I heard the clunk of his cane and the drag of his slippered feet. Then I realized he could fall, which could set back his recovery. I rushed to his side, but he slapped my hands away when I reached for him.

"Knock that shit off. I can do it myself."

"Now who's being stubborn?" I bit back a laugh. He might forgive me too easily, but he *haaaated* being patronized.

"Fuck off," he said, but he was smiling now too.

When he reached the railing, I stood behind him, inhaling his unique scent. The smell of the ocean, which he hadn't lost completely, despite his time in the hospital, and that underlying spice, his fire, that smoky goodness that was all the fight in him. I pressed up against his back and ran my nose along his neck.

"You have all day to quit that," he said, pressing back against me. "It feels so good to be outside. I mean, I was wheeled out into the yard a few times a week, but this... you... Heaven."

"I love you so much, Roman," I whispered, kissing his temple softly. "I couldn't bear it if I lost you."

"You're not gonna lose me," he said, letting his head fall back on my shoulder.

I wrapped my arms around him and was really invested in kissing his neck—where it met his shoulder and made him shiver—when he said the last thing I wanted to hear.

"I want to talk to them. The Source."

My blood ran cold, and I stepped back. "No."

Roman clutched the railing, his eyes wide from my reaction. "Creed, hear me out."

"There is no fucking way in hell I will ever allow them near you after what they've done. Why would you even want to?"

"I want to understand! I want to know how it works, what their life has been like, what the endgame is with all of this. Don't you want to know? I know you were learning how to be a healer from them at the commune, but don't you want to know what their ultimate plan is? Because after what happened at the lake, you have to admit, there must be one. There's something they've been trying to build, trying to attain, over all these years. All of the lives they've connected with... there was a reason for it all. Don't you wonder?"

"It doesn't matter. I'm going to make sure they never hurt another person again. If they refuse to cooperate, I'll let them starve to death."

"Creed, I know you're angry—"

"Yeah, I am. Why aren't *you*? They nearly killed you and your family. How can you—"

"Because this is important. What you do, what you *could* do... Think of the possibilities."

"I've had fifty years to think of the possibilities," I muttered. "Look, Todd has talked me into working with them, trying to show them how I've been caring for the elderly in the hopes that they can eventually learn to coexist with humanity. But Roman..." I exhaled, trying to keep my cool while fuming inside. "They're never going to be able to be alone. They're like a child, or a moody teenager who throws god-level tantrums. They should be locked behind bars for what they've done, but Todd thinks—and so do your aunt and uncle—that there's no way they can bring them before a court of law and have them found competent to stand trial, leaving an institution as the only option. In the wrong hands... they could destroy us all. Or they could cease to exist. I'm not sure I can handle being responsible for either outcome."

Roman turned to face me and placed his hands on my waist. "I hadn't thought about it that way."

"It's *all* I can think of. At this point, all I can see is that I'm going to be responsible for them and their actions for the rest of my existence."

Roman pulled me close, and I tucked my head into his neck, inhaling his scent, praying we had just a little more time. I didn't know how to exist without him, but I didn't want to drag him further into this nightmare.

"We'll figure this out, Creed. Together. You're not alone anymore." I started to pull away—how could I make him understand—but he gripped my waist. Hard. "Not alone, which means you don't make decisions alone, especially ones that involve me."

I pulled back and gazed into his eyes, which were full of determination—and I broke.

"I've been so scared," I whispered, relieved to share this burden, even a tiny part of it. "I thought I'd lost you that night, and I've been terrified of losing you every day since. And I'm just as afraid of losing myself."

It was his turn to shush me. "It's going to be okay," he said, and he sounded so certain, I wanted to believe him. "We're going to figure it out. You're not on your own, dammit. I may be an old man now, but I'm *your* old man, and I'm here for you. I won't let you get lost."

We spent the rest of that first day in bed, with Roman napping and me doing what little I could do to heal him. I'd need a huge infusion of energy to do all he needed and that wasn't possible at the moment. The only other souls in the house right now were Todd and Rey—this Dr. Santos, whom Todd had arranged to join us, was staying in another building. There was also, apparently, a squad of private security guys, whom Todd's benefactor selected, dispersed around the mansion. I sensed their movements from time to time, their unique energy signatures, but it was faint. Now, whether that was because of my focus being on Roman or my weakness, I'm not sure. But I needed an infusion of energy, and it was going to have to be soon. Or else I'd need an Exchange, which I really didn't want to do.

I was having all kinds of feelings about my faith. I didn't appreciate having to go through another religion-based crisis at my age. On one hand, following The Way had served me well for over fifty years. I'd helped a lot of people, and I'd been fairly happy, if a little lonely. But there had been an end point. After what had just happened, and Roman's curiosity about the jackpot at the end of the rainbow for The Source—not to mention that Cross and Mark had revealed I would die a painful death without an Exchange, without a steady intake of blood —my whole perspective had been shaken off its foundation.

I exhaled when the Queen song "Who Wants To Live Forever" started playing in my head. Like Freddy said, no one.

But that wasn't true. The Source had lived for millennia, and now we were dealing with the fallout of Stephen's betrayal. Would Amergin carry on? Would they fight to have their existence continued; The Way carried on? Or had Stephen spread information and data on Amergin's blood so far and wide that those seeking immortality would chase them until the end of time, and me with them?

Roman stirred beside me, and my morbid musings ceased, because he was here with me, he hadn't sent me away, he wanted me despite the chaos. Whether that would be the case always or—

A soft knock at the door took me from my thoughts. I climbed out of bed and put on my sweatpants before opening the door enough to slip out into the hall.

Todd had a concerned expression. "How is he?"

"Weak, but his pulse has been stable all day. He hasn't needed his oxygen. I'm going to have him use some when he wakes up, though, just to give him a boost."

"Sounds good. Rey's been cooking all afternoon, so we're going to have a feast in a while, but I wanted to let you know... Dr. Santos was able to procure a pint of A positive. She's been working on a research project that involves studying blood. Would that be—"

"A lifesaver. Well... it will be *very* helpful. Thank you. Wait—does she know about me?"

Todd shook his head. "She was led to believe it's in case Roman needs it."

"Good thinking," I said. "For me, the Exchange has always been more about the ritual and the energy than the actual blood, but after talking to the others, I guess I've been naive. The blood is necessary. I've only ever resorted to bagged blood when I've been between jobs and didn't have a person who'd given consent for an Exchange."

"And you don't feel comfortable doing one with anyone here?"

I shook my head. "Not Roman. He's not well enough. With anyone else, I'd feel like that's crossing a line."

Todd shoved his hands in his pockets. "I know I haven't before, but... I am now. Offering."

I narrowed my eyes. "Why? Curiosity killed the cat, you know, Agent Barringer."

He rolled his eyes. "Yes, I'm curious. But I'd do it because I saw the shape Roman was in when he arrived. I see how worried you are. And I know you want to be strong for him." He looked down at his shoes. "And I've gotten to know you better. I see what you've sacrificed. I trust you."

I leaned back against the wall in the hallway. "I'll think about it. But I already sense there's something different about you. You know that I'll know even *more* if I take your offering."

He cocked his head to the side. "I didn't know it worked that way."

"That's why I'm hesitant. Everyone has something to hide, don't they?"

"It's not like that, Creed. I honestly don't know what you see, what you think is different about me. My... benefactor, he says the same thing. I mean, sure, I'm a bit of an empath, I think? Maybe I have a little stronger intuition—"

"That's part of it, but there's more. Maybe you truly don't know.

But I *will* know if I take from you. You need to be sure you're ready for that."

"I appreciate your honesty."

I became very aware of the fact that we were having an intense conversation, and I was standing there with no shirt on, which felt a bit too exposed for the subject. Todd must have felt the same. He stood taller and cleared his throat.

"I... well, I just wanted to let you know about dinner. It'll be ready in about twenty minutes if you two want to join us. If you would rather I bring—"

"No, I think it'll be good for Roman to be up for a little while. I'll bring him out in a bit."

There was more Todd wanted to say, and he lingered in the hallway as I turned for the door.

"Creed... I swear, I'm doing everything in my power to ensure you can get back to your life."

"And that may or may not be possible. We'll be out shortly."

I closed the door and rested my forehead against it. Todd's guilt assaulted me through the door. It seemed to me he was a bit sensitive about this case, considering he was supposed to be a big bad G-man. He'd changed a lot of my opinions about law enforcement. So had Rey. I wondered if part of Todd's agreement to take on this special assignment had to do with his own ambiguity about the work he did.

"Creed?"

I turned around to find Roman sitting up in bed, his hair tousled in the sexiest way, his old man pajamas unbuttoned, revealing his velvety-soft skin and his dark brown nipples that I longed to taste.

"Are you feeling rested?" I held myself back from pouncing on him, but he presented such a mouthwatering picture. And my mouth *was* watering.

"I'm feeling... some kinda way."

He ran his hand down his stomach and caught his thumb on the waistband of his pajama bottoms, revealing a hint of black hair.

"You're *looking* some kinda way," I said, my voice hoarse.

"You're looking at *me* some kinda way," he retorted, with a hint of a smile. He lowered the waistband an inch more, revealing the crown of his very erect cock. "What are Nurse Creed's thoughts about fellatio?"

"Nurse Creed has a lot of thoughts about fellatio. Mostly that it could be too soon—"

"But that it also has a surprising number of benefits."

Oh, Roman was definitely feeling better. He shifted his legs and lowered his waistband to reveal the rest of his shaft. I could feel it on my tongue from memory, though I stood across the room. I remembered every vein, every curve, and his taste... so delicious.

"Benefits like dopamine?"

"Oh yes, and the endorphins that are released upon climax," he said, giving himself one long stroke. "Fellatio can also bring a person to a state of relaxation deeper than meditation. I've heard..." He gasped as he ran his fingers over the tip of his cock. "That orgasm can actually improve the function of one's immune system."

I approached the bed, my own erection pressing against the front of my pants, begging for freedom.

"I think Nurse Creed would approve, as long as his patient agrees that if his heart rate gets too out of control—"

"Yes, yes, we'll stop, I promise." Roman's seduction fell victim to his impatience. "Will you take care of me, baby?" And his impatience was just as irresistible. No wonder he got whatever he wanted.

I crawled toward him and smiled, licking my lips, making sure they were properly lubricated to take him into my mouth.

"I'd be glad to take care of you." Without touching him, I blew air over his sensitive skin, making him shiver. "But you have to let me do the work, and I'm going to take it slow. You come whenever you want to. Don't fight it. There's plenty of time—"

"Please, baby."

I could never, ever resist this man.

I slid down his body, rubbing my cheek, my lips, my nose over his cock as I gently pulled off his pants. I wanted access to all of him. I paid close attention to his pulse as I kissed him in all the spots I'd discovered he liked, when we'd done this the first time. I found more that made him sigh, made him jump, made him relax into the mattress. Those I concentrated on until I couldn't wait to taste him anymore. But even then, I only used my tongue, lazily brushing over his crown, giving him pleasure, but not doing enough to drive him wild.

The need coming from him had me buzzed, but it was hazy. Sleepy, like morning sex, and not full-potency Roman, which would have knocked me on my ass in the best way.

His breathing was steady, and his heart rate was slightly elevated but still in the normal range. His fingers on one hand tangled loosely in my hair, more stroking my scalp than anything... it was such a loving gesture. I looked up into his eyes, and I was touched to see him smiling at me. He let his eyes fall closed, and his head lolled to the side and then rolled to the back. Drowsily beautiful Roman was one of my favorite views.

I wanted to do more. I wanted to crawl on top of him, be closer to him, and take him inside me, ride him until we were both ready to explode, but this time was about him. The act of giving him oral plea-sure relaxed me into a sort of drugged-out euphoria that spread through my body, easing my aches and pains and leaving me feeling as delicious as Roman tasted.

His breath hitched and his heart sped up slightly. I was about to stop what I was doing when he opened his eyes and let out a long moan. He filled my mouth to overflowing. His energy bathed me in bliss, stim-ulating my cells and making me high. His hand tightened in my hair, and then he used both hands to caress my jaw, my neck, and my lips as he praised me, feeding me all that positive sex energy my body craved from him.

I sucked his thumb into my mouth, and that brought on another jerk and shudder, as well as more of his spend to coat my tongue. For the first time since our first day in bed together, I felt at peace. Mostly. The world was on fire and we were on the run, but for this moment, I was sated and happy.

"Come and kiss me," he ordered, tugging gently on my chin. "I want some."

I complied, moaning as he dragged his tongue over mine and sucked at my lips. He licked my cheek, where some of his cum had leaked out, and I whimpered. He was such a gracious lover.

"Come up here," he said against my lips. "I know you've got some for me. I can feel how much you need this."

"Roman, I—"

"You're about to blow, I can tell by that sound you're making and the way you're shaking. Give it to me, baby. I want it."

Against my better judgement, but helpless to deny him, I got to my knees and straddled his chest. Roman pulled down my sweats with one forceful tug. My cock brushed his lips once and then he sucked me down.

He was right—I'd been so close that a little suction and a few more strokes of his tongue and I came hard, grasping the headboard as I cried out. He sighed as he lapped up every drop, sucking me until my legs were shaking so bad, I could barely hold myself up. His heartbeat was normal again, but mine was all over the place.

I collapsed next to him and he wrapped me in his arms. "Best medicine yet. I think I would have been out of the rehab place weeks ago if I could have had you like that even once."

I laughed and snuggled closer. "I take it you feel okay? This was supposed to be about you, you know."

"It *was* about me," he said. "I got what I wanted. I want some more here in a little while, too."

I sat up and brushed his hair back from his face so I could kiss him. "You can have anything you want, *after* you take some oxygen, and you eat your dinner."

"Good," he said, stretching his arms over his head. He reached for the cannula and looped it over his head like it was second nature to him. He didn't even fight me on it. "I'm going to be planning all the ways I can lay just like this and have everything I want. You might have to get a little flexible, you know, bent over, ass in the air for the rim job of your life... or you on my lap, riding me with those strong thighs."

"It's like you've had a lot of time to think about this," I joked, but his fantasies were enticing. "As long as you're up to it."

"Oh, I'm gonna be up. I'm gonna be *all* up in you."

"I can't wait," I said. And I meant it.

NINE

R oman

I was a new man when we emerged from the bedroom a half hour later. Maybe it was the sex—which, God, Creed rocked my world—but wearing actual clothes instead of pajamas? And smelling Filipino dinner after weeks of hospital food with only the occasional treat from my aunties? Heaven.

Okay, I was wearing track pants and a t-shirt, still wearing my slippers, but it was a step up, and closer to the fashion of my age than the grandpa pajamas Bernadette brought me. They were comfortable, sure, and better than having my ass hang out of the gowns, but when Alistair busted out the same exact pair I had? Not cool.

Creed walked me down the hallway and toward the formal dining room, which had a folding table and chairs set up. He explained that Todd's team only had time to bring the necessities. The mansion was clean inside, fading outside, but we were in one of the most picturesque places on the Bay and we were being closely guarded, so we could relax a little.

Rey was stirring a pot of arroz caldo at the table when I approached.

"It smells like paradise in here." The chicken porridge dish was the absolute best thing to eat any time you felt under the weather. It had been one of Lola's signature dishes. "I can't believe you made my favorite!"

"How's it going, Sleeping Beauty?" Rey said, as he gave me a side hug and kissed my temple. Ever since I'd almost died for the second time, he was much more affectionate with me. I didn't dare tease him about it. I kind of preferred this treatment to the frequent headlocks, takedowns, and teasing.

"I'll take that over Six Dollar Man. I think I came out pretty beautiful from my sleep," I said, giving my uncle each profile view. He grumbled under his breath and served me a heaping bowl.

"You gonna get that hair cut or what?"

"I don't know. What do you think, babe?"

Creed vigorously shook his head.

I loved finally having someone on my side in family battles.

The FBI agent Todd Barringer entered the room from the front of the house. He made his way over to me and rested a hand on the back of my chair.

"How are you feeling, Dr. San Angelo?"

I shook his offered hand. "Roman, please, and closer to human than I thought I'd be."

"Great news." He patted my shoulder and headed over to get a bowl from Rey. "You were pretty out of it when you arrived last night."

"He thought he was dreaming." Creed tucked in next to me at the makeshift dining table and stared hungrily at his food. He waited for me to take a bite before he tried his. As he pulled the spoon from his lips, his eyes rolled back and he sighed happily.

"My roommate, Dr. Alistair Gardner, he'd be so jealous. Rey, he's from New Zealand but he lived in the Philippines for a while. Speaks Tagalog, can you believe it?"

"Seemed like a fun old guy."

"Yeah. We had a lot in common. He's a professor of cultural anthropology."

"Yeah. More weird shit. You should have heard the conversations." Rey rolled his eyes.

Creed gave me a quizzical look.

"Alistair knows a lot about the unusual uses for human blood that people have partaken in over the centuries."

We shared a look.

"Had he heard of The Way?"

"No," I said, wiping my mouth. "At least not that he shared. He did try to warn me, though. About digging where I shouldn't."

Our last conversation was fuzzy, but his choice of words niggled at the back of my mind.

"They have ways of making young academics disappear, or wish they had."

"Roman?" Creed must have sensed my unease. "Do you need your oxygen?"

"No, I'm... Never mind." I gazed around the table, uncomfortable with the concerned stares, and decided to change the subject. "So tell me what I've missed," I asked, as everyone took a breather from their food. I wondered what they'd actually tell me, given my delicate condition.

When no one spoke, Barringer wiped at his mouth and carefully arranged his napkin on the table. "Our current status is this: Adams, acting as his own attorney, has requested a competency hearing. If he succeeds in convincing the judge he's not fit to stand trial, he'll spend a nice chunk of time in a psychiatric facility until either he miraculously recovers, or they let him out for good behavior."

"I take it that's not what you want." It wouldn't be a stay at the country club, but it wouldn't necessarily be an adequate punishment for him.

"It's not, but it's better than him being free."

Creed's amber eyes were darker than usual below his furrowed brow. He crossed his arms over his chest and listened to Todd speak as if every word had the potential to stoke his fury.

"Hicks is still MIA. His wife Donna is cooperating with authorities and we have her in protective custody. She'll tell us whatever it takes to stay out of her husband's clutches again. I've got her working with Dr. Santos—you met her last night? She'll be back tomorrow, and if you're up for it, she wants to talk to you."

I glanced at Creed. "About what? What's her interest in this?"

"Carmen's a board-certified medical examiner and a parapsychologist. She's an expert on the effects of life-prolonging techniques used throughout the world, studying remains to see what, if anything, can be found."

"You mean as far as proof of efficacy?"

"Something like that," Barringer said. "I've asked her to look over the research being done at BioBourne to make sense of it. Looking for ethical discrepancies, whether they were harming individuals with their studies. Whatever we can find to build these cases against Adams and Hicks and whoever else we dig up. SCPD detective Ross Sterling is working the local side, but since the bodies of the four men were never recovered from the explosion, there go the attack cases. They're looking into charges for the house explosion, but since Adams is being charged with four counts of kidnapping and attempted murder of your family and Donna Hicks, and since she was kidnapped across state lines... it's all a mess.

"I don't know how the court side is going to pan out, honestly. It feels like a lot of effort that will likely go nowhere if Adams goes for a noncompetence deal. The only good thing that's coming out of this is he's considering talking to us more about the business of keeping The Source."

"Fucking weird," Rey muttered. Poor guy couldn't get away from it.

"And speaking of The Source," I began, placing my hand on Creed's leg, "what's being done about them?"

Todd and Creed exchanged a long look before he spoke again.

"At this point, The Source is off the books."

"What do you mean?"

More looks exchanged.

"Well, we have no way to prove they exist. No records of any kind. Whether it's because they've been around since before Christ, or if this is all an elaborate ruse—"

Creed snorted softly and shook his head. "You can't hold someone accountable for breaking a law if their existence predates all modern laws. They're older than any existing civilization except maybe some indigenous groups or the Egyptians, and more powerful than any living creature."

"We think," Todd said, and Creed shrugged. "All we have to go on are eyewitness accounts from the Loch Lomond incident, Creed's memories, and what little The Source is able to tell us."

"What do you mean? Are they cooperative?"

More looks. If I'd been the jealous type, I might have threatened Slick-Looking FBI Agent guy to leave my boyfriend alone, but A) I had no need to be jealous. I had full confidence in Creed's feelings for me. Maybe I was being cocky, but it was the one known factor in this whole thing. I could use it to solve for x or y in any equation. B) Todd Barringer was a looker, but Creed kept him at a distance; and C) he didn't give me the steal-your-boyfriend vibe.

"It's difficult to explain," Todd said. "I'm sorry, that sounded patronizing. What I mean is, they seem to not have a good understanding of what's going on, of how much time has passed, or even what's happened in recent history... which to them is apparently the last four hundred years. They claim to recall traveling to the so-called New World with their followers and finding a parcel of land on a ley line in Canada, away from other white settlers. They said that they avoided contact with the indigenous groups, and when threatened, they claimed to move on, eventually ending up in the Santa Cruz Mountains. That's as much as we've gotten."

Creed exhaled. "It's difficult to get them talking about themselves for long without it leading to a lecture of some sort. They're watching TV, meditating, giving lessons to those who want them at the compound, and preparing for the next equinox, as they say they've always done."

"And do you believe them?" I asked. "Is it at all possible that it's true?"

"You were closer to them than any of us. What do you think?" Todd asked. His question jolted me.

"I'm not really sure what to think. I know they are powerful. I remember my whole body buzzing, like my tinnitus turned up to a thousand and running through my entire being. If they had that effect on me, who knows what else they can do? It was... terrifying. It wasn't at all like when I'm with Creed."

Rey made a retching sound, and I was pleased to discover I had enough energy to throw a wadded-up napkin at his face. I must have felt better because it bounced off his nose.

Creed gave my leg a squeeze. "A combination of things occurred to make the ritual worse for you. Not only did they not use the pheromone, because it's not used for a ritual initiation, but The Source also lost control that night. Stephen was focused on saving himself instead of keeping up the illusion that everything was fine and the initiates were there voluntarily. Once that illusion came down, The Source claims they were rattled, dismayed that things hadn't been done properly, and they couldn't hold on to their power. Then, well, everything went haywire."

All of these pieces of information made me think it was even more important that I meet The Source. I'd have to make Creed understand that it would help me come to terms with what had happened to me, to get my questions answered by The Source.

"So, while I appreciate finally being sprung from the hospital, we have to have a plan."

"The plan," Rey said, "is we keep hunting for Hicks. We put Adams away for a long fucking time. We get you well. Then we figure out just how big this whole thing is."

"That's great, but how?"

"That seems to be where we're stuck," Todd offered. "I have FBI resources as well as assistance from my benefactor—"

"Who is this person?" Rey asked. "How do we know we can trust them?"

Todd liked to fade into the background until he was ready, and he clearly wasn't ready to tell us about the one financing his investigation.

"All I can tell you is this—my last big case with the FBI left more things unanswered than answered. My boss was under fire from *her* boss, and the next thing I know, I'm being reassigned and tasked with forming a unit of... folks... to look into crimes involving subjects that are out of the ordinary."

Creed snorted. "You mean freaks of nature?"

Todd gave him a sad smile. "You know I don't think that. You also know that I'm naturally curious, so I guess they decided I'd be a good fit. My benefactor has valuable connections with powerful people. I've seen things, met experts... there's no explanation for some of the things I've experienced except to say that there are, well, exceptional individuals out there. Most of them are good. Some of them seem hell bent on hurting people. I can't stand for that."

The room was quiet until Rey grunted. "More weird-ass mother-fucking shit. How do you deal with it, man? I became a cop because I wanted structure. I wanted answers, wanted to solve fucking problems. Now I've got vampires, ancient Druids... what's next?"

"Maybe don't ask that," Todd said with a nervous laugh. "Sorry, but if this subject is undesirable for you, Officer Cabral, you might not want to know more."

"Shit. And it's Rey. I'm officially on administrative leave."

I sat up straighter in my chair. "Leave? What do you mean?"

Rey's smirk fell, and he rested his elbows on the table. "Captain Rojas and I had a disagreement."

"When? Wait, tiyuhin. For how long?"

"'That's up to you' is what he said." Rey using finger quotes was never a good thing.

"It's because of me, huh?" My heart thudded painfully in my chest. Creed reached for me and I immediately felt his healing, but I was too upset.

"Told you I didn't do good with the politics bullshit." Rey winked. "It's a little vacation from the bullshit."

"But your pension," I said, and then I took in a shaky breath. Creed cursed, and he darted from the table. Seconds later he was back with my oxygen tank. "I hate this thing," I said, as I put the cannula on my face and took a few breaths. Creed pulled his chair closer to mine and wrapped me in his arms. His touch made the rest of this a little less awful.

"Hey, let's not go counting Dicknaldo out, all right? I've still got some mileage on me. I've got my twenty years, I'm less than a year from my three percent at fifty. I could retire. I still want to work, but if it's not with SCPD, so be it."

"Keep talking, and I might recruit you," Todd said with an eager smile. "That is, if you could put aside your disdain for the extraordinary."

"Extraordinarily *weird*." Rey leaned back on two legs of his chair and gestured toward Creed and me. "Does it look like I have a choice? It's not like I'm getting rid of the fanger over there."

We all laughed, but then fell silent. Talk about the elephant in the middle of the room. Since the valve had been open, I intended to make use of the time.

"So what was it like in Santa Cruz in the seventies? I mean, Rey was there, but he was a kid."

Creed smiled shyly and his eyes darted around. "Are we really going to talk about this?"

"Hell yeah," I said, snuggling in closer and resting my head on his shoulder. "I want to know what you've been up to, where you've been."

"Did you wear bell bottoms? Go to discos?" Rey asked.

"Wow, okay. I've never talked about this before. Uh, where do I start?"

"Where did you go after you left Gateway of the Sun?" Todd's smile was so kind, so caring. I was happy that of all the people Creed had to be stuck with besides me, he had someone like Todd. I tucked in, ready to hear all of Creed's adventures... and that was the last thing I remembered.

TEN

Creed

"When I left the commune, I was in panic mode. I ran as far away as I could, and then I walked through the woods until I was ready to drop. I was still in my black ceremonial garments and covered in blood. I used someone's garden hose to clean up, and I'm not proud to say that I took some clothes and boots out of someone's truck. I was afraid to look out of place or cause folks to call the police.

"I eventually found myself in Felton near Roaring Camp. They were having some sort of festival, and I found some food to eat, but it was the people I needed to be around. I immediately felt better, being around the festivalgoers. They were giving free rides on the train to the boardwalk, so I hopped on. I happened to meet a nice nurse and her husband onboard, and she told me they were hiring at the place where she worked in San Jose, and asked if I wanted the information."

"At this point, you thought everyone was dead?" Todd was gentle with his questioning. It really did make it easier, and I figured he knew my biggest secret, so why not tell him the rest?

"The last people I saw were Stephen and two others, but I couldn't make them out. He was arguing with The Source before I blacked out. When I came to, everyone was on the ground, bloody, motionless." I squeezed my eyes shut to rid myself of the vision. "I wish... I should have checked. Cross said he was playing dead, that Mark found him later. Mark hid in the bushes. I must have missed him. And Caleb. The fact that he was helping Stephen all along..."

"He's not helping him anymore. He pled guilty to the lesser charge of attempted kidnapping, said he would talk to no one, and he's due for sentencing next month." Todd frowned. "He had the same attorneys who were trying to help Stephen. I think EVE gave him a deal: keep quiet and we'll set you up after you've served your time."

"How long you think he'll serve?" Rey asked Todd.

"Maybe two years?"

"And in prison, he'll have plenty of energy to keep himself strong. He could even recruit others. He could come out stronger—"

"Let's not worry about that tonight," Todd said, placing a hand on the table in front of me. "I've got eyes on him. I want to hear more of your story."

"You mean how I survived for fifty years relatively undetected?" Rey and Todd stared at me, waiting for me to continue. "I'm the evening's entertainment, huh?"

Rey snorted. "Well, I'd make fun of Junior, but he's asleep."

I gazed down at Roman's peaceful expression tucked into my chest. He couldn't be that comfortable. I tried to move, but he doubled down on the cuddling.

"And I guess I'm stuck here. Okay. Where was I?"

"Did you go to San Jose?"

"I did. But I was afraid it was too close to Loch Lomond, and if anyone was looking for me, I wanted to be far away. I worked at a couple places as an orderly, which was fine for a while. Long enough to get a few paychecks under my belt. I started hanging out at a local community center, where I could shower and keep my few possessions in a locker, and I found a notice on the bulletin board. The VA was looking for nursing assistants to help with the veterans coming back from Vietnam. They offered paid training, so I went. Figured it was the least I could do, since I hadn't served."

"That must have been heartbreaking."

"It was. I'm going to be honest, in order to survive, I didn't always follow the legal path. I did have to lie to get hired. I fabricated a nursing degree, but eventually I went to school. Went a couple of times, actually. But I followed the VA to Massachusetts in nineteen seventy-four, and I stayed there for about four years."

"You did what you had to," Todd said. "Were you doing Exchanges then?"

Ah. He wanted specifics. I rubbed at the back of my neck with my free hand. "Uh, yeah. Back then, I did it more frequently. I needed to. I was still learning, feeling out what made me feel my strongest. It's a balancing act. Every day. I would usually find someone outside of work, though. Back then, it was pretty easy to find a willing partner as long as you knew where to look. Then I moved to the Midwest, worked in a hospital, and that's when I discovered that I could do the most good— and take in the most energy—by working with seniors. And there weren't a whole lot of opportunities to... connect."

"Why the Midwest?"

"By then, I thought I should see the country, you know? I'd been given this second chance, this new existence, and I knew I needed to use it. Plus, I would get this feeling every once in a while. Like something was wrong, I shouldn't be in that particular place, that maybe someone was watching me."

"How do you mean?" Todd asked.

"A couple of times I ran into people on my way to and from work, you know, like on TV where the main character realizes they're being followed. I don't know how to explain it, but I'd come across people who seemed out of place. I sensed odd energy signatures in people a few times—it changes when you follow The Way, sort of like a shift to your aura? And then a couple times I'd come back to wherever I was staying and something would be out of place or missing. So I'd move on. And the small towns weren't a good fit. Too many people knew each other, and everyone felt they were entitled to know all about your past. Then it was the eighties, then it was AIDS..."

"God, you went through all that," Rey murmured. "That had to be... I lost an uncle. Scared the shit out of me."

"Well, yeah," I said. I didn't want to make assumptions, but I knew Rey wasn't straight. "You were probably at that formative age—"

"And knew I was bi, yeah. I kept that shit locked down for a long time."

Oh, Rey. "I could tell, you know. When someone is infected? I can tell. On one hand, I could avoid intimate contact with them as a partner, but on the other, I felt compelled to heal them, help however I could. It was beyond my power to cure, but I could ease their suffering some. No one should have to die like that."

"Were you afraid you'd contract HIV?" Todd asked.

"I knew enough about the disease to avoid it. I can tell when someone is sick, whether I do an Exchange or not. I was careful. I went back to San Francisco in nineteen ninety-two. I hadn't been there in twenty years, and it... those were the hardest years. I worked in hospice with AIDS patients then. It took too much out of me. I left after three years and made my way through all of the major metropolitan areas in the U.S. Los Angeles, Dallas, New Orleans—I loved New Orleans—Miami, Atlanta, D.C., New York, Chicago... I tried them all.

"And everywhere I went, I looked for him. Libraries. And then when the internet was accessible, I found him. A picture. His new identity. Research became my obsession. But it's sort of like a soldier who's preparing for war, but it's not wartime, you know? It feels like it's not really going to happen. I thought I'd never actually find him, be in the same place at the same time. Then I was in Albuquerque, and I met someone who was telling me about this guy he'd met who was recruiting folks for a medical study. There were enough parallels that I thought perhaps I'd finally found them. I could end it. And you know how that turned out."

"It was just the beginning," Todd said. "I can't imagine, Creed. But you're not in this alone anymore. We'll take care of Stephen and Hicks."

"And I take care of The Source. Right." I exhaled harshly and shook my head, trying not to disturb Roman. "If it weren't for him?" I gestured to my sleeping beloved. "Y'all would be on your own."

"I know, and I appreciate you being here. I hope you know that."

Rey looked between Todd and I. "Yeah, yeah, appreciate all you want. I want to know if I need to worry about you biting my nephew."

I rolled my eyes. Rey and I had already had this discussion, and after the big meal he'd cooked, we were all a bit more relaxed. "He's the last person you need to worry about me biting right now, and you know it."

"Help me understand," Rey said. "Weird fucking shit, I can't even believe I'm asking this. You said you found out you *have* to drink. What are you going to do?"

I blew out a breath, and Roman stirred in my arms. "I'm not sure. Todd procured me some nourishment. When that's gone... I want to talk to Roman about it before I make any decisions."

"You're all so noisy. Talk to Roman about what?" He lifted his head and pulled off his oxygen. "What did I miss?"

"These two have been grilling me. Make me take you to bed so they'll quit asking me questions."

"What kind of questions? I want to know. Wait, what were you talking about with, 'talk to Roman about it'?"

He was pretty damn alert for someone who'd been asleep moments prior. He sat back in his chair and took a long drink of water.

"Fine. Apparently, Dr. Santos brought some blood with her under the impression that you might need it. I was going to partake of some tonight, away from these prying eyes." I raised an eyebrow at Rey and Todd, who both chuckled. "I can make it last a few days. It's not as potent or as helpful as the ritual, but it'll do until—"

"You need to do an Exchange." Roman's matter-of-fact statement was the truth.

"Yes." God, I hated every bit of this discussion. "I need to be able to heal you."

"Do you know the why of it? What the scientific explanation is?" Todd was so damned earnest. I felt no judgment from him. That should have made it easier to talk about.

"From what I've been able to figure out, the blood becomes like another element necessary for the body to survive. Oxygen, water, food, those are vital for human existence. When I was exposed to The Source's blood, I guess that's what you'd call it, it must have unlocked something in my DNA, something that stops the degeneration that comes with aging. It expanded my brain function, enhanced my ability to heal people through the manipulation of energy, and all it requires is a regular infusion of blood.

"Seems like a small price to pay for such a valuable skill, right? I think I thought of it that way before. But I've spent a lifetime in fear of not having access to a steady supply, and thinking it was only temporary, that I could quit anytime and I would just start to age like a normal person. Cross divested me of that notion and now... I know I need it to continue my existence. I'm just not comfortable with it. It was one thing when it was fueling my need for justice. Now..."

"It's a necessary evil, Creed," Roman said on a sigh. "It's like having to use insulin or blood pressure medication. I have to take medication now for the rest of my life—you think that's what I want to do? Drink the blood, baby. And when I get stronger, it won't be an issue anymore."

He was right; I just had so many hang-ups about it. But if I wanted this time with him, a lifetime to love him, I had to do it. It helped that he'd seemed to enjoy it immensely when we were alone.

"Roman, for full transparency, I offered my blood to Creed earlier today." Todd made eye contact with both of us. "I meant no disrespect and didn't intend to be inappropriate. I offered because I know he needs it and because I'm curious about the process."

Roman stared at Todd for a long time, and I feared the worst. Would this upset him too much? Cause his health to backslide? Would this put a wedge between us?

By the time he finally leaned forward to speak, it was *my* heart I was worried about.

"You're asking Creed to make himself vulnerable. He's not some mythological vampire who preys on the innocent, imbued with super-natural power. He's a man whose heart is too big for his body. He's a caretaker by nature, and he was that way even before he became what he is now. It's not *you* who could be hurt by this, but *him*."

Todd's eyes flared, and he glanced back and forth between us.

I was speechless.

"I would *never* harm Creed," Todd said in a low voice, barely over a whisper. "This is not an elaborate attempt to collect data. I'm not going to include it in a report to my superior. If at some point you want to have a discussion with my benefactor and share that part of yourself with someone who I can *guarantee* will have knowledge about you and your kind, I will set that up. But for now, this is just me, Todd Barringer, offering to help a friend in need."

"As long as you're not a girl, standing in front of a boy, asking him to love her." Rey's comment broke the tension, and everyone laughed. Rey seemed to have a hard time whenever the topic got heavy. I could relate.

Roman elbowed me and smiled. "You should do it."

"But I—"

"Look it, I have made myself abundantly clear that this weird shit annoys the fuck out of me." Rey swallowed and crossed his arms over his chest. "If it makes you stronger, and it helps you help my nephew, *I* volunteer."

Roman burst out laughing. Rey cursed. Todd covered his smile.

"Well gee," I purred. "When you put it that way..."

Roman reached for his oxygen again and got the hiccups from laughing, and that was enough for me to quit fooling around. This was what I needed so I could help him be well.

"Who wants to go first?"

I thought perhaps they would change their minds, but Todd sat up straight in his chair and unbuttoned the top button of his dress shirt.

"Where will you take from?"

Earnest. So open and yet... what would this do to our working relationship? It wasn't a sexual thing—not like it was with Roman—but I usually formed a bond with someone I took from. Mr. Jenkins and I had bonded over music, and when I finally revealed who I really was, he simply said, "I knew you were special, son. You take what you need. I'm not afraid." He was more to me than a patient, more than just a friend.

How would it be with Todd and Rey?

"The wrist." I cleared my throat, my hands shaking under the table. "I don't know what to say. I appreciate this. I want to be strong enough to help Roman—"

"Then I'm after him," Rey said, rolling up the sleeve of his sweatshirt. "Two doses have gotta be better than one, right?"

I can't believe this is happening. Roman's assessment of the situation had been right. I'd never trusted anyone with this whom I wouldn't be healing in the process. But all I had to do was take one look at my beloved, and I knew I had to. Maybe this could be a step in making things right for him. I would do anything to give him back what he'd lost.

"Todd," I said, and then I cleared my throat. "The purpose behind this ritual is for you to gain positive energy and for me to gain nourishment. I give unto you what you require, and take only what I need to survive, and, in this case, to heal Roman. Do you understand?"

"Yes." He listened carefully and sat still but not rigid.

"I will release a pheromone that will relax you before I partake. It may cause you to feel dizzy or light-headed, but it will be a pleasant experience. I will touch only your wrist, and I will take only three pulls. When I'm finished, I will heal the wound and you'll have no pain. Do you understand?"

"Yes."

"As I explained to you before, I will likely be able to detect anything unusual or abnormal. It's up to you whether I share that with you or not. Some people prefer not to know."

"I understand. You can tell me."

"Very well. Do you consent to this Exchange?"

"I do."

I nodded, but this felt... odd. Once more, shame flooded my senses, something I'd never experienced. I knew what I was doing wasn't wrong, and yet, I was having such anxiety about—

"I'm right here." Roman placed his hand on my thigh and spoke softly, his expression loving.

"I don't... I don't know if I can do this." I ducked my head and swallowed back a sob.

"Baby, you're only doing what you have to." He ran his fingers through my hair and pressed his forehead against mine. "We're here for you. You have nothing to fear. No one will hurt you, and no one is judging you. I hate to see you suffering. Please."

It was the *please* that did it. I couldn't refuse him. Wouldn't. I was doing this for him.

I took Todd's hand and turned it palm up. His veins were very close to the skin, thankfully. When I looked into his eyes, I saw no fear or dread, only his special brand of curiosity and kindness. If I had to do this with someone other than Roman, Todd was a good choice. I'd done it hundreds, maybe thousands of times before, but not like this. Not with a friend or someone I worked with as a colleague. It would change things.

"Is there anything in particular that is troubling you? Any part of your body that's causing you pain or discomfort?"

Todd shook his head. "No, actually."

I nodded once, and then took a deep breath in, holding it in my lungs, absorbing the strength of the waves against the shore below the house and the moist air from the fog. It was easy to tune out the cars above and focus on the nature surrounding us. When I exhaled, I unlocked the place in my mind as I'd been taught.

A flood of pheromone flowed from me, more than I'd usually use, but I was nervous, and I could tell Rey was unsettled by more "weird shit." It would be enough to loosen them all up.

I reached for Roman's hand and held it close to my belly, needing that connection for what I was about to do.

When I felt the hold Todd kept on his person loosen considerably, I leaned forward.

"Blessed be."

I placed my lips on the skin of his inner wrist and gently pressed my teeth into the flesh, willing his tissue to make way for me to pierce his vein. He gasped softly, but he relaxed even further, his thighs spreading and his head lolling to the side.

When his blood hit my tongue with the first pull, it had a zing to it that I wasn't expecting. It had less of a metallic taste than most people's I'd experienced before. Low in iron maybe? But he was the picture of health. His energy, coming directly from the source, was like nothing I'd ever tasted. It was... unfamiliar. Strange. Different. It wasn't unpleasant, just surprising. I didn't know what it meant.

I made sure to take the second pull slowly, gently, and the effect on my cells was immediate. His blood was potent, more so than the folks I'd taken from in the past, and I knew I would be contemplating why that was the case when I was able to concentrate, but right now I needed to be very intentional with this Exchange.

A rush of endorphins gave me instant strength and... certainty. That what I was doing was what I'd been made to do, must continue to do. My healing strength roared to life, and I sent a wave of appreciation to Todd. I felt his pulse quicken when it hit, and he sighed, his head falling back.

But instead of taking his energy in and absorbing it into my cells, I sent it flowing through my hand to Roman's, feeling the heat travel into his bloodstream. Images of light traveling through his arteries and into his heart filled my head, and I began to picture where I wanted it to go: to all the weakened, thready tissues that responded so well to my command.

Roman's grip on my hand slipped but I held on tight, determined to give him as much as I could from this Exchange.

On the third pull, I knew I needed to take some for myself. I allowed the healing energy to flow through me and it was like pouring a cup of water on a drought-stricken field. It disappeared instantly, only giving the ground a taste. It would have to be enough.

I took extra care to knit the tissue of Todd's vein and skin back together as if I'd never breached it, and when I was done, I gave his forearm a squeeze.

"Thank you," I murmured.

Todd lifted his head and blinked a few times before he sat straight in the chair. His movements were sluggish, but more in that way of the recently fallen asleep than of one who'd awakened after a sleepless night.

"Creed, that was... I don't have words."

Roman slumped against me and moaned. "Damn you... you were supposed to keep that for yourself."

"You've had enough fun for one day," I said. "Let's get you to bed—"

"Not until you're finished," he said, a crease appearing in his forehead. "It's Rey's turn."

I exhaled but shifted Roman's weight against me, so I could lean forward. Rey shoved his arm toward me.

"Yeah, yeah. You have my consent. Just do it."

I laughed and couldn't help it—I hit him with a whammy of a pheromone bomb, just to mess with him. He immediately slid down in his chair, cursing under his breath but keeping his arm steady.

"Blessed be," I prayed, as I bent to take his wrist. I took even more care with Rey than I had with Todd, not wanting to give my lover's uncle any reason to object to my brand of healing. I let his blood seep slowly into my mouth, and I had a moment of concern. What if I discovered something about Rey? He hadn't told me whether he wanted to know. Whatever I discovered, I'd have to figure out how to deal with it.

I opened my senses to him as I took the first pull.

Oh, Reynaldo.

He definitely took after his Auntie Frances, and I *would* be telling him that he was well into the pre-diabetic range.

With the second pull, I sensed a little resistance. Plaque in his arteries. *Tsk-tsk.* I'd be clearing that out, thank you very much. Otherwise, for a man in his forties with an incredibly stressful job, he was in good shape. Nothing a few dietary changes couldn't help. I sent some more healing energy Roman's way, hearing him sigh softly beside me.

The third pull was for me. I focused on channeling that aggressive spice Rey shared with his nephew, and it gave me a rush similar to the first few times I'd siphoned it from Roman. Rey groaned, and I knew it wasn't from pain. I'd hit him with enough pheromone to ensure he was feeling *good*. I let myself fully absorb the last bit of his essence before erasing any sign I'd been mucking around with his insides.

Rey really did feel a lot like Roman, but not at all the same. This was the first time I'd ever done an Exchange with folks in the same family, and it was interesting to note the similarities on a genetic level. I was also relieved to discover that the experience I'd had with Roman was indeed unique. There was so much more to what we shared than just the Exchange. It was the difference between a hug from a grandparent and, well, being filled in the most intimate way.

I was indeed stronger as I released my hold on Rey's arm with a pat.

"You okay?"

Rey stared at me, dumbfounded. "What. The. Actual. Fuck?"

"Right?" Todd answered him. The two gazed at each other, wide-eyed, and then back at me.

And now to make my exit before the questions started.

"See you guys in the morning," I said cheerfully, as I stood and turned toward Roman.

Roman smiled at me but looked puzzled. I scooped him up in my arms, and he grabbed for the handle of his oxygen tank, dragging it behind us as I carried him to our bedroom.

"Uh, good night?"

The two men muttered to each other, and I heard their chairs scrape as they both headed for their rooms.

"What's going on?" Roman whispered, more alert now.

"Let's just say that the pheromone affects everyone differently." I picked up my pace as I heard the two men close their bedroom doors. "We're about to see how."

Eleven

Roman

Creed placed me carefully in the bed we shared and went to the restroom, giving me time to wonder. About many things. Like how could this be real? How could my boyfriend heal me with his mind? What had I just witnessed? It was one thing for Creed to bite me when we were in bed, but this? And how freaked out was my uncle right now?

That thought made me chuckle as Creed opened the door. He was shirtless in a pair of lounge pants, and it's purely possible my eyes deceived me, but he looked *incredible*. When I first saw him naked, I'd noted how healthy he looked, like he'd stepped out of a late '70s/early '80s *Playgirl* magazine, minus the mustache. I wondered if he'd ever had one? But back to his physique—it was exceptional. He was the picture of health, until he'd disappeared. Those three weeks he'd been gone, he'd lost weight and muscle mass, and his skin had gone from peachy and freckled to sickly pale.

Now, he glowed. His arms and legs were toned, as if he'd been working a physically demanding job, not doing exercises at the gym.

He slid into the bed next to me and rested his chin in his hand.

"Are we doing this now, or can I convince you to sleep?"

"After that? Are you serious?"

He exhaled and fell onto his back, his breath minty fresh.

"You brushed your teeth? Is it because of... what does it taste like? I mean, I've tasted my own blood, but—"

"We're doing this now." While he tried to look put out about it, he had a hesitant smile on his face. "Before you ask, are we okay?" The look of vulnerability in his eyes had me curling myself around him.

"We are more than okay," I said, drawing my fingers along the side of his face, feeling his delicious stubble. "Have I not made it clear how amazing you are? How much—"

"Having a learned ability does not make me extraordinary."

I pulled back. "No, it doesn't. Not by itself. The sum of you—body, spirit, abilities, knowledge, wisdom, love, and soul—are the things that make you beyond extraordinary. Creed." I forced him to meet my gaze. "I fell in love with you before I knew what you could do. Always remember that."

He reached tentatively for my hand at his cheek, and he covered it with his larger one. His eyes drifted shut, and he lay there taking deep breaths. I thought he'd fallen asleep, but moments later he gasped and his eyes flew open. He covered his mouth and chuckled.

"What's funny?" I asked him, holding him tighter.

He held up an arm, and I saw the hair standing on end as he laughed again.

"What's going on?"

He turned to me, his amber eyes sparkling with mischief. "Remember how I said the pheromone affected folks differently?"

"Yeah?"

"It seems someone is working off some serious energy right now." He sucked in another breath and placed a hand on his upper chest, letting his fingers drape over his throat. His body relaxed into the mattress, and he smiled mischievously.

"Working...? Oh, fuck, you mean jerking off!" I burst out laughing, but Creed placed a hand lightly over my mouth and shushed me. "Who is it? Can you tell who it is?"

"I refuse to divulge that information. Along with consent comes confidentiality, my love." His back arched off the bed, and he moaned softly before settling back down. Like he'd just had aftershocks. "I'll never tell."

"You're absorbing their energy? Right now? What does it feel like? To you?"

"Like lying on warm sand, a cool breeze playing with my skin and hair, the lull of the surf putting me into that fully relaxed state. Sometimes taking in energy makes me aroused, but more than that, I feel the swell in my cells as they grow stronger, waiting to be told what to do next. Lying in wait until they're needed to serve another." He nestled his face into my hand and sighed again. "What did it feel like for you? Earlier? I've never done it like that before."

"When you passed your healing to me earlier, it felt almost like going under nitrous oxide, minus the giggles. You know what's happening but you're outside of your body. Totally calm. Happy."

"I can see that." Creed rolled onto his elbows and smiled down at me. "Doing an Exchange with others is nothing like what we experienced when we had sex and I took from you. I figured you would want to know. It's not an inherently sexual act, drinking blood. I don't feel aroused when I take from Mr. Fletcher." That visual made us both laugh. "Seriously, the pheromone isn't like a sex potion or anything, although to some it can feel like arousal. Like *someone* out there certainly experienced. But I wasn't, it doesn't..."

"Thank you for telling me, but I wasn't worried. You've been so upfront and honest about everything. I don't worry. Like I said. Next time I want to go with you to the strip club though."

"Or you can strip for me. Dance for me. We won't have to leave the house." He ran his hand down my side, over my hip and then over my fairly diminished ass. I wondered if he was disappointed in how I looked now, scrawny, muscles all atrophied from weeks in bed.

"We *will* have to, though. I'm not enough." I swallowed hard, struggling to accept my weakness. "To keep you sustained. I'll be okay with that. We're gonna work it out."

He kissed me gently, a light brush, a soft nudge, and we rolled together, our legs tangling.

"You are everything to me, Roman. You are my reason for staying on this ride. I'll get what I need, do what I have to, so I can be with you for as long as we have." His smile slipped. "Even if it means drinking that bag of blood the doctor brought. I'm sorry—"

"Baby. Don't ever apologize to me. Not for doing what you need to do to survive."

Creed nodded as if he were trying to make himself okay with all this. Then he kissed me insistently, probably hoping I'd quit asking questions, but he should've known by now that my ability to ask questions was without end. I'd let him work this type of magic now, give him a break from interrogation. Tomorrow. There would be time tomorrow.

The next morning, we left our room to investigate the delicious smell of maple syrup and powdered sugar. I told Creed I felt steady enough to go without my cane. He said to give it another day. I told him to kiss my ass. He did. But we were actually both very hungry, or we perhaps would have stayed in bed for more assploration.

Rey was once more at the helm in the kitchen, and Todd was at the table typing speedily on his laptop.

"Good morning," Creed called out before going to the fridge. Both men muttered a hello, but neither of them would make eye contact. Intrigued, my gaze darted back and forth between them, wondering if their expressions would give anything away.

Todd looked up first. His polite smile and nod gave no indication.

Then Rey started singing Earth, Wind and Fire's "Fantasy."

Creed and I looked at each other, and his eyes went wide. He shook his head and put a finger to his lips.

Go tiyuhin.

Creed took something from the fridge and went out the back door, trying to be sneaky about it.

The blood.

He'd told me he was going to drink it. I had to put my preaching into practice. I would not begrudge him anything he needed to do to stay well.

"How are you this morning, pamangkin?" Rey asked me, turning around from the stove.

"Good. Better than good. Last night really helped, so thank you both."

Rey smirked at me and turned back to finish preparing breakfast. "Weird fucking shit."

"I take it you two slept well?"

"Yeah," Rey said, the skillet slipping in his grip and banging on the stove. "Great."

I went over to help him carry a platter of pancakes and bacon to the table, but he simply pointed to a chair and snapped his fingers at me. I rolled my eyes and was ready to fuck with him some more when Todd spoke up.

"That's good, because we may have to move sooner than I'd planned." He closed his laptop and placed his hands on the table. "There's been a development."

Creed returned to the room, stopping by the refrigerator on his way to the table. "What's happened?"

"I was scheduled to have another interview with Stephen today, but the prison psychologist just let me know he's been taken to the infirmary."

Silence fell over the four of us.

"We should go see him."

I jerked around to face him. "Creed."

"He's starving. Either I go and give him enough energy to talk to us, or he dies and we never find out what he knows."

"He's surrounded by people," Rey said. "I'd imagine there's plenty of negative energy for him to feed on in that place."

"So he may be doing it to himself," I said. "Do you think?"

"He needs blood, and it's likely he hasn't been able to get any in there. Not that he follows The Way, but still, he hasn't been feeding on energy like I have, so he's got to find a willing blood donor or... forcibly take it. I'm not sure how that would go over. He's in jail, people might not think twice about it, but he also might get his ass kicked."

Todd leaned back in his chair. "How bad do you want to know what he knows? He might not talk to us, even on his death bed."

Creed stared him down for a long time. I felt torn. I didn't want Creed anywhere near this man who'd hurt him, had taken so much from him, but I also knew Creed would struggle without the answers he sought. If he couldn't get those missing years from The Source, it would have to be from Stephen.

He turned a pleading expression to me.

"You have to go," I said quietly, reaching for his hand. "I'll be fine. Go."

"We can be there and back before dark," Todd offered. "Roman will be protected."

"All right." Creed exhaled a long breath. "We need to know what he knows. With Hicks still out there, this won't end with Stephen's death. We have to find out what we're up against."

"Then let's—"

"Let's eat Reynaldo's fabulous breakfast, and then you go," Rey cut in. "Junior, you and I are going to talk to Dr. Santos later today, so you need to have your strength."

Creed sat next to me, and I placed a hand on his arm. He was completely stiff. I knew he was nervous about seeing Stephen.

"I wish I could go with you," I said, giving him a squeeze.

He turned that haunted gaze on me and shook his head. "Even if you were well, you've seen what he can do. This could all be a ruse. He may be counting on this, me coming, to do something even more horrible."

"Are you sure it's safe for you to go?"

Creed tilted his head to the side and sighed. "I'll be fine. I've got a few tricks up my sleeve."

We finished eating while Todd talked over logistics. Besides the visit to the prison to see Stephen, there was a hearing scheduled today for the FBI to seize all assets of BioBourne and EVE. It seems Donna Hicks's information gave the government enough proof that human subjects were being used illegally in experimental research. She'd turned over all the information she had, and the FBI and INTERPOL were working on tracing the money in order to shut down their international accounts.

"It's not likely to completely put them out of business, since they've gone international," Todd explained. "But the more we find out, the more pressure we can put on them to turn over Hicks, and to eventually put an end to their operations. The government has a stable of rabid attorneys who live for this work."

"That's all well and good," Rey said. "But all these unknowns give me fucking hives, man. I hate sitting around waiting."

Todd turned to him with a perplexed smile. "And you've been a cop how long? The biggest part of our job is sitting around waiting for the bad guys to make mistakes, isn't it?"

A knock on the door had us all tensing, until Todd looked at his watch and pushed back from the table. "Dr. Santos. I'll let her know Creed and I will be leaving. Roman, are you sure you're up to this?"

I nodded. "I feel good. I'm okay."

Todd nodded and headed for the front door.

"I do need to get dressed though," I said, pushing myself to standing. It was a smidge easier today. Woohoo, standing up is a real feat.

"I'll come with you," Creed said, pushing back from the table. "Rey, thank you for breakfast. I'll clean up before we go."

"No, I got it. Go get ready."

Creed nodded and followed me to the bedroom.

I was barely using my cane, but I suppose it was good I had it today, since Creed wouldn't be by my side the whole time.

Once we got to our room, Creed went quietly to the walk-in closet.

"Hey," I said, following him. He'd pulled his shirt off, and I wished we had time for me to trace the freckles on his back. "You ever been to a jail or prison? I only ask because it can be a little overwhelming. I've visited several in my research. It's not the most pleasant experience."

He shook his head and pulled out a dress shirt I'd never seen him wear.

"No. I've worked in a psych ward, though. And some of the veterans' homes were intense. Honestly, that's the least of my worries." He turned to smile at me. "A lot of negative energy in a jail." He wiggled his eyebrows as he started to button up.

"Let me," I said, taking the two sides of his shirt. "Stay close to Todd." I started at the bottom and enjoyed making him squirm as my hands brushed his groin. "If the vibe gets aggro, you guys get out of there. You will know, won't you? You can sense it?"

"I can," he said quietly, sucking in a breath as my fingers brushed his belly. "Dr. Santos doesn't know about me," he said. "I think it's safer if you don't—"

"I'll never share your secret. Never. That's for you to decide, not me."

"You won't out me?" he laughed. "A bit late for that."

I pulled him close and kissed him. I didn't want to be away from him. Twenty-four hours reunited wasn't enough.

"Mmm, Roman," he moaned, as I tore away from his lips and worked his throat. I was ready to unbutton what I'd just buttoned when he placed his hands gently on my face, bringing me back to his lips. "I don't want to stop, but if I don't, I won't leave. I need to do this."

"Just giving you a reason to come back to me."

"I have all the reasons, my love. This trip will hopefully bring us closer to ending this nightmare. Then we'll have time..."

"You'll come home with me?" We hadn't discussed the particulars of this second chance at a life together. "When this is over? You and Rhonda? Move in with me, Creed."

His eyes widened, and he tightened his grip. "You would want that?"

"I require that," I said, tugging him closer. "I require you in my bed every night, or day... I know you like to work nights."

"I guess I never thought I could have my life back. I hadn't thought that far ahead." He ducked his head. "You'd really want that? A free-loading night nurse?"

"Yeah, I really would."

"Who'd occasionally need to drink blood?"

"Mmm, especially I would."

"Who'd love you all the rest of his days?"

"He better. Come here."

In the before times—before I died—our embraces had often been rough and tumble, a not-quite fight for dominance. Playful and determined. Now they were a tussle to see how close we could possibly get. They were desperate because we knew what it meant to be apart. They were hopeful, because after all we'd been through, we'd found our way back together. I had to have faith that we would continue to do so.

"I'm going to be back as soon as I can. Hopefully I'll have good news, and a good buzz. I want to do all I can for you. You're stronger already, and I know I can do more."

"I'm stronger with you here. All I need is you."

"The things you say." He kissed me once more and then stepped back. I let him go reluctantly, feeling him pull away more than physically. I knew he had to prepare himself for this meeting so I let him go.

"I will see you tonight." I backed out of the closet.

It was nearly impossible to keep moving away at the sight he made in slacks, a dress shirt, and a blood-red tie he was in the process of tying.

"Nice color choice."

He winked at me and straightened his perfect knot. "I like being a little ironic." He slid his suitcoat on and straightened his lapels. "Do I look like FBI?"

"The hair's a little long," I said. "You look illegally handsome."

"Good."

He turned out the light and walked toward me. He pulled me in for one last kiss, making it a good one with the tongue flicks I loved so much.

"I'll be back soon."

"Please."

He pressed his forehead to mine for a long moment and just held me. I knew he was shoring himself up, and when he let go and walked away, his movements were that of a man on a mission.

Stephen wasn't going to know what hit him.

Twelve

C reed

"Special Agent Todd Barringer, and this is my consultant, Creed Lowell."

The guard took a long look at my ID, and I began to sweat. Todd said the suit would get me through with him at my side, no problem. A deputy took us through several hallways, past inmate areas, and I was immediately hit with an enormous wave of negative energy. As we entered the infirmary, I searched out a familiar energy signature, and when I found it, I was shocked at how weak it was. The nurse in charge greeted us and explained that Stephen was being kept isolated from other inmates. She insisted we keep our visit short.

"Mr. Adams may not last the night. He's experiencing multiple organ failure and is no longer able to keep liquids down."

Todd thanked her and reassured her that we'd make our visit brief. I planned to ensure that he had enough energy to speak to us, whether he chose to accept it or not.

We entered the room, and I was shocked by what I saw. If I'd needed a reason to fear the end of my existence, I was looking right at it.

Stephen wasn't much more than skeletal remains. His eyes were closed when we entered, but then he took a deep breath and coughed, the phlegm rattling in his chest.

"I knew it was you. You smell so sweet. Always smelled so sweet."

"Mr. Adams, I'm Special Agent Barringer—"

"And you brought the golden boy with you." He shifted in his bed, the pain evident in his face. "You've come to see me off, have you, Guardian Creed?"

"I've come to offer you an Exchange, if you'll have it."

Todd's expression was alarmed, but I held up a hand to him,

Stephen appraised me for a long time, his breathing labored. "It's not an Exchange if I have nothing to give you," he said, his raspy voice harsh. "As you can see—"

"I want you to answer my questions, Stephen. Since you've left The Source to my care, it's the honorable thing for you to do."

"I figured you'd know by now that I rarely do the honorable thing, Creed. Taking from you will just prolong the inevitable," he said, shaking his head. "I want it to be over."

"Will you at least tell me what I need to know?"

Stephen coughed again, and it appeared to take all of his energy. I almost thought he was losing consciousness, but then he opened his rheumy eyes and stared me down.

"Yes, Creed. I stole The Source. I saw an opportunity to make money, to no longer be starving, and I took it. And I've regretted it every day of my existence since then. Ironically, I wound up with a different sort of starving."

"How do you mean?" Todd asked.

Stephen gestured toward the chairs next to his bed, and Todd and I sat.

"The Source, as you have no doubt already figured out, requires round the clock supervision. I couldn't sleep for weeks. Did you know they rarely ever sleep? They kept me up either asking me questions, or wanting to meditate together, or teaching me things I had no desire to learn. I came to loathe their presence, and I used my talents to keep them... manageable." He smirked. "I've always been a bit of a bad egg. Ask my family." He licked at his parched lips and swallowed.

Todd stood and reached for the water pitcher on the bedside table. "Would you like some water, Mr. Adams?"

He shook his head. "Will only prolong my pathetic existence." He dragged in a phlegmy breath and closed his eyes for a moment before continuing. "I was a bad kid. I knew things I shouldn't know. Made other kids feel uncomfortable, the teachers told my parents. They could never quite put a finger on why. I learned early on that I could get whatever I wanted from people as long as I kept them afraid of me. They'd give me things, tell me things, as long as it would get me to go away. Women... they knew better than to go home with me, and if they ignored that feeling, well, it was no surprise what happened to them. Like your friend, Muse."

I gripped the armrests of the chair, and Todd pressed his forearm against mine. I felt a tendril of energy prickle over my skin, as if Stephen was determined to disturb me to the bone, to terrify me with his words if he was no longer strong enough to get into my mind.

"I take it you saw my handiwork? I left her out in the open... how do the kids say it? For funsies. She and that Shaw fellow were on their way out of camp. I fed on their fear for a good long time before killing them and making my way to the initiation. She was still drowning in her own blood while The Source was getting drunk off yours."

He laughed but it came out as a raspy, choking sound. Todd placed a firm hand on my arm to keep me from launching myself across the scant space to attack the shell of a man. He needn't have worried. I knew that reaction would've only satisfied Stephen's hunger. I refused to give him the satisfaction.

"Who besides Caleb helped you? I know Lourdes is dead. Who else kept The Source with you?"

He tilted his head to the side. "That's what EVE was for. The gatherings. The Source fed on them. I could keep The Source fulfilled and fooled into thinking we were carrying on The Way, when in reality we were building something worth building, not just a bunch of freaks and misfits in the woods, healing each other's boo boos. No, with the power of The Source, we were able to use their blood to create the answer to man's greatest drive."

"Immortality."

"Yeah, well, close enough. The serum can do pretty incredible things, but unlike The Way, there's only a regular dose necessary—no Exchange—and in clinical trials, clients stop aging and feel great. It's not foolproof. If you stop taking it, whatever improvements occurred go away almost instantly, but it doesn't do"—he gestured down at himself —"*this.*"

"Is this what you want?" Todd asked him. "Are you truly ready to wither and die?"

"What's the alternative? Stay alive so I can rot in this place? You'll never let me out, and my former business partners wouldn't allow me to remain free, so why should I continue on?" He leaned forward, lifting his head slightly off the pillow. "You don't want me out of here. Without The Source tying me down? No telling what trouble I'd get up to."

"How about Timothy Hicks... What can you tell us?"

He rested his head and closed his eyes. "What do you want to know?"

"How'd you connect with him? What is he trying to accomplish?"

"Hicks is your worst nightmare, Creed."

"Worse than you?"

Stephen let out another dry, raspy laugh. "It's not my fault I was born special. It's too bad I'm at my end, or else I'd leave you with a few more images of your beloved being exsanguinated. Wouldn't that be fun?"

"It would be tired. Useless. You never had anything to offer but hate and fear. The world will be better off without you."

"Maybe so, but Hicks is different altogether. Where I could show you what I wanted you to see... well... let's just say he gets what he wants. Whatever he wants. He wanted control of EVE, he's got it. But without The Source, he's going to need the blood of a powerful one, and I don't see anyone volunteering."

"Are you aware of other ones? Powerful? Old like The Source?"

"They've insulated themselves. They won't be found if they don't want to be. I've met a few during my time with The Source. They struggle to keep going in this current world. Many have moved to more primitive areas. Easier to remain hidden. But as our world grows smaller, the easier it will be for them to be detected. It won't be long now until they all die out. That's what I predict."

"So Hicks is planning to move forward with EVE's plans to…"

Stephen sneered at Todd. "Wouldn't the FBI like to know! You'll never untangle the web, so I'll tell you this. As long as there are wealthy people supporting EVE's mission, the quest to perfect the serum will continue. The few will benefit from the sacrifices of the many."

"Sacrifices? What do you mean?" I asked him.

"Rich folks are willing to do *anything* to stay young. They don't care what they're putting in their bodies as long as they get results. Look at them snatching up all the weight-loss drugs meant for diabetics."

"You used The Source to further their greed."

"That's right. I've already told you, I'm a bad, bad man. Those scientists at BioBourne got what they needed because I kept The Source occupied. Kept them seeing what I wanted them to see. They thought—"

"They thought you had a new cohort," I said, realizing why The Source had been so confused about everything. "You kept the illusion up for them—"

"Yes. I took their blood, used their energy, presented them with new recruits who were actually EVE members looking for the fountain of youth. There was no instruction in The Way. You think those bastards would have lived like we did? Done something to selflessly help their fellow man? Fat chance."

"How can we find Hicks?"

"Besides following the money?"

"We've shut down all of their accounts," Todd interjected. "We're tracing what we can, but you covered your tracks well."

"Thank you," Stephen said, nodding his head. "I wasn't too terrible at running a financial empire, it turns out."

"That appears to be true," Todd said. He was good at shutting down his disgust when he was after information. I knew how he really felt, but he spoke to Stephen as if the man was truly his equal. It did the trick.

"Your next best bet is to try the clinics. Longevity Health. The forward-facing arm of EVE. They'll be administering the serum. Withhold their serum, they'll turn him over. Those old biddies won't go without. They'll give up their own kids to keep what they've found."

"You're willing to give up your allies?"

He shrugged. "They're not my allies. If you can't have it all in this life, why not burn it all down before you die?"

Todd cocked his head. "So why didn't they keep you around? Seemed like you were a valuable commodity. Wait. That's what the disagreement with your lawyer was about, wasn't it?"

"One form of slavery for another. No, thank you—"

"You aren't strong enough," I said. "Without following The Way? Your blood isn't worth a Get Out of Jail Free card."

He shrugged. "They don't know that, but it doesn't matter. No, I'm getting what I want. Peace. Finally. And you, Creed? You can sit in judgment upon me all you want. I give it no more than five years with The Source and you'll be willing to do just about anything to get out from under this life." Stephen closed his eyes and sank back into his pillows, his breathing slowed considerably.

"Do you have anything else to ask him?" I asked Todd. I was sorely tempted to force-feed Stephen my blood, keep him alive longer, prolong his suffering, and just the fact that I was having thoughts like that let me know it was time for me to get away from him. I may not have been perfect, I may have strayed, but I would not betray my soul in the name of vengeance. Muse wouldn't have wanted that, either.

"No. Mr. Adams has nothing left to offer us of any worth."

Stephen coughed, and pain screwed up his face.

I moved closer to him. "Is there anything I can do to ease your suffering?" I didn't want to offer, but it was The Way.

He reached for me, and though it repulsed me to touch him, I gave him my hand.

"You know how to do it. End my suffering. You can tear tissue apart just as easily as you can knit it back together. I know this about you. I've followed you for decades, did you know that? I know how powerful you are. You can do it now. Kill me."

That confirmed my suspicions. All those years I looked over my shoulder, I wasn't imagining things. His admission made this trip worth it. I put my hand over his, ready to pull away. "If you've followed me, then you know I would never."

He tightened his grip, and suddenly I saw Roman on the other side of the bed, blood spilling from his split throat. I gasped. Though I knew it wasn't real, it was an image burned on my brain that would induce my guilt no matter its truth.

Todd sprang up from his chair. He attempted to peel Stephen's fingers from my arm, but once I got past the initial shock, I knew what Stephen was trying to do.

"Not even that will make me kill you." I sent energy his way, a whole load of it. Not enough to heal him. He hadn't given his consent, but then, I wouldn't be following The Way if I didn't do everything in my power to ease the suffering of another. Despite the fact that I knew every moment he continued to exist was pure torture for him, I gave it to him. He'd have just enough energy to keep him wallowing in this state of decay. "Perhaps in the next life, you will learn to use your powers for good instead of causing pain."

"Let me die," he croaked. "Please, Creed!"

"You'll die when it's your time. Blessed be." I let go of his arm and turned to leave the room. Todd said something else to Stephen, whom I left panting in the bed. He'd last a few more days probably. Showing me Roman's near-death experience could have drained him of all the energy he had left, but the energy I'd given him cured him of that notion.

Out in the hall, I encountered three nurses who stared at me in horror.

"He's awful," one of them said to me. "No one will go into his room alone."

"You should *never* be alone with him. Just know that whatever he makes you see isn't real. He doesn't have much time left. Don't give him the satisfaction of your fear."

She said something in Tagalog and crossed herself. I wanted to remember the words and ask Roman what they meant later, but I needed to take advantage of the opportunity around me.

I closed my eyes and took in a deep breath. On the exhale, I flicked my internal switch to absorb.

I took it all in, the hatred, anger, fury, and rage, and I soaked it up from all of the broken souls in this building. I normally avoided darkness like this, but beggars can't be choosers, and after sending so much of my positive energy into Stephen, I needed to replenish. I just prayed to the Goddess this filth wouldn't taint my essence.

I gazed around the infirmary, which currently housed six inmates in beds either sleeping or watching TV. Except one. He was shifty, watching the nurses come and go, his face all twitchy and sweaty.

A flash of silver caught my attention as he leaped from the bed.

I had him from behind in a bear hug before he could lunge for a nurse.

"Let go of me!" he snarled.

Keep fighting. Keep struggling. That's it.

His adrenaline hit me in a rush, and it went down *so good*. His desperation was exactly what I needed.

The nurse called for the guards, who quickly disarmed him and took him from me. I stood with my hands out.

"I'm a nurse," I said, by way of explanation. "I saw him getting ready to jump her."

The guards thanked me stiffly and wrestled the inmate back into bed, fastening cuffs at his wrists and ankles as he bitched and moaned.

"Thank you," the nurse said, squeezing my arm. "You never know what they're gonna try."

I smiled back at her and hoped she made it through this rotation unscathed. I siphoned off her fear and beneath that, I touched her plentiful strength. Working with violent patients took its toll and most nurses didn't have the ability to shake off the constant level of stress. Me? I loved it, but I loved my dementia patients the most.

Todd exited Stephen's room and took me by the elbow. "We need to go."

I heard Stephen's weak laughter behind us as Todd dragged me away.

"What happened?"

"I'll tell you in the car."

Todd's face was pale, and as he accepted his weapon, his hand visibly shook. He walked fast out of the building, through the checkpoints, and into the parking lot where he'd parked the Crown Vic. Once inside the car, he put the key in, then rubbed his hands on his thighs, his breaths coming in rapidly.

"Hey, Todd, you need to slow down—"

He continued to gasp, and before he had a full-blown panic attack, I placed a hand on his back and sent him some healing energy. I spoke low and close to his ear, using my voice to give him a focus for his breathing. After two very long minutes, he finally began to breathe normally.

And then he began to cry.

I had no clue how to respond other than to gather him close to me, hold him tight, and continue sending him energy. He pressed his face to my shoulder as his body shuddered. The sadness nearly overwhelmed me. Sad... he wasn't afraid, he was profoundly sad. Whatever Stephen had made him see had provoked a sorrow so deep, I could relate.

I concentrated on slowing down his heart rate and spreading euphoria through his limbs. He clutched at my arm as I held him, and he sobbed.

"Todd, hey, it's okay. Whatever he showed you isn't real."

"You're wrong about that." He took a few deep breaths and pulled away to rub at his face. He stared out the windshield and did some sort of his own meditative breathing to get himself back to a functional state. "Thank you, Creed. I'm sorry—"

"Don't ever apologize to me for crying," I said, giving his shoulder one more squeeze.

"It's not that," he said, wiping his eyes once more. "I don't have a problem crying in front of you, but I was supposed keep you safe in there and I barely made it out."

"I think it's fair to say that on this particular case, you need to expect that you might not be fully prepared for everything that happens."

"Yeah," he said with a laugh. "The FBI training manual doesn't exactly cover the appropriate regulations for letting someone drink your blood." He gave me a smirk and started the car.

"Guess you're going to have to add an amendment."

"Actually," he said, turning and placing his hand on the back of my seat to look out the back as he reversed, despite the rearview camera inserted on the dash. So careful. "Since I've taken a detour from my usual FBI caseload to investigate these special situations, perhaps I'll have to work on a new manual. My benefactor has funded our work for a minimum of another two years and has promised me additional staff." He glanced at me before putting the car in drive and pulling out of the parking lot. "I think there's a lot I still have to work on with this case. And I could use your help with my *other* case. What do you say? Interested in joining my band of merry folk?"

I frowned. "You mean merry mercenaries? Todd, what part of 'hippie' makes you think I'd be interested in working for The Man? In any capacity? It might be the twenty-first century, but I haven't changed all that much. Besides Roman's family and you, I'm not all that fond of law enforcement."

"Which is why you're perfect to consult on my cases with this task force. You'd be working to help people like you. Plus, I know you're going to need some help with The Source, and it's in my benefactor's best interest to help financially. They've asked me to pass that along to you. They don't want you to worry about the monetary aspect of caring for them."

I opened my mouth and closed it. "How did we go from your tears to my financial security? Wait... Todd, what did you see? What did Stephen do?"

Todd rubbed at his mustachial region and exhaled. "I'll tell you someday. It had to do with my past, the events that set me on this path. I *will* tell you, but right now, we need to talk about what just happened, because I think Stephen gave us a lot of information and I don't know how seriously to take it."

"Fine. Just drive, because after what he showed me, I'd really like to see with my actual eyes that Roman is okay."

Todd tapped his thumbs on the steering wheel. "Is it wrong that I won't be sorry when he's no longer alive?"

"Nope. The world will be a better place with him gone. I just hope he's not taking crucial information with him, because the stuff he just told us? Could be very, very bad."

As he sped off down Highway 101, I wished for him to drive faster. I needed to know Roman was safe. I needed to touch him and be sure. I also needed to prepare him that things might get worse before they got better, if that was possible. What, for him, was worse than nearly dying?

"It doesn't sit well with me knowing that there are people out there like him. That's so much power, and regular people can't defend against that."

"Is that what brought you to this work? That's good... really good. I doubt we irregular folks would be very good at policing ourselves. "

"That's not what I meant, Creed."

"Maybe not, but 'tis true. Just get us back to the house. I need Roman."

Timothy Hicks

Timothy left the meeting with the EVE board members feeling like he had a lot less ass. Time was running out to obtain what was needed to formulate the final version of the latest serum, and those greedy bastards were out for not just special blood, but the blood of anyone not delivering on their promises. Previous incarnations of the serum had required frequent injections, and once the user quit taking it, they backslid. Degeneration was rapid and painful. Investors and users were pretty discouraged and pressuring the board to come up with better solutions.

Then his darling Courtney came forward with an answer to Timothy's dilemma. She came to his office as he was contemplating his next move, smelling delicious and wearing the low-cut blouse he liked so much.

"My law enforcement contact was able to get me a blood sample from Creed Lowell. From off of his motorcycle after he'd had an accident."

That information perked Timothy up. "Do tell."

Courtney entered his office, closed the door, and proceeded to walk around his desk and sit on his lap, just as he'd trained her. She had a mind of her own, for sure, but she liked to please her boss, and Timothy always got what he wanted.

He looked over her shoulder as she spread lab reports out for his perusal.

"Tell me what you found, darling."

He ran a hand up under her blouse and caressed her back, causing her to suck in a breath before she began speaking.

"Our predictions were correct. Lowell's blood has nearly all of the markers found in the early samples of The Source's blood. Whatever he learned from them, whatever they were doing at that commune, he received a tremendous influx of power from The Source, maybe even more than Stephen. And whereas the most recent blood samples from The Source seemed to have weakened, had fewer of the markers needed for the serum, Lowell's resemble those taken near the beginning of the research data findings."

He glanced at her paperwork, but the science mumbo jumbo wasn't his strength.

"This seems to be good news. Now we just need to convince Creed that joining us, being a part of our mission, is a better use of his gifts."

"And if he refuses?" she asked, swinging her long black hair over her shoulder to look back at him.

He pulled her hips tighter against his groin, and she arched her back.

"The thing about most people is that they're motivated by doing the right thing. Personally, I've never fallen prey to that motivation, but it's helpful to know when someone needs the slightest push to come onboard. I just need to convince Creed Lowell that cooperation *is* his right thing."

"And how will you do that?" She raised an eyebrow at Timothy and rolled her hips, inviting him to take things further.

He slid his hands along the sides of her thighs, catching her skirt and pulling it up. He was pleased to feel the garters under his fingers, and then... nothing. He'd instructed her not to wear panties, and she'd complied. After his ass-chewing of a board meeting, there was nothing like a little obedience to get him back in the game.

"We'll remind Mr. Lowell that he has things—or people—to lose if he doesn't cooperate." He lifted her as he stood and bent her over his desk. He unfastened his trousers and pulled out his erection, ready to take something else he wanted, but admiring the way her ass looked, presented just so, gave him ideas for other things he might want.

He slid inside her without any warning, and she stiffened for just a moment before pushing back against him. She wasn't the most enthusiastic fuck he'd ever had, but she was lovely to look at and followed his directions quite well. She'd also proven to be quite useful in his current dilemma. The fact that he hadn't even had to threaten her to make her comply was nice... for now. Plus, knowing she wasn't one hundred percent into the fuck was a turn-on for him. He wasn't looking to please anyone. He took pleasure in knowing that while she might not love getting fucked over his desk, she'd do it because *he* wanted it.

Let it be a reminder to her that she was here for his pleasure.

He had his people out looking for the safehouse where the FBI was keeping the things he wanted from him, and it was only a matter of time before he had a location and a plan. The board was just going to have to wait patiently.

One thing was for sure, he loved the power he currently held, over this woman and over the greedy fucking people waiting on the new serum, but he wasn't going to partake of their so-called miracle drug. No, thank you. He knew he was in prime physical shape, could have any woman he wanted, and would soon deliver a product that would make him enough money to hand over the reins of this fucked-up operation and move on to the next challenge.

Who knew what that would be? Perhaps politics? He'd love to see what he could make happen at the highest levels of civilization. Maybe he could convince a country they needed to annex their neighbor and their resources. Maybe he would start a war.

Thinking big like this made his dick even harder, and he pounded into Courtney, driving her pelvis into the edge of the desk, which probably didn't feel great. That made him wonder how quickly bruises might form, and suddenly, that was what he wanted to see more than anything...

THIRTEEN

Roman

Two cars pulled into the driveway at the same time, and Rey moved quickly to my side. One car brought Dr. Santos with bags of food. The second—

"Thank God," I whispered. I was up out of my chair and hobbling as quickly as I could to the passenger's side of Todd's car. Creed was out the door and in my arms in an instant. He stumbled back against the car and caught himself.

"I should really take a shower and change before I hold you like this."

"There's no time for all that," I said against his neck.

"But germs, Roman. You can't afford to get sick—"

"Shut up and kiss me. I was worried—"

"Come here." Creed wrapped me in his arms, and he was practically vibrating.

"Not that I'm complaining, but what's gotten into you?"

"I needed to see you. Touch you. Feel with my own hands that you were safe."

"That great of a meeting, huh?"

"Stephen was his evil self. I expected it. Prepared for it. Didn't make it any easier." Creed breathed against my hair and moaned. "Goddess, I missed you. I wish I could steal you away, back to bed."

I was grateful he had a decent amount of self-control, because I was ready to climb him and *make* him take me to bed. But there were things to consider. Like our guest. We stepped apart, and he approached her with an offer to help with the bags she was juggling.

Todd exited the car with a phone to his ear, and he waved. He continued a conversation with someone as he walked past the house.

"I picked up stuff for build-your-own pasta. I hope you guys are hungry." Dr. Santos smiled at me, but her gaze followed Creed. "I hoped we could all talk over dinner."

"Sure, that would be great," I said, though I wasn't too sure that was accurate. "Thank you."

I was relieved that Todd and Creed were back. I didn't want to talk to Dr. Santos alone. She'd asked a lot of pointed questions earlier in the day, and I'd feigned brain fog and exhaustion to avoid slipping up and sharing too much information. We'd stuck mostly to her questions about La Mente, which was a relatively safe topic. I knew she could be helpful, especially with understanding the physiological aspects of Creed's differences, but the trick was not to reveal his secret unless we knew we could trust her, until he was ready. Todd had only just met her, so we were taking a risk even letting her be here.

Rey greeted Dr. Santos and took the second grocery bag from her to carry into the house.

Creed gestured for me to walk ahead of him, which I assumed was so he could tell how I was progressing. I made sure to pour all the swag I had into that walk and even did a little swing with my cane, showing him I didn't really need it anymore. Well, not at the moment. I kept it with me just in case, though. I wasn't completely confident in my movements yet.

Creed and Rey set things down in the kitchen, and Creed grabbed something from the fridge and headed outside. I supposed he would be finishing off the blood before Dr. Santos saw what he was up to. Rey was talking to her, so I followed Creed outside.

"Hey." I didn't want to startle him.

He sighed as he turned around, and I spotted the blood in his hand. "Sorry. I—"

"Don't apologize. I just wanted to make sure you were okay. The trip drain you?"

"Yes and no." He rolled up the empty bag and shoved it in his pocket. "Talking to Stephen did, but there was plenty of energy to be had from the... guests of that establishment. Actually, I could use your help. Come here."

I stood before him, and he placed his hands on my chest under my sweatshirt.

"You need to hang on to your energy," I whispered, but he shushed me.

"Remember the part about me being a processor." He sucked in a breath, and as he blew out, his hands warmed over my skin and I was forced to take in a deep breath.

"I can't hold on to this much negative energy." His voice was back to that soft, soothing, singsong tone that did as much to relax me as the actual healing. "I need to use it, turn it into something good. This is the difference between Stephen and the others, and me. Even Cross and Mark. They take all the energy, they take the blood, but they don't filter out the bad parts. I have to. It makes me stronger, and it's using my skills for how they were meant. Do you understand?"

"Do I have to understand?" I sighed and smiled. "Or can I just appreciate the benefits?"

He caressed my chest with his hands and chuckled softly. "You can enjoy it all you want. It makes me happy to do this for you. Not happy you need it, but happy I can." Another deep breath and one more flow of energy...

"Whoa." My legs wobbled, and I leaned into his touch.

"Careful, now," he said, wrapping his arms around my waist and burying his face in my hair. "Just breathe with me."

"Oh, I'll breathe with you. You keep hitting me with that, and I'll do anything—"

"Hey, you two." Todd stood at the doorway to the kitchen with an apologetic smile. "Sorry to interrupt, but I got a call from the compound. Mark and Cross let the agents know that they need to leave. Apparently they booked some club dates."

He shook his head with a frown. I could understand his frustration. This meant all the weight would be back on Creed. I just hoped I could help.

"How long do we have?"

"They're leaving in three days."

Creed nodded. "They've put their lives on hold long enough." He gave me a squeeze as if he didn't want to let go but knew he should. "This is my responsibility."

I tapped his chest. "*Our* responsibility."

He gazed down at me with glassy eyes and pressed his lips together.

"Give us a minute?" I asked Todd.

He nodded. "Sure. Dr. Santos will be finished with dinner in a few minutes. It smells really good. I might save some for you, but I'm pretty famished. Take your time."

He closed the door on us, and I laughed, but Creed held me tighter.

"I don't know what the right thing to do here is."

"The right thing to do," I said, "is for us to pack up our shit and leave with Todd and Rey tomorrow. I go where you go. We do this together."

Creed stepped back and sighed. "I have a few conditions."

I raised an eyebrow. I was trying really hard not to be my petulant self.

"First... fuck, I don't like this at all."

"I know you don't—"

"Roman, please. You will never be alone with *them*. Either myself or Todd—"

"I promise. I won't do anything to add to your stress."

"I should tell you... they offered to heal you."

"You mean, like you do?"

"Like, fully. They're capable, or at least they used to be. But you should know, they may also try to persuade you to become part of their family, become a disciple. Anything you take from them will not be offered without strings. I don't think they're capable of being selfless at all."

"Thank you for telling me. I don't know how I feel about any of this, but I trust you. We'll figure this out."

"And you'll promise? Never alone with them, Roman. I mean it. I couldn't bear it—"

"I promise. Baby. It's going to be okay." I went to kiss him, and he put a finger over my lips.

"Not yet."

Then I remembered what he'd been doing out here before I interrupted.

"Of course. I'm sorry."

He kissed my forehead. "I'll meet you at the table."

He guided me into the kitchen, and then he cut down the back hallway toward our room. I followed the sound of laughter to the dining room and found Rey and Dr. Santos chatting in Tagalog, while Todd sat by observing with that kind and curious expression he often had.

"Hey." Rey started to get up but I waved for him to sit.

"Sorry to keep you waiting. This looks delicious."

I sat down just as Creed approached from behind, pushed in my chair, and kissed my cheek, leaving a wake of minty fresh mouthwash.

"Thank you for having me. If you don't mind, I'm going to talk while you eat because I'm practically bursting at the seams with information, and I can't wait any longer. Is that all right with you?"

Didn't sound like it much mattered; she was going to talk. I tried to keep my snark to myself as I recognized her eager energy. I tended to resemble her at times.

Rey took a bite, and then leaned back in his chair. "As long as you know we can't comment on ongoing investigations..."

"No, of course not."

Dr. Santos was probably in her late thirties/early forties, although it was sometimes tough to tell with Filipina women. She was dressed in a sweater, slacks, and plain black dress shoes. Her dark hair, high-lighted with auburn, was pulled back in a complicated twist. I had a fleeting thought that perhaps I should start learning some tricks and buying hair ties, as my hair was long enough for a topknot. Who knew how long I'd let it grow? Rey hated it and Creed loved it. Perfect.

"My fascination with this case began when I discovered that Roman San Angelo was the same person who wrote the fascinating paper on La Mente that I'd read recently. I'd been studying the physiological effects of the participants in a similar study. The University of Edinburgh got their hands on the documentation through INTERPOL's criminal investigation, and I was assigned to be the lead researcher. The subjects of this botched experiment were all young people, university age, from Southern France. Towns like Marseilles, Nice, and Toulon had a rash of missing young people, and many of them turned up in Monaco as part of this experiment. It was shut down, the victims were reunited with families where possible, and it was kept completely from the media, which is bizarre."

Creed leaned closer to the table, his attention rapt. "Carmen, when did this occur? This research?"

"Shoo, well, I was working on it about five years ago, but the discovery of the botched experiment happened in the nineties. I've been given permission to share what I found, but only with the four of you. The French government doesn't want these families further traumatized. So what I'm telling you has been cleared by INTERPOL and my university, but it is for your ears only." She gestured to the group of us at the table.

"Thank you for that," Todd said. "And I will share what I can as well."

She nodded. "Great. Now, Roman, what I found in my research applies directly to you and what you experienced. What happened to you, your injuries... it's been done before. This was not an isolated situation. The botched experiment details the exsanguination of members and the effects on the body of hypovolemic shock, and then what happened when they utilized their so-called replacement serum."

Creed and Todd stared at each other. Todd's neck and cheeks were blotchy.

"You mean, they were draining these kids of blood and giving them something else?"

"Exactly. They were also conducting studies on prolonged exposure to fear-inducing stimuli. I have boxes and boxes of blood test results, samples, doctors' notes from the—"

"And what did they discover?"

"Well, for the blood, the patients who received the serum after their blood loss appeared to make initial improvements, but once the serum was halted, they suffered damage to their internal organs on par with long-term alcoholics, or those with uncontrolled diabetes. It was like not only had they never had the serum, but the organs deteriorated at a faster rate. Whatever the initial damage from the blood loss, the serum seemed to mask underlying injury to the kidneys. When the serum was halted, the patients backslid, many ending up on dialysis."

Creed placed his hand on my arm as my heart started pounding. He spoke in my ear. "That's not going to be you, okay? Your kidneys are going to be fine." He kissed my temple and leaned back, but this time he put his arm around me protectively. The weight helped calm my jitters.

What I'd gone through had been awful enough. What if it was only the beginning of my health issues?

I took a drink of water and set the glass down harder than I'd planned.

"You okay, Ju—Roman?" Rey had his hands on the armrests of his chair, ready to spring into action.

I held up a hand and nodded.

"What about the fear studies? You've read my paper, so you know what I found out about La Mente."

"There was data in the reports from France about psychotic breaks, PTSD, stress symptoms like hair loss, eating irregularities, broken teeth from grinding... it's all bad. I don't get the purpose behind it, nor how any medical professionals could have been involved. Why intentionally hurt these kids?"

"The actions of some sick fuckers, if you ask me," Rey said. "Seems like the world has a few too many megalomaniacs with god complexes just looking to hurt people."

She tilted her head to the side. "Do you know more about the people behind what happened to Roman? And your sister-in-law and nephew?"

Rey's gaze darted between Todd and Creed, and he swallowed.

"Well, I meant more in general, but yeah, my family has a long history of being hurt by shit like this."

Carmen continued to stare at him, pleading with him to share more, and I wondered if he would. Rey didn't like to talk about his past.

"In all of your research, didn't you find out that this wasn't the first time my family has dealt with this shit?"

Carmen peered at me, and then shook her head at Rey, who cursed and ran a hand over his face.

"My parents were members of The People's Temple. They went to Jonestown."

Carmen's eyes flared, and she sat back in her chair. "Rey, I'm sorry, I had no idea."

He shrugged. "It was a long time ago. My older sister Vanessa and I were little. We didn't know what was happening. My tita Frances, Roman's grandmother, took us, told them if they wanted to go off on some crazy adventure to leave their kids with her until they were settled. I wouldn't be sitting here if it weren't for my tita."

"How awful," she whispered, shaking her head. "She sounds like a wonderful person."

"She is," I said. I grew heartsick thinking that it could be a long time before I saw her again. I'd had video calls with her, and Rey had taken me to play bingo with her once while I was in the rehab facility, but now I was running off with Creed to an undisclosed location.

Rey assured me she was doing as well as could be expected, that her sisters were keeping her occupied. All she knew was that I'd been in an accident, and without Creed's healing touch, she often forgot that fact. She would continue to slip away while he was gone, but at least she was in a safe place. With me around, she and the rest of the residents at Puesta Del Sol were at risk of becoming part of this drama.

"I just wish the reports had more information about what they were doing with the data. The blood, we know, was for this serum, but the fear? What could they possibly gain from scaring the daylights out of kids?"

Todd glanced at Creed, and then spoke. "We believe the persons conducting the fear studies were benefiting from them. It's complicated, I can't share a whole lot. But what I *would* like is to show you some of the data we've collected to see what you can make of it. I'd like to see if you find any correlations between the dataset you've been researching."

She blinked and sat forward excitedly. "I've got my mobile lab gear with me. When would you like me to start?"

Todd smiled. "We have to leave soon. How about you take the day tomorrow? I know it's not a lot of time, but hopefully enough to get a first impression and then we can talk next steps."

She placed her hands on the table in front of her. "I'm happy to help. I would also like to give you a physical, Roman, if you're okay with it. I think it would be helpful to see how much you've improved since you first entered the rehab facility."

I shrugged. "I guess so. As long as you don't intend to poke me with any more needles."

She laughed. "Well, a blood sample would be great, but I absolutely understand why you wouldn't want to part with any."

I glanced at Creed, and his lip twitched as he made himself busy with a bite of pasta. She had no idea.

Dinner wound down afterward. Dr. Santos, Rey, and Todd continued to speak about her experiences in Edinburgh and her love of traditional Filipino food, and I was proud of my uncle for keeping the conversation going while my head was spinning.

"Roman, let's get you to bed," Creed said with an expression that hinted at "we have things to discuss" more than actual concern.

"Yeah, I guess it's time for me to turn in," I said, all casual and shit. "It was great chatting with you."

I held out my hand and Carmen clasped it in both of hers. "I'd love to talk more tomorrow, if you're feeling up to it. Is there anything I can help with? Did you need the blood? You're looking well, especially given what I read from the reports—"

"Actually, yes. Thank you. Yesterday was a rough day." Oh shit, I was actually lying here.

"Thank you," Creed said. "It came in handy. He was a bit depleted after his transport."

"Oh no, of course," she said, her eyes flaring at Creed. "I'd hate for you to have to donate again. That was wild, you actually being a match for him and everything. I read the paramedics report, and my goodness. You saved his life, didn't you?"

"He did," I said, before Creed could spew some bullshit about, well, it was nothing, aw shucks. "More than once." I couldn't help getting a little sappy, and when Dr. Santos's hand went to her heart and she made that *awww* face, I felt I'd covered for us pretty well.

"I guess it's pretty handy to have a boyfriend who's a nurse."

"Absolutely," I said, thinking just how well mine took care of me.

"Good night," Creed said hurriedly, his cheeks flushed. He made eye contact with Todd, and I wanted to know what that was all about but bed actually sounded great, especially with Creed naked beside me. One could hope.

FOURTEEN

Creed

While Roman seemed a little tired and probably needed the rest, I'd used him as an excuse to leave the table and the disturbing conversation.

"I'm not questioning you, but are we leaving because of me?"

"That obvious?"

"I mean, I am a little tired, but I wasn't like dropping my head in my plate or anything, was I?"

"No. You ate your pasta like a big boy."

This earned me a pinch on my side, and I tried to keep my laughter to myself until we were behind closed doors.

Roman plopped down on the foot of the bed and removed his cannula. He was moving so much better, less old man and more middle-aged man who'd just started going to the gym after a long hiatus.

"We do have things to discuss," I said as I approached him. I cupped his jaw, loving the brush of his hair on the backs of my hands.

"Like how you're gonna let me have dessert?" He tugged on my fly, and I laughed, but then he wrapped his arms around my hips and pressed his cheek to my belly. "I hated you being away today. It was too soon. I know it's not, like, healthy and shit to want you with me all the time, but damn, Creed. I've lost a lot of time. *We've* lost a lot of time together."

This man. This young man unraveled me with his declarations. How I'd longed over the years to have someone to call my own. Someone who would gaze at me like the moon rose at my wish, like the stars shone because I willed it. Someone who believed me to be worthy of their affections and devotion and loyalty. Someone who loved me not for what I could do for them, but for the sheer pleasure of my company, and Roman wanted that.

Yes, he was young. We were a lifetime apart, though his experiences had brought him wisdom beyond his years. Would he change his mind someday? That was possible. But if my journey to this point had taught me anything, it was that tomorrow was never promised, that it often delivered heartache and loss. That love was the only true joy one could hope to receive in their existence. And I wanted it. Needed it. Craved it. With him.

"You honor me," I said, gently brushing his hair back from his face. I lowered myself to my knees before him. "You humble me with your trust. Anything is possible if you... love me."

I loved cocksure Roman, I loved wise Roman, but most of all, I loved that Roman could confess to something so vulnerable and with his next breath, own me.

"It is, and I do. I want—"

"Then take."

Roman tangled his fingers in my hair, tilted my head back, and kissed me. Deeply. With long strokes of his tongue as if he were impressing upon my body the importance, the necessity of his touch. As if he were reminding my cells of what they'd missed being away from him, scolding the heavens for keeping us apart, and daring the aether to try that shit again.

He tugged my hair and pulled back from the kiss, keeping me at his mercy. "I need to fuck you, and I don't want you to say I'm not well enough."

I laughed and licked my lips. "I wouldn't dare." How could I? I needed him just as bad.

He loosened his grip, allowing me to rise up on my knees.

"I have only one request?"

His perfect, naturally sculpted eyebrows lowered over his dark eyes and his nostrils flared. "I'll allow it."

Fuck. The confidence. The arrogance. He and I both knew I was bigger, faster, and stronger than him even prior to the current state of his health. I would give him whatever he wanted, but having him tell me what he was going to do? Hotter than fire.

"Let me do the work and you reap the benefits."

He frowned, and I feared I'd ruined our forward progress, but then he sighed. "Probably a good idea. For now. But when I'm better—"

"I know. I'll be ready."

I pulled his shirt over his head, gently urged him onto his back, and slid his bottoms off as he crawled up the bed. The nurse in me couldn't help but give him a once-over. I was pleased to see that his color had improved even since yesterday. Once he was stronger, I'd start physical therapy with him and encourage him to start working on his endurance and strength. I knew it would make him feel better, but for tonight, I planned to engage in a little therapy that would benefit us both.

"Get naked and get up here."

His demands brought my erection roaring to life. I left my clothes in a heap on the floor with his and straddled his thighs.

"Happy to comply."

His breath hitched as he watched me stretch myself for him, his cock twitching in his hand and his legs jerking beneath me.

When I was on the precipice of overstimulation, I bent over to kiss him. "You control this. Fast, slow, whatever you want."

He ran his hands over my thighs as I rose above him, lifting myself up with my feet planted on either side of him.

"What a picture you make," he said, as he cupped my balls and bit down on his lower lip. When I sank down, taking him inside me, I was flooded with so much sexual energy, I nearly came.

Then he squeezed my thigh. "Slow."

Something told me that wasn't because he was flagging. No. He wanted me to feel every bit of him as I rode him, wanted to watch the place where we were connected. And I did move slowly, pulling off completely before taking him in again. I gasped every time his crown breached me, and my eyes watered with the stretch as I took him all the way. He was thicker at the base of his cock, and each penetration stretched me deliciously. My thighs shook with the effort of moving so slowly but it was worth it.

He slid his hand between us, and his fingers caressed the spot where we were joined. He moaned, and I did a quick check to make sure his heart rate was okay.

It was just fine.

"So good, baby. You take me so good. So strong."

I gazed down at him and loved how relaxed his face was, how his eyelids drooped, and how he gave himself over to the pleasure. The moon shone brightly through the window across my thighs and his chest with an ethereal light. Roman swore and sucked in a breath.

"Okay?"

"Faster, baby. Please. I need it."

There it was. That switch from Demanding Roman to Pleading Roman was all it took. I threw my head back, fell to my knees, and rode him with abandon. We both cried out—to hell with whoever was listening—and then he grabbed for my cock and angled his hips just enough to hit me right in that spot I needed.

"Roman..." I breathed his name as I came, whispering it like an incantation, a blessing, a prayer. A plea. A wish upon the moon. *Please let us have time to build on this bond, to love each other's bodies, and to shelter one another from the ugliness surrounding us. Please. Let us have time.*

I wasn't sure whom I spoke to, but for a brief second, it felt as if I'd risen from my body at the moment I'd reached my peak, said my piece, and then was slammed back into myself in time for Roman to lose that slim margin of control and begin to tremble, sending another wave of orgasm through me.

"Baby," he whispered, over and over, his voice full of emotion, full of thanks, full of love. His heart stuttered the slightest bit, and I froze, waiting to see if he'd need assistance, but then it settled into a healthy sinus rhythm. His breathing was steady and only a slight sheen of sweat covered his torso, making him glow in the light of the moon.

Or that could have been me, high as a fucking kite on the energy we'd just produced.

I collapsed beside him as he reached for the tissue box to clean up our mess.

"You were saying... we needed to talk?" He was panting, but one scan and I could tell that he was okay, the exertion just enough for him.

"Talking is nice. What we just did was nicer. Let's just not talk about what we *need* to talk about for a while. Pretend like there's nothing important to talk about."

"So you don't want to talk?" he asked, rolling over to plant kisses on my bicep.

"I *want* to talk, but *not* talk about what we're *not* gonna talk about tonight."

"You're giggling," Roman said, and my giggles became full-body laughter as I held on to him for dear life.

"You're amazing," I said to him, kissing him deeply and forgetting that we had anything else to talk about.

The next morning, I woke before Roman and I was restless. I knew we were going to have to pack up and leave this little sanctuary, and I was not prepared for the two most significant people in my life meeting each other. One made me feel like I could handle anything, the other had made it *possible* for me to handle just about anything. One made me feel cherished, the other made me feel tarnished. One needed my guidance, one needed *me*.

How much more would Roman tolerate before he finally decided it was too much? I wanted to believe him that he would stand by me as I took responsibility for an ancient being who needed guidance to navigate the world, but I couldn't blame him if it became too much. Todd swore I'd have help, but for how long? Maybe it was time to meet this mysterious benefactor for myself and get some answers.

The house was quiet. It was just before dawn. I went out onto the back patio to think, to strategize, to slow my brain. It was a typical late fall morning, fog clinging to the hills of the Peninsula like a blanket and the sun beginning to creep over the East Bay hills. The Port of Oakland would soon be bustling with energy as ships loaded and unloaded, the large cranes that inspired George Lucas's tall machines in the *Star Wars* movies plucking containers off the giant barges like they were kids' toys.

"Hey."

Todd closed the kitchen door quietly and approached me at the railing, two coffee cups in his hands. I thanked him as he offered me one.

"I was just thinking of you," I said.

Todd's eyebrows rose. "What did I do now?"

"Nothing like that." Things were still a little awkward between us, but in a different way. At first he was concerned with keeping me safe and finding out just what the hell had happened at Loch Lomond. Now, after completing an Exchange with him, I felt closer to him, that I could trust him. But it was as if he wasn't quite sure how to handle feeling so friendly toward me, and yet remain objective. "I wanted to ask you about your benefactor."

Todd sipped his coffee and gazed at me over the rim. His blue eyes matched the sky at dawn. "Sure. Ask. I'll tell you what I can."

"You said that they would know about me, about people like me. Did you mean, people who are differently abled in an extraordinary way? Or *specifically* like me, what I've gone through?"

"The first," he said. He wore another crisp white dress shirt and gray slacks and his skin still held a bit of the healthy glow I'd given him. "My benefactor..." He paused to, I assumed, censor himself. "They have their fingers in several areas, but all have to do with people who are, like you said, differently abled. Exceptional. I met them during my last big case, like I told you, and they just... they know so much. It was like waking up and realizing that the world I'd been living in for all of my thirty-four years had an entirely other layer to it, you know? I don't know if you've ever seen it, but there was this movie I saw a long time ago about a guy putting on glasses, and he could see that certain people were actually aliens or something—"

"*They Live*. Rowdy Roddy Piper. Fair wrestler, hilarious as an actor. Yeah, I remember. I'm the one who was alive when that movie came out, remember?"

Todd chuckled, his cheeks flushed. "I forget sometimes. But that's how it felt, you know? And all of a sudden I'm thinking, if this is real, then who's to say that other things I thought were fiction... and sure enough, I get assigned to this case. A former cult-turned-bioresearch giant terrorizing innocent people and stealing blood." He shook his head. "You can imagine I was all in. I have this... compulsion to understand, as well as to ensure that people aren't abusing their exceptionality, I suppose. I still don't know what to call it."

His enthusiasm was contagious. "And your benefactor—"

"*Way* other," he said with a nervous laugh. "It's hard to keep pertinent details from you, because I think you'd really gain a considerable amount of understanding about what it means to be different from... them. And they are incredibly generous, have made it their life's work to protect people from being exploited for their gifts, for lack of a better word."

I could imagine Roman also being thrilled to meet this mysterious person. He'd found a way to turn his curiosity into his life's pursuit. If not for myself, or for The Source, I could do it for Roman.

"How would this work? Can you set up a meeting?"

Todd's smile was genuinely pleased. "Let me reach out. We need to leave later today for the compound. I think it would be best if we travel at night. I can ask them what their comfort level would be in meeting with you there, or perhaps a stop somewhere along the way."

"I'd like to do it without Roman." I wasn't sure what made me say that. I had a hunch, an intuition that it was the right thing to do to protect him. "First. I don't want to put him in any more danger, and until I've met this person for myself, I'd rather not take a chance with Roman's safety. It's not that I don't trust you—"

"Of course, no, I understand. Let me make some calls."

"Thank you. I just want to be careful."

Todd nodded and held up his coffee toward me. "We want the same thing. I don't want anyone else getting hurt on my watch."

We stood together, drinking our coffee and watching the East Bay come to life. The traffic grew congested on the bridge above us, seabirds began their search for sustenance, and several fishing boats puttered by on their way from the Berkeley marina out past the potato patch under the Golden Gate and beyond to the coast.

"This was really a good spot for us to stay," Creed said. "If I focus, I can almost pick up the tension in the commuters as they plug along the bridge headed into the city. A little buzz with my morning joe."

"Right. Get it where you can, I guess. Strategically," Todd said, "it's not easy to sneak up on. There's only one road in or out and boats can't dock here. Not to mention, it's a breathtaking view."

"The Bay is beautiful. Where are you from, originally?"

Todd gave a sly smile. "Haven't figured it out yet?"

Creed frowned. "Should I have?"

Todd wiggled his fingers and laughed. "I thought you would know things if we did an Exchange."

I barked out a laugh, unused to a playful side of Todd.

"Whatever your 'other' is, I've never encountered it before."

He nodded and gazed off toward the hills beyond Oakland. "That makes two of us. Three, really. I don't know much. My benefactor... he alluded to something peculiar, but even he was unable to get to the root of my *otherness*. Guess I'm not meant to know yet." He smiled and sipped his coffee, his eyes darting to mine and then away, as if he wasn't sure he liked being under my scrutiny, though it was clear he was curious too. Always curious, our Todd.

"I guess I'll have to try harder to unravel the mystery."

Todd laughed and shook his head. "I'm heading inside. I think Rey is cooking again. Man, he sure can cook. I've eaten better here than... well, than in a long time."

My stomach growled at the thought. "I'll see you inside."

Todd looked as if he had something else to say, but then he waved and opened the door, leaving me to a few more moments of peace. I had a feeling they might be my last for a long time.

Fifteen

Roman

"Open up and say 'ah.'"

"No offense," I said to Carmen after complying with the whole stick-out-your-tongue bullshit, "but I am so sick of doctors."

She laughed and jotted down some notes on her laptop.

"I would be too, in your case. But it's important to have a record of your progress, and since you aren't in the rehab facility any longer, someone should update your chart. Perhaps Creed? I know you're moving on—"

"Yes," I said. "We *are* moving. We are needed elsewhere, and it seems these folks may not be done making my life miserable yet."

Carmen sat her instruments to the side and folded her hands in her lap. "Roman, I've read the police reports, and I'm aware of what happened while you were at the rehab hospital. I'm very concerned for your safety. I don't want to alarm you, but in the studies I've looked at? They went to extreme lengths to silence their witnesses."

"I'm aware," I said. "I know the risks."

"Do you?" She rolled up her sleeves to show horrific scars.

"Oh my... What happened to you?" I reached for her hands and turned them over to look at her forearms. A series of cuts had been done up and down them, to varying depths.

"Just like you were motivated to study cults because of what happened to your family, your great-aunt and uncle, I too was drawn to this work." She turned her hands over and grabbed for my mine. "You know what happened to me."

My voice broke as I whispered, "La Mente?"

"I'd just finished my first semester of a fellowship at Oxford. I was traveling through the south of France when I met Guillame. He was hanging out around the hostel where I stayed outside of Cannes, chatting with the other young people like me. He was enigmatic, knew my name even before I mentioned it to him. Knew where I was from when only a few phrases in broken French were exchanged. He took advantage of our desire to see everything, experience everything. Three of us returned with him to the chalet he said he was renting, myself and two girls from England whom I'd been traveling with, and what started out as a couple of weeks of parties, spiritual conversations, and great sex, turned into my worst nightmare."

"You were one of those experimented on."

She nodded. "A fact I did not disclose when I applied to medical school. My current employers are only aware of surface level bits of information. I'm sharing this with you because... I have a feeling you'll get it."

She was taking a big risk talking to me. "The fear studies? And the blood? Oh God, Carmen. How did you get away?"

"The police raided the chalet and found us. They got us medical care, interviewed us, and then loaded us on a train bound for London. It was traumatizing on top of the trauma we'd already experienced. It was clear they wanted our information and then wanted us gone."

"So you never knew what happened—"

"Guillame found me, called me, let me know he was questioned and let go... and wanted to know when he could see me again."

I sat up straighter. "How did he find you?"

Her lips lifted into a humorless smile. "Well, I'd told him almost everything about myself, so he knew just where to look. He got my phone number from someone I went to school with."

"Was he the one who hurt you?"

"Not physically, no, but he made sure I stayed. He was very persuasive, telling me that the work they were doing was vital to understanding humanity or some bullshit like that." She rolled her eyes. "He made me feel like I was the only person on earth who mattered to him, that what was between us had nothing to do with La Mente. Or L'Esprit, as they called it in France. He assured me that he would take me away as soon as he could, that he was just as held captive as I was, which wasn't true."

"Did you believe him?"

"No. While it turned out I was the only one he had a sexual relationship with, he'd said similar things to Chelsea and Emily. We kept in touch after we got back to England and supported each other through the process of deprogramming ourselves, and they told me about the conversations they'd had with him as well. Same lies. The only difference —and this is what made it the hardest to get over—was that if he was only intimate with me, that *had* to mean he cared about me, and that maybe he was a victim like I was."

"Mindfuck. I'm so sorry."

She shrugged. "The other girls went on to finish their studies and settled down with nice men. I finished med school, my psychology doctorate, and I've been searching for answers ever since. Why the fear? Why the blood? How were they related? And I gotta tell you, even after reading your paper, after reading the police reports, I still feel like I'm no closer to any answers, other than there are awful people out there who are compelled to hurt others for their own pleasure. And not in a consent-based way."

And here I sat in a position to tell her, at least one explanation as to why this was happening. But telling her about The Source or any of the history meant outing Creed, and I wouldn't do that.

As much as I wanted to ease her pain, I couldn't.

"At least with stories like Jonestown and what happened to your family," she continued, "we have closure, albeit awful, painful closure. With La Mente, I believe they went underground. I think they had people in high enough places that they got a slap on the wrist and were exiled to play their reindeer games someplace else."

My stomach dropped. She was closer to the truth than I could admit.

"I have to believe," I told her, choosing my words carefully, "that what happened to me, what happened to you, that we can get to the bottom of it and shut down these groups. I believe Todd when he says that his task force is going to continue hunting them to the ends of the earth. If it takes my lifetime, I'll keep fighting."

"What about your degree?" she asked in a hesitant voice. I wasn't sure why it didn't bother me to tell her these personal things, other than maybe because of the scars on her arms. They were proof that she understood what I'd been through.

"First step is getting healthy, then I'll circle back with my department. They've been absolutely supportive, and there are many folks who will stand by me if it comes to an appeal for more time." I thought about Alistair and missed him, missed our chats. "You know, I've thought of someone who would be a good person for you to speak with, someone who was very understanding when I needed it. Dr. Alistair Gardner."

She frowned. "I don't know the name."

"He was my roommate at the rehab facility, though I'm not sure how to get in touch with him. He just... *knew* things, knew how to support me and challenge me without making me question my resolve, you know? I miss the old guy. Wish I would have been able to get his contact information before I left. Now, I don't know how to get in touch with him."

She put a hand over mine. "Maybe I can help. After you leave, I'm going to head back to Santa Cruz. I'll poke around and see what I can find. I'm going to present my findings to the attorneys working on the cases against BioBourne and EVE. I hope it helps. If I can locate him, I'll get word to... the police? Your aunt, maybe? In the meantime, you could probably use some rest." Her gaze dropped to the table, and she busied herself gathering her things. "I'm sorry I took up so much of your time—"

"Hey, Carmen. Thank you. I know it's not easy to talk about what happened, and when I can tell you more, I absolutely will. We will find them all, and we *will* end this. For all of us who have lost because of them."

She flung her arms around me, and I hugged her back though I was surprised. I wasn't the kind of person people usually hugged unless they knew me. My perma-scowl and shitty attitude tended to turn folks off. Perhaps we knew enough about each other that pretending we weren't a little raw inside wasn't an option.

"I'm sorry, I'm not usually this emotional," she said, pulling back and wiping a few stray tears. "I just haven't talked about it in so long, and then only with Emily and Chelsea. Thank you, Roman. I know this is all fresh for you."

"It is, but knowing there are more folks out there searching for the answers I seek motivates me."

She patted my hand, and then I stood slowly from the chair, making sure I had no light-headedness, no dizziness, before I tried walking.

"I'll see you at dinner?" she asked.

"I'm... Well, I'm not sure when we're leaving."

She nodded. Surrounded by her lab equipment and stacks of folders, she looked a little lost. I wondered if perhaps we should just bring her with us, another member of our band of misfits, but Creed wasn't ready to reveal any more of himself, and she would definitely know something was different about him if we traveled together and remained in tight quarters.

"I'll see you before we go." I gave her a wave before leaving the room and glanced back to see her staring at her paperwork. She seemed distraught.

Fuck these monsters for all they've done to take perfectly capable, strong and resilient people and turn them into pawns in some game for their sadistic pleasure. I was sick of it all! The sooner we dismantled what was left of EVE, the better for all involved.

I stormed around the corner and bumped into Creed.

"Roman, your blood pressure is high—"

"I know! Baby, *she's* one of their test subjects. They hurt her."

He took me in his arms and held me, soothed me, until my heart was doing what it was supposed to, I guessed.

"I wondered. She seemed quite invested, and I knew there was something she wasn't telling us. I'm glad it wasn't something worse, but I'm sorry she had to go through it."

"It was hard not to tell her what we know. About The Source. Do you think it's the same being behind La Mente? Or is there another?"

Creed's eyes flared. "I suppose it could be another. It kind of makes sense. My cohort never used any of the fear in their teachings. There were no research studies. I assumed that was all Stephen, but what if it was another being?"

"We've got to try to get The Source to talk about what happened."

Creed sighed. "I've tried. Todd's tried." He planted his hands on his hips and shook his head. "I wish we would have gotten more out of Stephen. Todd got a call a few minutes ago. Stephen's gone."

"He *died*? Oh God. That's... Well. You thought he would. How do you feel?"

Creed's posture was defeated, like he'd been carrying a heavy weight and finally dropped it to say, "I can't do it anymore."

"It's anticlimactic, you know? He got off easy. Not that his death was easy... I'll have to tell The Source. I wonder how they'll take it."

"I'm sure they'll have mixed feelings. It seemed, from what you said, they had a difficult time with Stephen."

"They did. It wasn't pleasant, but then, given all they've lived through, I don't know how to judge that. Where does that fifty years rank on their scale of best to worst of times, you know?"

I looped my arms around his waist and pressed my head to his shoulder. "I'm just glad he can't hurt you anymore."

"I feel the same about you," he said, brushing my hair back. He kissed my forehead and sighed. "I would really like you to use your oxygen for a bit before we leave. Will you do that for me?"

"It's time, huh?"

He nodded with a quick kiss to my lips. "It is. You can say no, Roman. You can let Rey take you home and you'll have police protection."

I stepped back. "Is that what you truly want?" I'd give him this, though I knew the truth.

"No," he whispered. "And I'm an awful, awful person for wanting you with me when I have no idea what's about to happen."

I smiled and cradled his face in my hands. "We've got this. It's going to be fine."

He placed his hands over mine and kissed my knuckles. "Rhonda will be happy."

"Will Creed be happy?"

He gazed down at me with those warm amber eyes, and I saw in him the young man he was before his life was altered irrevocably. The young man who was a kind and gentle soul, a bit adventurous, maybe a little freaky, who just wanted to be loved. Who wanted to find a world that would accept him, where maybe he'd find acceptance.

It was that young man whom I would protect with my last breath.

"Creed will be forever grateful, and blissfully happy to have you by his side. He will be terrified, but blissfully happy."

"Good. Then let's get some oxygen and hit the road. *Ooo*. Think we could stop for some ice cream? I'm dying for a Blizzard."

"A blizzard?"

"DQ, baby," I said. "Haven't you had one before?"

"I've had ice cream, but I don't think I've ever had one of those."

"You're in for a treat," I said, licking at his lips. "And when we get to wherever we're going? You're in for an even treatier treat."

That made him laugh. "Come on, my treat. Let's see if Todd and Rey have loaded the cars."

"What about Carmen?"

"Todd went to tell her goodbye for us. Don't worry. We'll be keeping in touch with her, and he said she's going to be working with Vanessa. She'll be okay."

I nodded. Somehow I knew our paths would cross again. Strange— I'd had the same feeling with Dr. Gardner. Like they were put in my path at this particular time for a reason.

Todd drove his Crown Vic and Rey followed in his SUV. Creed and I cuddled up in the back of the Crown Vic, and I promised to nap as long as Todd promised to stop at a DQ. He turned up his lip at the idea, but agreed before I threw a tantrum.

Creed stroked my hair and my back, putting me in a hazy state, but I wasn't fully asleep. My mind was still spinning from my talk with Carmen and Stephen's passing. It had been a heavy day, and while I should be napping as Creed requested, I was full of turmoil.

I would be meeting the being responsible for my near death. The being who made Creed what he was: both a gifted healer and a troubled man. What if the thing Creed feared the most came to pass? What if The Source decided they weren't done with me and wanted the rest of my blood, or decided to use me for the next ritual against my will? Could we trust them?

"If you keep thinking so hard, we won't stop for your ice cream treat."

I blinked several times to clear my vision. "How?"

Creed kissed the top of my head. "Your heart's been doing a little dance. Nothing to be concerned about but your pulse keeps changing, which leads me to think you were faking your nap and worrying."

"That's creepy. I know you can sense my pulse rate but, like, do you hear it? Feel it? How does it work?"

"I can feel it, but not just by touching your pulse points. I don't have to touch you to feel it. It pushes out energy. Everyone's does. But I'm attuned to the unique signature your heartbeat makes."

I pushed myself up to sitting as Todd pulled off the freeway.

"We had to go out of our way a bit to get here, but voila."

"DQ! Yes!" I rubbed my hands together. "Get ready for the best ice cream experience in your life. Well... one that's pretty damned good. I'm sure there are more elaborate and expensive ice cream confections. But none can surpass the nostalgia of DQ. Lola Frances used to take me here when I was little."

"Well, let's see what's on the menu."

"Oh, hey, can we go in and order, please? I've got to use the bathroom."

Todd looked around as Rey pulled into the lot next to us. They rolled down the windows and spoke to each other, then pulled around the back of the restaurant to park on the side closest to the exit of the parking lot, which would make it easier to get back on the freeway. I really had to pee, and practically had the door open before Todd had the Crown Vic in park.

"Hold your horses, Junior," Rey said, trotting over. "I'm going in with you."

"God, I can do it myself."

Creed came around the car and grinned at me. "Now, Roman, as your nurse—"

"All right, all right. If y'all are going to gang up on me."

"Hey, Creed? You got a second?" Todd called from the car.

Creed squeezed my hand. "I'll be right behind you."

Our fingers slid apart as Rey led me away.

Sixteen

C reed

I met Todd around the front of the Crown Vic, and he was frowning down at his phone.

"Oh, sorry. The security detail got separated from us a couple of lights back and I had to give them directions. I thought I was going to have news for you. I heard back from my benefactor but all he said was he'd find us soon. I don't know what that means; the guy... I mean, *they* move like smoke."

"It's okay," I said, squeezing his shoulder. "If I'm going to meet *them* soon, I'd find out anyway." Todd's phone buzzed, and he held up a finger as he answered it. I gestured to him that I was going inside and though he was distracted, I was pretty sure he saw me.

I approached the door to the fast-food restaurant and noticed a man standing next to his car, smiling at me. I nodded and reached for the handle of the door. He took a step closer, as if he were expecting me.

"Hi," he said. "I was hoping we could chat for a minute. I know you have some place to be."

He seemed friendly, no bad energy surrounding him... and I recalled Todd's weird message.

"Right. Yeah, I have a minute. Are you—?"

"How are you?" He shook my hand briskly and stepped out of the way of the door. "It's so great to finally meet you."

"And you as well," I said. "When Todd said you'd be here at any time—"

"It seemed like a good opportunity."

He was dressed in slacks and a dressy polo, not exactly the kind of person you'd imagine with vast amounts of knowledge regarding the supernatural. I suppose I thought he'd be older as well. This man looked to be mid-thirties? But who was I to judge. I looked twenty-five, and I'd looked this way for fifty-plus years.

"I've heard so much about you," the man said. "I think we can really help each other."

"That would be great, truly. It's been exhausting, and I hate the toll it's taking on my boyfriend."

Something in his expression flickered. It was so quick, I thought I'd missed it.

"We would hate for anything further to happen to him or his family."

"Right."

And then I caught him glance toward the restaurant. I followed his gaze... and saw a man dressed like him, standing behind Roman and Rey in line to order. Rey was looking around the restaurant but he didn't seem to notice the threat.

"We can ensure his family is safe. All we need is for you to come with us."

I looked back at the Crown Vic, and Todd was standing next to the driver's side door on the phone with his back to me. A man dressed in the same polo stood behind and off to the side of the car, ready to ambush Todd.

"Tell your men to back down."

"You took what belongs to us, so it's only fair that you pay reparations. Come with us willingly, and we will leave Roman alone."

"He won't believe I'd go with you willingly."

"You better make sure he does, or else we'll never let him find peace."

How could I have missed it? Were these people so skilled at hiding their evil energy that even I couldn't detect them? Not even when shaking their hands?

"Make your decision."

Time stopped as Roman and Rey opened the door and spotted me.

They'll never stop chasing me.

Roman will never have peace.

"Creed?"

Roman's smile—huge now that he had his ice cream, and he'd bought one for me—faltered.

My heart shredded into tatters.

"I'm gonna go," I said, backing away, putting myself between him and my captor. "I'm sorry. You guys go on ahead. Todd will make sure you have everything you need."

"What the fuck, Creed?" Rey had spotted the others and had his hand on his sidearm.

I smiled and tried to make it genuine. "I'll miss you guys, but they've got answers I need. And I just can't do it. The responsibility for The Source? I can't do it. Tell the others I'm sorry to impose. I hope you get well soon." I'd backed up to the Mercedes and one of the men I hadn't seen crept up behind me, and opened the rear passenger-side door. Rey couldn't see it, but there was a weapon at my back. They didn't need it. All they had to do was threaten Roman. One of the men who'd been in the restaurant behind them flashed his weapon and smiled at me. I'd do anything to keep Roman safe. Even if it meant lying to the most important person in my life.

"Creed." Todd approached, his weapon drawn. He gestured for me to come toward him. "Step away from him," he ordered the men in polos, two of whom had pulled their weapons.

I held out a hand and swallowed a sob. "No, Todd. Please. No one needs to get hurt." But Todd wasn't backing down. I hoped he didn't see the tears streaming down my face in the darkness of the parking lot. "I told you, man. I'm tired of the alpha male law enforcement vibe. I'm sick of it. Just let us go."

The man who approached me continued to smile at my chosen family, and I spotted a gun in the back of his pants.

Todd's incredulous look tore the rest of me in two. I'd never felt so small in my life.

"Let me be with the people who get me."

He lowered his gun, and I was gutted. My acting skills weren't that great. How could they believe me? But Roman might. He'd made it perfectly clear. I was not to run away again or that would be it. I had to believe he meant it, or he was about to die.

Rey pushed Roman toward Todd's car, blocking him from the now five men who were closing off the area around the Mercedes. Todd hurried to Roman's side and him and Rey blocked Roman as they backed toward the Crown Vic.

"Creed. No."

Roman's already pale face was ghost white. He pressed a hand to his chest, and I couldn't watch anymore. I climbed into the car at the same time as the driver.

"Get me the fuck out of here."

"Absolutely." He closed the door and started the car. I couldn't look in the direction of the Crown Vic. I stared straight ahead and complied when the others climbed in around me, boxing me into the SUV. "Hell of an acting job. Even I believed you wanted to come with us."

"Fuck you. And fuck all of you for threatening him." I was seething, and it was making my power surge. I fed off of their cocky posturing and their smug attitudes. I had half a mind to tear into their gray matter and leave them quivering messes where they sat. As long as they left Roman alone, I would hold onto the oath I took... for now.

"Settle down back there, Guardian Creed." The one who'd climbed into the passenger seat turned around, and I was hit with a wave of dark energy I hadn't felt since the night they ran me off the road in Santa Cruz.

"That's right. You might be more powerful, but I always get what I want. I've been patient, and since you took The Source from me, I'm going to take *everything* from you. You're never going to see Roman or any of your friends again. Make your peace with that. Where you're going, there's no coming back."

And then I was hit with fifty-thousand volts of electricity in the form of a taser, and another and another, until I collapsed against the man next to me in the backseat. I was still aware, but nothing would work.

I was paralyzed, in pain, and all I could think was, *you deserve this.*

Becoming aware was like every cell in my body crying out for healing energy at the same time. A chorus of pain rang out through my entire system, screams and cries so loud they vibrated under my skin. But I heard nothing. My eyes? I opened them to blackness. The only sound was my panicked breathing, my heart pounding in my chest, and the sloshing of water.

"Stephen placed me in this state for periods of time to keep me compliant."

Compliant? Maybe. But if Timothy Hicks wanted to use me for his dark deeds, he would soon learn that keeping me isolated in a sensory deprivation state would end me.

Perhaps that was the best outcome to this horrible situation.

Stop fighting.

But just thinking those words brought forward a face from the blackness that I'd burn down the world for.

Roman.

The sheer joy on his face while holding his ice cream. Before that, his fingers brushing my hair back from my face as I knelt between his thighs. Before that, when he heard his uncle singing in the kitchen, and he realized just how affected Rey had been by the pheromones before our Exchange.

As his face faded from view, the waves of pain and anguish flooded me again. I fought against the walls of whatever they were keeping me in, screaming at the top of my lungs.

Dim light filtered in around the edges of whatever was closed over me, and I heard locks clicking open. A door was lifted and the light, even though it was muted, seared my corneas. Two men lifted me from the chamber, and I tried to conserve what little energy I had after being tased.

"Welcome, Guardian Creed."

Three men in those same polos stood with Hicks. They must have all been trained in how to mask their energy, as I was not picking up anything about them, no threat, no nothing.

I chose to remain quiet. I wasn't interested in prolonging my existence, or fighting back, but I did want to absorb all of the information I possibly could.

"I'm sure you have questions," he began, and paused to allow me to speak. How generous. I had nothing to say. He'd made sure of that.

"Or not. We've gone to great lengths to make you feel at home," he said, gesturing around the room. With no windows. With fucking tie-dyed wall tapestries and a lava lamp. Hicks laughed. "We tried to bring your dog, but she seems quite happy where she's at. I suppose she's not going to miss you."

That meant they knew where the compound was, but either they weren't able to mount an assault or they chose not to. Why not? Wouldn't they want The Source back?

"We've even gone so far as to provide you with a personal caregiver. Ironic, huh? You go from being the nurse to the nursed."

The door opened, and two more men came in with someone tucked behind them.

"Her job is to keep you in tip-top shape. She'll examine you and make sure you have everything you need while you settle in. Then we'll get to work. Sound good?"

I crossed my arms over my chest. What did he expect? A happy dance?

Then they pushed the young woman forward, and my heart was torn yet again.

"Lexi."

"We'll let you two get settled. Dinner will be delivered soon."

Hicks and his henchmen left the room and closed the door, engaging an electronic lock behind them. One of them remained behind and watched us through the window.

"Creed, what's happening?"

Lexi burst into tears as I approached her. I didn't know whether she'd accept any comfort from me, but I held a hand out to her.

She rushed me and wrapped her arms around my waist.

"Lexi, I'm so sorry."

"What's happening? Why are you here?"

"How did you end up with these people? Did they kidnap you?"

"No! I mean, not exactly. I was approached by the director of Longevity Health. They called me up, asked to meet with me, and they offered me a shitload of money." She looked up at me. "Things at Puesta haven't been the same without you, and my landlord imposed a ridiculous rent hike, plus my car broke down. Then all of a sudden, today they tell me they need me at a different facility, and then these scary guys showed up at my house and told me to pack a bag. Creed, what's going on?"

I sighed. I should have known it wouldn't just be Roman.

"I'm sorry, Lexi. You're here because they needed to give me a reason to cooperate."

"Cooperate with what?"

I looked around the room. Beside the sensory deprivation chamber, there was a twin bed, a sad couch, a full medical cabinet, and all the equipment you'd find in a typical ICU unit.

"They're going to force you to keep me existing." I walked over to inspect the supplies and sighed. "They knew I'd give up. With Roman safe, I'd give up."

"What are you talking about? This is freaking me out."

I turned to face her. "Think about what you saw."

Her eyes widened, and she backed up a step. "When you... with Mr. Fletcher?"

"When you saw me bite him."

She shook her head. "What is happening?"

"I can tell you, but it's not going to make it better for you. I'll say this... they brought you here to make me cooperate with them. They're using you."

There was nothing I could do. I had nothing to bargain with. Either I did what they wanted—which I assumed was remaining strong so they could use my blood—or they'd hurt Lexi. They'd hurt Roman.

"Why do they have you here?"

"Because, Lexi, I'm... different."

"I know. You're gay. You told me. I don't know what the biting was about—"

I cringed at that memory. I hadn't wanted to hurt my friend who'd developed a harmless crush on me.

"It's not that. I'm able to heal people through the Exchange of energy and blood. When you saw me with Mr. Jenkins, I was taking nourishment from him so I could continue to take care of the patients at Puesta. I chose to work with the elderly so I can make their final years as peaceful as possible."

She frowned. "Yeah, but... I don't understand. Why did you bite him?"

I exhaled and tried not to lose my temper. It really didn't matter whether she believed me or not. It might have been safer if she didn't know, but I needed her help if I was going to keep her safe.

"What did they tell you to do with me?"

"You mean, what did they say about the job?"

I nodded.

"They told me to take your vitals. And your blood."

Here we go.

"Then I suppose we should get started. I'll tell you the whole story."

SEVENTEEN

R oman

I fought physically against Rey and Todd. I fought dirty. I screamed at them to follow Creed, but they refused. *"It's not safe. We have to get you to safety."* Fuck that. Creed needed us.

Eventually I collapsed in the backseat in a daze and completely drained. How the fuck had this happened? We'd taken precautions. Where were the security guys? Todd was going to have a lot to answer for.

I didn't believe Creed's words, not for a minute. I knew why he would say those things. I thought back to how uncomfortable he'd seemed, telling us about his life, how he'd resisted doing the Exchange with Rey and Todd. But he'd been all in when were alone... when we fucked. I replayed what he said over and over, trying to determine whether there had been any hints or secret messages, but there was nothing. He said he was seeking answers, that he didn't want the responsibility of The Source, and I knew that was true, but the Creed I knew—

the Creed I loved—wouldn't have walked away from something so important unless he felt he had no other choice. He wouldn't have walked away from me. No matter what.

"We're almost there," Todd said, both hands gripping the steering wheel. He cursed under his breath as the Crown Vic sped down a two-lane highway, taking the curves and turns too fast but completely in control.

Rey was dead silent. Even when I'd pushed him and screamed at him for backing down, for letting those assholes take Creed, he didn't fight back, he didn't get mad, he just held me until I couldn't fight anymore.

Todd finally turned off of the road and took a long gravel drive through the redwoods until we pulled up before a huge concrete and glass structure. The only way I could make anything out was the floodlights around the property, as it was the middle of the night by the time we reached the compound. There were guards outside and two additional black SUVs parked out front. A tall guy with wavy dark hair came out of the front doors in dark cargo pants, boots, and a tight black long-sleeved shirt.

"We've got your room set up, Mr. San Angelo," he said, as he helped me down from the car. Rey came around from the other side of the car and butted him out of the way.

"You need your chair?" he asked me quietly.

I shook my head. "I'm all right." By this time I was exhausted but not sleepy. My lungs ached and I'd need my oxygen before bed, but I wanted answers.

"How did this happen?" I asked my uncle. Todd came to stand in front of me.

"It's my fault, Roman. I got separated from our security detail and got distracted on the phone trying get them to our location. I never should have let him get out of the car alone. I was trying to set up a meeting with our benefactor and I lost... focus. We'll find him."

Rey kicked up his chin. "You believe that shit? What he said?"

Todd hesitated, and his kind expression turned forlorn. I hadn't thought about the fact that he and Creed had gotten close while they'd been working together. I knew he took his job and his role in this situation seriously, but I could only sense shame and disappointment from him.

"I don't want to," he started.

"Because he didn't," I spit out. "He was trying to protect us."

Todd swallowed hard. "We'll find him. I sent a team to follow their caravan at a distance. It's not ideal. Another unit will try to track them by drones, and they're working on picking up a cell signal." He shook his head. "I'm... I fucked up, Rey. I'm sorry. I thought—"

"You sure as fuck did. Come on, pamangkin. Let's get you to bed."

We followed the security guard up the steps to the front door and into the house, leaving Todd alone in front of the house, staring off into the distance as if he could will Creed's return.

Cross and Mark rushed to meet us.

"Are you all right?" Mark asked, placing his hand on my arm. Cross moved to Rey's side, and the two of them spoke in hushed tones.

"I don't know." I couldn't put my thoughts into words. My usual fiery temper had made a showing in the moment, but now, I had nothing left. I was... fucking heartbroken.

I'd thought we were in the clear. I'd let my guard down. I think we all had, and Creed paid the price.

Creed had orbited me in turns like the caretaker I needed physically and the partner I needed emotionally. We were the push and pull of the tide together, working in concert, loving together. We had to get him back.

"Roman?"

I'd been too caught up in my despair to realize the room suddenly brightened.

The Source's glowing figure descended the stairs dressed in red flowing material, which moved as if it were animated. Their hair was shorn close to the skull and their wide eyes were so blue, so perfectly round, the whites showing around the irises. They smiled kindly and took a few more steps, stopping at the foot of the stairs.

Rey stepped in front of me, but he remained quiet.

Creed didn't want this. He didn't want me to meet them, be in the same room with them. How could he have chosen to leave me if he was so adamant I not be in the same room as The Source?

Because he didn't choose this. I knew it in my bones, in my heart, in my blood he found so precious. He'd been forced to act... to protect us. He'd once again sacrificed himself for me.

"I'm afraid this is all my fault." Their voice was slightly accented, a similar lilt to the Irish, and the timbre was equal parts soothing and disturbing. I broke out in goosebumps.

Todd approached them and held up a hand. "I would like to get Roman settled in his room, and then I can tell you more of what happened, but please... let us tend to Roman."

The Source turned to him and smiled. "You seek to protect him, but I only wish to offer healing. He suffers. I would take that from him. It is my wish to make reparations."

Their gaze bored into mine and everything else fell away. Their beauty was so pleasing, and I knew that the depths to their soul, their power, was infinite, that if I took the hand they held out to me, I could stop fighting, stop struggling.

And then I smelled it, though instead of sugar cookies, they emanated the fragrance of the forest after a rain: damp, dark, earthy. Sweet, but not the kind that made my mouth water—instead, the kind that made me want to get lost in nature, roll in the moss, bathe in a forest spring, at peace and one with—

They were using their pheromone with me, and once again, I hadn't given my consent.

I leaned heavily on my cane and pulled myself up to my full height, which was similar to theirs. "I look forward to speaking with you, but I need to rest. I do not consent to your healing at this time."

Their smile faded and their eyes widened impossibly farther. They pressed a hand to their mouth and took a step back. "Forgive me."

They turned and hurried toward the back of the house and disappeared into the darkness.

"Well, shit." Cross went after The Source, and a moment later, thunder rumbled throughout the fortress and rain pelted the windows.

"That could have gone better," Mark said. He took my arm and gestured to Rey. "Let's get the two of you settled upstairs. You have the third floor to yourselves. Either Cross or myself will be with The Source at all times. You don't have to see them unless you wish to."

"I'm sorry," Todd said, shaking his head. He looked as if all was lost, and if I wasn't careful, I'd be right there with him, wallowing.

"It's okay. Thank you."

I wasn't sure what I was thanking him for, and by his expression, neither did he. I think, though, that I realized the big picture. They were always going to come for Creed, for us, and we'd been complacent.

"You good?" Todd asked Rey.

"Fucking amazing," he said, rolling his eyes. "Let's go."

It was a slow process to climb to the second floor and when I faltered at the landing, Rey picked me up and carried me the rest of the way, knowing full well I hated every second but he was too preoccupied to give me shit about it.

The third floor was a large, open space with a kitchenette, a bathroom, and, behind glass French doors, a bedroom. The ceiling was slanted in various spaces, creating little nooks and crannies that held a reading nook on one side and a desk on the other.

"What is this place?" I asked, but then I yawned so wide my jaw cracked.

"I'll explain everything in the morning," Todd said. "Rey, that couch pulls out into a bed, or there's another bedroom on the other side of the—"

"I'm good here." He set me down next to the couch, and Todd sat our two duffel bags next to the bedroom doors. "I'll be one second," Rey said to me as I sat down, or more like I collapsed into a heap on the comfortable leather sofa. Rey stepped out into the hall with Todd, and the two had a heated discussion that I was too tired to try to follow.

Recessed lighting had been turned down to provide soft ambiance around the perimeter and the bedroom was dark beyond the doors. I wanted dark. I wanted quiet. I wanted to disappear. My heart was as empty and cavernous as this fucking fortress. Part of me was gone somewhere, probably in danger, likely in pain, and whether he meant to leave me or not, whether he'd agreed to go in order to protect me or, as I feared, to get out of his responsibility, I couldn't help but mourn his absence. I'd fought so hard for weeks just to be by his side, and he was ripped so senselessly from me. I wanted to scream, but I also wanted to curl up in a ball and ugly cry.

"Are you hungry or anything, Junior?"

Rey stood beside me, and I couldn't think of an appropriate answer.

"Why?" My voice cracked and the tears I'd held back with anger and indignation and worry fell—and based on his expression, scared the shit out of my uncle.

"Oh, honey, I wish I knew." And my uncle sat beside me and did something he'd only done once before. The night I'd returned home after fucking around with my hooligan skater friends and found the front door open, Bunny barking his head off, and my parents tied together on the kitchen floor, pools of blood spilled from bullet wounds in their skulls. I'd called Rey and he'd come screaming over in his patrol car, beating the fire and ambulance and even the first patrol car dispatched to the scene, and he'd run into the house.

That night, he'd held me as I screamed and screamed, cursing the fucking God who was supposed to love and protect his devoted followers, blaming myself for being out instead of home with my family, and despairing over losing the two people who'd done their best to love and care for their cantankerous and rebellious son who was determined to fuck up his own life, and in return, had possibly destroyed theirs.

"Goddamned Nurse Creed," Rey muttered under his breath as he held me and tried to console me. He smoothed my long hair down, rubbed my back, kissed my temple and continued to try to soothe me for what felt like hours. Eventually, when I had nothing left, he once more carried me, this time into the darkened bedroom, and tucked me into yet another soft, comfortable bed, only this one was cold. I shivered as I pulled the chilly sheets tight around me, and likely would have continued to sob, but I was depleted. Empty. I feared that not even restorative sleep would bring me back from the ledge this time.

"Let me be with the people who get me."

Creed's words tore through me, and I gasped. He had to know that wasn't true. He would never have left me of his own volition, and I knew he was in terrible trouble. If we didn't get him back, if we lost him... I'd thought I was broken before.

"Shit. *Todd*! Get his oxygen up here! And where's the fucking medic?"

The light flicked on and I sensed others around me, but my vision was spotty, I couldn't get in enough air, and that was all she wrote. I slipped into the cold darkness as if I were back on that slab, my blood being siphoned from me, my life spilling on the ground.

I woke at some point and found myself hooked up to machinery once more. I nearly pulled out my IV trying to wake up from the nightmare, only I *was* awake. I was awake inside the nightmare.

"Mr. San Angelo," a male voice said, one I hadn't heard before. "I'm Larsson Berg—I'm a medic. Do you know where you are?"

"No," I said, and the effort felt as if I'd swallowed sandpaper.

"Okay. Your uncle is downstairs with Agent Barringer. We're at a safe house. I'm just going to check your vitals, and then if you want—"

"Bathroom."

He chuckled. "Absolutely. One second." I felt a cuff tighten on my arm and his cold stethoscope under my t-shirt. "Can you take a couple of deep breaths for me?"

I tried but it led to a coughing fit, which made his machines go berserk for a few seconds until the beeping returned to a sinus rhythm.

"Okay, let's unhook you and I'll help you."

Here I was, back to needing help to go to the bathroom. A weak part of me had a brief thought that maybe I should just take it all off, refuse all help, and go back to sleep until I didn't wake up. What was the use?

But I wasn't about to give up. My boyfriend needed me. He may have tried to hurt my feelings, but I was pissed now. Pissed to be back in this state, pissed at myself for insisting we stop for ice cream. Pissed at the fuckers who'd taken Creed from me. And to be honest, I was pissed at Todd.

When I'd finished in the bathroom and Larsson was helping me back to bed, I heard footsteps thundering up the stairs.

"Junior?"

"Hey," I said, as Rey rushed to my side.

"How do you feel? You hanging in there?"

"I'm fucking livid, is how I'm feeling. Where's Todd?"

"I'm here." Todd came in behind Rey, standing back as if that would save him from my wrath.

"Tell me you know something."

He cleared his throat and looked to Rey, who raised an eyebrow as if to say he was on his own.

"We have a general location. It's a pretty large area, but they've narrowed down a potential search grid. We're doing what we can. But I brought you someone who's been going nuts since you arrived."

I heard a familiar tick-tick, and then Rhonda launched herself onto the bed and into my arms.

"Oh, baby," I said, burying my face in her neck. "I've missed you!"

"Mark says she's been searching for Creed since we left to meet you," Todd said. "We discovered Creed had been giving her his blood. She's actually like thirty years old."

I shot him a surprised look, then went back to petting her. "No wonder she was such a mess without him." She and I had that in common, only without him, my heart hurt. For her, it could be a lot more serious.

"We'll find him," Todd said. "I won't stop searching until he's safe."

I nodded, but I was weary. I would continue to fight for him until I took my last breath, but how many of those did I have left?

I gazed into Rhonda's eyes, much wiser than those of a typical dog, and the answer was clear.

I had no choice but to fight. I just hoped that whatever the outcome on the other side of this battle, there would be no more pain, because my heart, literally and figuratively, couldn't take much more.

Eighteen

C reed

"I'm sorry, Creed. It's time for more blood tests."

I don't know that Lexi would ever recover from the tasks she was being forced to complete daily. The EVE folks wanted blood samples at regular intervals, hourly vitals while awake, and while I slept, they kept me connected to monitors. Anytime I resisted their requests, they brought in the laptop that showed Roman's grandmother and his aunts at Puesta Del Sol, and they threatened Lexi with bodily injury. After the first time they nicked her with a knife, I complied, and would continue to do so. They shaved my head, hooked me up to electrodes, and took CT scans of my brain. They ran every test known to man, to get a base-line they said, and I was given nutritious meals five times a day, which I tried to refuse, but I couldn't risk anyone else being harmed. Hicks had me right where he wanted me.

"It's fine. You're so gentle with the needle, I don't even have a bruise."

She gave a quick smile but got to work concentrating, her hands shaking just the slightest. After being locked away in here with me, I'd told her everything—the commune, the mutiny, how I'd spent the last fifty years... She'd heard me out, had her moments of yelling at me, of crying, of disbelief, and finally acceptance that we were in this shit together. When they'd tried to take her out of my room to sleep elsewhere, she'd begged to stay with me and they'd allowed it, as long as we cooperated. She slept on the couch. I tried to give her the bed, but they'd insisted I needed to be in the bed and connected to the monitors.

"Hey," I said. "I'm sorry you were dragged into this, Lexi. I would do anything to make them let you go."

She shook her head and tucked her hair behind her ear, realized she now had to wash her hands, and put on new gloves before trying again. "I hate that they're hurting you, that they're making *me* hurt you." She tried to laugh but it came out a sob. "You were always better at this than me."

"No, I wasn't. Come here."

I used a bit of pheromone, just the slightest bit to take the edge off for her, otherwise they'd come looking for a blood sample and discover she wasn't able to do what they'd brought her here to do. I wouldn't put it past them to eliminate her if that was the case. I'd take the sample myself before I allowed that to happen, but then they were watching. Always watching. It had been three days of this, and they wouldn't tell me anything other than I'd be briefed soon, as long as I cooperated.

I pulled her into a hug and held her until the shaking stopped, and she was able to take a few deep breaths.

"I'm so scared, Creed. What are they going to do with you?"

"I have an inkling," I said, just as the door opened. Lexi stepped away from me and moved to the counter to wash her hands and get new gloves.

"We need the sample."

She nodded and glared at the guy in the polo shirt. There seemed to be no end to the amount of young men in those damned Longevity Health polo shirts and gray slacks. They all were the quintessential fitness-model types, not too built, perfect teeth, tanned skin, bright eyes, big enough for me to fear I'd likely be defeated in any sort of combat. They were bigger, and I was weakened by this captivity.

They'd kept me in this room with just Lexi for three days, and I hadn't slept. My mind was going a mile a minute trying to figure a way out, and eventually I'd given up, given in, and would have accepted my fate were it not for Lexi. I had to figure out a way for them to let her go, only that wasn't likely, considering all they'd spoken about in front of her and the fact that they'd kidnapped her. Unless they were able to make the whole operation disappear, letting her go would lead to their discovery.

Lexi approached and made eye contact with me, showing me the needle. I nodded and rested my arm with my palm facing up. She'd gotten herself together and the procedure was nearly pain-free. She wrapped the label on the sample bottle and handed it to the worker.

"Well, Creed, things are looking good." Hicks walked in with two of his men remaining outside the doorway. A third person stood behind Hicks.

I stared at him coolly, remaining silent.

"All of your tests have come back with exactly the results we were hoping for. Your blood, your body, is purer than even The Source's. While you don't have their age and wisdom, your blood will be perfect for our purposes. We will continue taking samples several times a day as we make some adjustments to your regimen, and we'll see if we can boost your potency."

"Glad you're getting what you want."

I couldn't resist. I hadn't learned to keep my mouth shut as well as I'd thought.

"Nearly. We're nearly there. But I brought something for you." He reached behind him and brought forward a young man not in uniform, but was instead dressed in only a robe. And he was grinning.

"Creed, this is Neil. He is here for your nourishment."

I frowned. Of course they would bring people to me for Exchanges.

"Now that we've got baseline data on you, it's time to see just how powerful you can become. The Exchange is the most important source of your power, and we have a wealth of volunteers to supply you with your daily needs."

"Daily? I only require an Exchange once a month."

Hicks sighed and smiled, but it looked as if his face might break with the effort to appear sincere. "That was then. *Now* you will take your nourishment as often as I require. We want you to be as strong as you can possibly be. I know there are other ways that your kind gain strength as well, and Neil, along with being able to nourish you, is here for any other pleasures you may wish to take with his flesh."

I should have expected it, but his words stirred a rage within me that urged me to tear this place to the ground, Lexi or no. I ached to lash out, end this man. I could do it. Stephen knew I could do it, but I would cease to exist before committing murder. I would *never* have sex with a person they brought to me. Even if they starved me and that was the only hope I had of existing, there was no way.

Neil, oblivious to what was really going on, gave me the most welcoming smile and began to unfasten his robe. I placed a hand on his chest.

"No. That will not be necessary."

His cheeks flushed, and he looked between Timothy and me.

"Suit yourself. This time, Creed. You will do what I wish if you want those you care about to remain well."

I glared at him once more before leading Neil over to the couch and asking him to sit. I ran through the ritual, refusing to give in to Hicks's hedonistic ways. Neil merely smiled and nodded, and when I released the pheromone, he sighed and fell back against the couch, obviously aroused. I had a fleeting thought that if I made it unpleasant for him, perhaps he'd leave, spread word to the others that what they'd volunteered for was not what they'd been told. How many people could he possibly have under his control? And where were we?

I nearly forgot to give thanks for taking from him, but I mumbled against his skin, "Blessed be," and then broke his skin with my teeth. The taste was...iuyunpleasant. Not that the taste of blood had ever been delicious to me. It was nothing like vampire films and books where the monsters drink the blood of the innocent, extolling the savory nature of life's elixir. No. Blood tasted like blood. But when taken under the right circumstances, the *experience* was pleasant.

Now, I was seething with anger, and that gave the blood a tang that turned my stomach. I took as much as was safe for the young man, but more than I normally would have. If Hicks wanted me strong, he'd get strong. He'd get me so strong that eventually I'd have the power Amergin wielded, and I would make him pay for what he'd done to me and countless others.

As I was knitting Neil's tissues back together—and ignoring his erection and happy moans—I caught movement at the door. A woman with long black hair poked her head inside, and she gasped when she saw what was going on.

"What are you—"

"What are you doing down here?" Timothy said, hurrying to block her view.

"I need to speak with you." Her eyes widened as she saw me briefly before Timothy pushed her out the door and into the hallway. Their angry voices carried into the room.

"Are you okay?" I asked Neil.

He blinked a few times and smiled. "I'm great. Wow, that was incredible. They told us that serving you would feel good, but I had no idea..."

I leaned close and whispered in his ear.

"Neil, listen to me. Lexi and I are being held against our will. Do you have any contact with anyone outside of this place?"

Neil's brows furrowed slightly but didn't lose his smile. "What do you mean?"

I knew it was a risk, but I had to try.

"Can you contact the police? Can you tell them Lexi is being held here?"

"The police? But why?" His eyes widened, and he looked to Lexi. She nodded as tears ran down her face.

"Sorry for that interruption. Neil, thank you for your service. Lawrence will take you to your room."

Neil smiled at me once more and bowed. "Thank you for this opportunity to serve."

I had no idea whether or not Neil would help us, or if Timothy would figure out that I'd tried to get him to pass on a message, but as

Neil was whisked away, Timothy appeared to be irritated about something.

"Now," he said, walking toward the sensory deprivation chamber, "to insure you gain the fullest potency of the Exchange, it's time for you to rest—"

"Actually, *Timothy*," I said, giving his name all the venom I could produce, "depriving me of my senses only weakens me. I'm at my strongest when I'm able to heal others."

"Healing? No, Creed. There is no need for you to—"

"There *is* a need. Unlike the others you've come into contact with, I have to make an *actual* Exchange, the blood for the healing, otherwise it... well, it won't have the results you're looking for."

Timothy frowned—and then he got an expression of complete amazement.

"That's it! That's the difference." He approached me and moved to grab my biceps, and I stepped back.

"Don't you fucking put your hands on me."

He placed them on his mouth instead, and laughed, ignoring my ire. "That's it!"

"What's it?"

He gasped and kept his hands clasped in front of him. "We've been looking for the difference, and you just gave it to me. The reason your blood is the purest. The reason you're stronger. It's your *selflessness*. Stephen did away with the teachings and healing so long ago. I don't think there are many left alive who learned what you did, if any. Even Mark and Cross, they don't heal people anymore, nor The Source. It's *you*. You're the healer, and therefore you're the strongest. This is amazing!" He put his hands on his mouth again and looked as if he'd just won the lottery. "If healing is what you need, we can certainly provide you with opportunities."

His maniacal laugh hit me like a sledgehammer to the stomach. What horrors would he think of next?

"Be well, Creed. I shall see you tomorrow. Lexi? Come with me."

I stepped between them. "She stays with me."

Timothy's eyes flared. He wasn't going to give up his need for control.

"I thought you didn't like women, Creed." He leaned in close, invading my personal space until I was ready to physically remove him. "What would Roman say? Of course, he wouldn't have to know. Stephen said sexual energy is the most potent. I know it gets *me* off. You can have all you want. You can indulge however you want, and there's no judgement here. You and I could sit on top of the world if you'll work with me."

I didn't reply. I held his gaze and let him think he could persuade me. Perhaps that was the answer. He said he always got what he wanted. Maybe I could be as good an actor as I'd been with Roman, only this time, the purpose would be to get under Timothy's skin, find a way out. Find a way back to Roman and grovel for his forgiveness...

No. I needed to close that door or the misery would consume me. Wishing for a positive outcome would break me in the end. I needed to accept that there'd be no going back to him this time.

TIMOTHY HICKS

He strode toward his office on a high. This was turning out so much better than he'd anticipated. He'd been a little harsh on Courtney, but once she heard what he'd learned, she'd be amenable.

He'd told her to wait for him in his office, and he was pleased to find her exactly where he told her to be.

"I'm sorry," she said, sitting in his desk chair, her hands in her lap, her dark eyes wide. "I didn't mean to intrude."

"Tell me what you observed."

She exhaled. "Are you keeping that nurse here? Against her will?"

Timothy rested a hip on his desk next to her, appreciating the fact he could look down on her, and down her blouse.

"The nurse is here because she has ties to Creed. She's a bargaining chip, here to keep him in line."

"Is that necessary?" Courtney had lowered her voice, but I could tell she was disturbed by what she'd walked in on.

Pity.

"It is. Creed is vital to the success of this project, *our* success. Darling, without him, we are finished. EVE, Longevity, you and I. Done. Now, you don't want that, do you?"

She shook her head and smoothed out her skirt. "No, I'm only concerned about the safety of those in our program."

He reached out and cupped her jaw, forcing her to look him in the eye. "You're so very valuable, Courtney. Immensely. I couldn't have kept this going without you, with all of the obstacles Stephen left for us to clear, but we're almost there. *Almost there.* And when we deliver the goods to EVE's distributors, we're going to be able to write our own ticket. Don't you want that? You love success, don't you?"

She looked at her hands, and then looked up in that demure way that always got Timothy hard. Made him want to test her boundaries, wanted to see just how far she'd go.

She placed a hand on his thigh, and that was consent enough. He unfastened his pants and took her hand, placing it where he wanted it.

He got everything he wanted from her, had her every which way over his desk, then he left her to clean herself up. He couldn't help himself. He wanted to see what his billion-dollar baby was doing with his newly replenished energy. What would Creed do next? What could Timothy *get* him to do next? The possibilities were endless.

Endless.

Nineteen

R oman

Five days. Five days lost while trying to get strong enough to go down the stairs on my own so I could yell at Todd some more.

Five days to question everything.

Five days to feel sorry for myself.

Five days was enough.

Rey remained quiet, eerily quiet. When he brought me dinner, I was determined to make him speak to me.

"We should go get him ourselves."

Rey set down my food and turned on me with his eyebrows high. "Come again?"

"What are we waiting for? God knows what they're doing to Creed. What they're making him do."

"Do you think I have a fucking army in my pocket? Did you happen to see how many of those bastards came to collect him?"

"I'm not ignorant. I know what we're up against. But I can't sit here and wait anymore."

"I know, honey." Rey's permafrown was so severe, he appeared to have aged ten years during the five days. "I'm antsy too."

"I don't want him to think we've given up on him. The longer he's away... I'm worried for him, Rey." My guilt had been weighing on me. I knew he most likely sacrificed himself to keep me safe, and the longer he was with them, the more he probably thought I'd let him go. "I told him, Rey," I said, my voice so hoarse it pained me to say the words. "I told him if he walked away again, I couldn't do this again. He believed me. You heard what he said."

"Yes, and I saw the guns pointed at you. Why the fuck do you think he said what he said in such a way? To make his exit as convincing as possible."

"Maybe so. Whether that's why he said it or not, he's going to believe we gave up on him. I can't have that. I can't have *him* giving up. He'll... cease. To exist."

Rey sat down with a huff and rubbed his hands on his thighs. "You mean..."

"Yeah. Even if he meant what he said, we have to at the very least get him away from those people and let him decide. Even if he decides he doesn't want to be *here*. We have to try."

Rey's nostrils flared. "You're right. Shit, I always thought that maybe if people would have tried a little harder with my folks, maybe they would have made a better choice."

A twinge in my chest made me wince. "Rey... I know, I'm sorry."

"I'm old enough to remember, you know? Remember begging my mama to stay with us. Her and papa said they were going to build a better life for us. That it would just be a little while and they'd come back for us when the town was ready for more kids. I was angry at my titas for not convincing them to stay. Everyone just let them go. But maybe my mom didn't *want* to go, and it was Dad putting the pressure on. Maybe it was the other way. But somebody could have stepped up and made at least one of them stay. I could have had one parent, at least. The point is, the family said 'oh well, they're off. Guess that's what they want to do.' They could have tried harder, not given up."

I was speechless. Rey had never talked to me about his parents, not like this.

"I never... I just assumed you were too young to remember."

Rey nodded and looked down at the floor. "Yeah, well. Whatever. Creed has done a lot for this family. He gave us more time with Tita Frances. He saved your life. We owe him."

"We owe him."

He blew out a breath and nodded. "We'll get him back. I'm not losing another person I care about to a fucking cult. Now eat your damn dinner. I need to think."

He stormed off, and I called out for him.

"I'm not going anywhere without you, Junior. Just eat."

The vegetable stew was flavorful and warm and yet it went down like ash. Everything was wrong. Felt wrong.

"May I come in?"

The Source stood in the doorway, avoiding eye contact and appearing... frail. Their light was dimmer, but it was still there... and it was the light I needed. I knew what I needed to do.

Nothing Creed had ever told me involved The Source hurting anyone. Other than me, and he'd said that had happened under duress.

Rhonda came barreling past them and onto the couch next to me. She'd have my back. I could do this.

"Please come in."

The Source smiled hesitantly and flowed into the room as though their feet never hit the ground. I couldn't look at their face for long. It was too perfect, masculine and feminine beauty combining to create this ethereal being who alternated between kind and fierce without their expression changing.

"Mr. Jenkins is teaching me to cook. Do you like the soup?"

I nodded, looking down at my spoon. "I do. Very much."

They sank to a cross-legged position on the floor on the other side of the coffee table from me. I appreciated the space.

"The nutrients in this food will be good for your cardiovascular system. Nourishment and meditation are vital for your recovery... I'm sorry. Creed tells me I fall into my role as Teacher too often, that I must learn to listen."

They fell silent, and I chuckled. "I'm a teacher as well. Sometimes I, too, forget to listen."

Their eyes widened and they leaned forward. "What kind of teacher are you?"

I had just taken another spoonful of the soup to be polite, so I paused to think on how I could answer in a way that they might understand.

"I'm a university professor, a teacher of young adults, in the field of psychology. I teach students specifically how people can be negatively influenced by charismatic leaders or groups and manipulated into committing crimes and harmful behaviors." *Whoa.* How was that going to go over?

"One so young as you has the experience to lead others in this field?"

I smirked. I didn't think the slight was intentional. "I've absolutely had the experience. I may be young, but I've seen a lot in my years. My family has experience in this type of thing, as well."

They cocked their head to the side. "Can you tell me more? I want to understand."

So I did. And they listened, though I wondered how much they truly understood. I talked about Jim Jones, David Koresh, Charles Manson, and on and on until my soup was cold and I had a chill. I reached for a blanket and started to wrap up.

"Oh, I have kept you too long. I only want to know you. To understand why Creed loves you so."

And there went what was left of my energy. I sighed, and The Source climbed to their feet.

"Are you unwell? Shall I call for your uncle?"

I shook my head. "No. I'm... I'm okay. It hurts to talk about him."

They blinked. "About Creed?"

I nodded.

They lowered themself to the couch next to me, and my hair stood on end. Though their glow was dimmed, they exuded warmth, and their energy was like a crackling fire next to me.

"I have spoken to Todd, and I know that Creed said he wished to be free of me."

"I'm sorry," I said, wishing to touch them, to comfort them for what must have been a difficult thing to hear. Then I remembered they nearly ended my life. I shrank from them involuntarily, and their eyes widened.

"It is I who am sorry. This is inappropriate. I know Creed did not wish for me to harm you, and that is certainly not my intention, Roman. It *never* would have been my intention." Their impossibly large blue eyes filled with tears and rain begin to splatter the window, a steady thrumming. Rhythmic, almost, unlike a typical chaotic rainfall. It reminded me of a heartbeat.

"Creed asked me to never be alone with you. But I'd told him that I want to understand. I want to know how he became who he is. I know he would... well, I don't know what he's thinking. I don't believe he left me willingly. I don't want to believe that he did."

"He did not go willingly, Roman. He never would have left your side unless he meant to protect you."

Their tears were catching because suddenly, my eyes were filled with them, too.

"I'm terrified for him," I whispered.

Lightning streaked through the sky, illuminating the giant redwoods outside the window. The Source turned and gazed out the window and then turned back, their eyes narrowed.

"I'm *furious* for him. If I were able to... I want him returned safely. I want to punish those who have wronged him, who have caused him harm, who have taken my teachings, taken The Way, and used it for selfish and harmful purposes—"

Footsteps thundered up the stairs, and Todd and Rey burst into the room.

"Roman—"

I held out a hand to Todd and turned to face The Source. I took their hand in mine and instantly the storm calmed outside.

"I am... broken," they cried.

"I know. I am too."

The Source fell into my arms and wept, and with what little strength I had, I held them and tried to ease their pain the only way I knew how. Touch wasn't a language I spoke with strangers, but then this being was no stranger. Yes, we'd met under horrible circumstances, but I recognized the loneliness and despair within them, and I couldn't bear to see another person suffer, despite what had happened between us.

I held them for several minutes while Rey and Todd tried to figure out what to do. Eventually, Todd ran downstairs and brought back Larsson.

"We need to get Roman back to his bed and hooked up to his oxygen," Larsson said to The Source in a calm voice. The guy had such a soothing tone, it was perfect for easing the most agitated patients, I assumed. It worked on The Source, as well.

"Yes, of course," they said, letting me go. "Thank you, Roman. Creed is right to put his trust in you. You are an honorable man." They gave me one last smile and stood from the couch, taking Todd's hand.

"Thank you, and... I'm sorry, I don't know your name."

They bowed to me. "Please call me Amergin."

"Amergin. Let's talk again. Please."

They nodded once more and allowed Todd to lead them from the room.

"Fuck me, are you all right?" Rey knelt next to me.

"I am, I really am. They're so... sad. And lonely. It was okay, really. I know I said I wouldn't be alone with them, but I don't believe they mean me harm."

"Well, to be sure, I should at least be outside the door. Because if anything else happens..."

"I want to allow them to do it. To heal me." Todd entered the room as I spoke, and he halted, his face noticeably pale.

Rey's eyes bugged out. "Pamangkin."

"Roman," Todd began, "I can't let you take that risk."

"It's not your decision, Agent Barringer. I can't sit here a moment longer while Creed is in danger. If The Source agrees, they can heal me, and then I'm going after him."

Rey threw his hands up in the air, cursing in Tagalog.

"Actually," Todd began as he sat next to me on the couch, "I have news."

"What the fuck—"

But Todd continued, "We've had a break."

I grabbed his arm. "What's happening?"

"Vanessa just called. A woman phoned the PD today, asked for Vanessa, and she gave up Hicks. Told her where he is, where the headquarters for EVE is hiding out, all the details we need to crush them financially—"

"Did she say where they've got Creed?"

He pressed his lips together and gazed at me for a moment longer than I wished he would.

"What is it?"

"They've got a nurse from Puesta Del Sol with him—a Lexi Teodoso," Todd said.

I pushed myself up to standing. "Not Lexi. We have to go—"

"There are complications, Roman," Todd began, holding his hand out to deter my screams, but even I knew I needed to keep a lid on my anger. It was killing me—literally—my inability to temper my emotions, to manage my responses to situations. I needed to get better... or else.

"Tell me."

Todd blew out a breath, obviously relieved. "According to this woman, who's Hicks's assistant, there are several levels of security and approximately fifty people who are live-in test subjects. I'm assuming they have them there to provide blood and... whatever else for Creed. She said there could be anywhere from ten to twenty guards on site at any time, and not just rent-a-cops. They have ex-military personnel." He cringed. "And this woman has agreed to go back to work in order to keep Hicks believing he's safe. We're working out a WITSEC situation for her, but she said if he gets any tingle that she's talked, he'll up and move them."

"Then let's go! Let The Source heal me and go."

"She's going in tomorrow to bypass security and get us in."

I waited a beat for more information. When it wasn't forthcoming, I asked again, "Then why are we still here?"

Rey raised his eyebrows at Todd.

"Because we're staying here. It's safest this way—"

"Todd—"

"Junior, listen to him."

Todd and I both took a deep breath. This was definitely testing my new no-freak-out policy.

"Roman, they know where we are."

That jolted me. "How—"

"The woman gave the address, says Hicks has known for over a week, and since he wasn't getting the results he wanted with The Source's blood, and Creed was potentially a better option, he decided not to attempt to reclaim The Source. For now."

That meant Creed was even more valuable to him, and that Hicks would be more desperate to keep him.

"We also don't know that we can fully trust this woman. I'm not putting all of you in danger on her word. He could have instructed her to mislead us, for all we know."

"But you're going to pursue the lead, correct?"

"My colleagues in the FBI are getting a warrant, we've got surveillance at all entry points to the property, which is in Milpitas, so out of SCPD's jurisdiction, and we've got drones up top. They're prepping SWAT to serve it at daybreak if all goes according to plan." Todd paused and cleared his throat. "All members of the San Angelo and Cabral families are to steer clear. We don't need any more hostages taken, or to chance anyone else getting hurt."

I pressed my lips together and tried to maintain a calm exterior. I needed to gather every bit of strength I could muster. Creed wasn't here to hear my heartbeat skipping around, but I knew it was.

"You listen to me, Agent Barringer. Creed is there because he tried to protect us. Whether he chooses to be rescued or not, we have to try. And if something goes wrong, he's going to need me—"

"And he will need me as well."

We all turned to face The Source. They were the cause of this mess. They were also likely the answer to saving Creed's life.

Twenty

C reed

"Goddess, if I eat another bite, I'm going to explode."

I pushed away the tray and Lexi gave me a sad smile.

"I can't believe they cut off your gorgeous hair," she said, running her fingers over my scalp. "I can't get used to it."

I shrugged. "Hair grows back, I guess. It's the rest of me that I can't get used to."

She shook her head and looked me up and down. "The good news is, if you ever get out of here, you can enter some major body building contests and win. I swear you've put on twenty pounds of muscle right in front of my eyes."

The food, the blood, all of it combined to perform a gruesome miracle. Lexi's observation wasn't too far off. I was actually *growing*. They'd had to bring me larger scrubs twice. I had way too much energy, so I worked out hourly to try to siphon some of it off. Men would kill to pack on this kind of mass in a few days. Men *were* killing to achieve it.

Then the steady trickle of folks who needed healing were paraded through. I gathered they were folks from their Longevity Health clinics, or perhaps members of EVE. They suffered from things like skin cancer, heart disease, and COPD. I was able to give them nearly full respite from their symptoms, but I let them know that any of these conditions could come back without significant lifestyle changes or medical interventions. They would praise me, bless me, and smile at me as they were being led out, completely oblivious to the absurdity of the situation. Hicks would tell them not to worry, that they were being considered for the serum, which would eliminate the necessity for any additional treatments.

"This is wonderful," he said, after the last person was shown out on the fifth day. "You're great advertising. These folks have all applied to be a part of our first phase, and now they'll be willing to pay anything to continue feeling good. Damn, Creed. You'd be such a great asset to the company if you'd give up your piousness."

"It's my *piety* that is allowing you to carry on this disgusting endeavor. You can't have it both ways." Because if I gave up carrying on The Way, I'd stop caring about anyone but myself and then why continue my existence? I could take the Stephen Allman way out.

The thought that I'd been healing people who were making this unconscionable system possible with their ludicrous amounts of money made me nauseous. It was becoming impossible to feel any sort of relief from this type of Exchange. Even the volunteers they brought me to drink from were so fucking giddy about it, I wanted to hurt them. I wanted them to be hurt like my Roman.

Who was mine no longer.

The rage building in me was hard to ignore. Hard to keep a lid on. At any point I could lose it, and the longer this dragged on, the more curious I became as to what that would look like.

Timothy Hicks proved to be a formidable adversary. There was no reasoning or bargaining with him. We remained at an impasse. He was mostly tight-lipped about what was being done with my blood. I was, however, able to get a few details from him, things he let slip in front of me during one of his many tangents. The guy certainly liked to hear himself talk.

I learned that the blood they took from me was being mined for particular elements, and then those were replicated at their facility, but they could only do the process a few times before those elements lost their potency, which was why they needed a steady supply.

Boohoo. Only, I could see the greed in his gaze as he looked me over. I could feel his fascination growing as he appraised my transformation. During his visits, he'd speak on all sorts of topics, most of which turned my stomach, which was already unsettled from the sheer amount of calories I was being force-fed.

Over and over he marveled at the differences between me and The Source, how brilliant he was for discovering why I was more powerful, or more useful to him, and how he was going to make EVE so much money.

"It's just a shame there weren't more of you," he said on the morning of the fifth day. "Stephen really fucked up when he stopped having the acolytes learn The Way. Even if only a few from each commune went on to become strong like you, that would have allowed us to make even more of the serum—although we never planned to make it available widespread."

"I'm guessing folks have to pay a hefty price to get their hands on it," I asked him, while I did push-up after push-up.

"Oh, definitely. We are quite selective. Money alone won't get you access. There are additional criteria. Power, influence, IQ. But along the way to creating the serum, our researchers discovered many valuable ways to enhance life, to prolong it, and that's what the Longevity arm of EVE is all about."

"Sounds like you've got it all figured out." I sounded bored, and that just made him talk more.

"I will. Now that I have a steady supply of the necessary ingredients, my troubles will be over."

I shrugged and turned over to do sit ups, one after another after another.

"Why didn't any of you try to learn from The Source when you had them? Seems to me that if you would have learned how to heal, you would have already possessed what you needed."

He sighed. "Stephen refused to consider it. He claimed The Source had some sort of dementia and could no longer impart that knowledge, and anything *he* knew to do he'd forgotten long before."

I didn't think that was true. Despite all of his shortcomings—well, and the fact that he was purely evil—I didn't see how Stephen could have forgotten anything we'd been taught. The knowledge, the skills, or hell, the substance of what we learned was imprinted on me at a cellular level. Perhaps Stephen had been protecting himself and preparing for this program to eventually end.

"He said even you couldn't teach others, because you'd only been with The Source a short time."

"And it takes The Source's blood to trigger the DNA."

He nodded and licked his lips. "See, my wife, she was a brilliant scientist. Between the work she'd accomplished at BioBourne and the improvements to the serum, the program advanced exponentially. Before she jumped ship, she told us she was close to discovering what it was about The Source's blood that caused the change. But she wasn't willing to cooperate fully."

And thank the Goddess for that.

Hicks seemed to be waiting for some sort of reaction from me, but I was beyond being shocked. Although, I was committing everything he said to memory in case... well, in *hopes* I ever got out of there alive. That likelihood dimmed as each hour passed. Perhaps the smart thing to do would be to shut off my thinking and feeling and merely... exist. Solely for their purposes. Not allow myself to want or need anything. Had The Source done that? How had they endured? So many questions I wished I'd asked. I supposed I'd even developed some empathy for them.

"Sadly, she'll have to be dealt with," he continued while I spaced out. "My wife. In due time. I don't want to jeopardize our operations, but her days are numbered. Shame. She was almost perfect."

I sat back on my haunches. "Why tell me all of this? Aren't you concerned about your secrets being revealed?" I rolled my eyes. The more I acted unimpressed, the more details I could get out of him. He couldn't help himself.

"I *would* be if I thought you could ever leave, but I've made sure that won't happen."

His whole demeanor changed, however, when the woman with the black hair walked by. He went from jovial in a sick way to downright predatory.

"I wonder..." he said with a sinister smile. "Stephen said that the energy from sex was particularly potent for those of you who practiced The Way." He opened the door and called to her. A moment later, she appeared in the window and he spoke to her out of my earshot, but I felt her energy shift from alert to anxious. Her facial expression, however, did not change. This woman was intriguing.

He took her hand and led her into the room, and I could see instantly that he was aroused by her presence, while she appeared unaffected. Only the slightest change to her body temperature and her heartbeat let me know that anything was amiss.

She was dressed in a long, fitted black skirt with a black and white striped button-down blouse and four-inch heels. Her straight black hair fell to her waist, and she had heavy bangs that fell across her forehead as if she'd come straight from the salon. Her perfectly round and symmetrical brown eyes were expertly lined and she wore a pleasant shade of red lipstick on her lips. I assessed what I could about her and could tell that she hadn't partaken of the serum.

Oh, yes. I'd been able to discern who the engineered folks were versus the ones who'd simply become swept up in Hicks's madness.

"Creed, you haven't properly met my assistant, Courtney." Hicks loomed over her from behind, standing way closer than any sort of Human Resources manual would describe as appropriate for work.

Courtney gazed in my direction but there was something hollow about the way she looked at me.

"How do you do?" She reached a hand out, but Hicks placed his hand on her bicep and lowered her arm to her side.

"She's gorgeous, isn't she?" He smiled salaciously at me and let his fingertips glide along the side of her breast, and then gripped her hip. "Courtney keeps things running smoothly around here, don't you, sweetheart?"

I saw the faintest trace of discomfort in her expression as he pressed his hips into her, but she kept her gaze locked on mine. It was almost as if she were trying to—

Help is on the way.

I heard her words as clearly as if she'd spoken aloud. I schooled my expression to give nothing away and wondered if I spoke, if she could hear me.

Are you safe?

"I know you prefer men, but I'm telling you, there's nothing as sweet as her mouth on your cock. You'd enjoy it. But then, you'd get something out of it just being present, now, wouldn't you?"

He squeezed her arm and her nostrils flared.

He can't hurt me.

She looked fierce, as though she'd endure his stupidity knowing she'd have the last laugh.

Her lip curled in a smile as I thought that.

"Hicks, unless you need something from me, I'd appreciate a little privacy. You've got me so stuffed, any more energy, blood, or food, and I'm going to go into a fucking coma. Too much of a good thing will make me vomit."

He grinned down at her, and I prayed I'd gotten her a reprieve. She was fierce. She had a warrior face on that gave me hope she would survive this relatively unscathed.

"You're missing out, but all right. Rest, or whatever you need to do. We'll have more folks for donations and receptions tomorrow," he said with a chuckle. "The people you're healing are definitely singing your praises. We've been inundated with requests. I'm hoping to keep a lid on it, though. Can't have the Vatican sniffing around to investigate my miracle. No siree. You belong to *me*, Creed Lowell."

He laughed and tugged on Courtney's arm to get her to leave the room.

I shot a look to Lexi, and was about to speak to her when Hicks opened the door once more.

"Come, Lexi. I need you for another matter."

Her eyes went wide, and I turned on him.

"She stays."

He gave me a playful pout. "Oh, come now, Creed. I think we've established that you're not in charge here."

I put myself between them and made myself as large as possible, which put me at eye level with him and about thirty pounds heavier now.

"You know, *Timothy*," I said with a sneer, "another type of energy that gets me high? Violence. And I've had enough of you. Beating you to a bloody pulp sounds like a great way to end my day."

His smile flickered, but then I saw him glance behind him to where there were two guys who were a little bigger than me.

"Violence, huh? I'll keep that in mind. But for now, she comes with."

"She stays."

I felt Lexi's heart beating out of control. Her fear filled my nostrils with a pungent odor, like singed hair. *No way.* I would fight any of these men to the death before I allowed them to put a hand on her.

"You know this won't end well for either of you, nor your precious Roman, if you don't behave."

I glared at him down my nose. "Maybe I'm fed up with your bullshit. Test me and see what happens."

He grinned but it didn't reach his eyes.

"Creed, I wish for there to be no violence."

"And I told you. I. Don't. Give. A. Shit."

"Creed," Lexi whispered, but I couldn't turn to look at her. Not if I wanted to have my desired effect. I wanted Hicks afraid. If he thought I'd become a loose cannon, maybe he'd back off his demands some. I would absolutely not allow him to take Lexi from my sight. I couldn't surrender. I had to figure out how to get her out of there, especially after what I'd just seen with Courtney.

Hicks just stared me down, and I felt his energy signatures fluctuating. He didn't like being challenged, but he also didn't want to fuck up the good thing he had going. I figured I might win this battle—

"Carey, please escort Lexi out."

One of the buff guys stepped into the room and locked eyes with me —and that proved to be the straw that broke this camel's back.

Gone was my need to follow The Way's tenets. I was being threatened. Innocent people were being threatened. I would not allow Lexi to be harmed because of me. She was my priority.

"You do *not* want to take one step farther," I warned the man.

Sadly, he chose to go with his ego and take that step.

Before his foot hit the ground, I focused on his Achilles and severed it with surprisingly little effort.

He slammed to the ground and howled in pain. That brought two more big guys into the room. I didn't take the time to warn them before doing the same.

"What the—Phil! Get the taser." Hicks seemed rattled. Finally.

"Call them off, or I swear on all I hold dear that you will not take another breath."

The guards rolled around on the floor in pain, and I was tempted to do more damage to ensure they did not get up again.

I hadn't even broken a sweat.

Hicks's expression remained fixed, not giving away his thoughts. "You don't want to push me, Lowell," he said.

I smiled wickedly. "Nor do you want to push *me*."

Hicks stared at me blankly. Two more men came to the door, and he instructed them to remove their fallen comrades. One of them, I'm guessing Phil, had a taser, which he made no move to unholster. They dragged the wounded men out into the hallway, their eyes wide. I wondered whether they would follow orders if Hicks sicked them on me.

Hicks, however, watched them remove the men with a scowl and then turned back to me, his hands on his hips.

"This doesn't change anything. You are still my property. If anything happens to me, you will not be freed. Keep that in mind."

He pulled the door closed, and I allowed myself to relax the slightest bit.

Lexi moved to my side and burst into tears. All I could do was hold her—there was nothing more to say. Once her breathing evened out, she sniffled and looked up at me.

"Did you know you could do that?"

I hadn't even taken the time to wonder if my actions would frighten her. She didn't appear to be afraid.

"Theoretically? Yes. But I've never, *ever*, used my power to harm a living being. Some have asked me to before, and I could never bring myself to do it. I guess I reached my limit."

She wiped at her eyes and her brow furrowed. "I'm not sorry you did it. Thank you for protecting me, but you should do whatever it takes to get out of here, Creed. If you have the chance again, you should take it."

And there it was. I was our only hope.

I'd have to consider how desperate I was to be free.

"Look, Lexi, I don't know what will happen the next time he comes in. You should rest—"

"Fuck that, Creed. We need to strategize. If we get a chance to get out, we need to take it."

"Yeah, but he said—"

"I remember how we got in. I wasn't sure at first, but I've been replaying it in my mind. I think I can get us out of here."

I let out a breath. "Lexi, I'm stronger than I was, yeah, but he'll have security out there. They'll be armed."

"And so are you. You just proved it. You're strong enough, we just need to, I don't know, what's it called? Have a blitz attack."

I chuckled. "Why, Lexi. I'm surprised at you."

She punched my arm, and then winced. "Goddammit, that hurts. Shut up, my brothers play video games." She lowered her voice even further, so even I could barely hear her. We knew we were likely being watched and listened to. "The next time they come, you take them out. However many you have to in order to get out of here."

"It's too dangerous. You could get hurt."

She blinked her lovely brown eyes. "Are you still full? Are you at your peak strength?"

I shrugged. "It's hard to tell anymore. I existed for so long with just enough energy stored to do my work and survive. Now I feel like a monster."

Her eyes darted to the corner, where we'd found a camera before.

"Take from me," she whispered. "Take my blood. I want you to be as strong as you can be."

"Lexi, no—"

"You protected me, Creed. You saved my life. Use my blood to save us both."

Twenty-One

R oman

I knew I should be afraid. After what had happened the last time I was shirtless in front of this being, I should be terrified.

We stood in the moonlight beside the creek at the edge of the property. Rey, Todd, Mr. Fletcher, Mark, Cross, Amergin, and I stood inside a five-pointed star that had been marked on the packed earth. There were candles at each point that flickered in the breeze. The air was crisp and the wind rattled the leaves on the trees. Amergin had been insistent that they have all the necessary tools at their disposal, and apparently running water and nature were necessary. We hadn't had a lot of time to discuss what would happen, but time was of the essence.

Todd had been insistent that we were to stay behind, Rey had fought with him, and then Todd received a phone call that set all of this in motion.

His benefactor apparently sensed a disturbance in the force, or whatever psychic metaphor explained the fact that he knew we all needed to be present to retrieve Creed. That I would *specifically* be needed.

"I better not see a drop of his blood shed, and if you harm one hair on his body—"

The Source—Amergin—grinned at Rey. "I would expect you to do all in your power to protect your kin. You will have no need to intervene. He will feel no pain, and when I have completed the ritual, he will be well once more." Amergin turned to face me. "Of course, to be at your most potent, I would give you my blood—"

"*No.*"

"Rey," I breathed. "I need to be strong for Creed—"

"Who would *never* want you to be as he is. You would die, Roman. You would have to drink blood to exist. Look what that's done to Creed!"

I knew that was true, but I was willing to do literally anything if it meant having Creed free to choose how he wanted to spend the rest of his existence, even if it was without me.

"I do not wish this to be contentious," Amergin spoke, their voice traveling over my skin like a current. "Roman, I wish to heal you. My offer to bring you into The Way will stand, if you should so choose at a later time. Do I have your consent?"

"To heal me, yes."

Amergin glanced mischievously once more at Rey, who scowled at them, and then they turned that warm smile back on me.

"Now," they said, closing their eyes and taking a deep breath, "I need all of you to take each other's hands and focus all of your love and light on Roman. Keep your minds clear, remove all darkness from your beings. There is only light." They raised their hands to the sky and let their head fall back. "We call upon the power of the moon and the Goddess. Converge upon this place and grant our beloved Roman your healing energy. Set the tissues of his organs alight with your blessed heat. The water's flow shall cleanse his blood of toxins that impair his own immunity. Take our love and bathe his cells, make him strong, make him ready for the challenge ahead. Heal this teacher. Fill him with strength of mind, strength of body, strength of purpose."

Mark and Cross began to chant the last line of Amergin's prayer and the others joined in. Heat began to caress my limbs as they chanted, and the more they spoke, the warmer I became, until I felt the heat licking at my organs inside my chest and abdomen. This was different than the times Creed had healed me. It wasn't soft and gentle. This was intentional, intense. It wasn't pleasant, but it wasn't painful like my exsanguination.

Suddenly the wind picked up. The ground rumbled beneath my feet, the water began rushing violently through the stream, which had been a trickle before...

"Junior—"

"I'm okay," I said, but the pressure was building in my chest and I started to pant. It was as if I had my oxygen on and someone turned it up to eleven.

"Stay calm," Cross said to Rey. "It's all right."

"How do you know?" Rey asked him. "You seen this before?"

"No—"

"*Junior!*"

A flash of white light blinded me and then I felt... weightless. As I floated in some sort of realm between consciousness and dreamland, unintelligible whispers tickled my ears and prickled along my skin. Currents traveled through my bones, the buzz making my teeth rattle.

And then there was silence. My mind was, probably for the first time ever, at peace.

It was not like this last time.

Last time, I felt things.

This time... I felt nothing. Nothingness that seemed to spread out in every direction.

Maybe this is it.

My heart broke.

No. How was I going to save Creed? How could this have happened?

"Brave Teacher Roman. Worry not. You shall be reunited with your Moonwish."

I couldn't open my eyes, and I didn't think I'd spoken aloud, but somehow Amergin was here, wherever *here* was.

"Am I dead?"

"You are in The Healing, a space in between awake and slumber. Your body is absorbing the energy and putting it to work. It won't last long."

"How are you here?"

They made a small sound like a sigh, like they were pleased. "We are linked here. It is my duty as your healer to see you through to wellness. It will be over soon."

"I don't want to go," I cried. "I want Creed. Please don't take me from him."

"Rest easy, Roman. This is not The Passage. You will wake as soon as your healing is complete and then you will be reunited with your Moonwish."

"What does that mean?" I asked them. "Moon wish?"

Amergin made another pleased sound. "It is quite a beautiful belief of my people. Only the rare follower of The Way will find their Moonwish: the person their heart calls to in the night. The need for this being overrides all others. The love between the Moonwished is something your body craves like oxygen. You are stronger together, and being apart for too long may cause you both to weaken spiritually. It is the purest of emotions, the purpose that drives them, the link that gives them both unimaginable power. To find one's Moonwish is the greatest gift. The Moon's most sacred blessing. It is a choice, not fate, but once joined, the two become one. The love of this pairing is enough to sustain both halves of the whole."

Their words resonated deep in my soul. All they described was exactly how I felt the moment Creed and I stopped fighting the pull between us. We'd surrendered to the tides, but they'd pulled us apart again and again. Would we, *could* we, find our way back to each other?

"I have only seen a true pairing such as yours a handful of times over the centuries that I have walked this Earth, and each time it was a miracle to behold, made more beautiful by each obstacle in its path. Finding your Moonwish brings peace a rare few ever experience in their lives, but it can also bring pain that would level a lesser heart. You and Creed have experienced such strife so early in your pairing, but I hold fast to my belief that it will make you stronger together."

"Please," I whispered. "I wish for him. I bled for him. I yearn for him. Tell me how can I *be for him*?"

Gentle fingers stroked my forehead, pushing my hair out of my face.

"You ask of the Moon. You pledge yourself to the Moon. You serve your Moonwish and protect their heart with your life. You do not falter in the face of adversity because, in your soul, you know that your Moonwish is the other half of your being, necessary to complete you, a welcome and beloved addition. Call to the Moon, Roman. Call for your Moonwish. Once you rejoin us, we shall fetch your Moonwish and bring him home to you."

The voice was gone so quickly, I wondered if I'd dreamed it. Awareness began to creep in around the edges of the light. I inhaled through my nose and my lungs expanded without any pain or tightness. With each exhale, a little more sensation returned. My skin broke out in goosebumps as a cool breeze blew across my bare chest. Voices filtered into my consciousness and this time I understood what was being said.

"He's here, he's right here. Just a few more moments and he'll be awake and alert, won't you, Roman?"

The soothing voice... Larsson? Where'd he come from?

I flexed my fingers and toes and arched my back. More deep breaths. No pain. No weakness. No tinnitus. No dizziness upon waking, as I'd had for so long.

"Junior, I swear to God, if you hear me—"

"I'm here, tiyuhin." I still hadn't opened my eyes. I needed to... remember.

Moonwish.

Please, give me the strength to free him from those who harm him. Let him decide if he truly wants to be free of me, and if he does, I'll let him go, even though my heart will never recover. He's my one. He's my Moonwish, no matter what happens. I won't be able to live with myself if I don't free him. Whoever is listening, please give me the strength to free him, whatever it costs me.

My eyes flew open, and I found myself on the ground staring up through a circle of trees at the brightest moon I'd ever seen. It seemed closer than I'd ever seen it, or maybe I was just seeing it clearly for the first time.

"Thank fucking God, Junior."

Rey rested his forehead on my chest, and I heard him reciting the Lord's prayer.

I placed my hand on his head. "I'm okay, Rey. Promise."

The look he pegged me with when he lifted his head hurt my heart. He'd aged, it seemed. He seemed to have more lines on his face, more gray in his hair. I hated that I'd done this to him. Again. I vowed then and there not to cause him any more stress.

"How do you feel?" Todd knelt beside me, also looking distraught.

"I think great? Help me up and I'll tell you for sure."

Rey and Todd each took one of my hands and they pulled me to standing. I overcorrected and nearly faceplanted from the force.

"Whoa." I never thought I'd feel like myself again after waking up in the rehab facility, but this? I felt like... *more.*

"Let me take your vitals, please?"

I let Larsson sit me down and take my blood pressure, but I was vibrating. I wanted to run. I wanted—

"Where's Amergin?"

Todd turned to look behind him, and I followed his gaze. Amergin sat next to the creek, a faint glow to their red robes.

"Fucking weird-ass bullshit," Rey muttered as he dusted off his pants. "Can we get to the part where we fuck some shit up? Please? I know Creed is a goddamned pacifist, but I really want to fuck some motherfuckers *up.*"

Todd spoke quietly to Rey while I walked closer to Amergin.

They sat in a meditation posture, but their eyes were open. I stood beside them for several long moments, feeling the vibration of their energy—less now but still present—as it ran through me. I wondered what this all felt like for them. Did it pain them? Were they depleted?

"You did very well," they finally said, a soft smile on their lips. "How do you feel?"

"Like myself from before, but better?"

They made that pleased sound once more. "I am glad. It brings me peace to know that I have taken steps to right the misstep I took with you. I am not absolved of my crime, but this is a step in the right direction."

"Does it help that I forgive you?"

Their eyes drifted closed, and I watched as their chest rose and fell. "It does. You would be just in withholding your forgiveness, but I appreciate that you would consider it after everything that has happened. Do you comprehend what occurred the night at the loch?"

"I don't know, honestly. The whole thing was a shock. Creed only said that you were not yourself, that there was something else happening."

They nodded. "Creed has always been astute. Though Stephen had kept me in isolation for most of the time I spent with him, I became aware that The Way was not being followed, and as a result, my power was weakening, my connection with the Earth was waning, and therefore just as when one receives my blood through initiation, and then must continue to receive energy to grow stronger, I too made my covenant with the Earth.

"I observe the sacred holidays, perform the rituals, and that helps to maintain the balance, the harmony of our kind with nature. At least the nature within my reach. Because I let Stephen contain me, I let him lead me away from my path, my purpose, and now the harmony with nature is out of tune, so to speak. As a result, the health of my form and that of the ley lines upon which we dwell is out of sync. The resulting chaos, it weakens me, it weakens our link to nature, it weakens the covenant between us, and I fear, after all this time, what impact that will have. Already I have seen the evidence of what your people call climate change. It was my duty to protect the land, and I have failed. Now I haven't the numbers to carry on my part of the covenant, and I am afraid of what that will mean. I am... adrift."

Tears spilled down their cheeks and they let them fall. Their loneliness hit me hard, their pain affecting me almost as strongly as their healing.

I lowered myself to the ground to sit beside them and held out my hand. They glanced at it, and then at me in surprise.

"Take it," I murmured.

"You are kind, Roman. So full of love for one who has suffered such loss. You share your essence with me despite what I have done."

"Because we continue to be linked, Amergin. Through Creed.

Because of what you made him, I have found my purpose, my... Can I ask? Was I dreaming before? Did you speak to me of Moon—"

"Moonwish, yes, Roman. It became clearer to me as we shared an Exchange of energy that Creed is your Moonwish, and you are his."

"And because of you, we found each other. I'll always be grateful to you for making it possible for us to be together, no matter what happens when we find him."

I took a deep breath, because what I was about to say was a wild notion, one I didn't know whether the others would go along with.

"Amergin, when we have Creed back, when this current threat is over, I want to learn from you. I want to teach you. I don't know that I'll ever be ready to become a practitioner of The Way, but I want to... help you, with your journey in the present. It's all I have to give you, and while I don't know what it will look like, I don't know what will happen, I want you to know that I'll be here for you however I can be."

I tried to choose my words carefully, remembering Creed's warning, though I didn't think it would be any sort of purposeful manipulation. I knew that The Source had a much different frame of reference for human interactions, and we'd have a lot of work to do to get them to a place where they could function.

"Your offer, your words, they mean more to me than I can say. I am honored." They bowed their head and when they lifted it, they smiled, and I felt a spark of hope in my center that mirrored one in theirs.

"Are *you* well?" I asked them. "Did The Healing put a strain on you?"

They smiled and made that sound once more. "So thoughtful. The act of Healing does not deplete my energy, Roman. It is more the dissociation in my mind, the disturbances I feel from the Earth that have me unsettled. To have lived as long as I have in harmony with the being that supports life... and to now be, not quite at odds, but almost like two lovers who have wounded one another and must work to mend the rift between them, I am not... whole. I don't see a clear path back to wholeness, and that frightens me. It makes every step, every action unsure, and I have not felt this way before. I suppose it is what the Christians referred to as pride? When one feels they are incapable of stumbling that they are most at risk for a fall?"

"I think I understand." I laughed. "The only thing I can compare it to is when I was a cocky teenager who thought he was invincible, and I would do ridiculous tricks on my skateboard. I thought there was no way I could fail, so I took risks that could have ended my life. I assumed I was at one with my board, that I was in control. Same with surfing. I thought nothing could touch me until I nearly died after hitting my head on a rock."

Amergin covered our hands with their other hand. "Youth are quite prone to this, I have learned, though I was never a parent. I like that you try to find ways to see my truth through your truth. Is this what you call your psychology?"

"Yes! That's exactly it," I said with another laugh. "See? We're learning together already."

They threw their arms around me and laughed so loud, it reverberated through my spine.

"Thank you, Roman," they whispered close to my ear. "Thank you for sharing your truth."

"It was my pleasure. Thank you for making me closer to whole."

They pulled back and nodded. "Let's go finish the task."

The sound of helicopter blades permeated the quiet in the grove, and we all looked skyward.

"That must be them," Todd said, and then he leveled us with a serious gaze. "Let's go."

We all took off at a quick pace toward the house and, as we approached, we saw three helicopters touch down on the vast lawn that spanned the front of the property. They appeared to be military-issue, and two of them held several men in unmarked uniforms.

I wasn't sure what I'd thought we'd find when Todd's benefactor exited the third helicopter, but it wasn't an older man in a tweed suit holding hands with a teenaged girl. They were escorted by two men dressed in the same black utility gear as the others, the tall one with long curly blond hair pulled back in hair tie, and the shorter one was bald with a long beard.

Todd walked toward them and shook their hands—the young girl he gave a quick hug to—and then he led them toward where we had stopped near the front porch.

"Let's do introductions inside," Todd said, as he took the front steps two at a time and hurled the door open. We exchanged looks with the newcomers, and the older man nodded at me with a knowing smile.

Once inside, Todd led us to the sunken great room. Mr. Fletcher was sitting at the table playing checkers with Craig, and when we entered, he got to his feet. I hadn't had a chance to speak with him much since we'd arrived, but I knew he was worried about Creed as well.

"It's a pleasure to finally meet you, Dr. San Angelo," Todd's bene-factor said with a British accent. He held out a hand to me.

I protested, "I'm all but—"

"For now, but as Agent Barringer once said to you, not for long."

I took his hand and his grip was firm—but it was more the grip he held on my psyche that surprised me. He had this way of looking at you as if he *knew* shit. I was so fucking glad I'd been healed, because meeting someone as intimidating as him when I didn't have all of my faculties would have left me pissy.

"Indeed, you look well." He let go of my hand and turned toward The Source, who gazed at him thoughtfully. The old man bowed to Amergin and said something in a language I didn't recognize.

Their eyes lit up and their glow seemed to brighten. They responded in what sounded like the same language, their already musical voice sounding more ethereal than ever.

Rey elbowed me when I didn't move with the others to sit on the sectional. "More weird fucking shit," he muttered.

I had a feeling things were about to get the weirdest yet. Poor Rey.

Todd gazed at all of us, his face pale and strained. "We don't have much time if we want to make it to the complex—"

"We have four hours. The flight will take us three and a half hours. We have a little time."

The teenager spoke so confidently. I wondered what her role was here.

"Thank you, Joanna. I am Nigel Hart. This brilliant young woman is Joanna Howe. The one in need of a haircut, her father, Captain Jackson Howe, and the one with no need of a haircut but perhaps a shave?"

The guy chuckled. "Has no use for rates or ranks anymore. James Morton, Navy SEALs, retired."

"And you are Officer Reynaldo Cabral, SCPD… at least for now." Mr. Hart's eyes twinkled as he addressed Rey.

"For now," he agreed, crossing his arms over his chest. I bumped him with my knee.

"They're here to help us," I whispered, not sure how I knew that, but the words felt right.

"You are correct, Dr. San Angelo. I've been in close contact with Agent Barringer, whom I sent to Santa Cruz to consult on this case several weeks ago." He frowned, his mustache thick and twitchy as he spoke. "And in the interest of time, I suggest that we ease your concerns and then load into the helicopters. I believe Agent Barringer let you know that the two of you will be crucial to Mr. Lowell's rescue."

Amergin and I looked at each other.

"Whatever we need to do to free him," I said. This time Rey bumped *me*.

"How do we know you don't work with EVE?" Rey asked. "You can't expect I'm going to let you take my nephew anywhere without some more information."

"Rey," Todd said, trying to placate. The two had grown close, but not close enough that Rey would trust him with my safety, not after all that happened.

"It's all right, Todd. Officer Cabral is right to question me. Here is what I can tell you. We share an interest in putting EVE out of business and rescuing Creed." He patted the girl on her shoulder. "When we're made aware that a person with extraordinary gifts is in danger, we do everything in our power to bring them to safety. My people have been following EVE's work for some time now, waiting for an opportunity to put them out of business. This is why I sent Todd to consult on the case. Once we learned of Creed's abduction, we mobilized our response team."

"And they are… who, exactly?"

The blond stood taller behind the couch where Nigel sat.

"We've gathered a hand-picked group of special operations personnel who are retired from the service to assist in these rescue operations. Larsson, Gordon, and Craig are members of our team, as are James and I. The men and women in those helicopters outside work with us as needed and have been thoroughly vetted."

Mr. Hart chuckled at that.

"When we have more time," Captain Howe continued, "we'd love to fill you in on our operations. We believe we can help each other, but tonight's mission is to liberate Creed Lowell from the bunker in Milpitas. And if we are to do that successfully, we should mount up."

Rey shot Todd a look and then glared at me. "Fine, but I don't like this," he muttered.

I took a long, hard look at Mr. Hart, taking in his uni-leisure wear of tweed and silk, his knowing gaze, and I felt only kindness and determination.

"That is because you, Roman San Angelo, have a very strong gift of intuition, one that has been strengthened by your recent health crises. I won't use words to try to convince you that you can trust me. I know you've been underestimated by men like me in the past."

This man read me so clearly. Sure, he could have had a hunch, but his observation was something I'd only ever shared with family. And with Creed.

"But *I'll* try to convince you to trust us," the young woman said. "By telling you that Creed is in a lot of danger at this very moment, and I know that you would do anything in your power to give him his freedom. Whatever he chooses to do with it."

My fucking prayer. How did this little girl know—

"Just as you have been underestimated, so have I. You're going to have to accept that I know things, and be satisfied with that. I'm here because the situation on the ground is changing rapidly, and I will See how best to approach it."

I smiled at her. She knew exactly how to reach me. I liked her already.

"Then let's go."

Twenty-Two

C reed

Six days had passed and I was strung so tight that every beat of my heart I could feel in my eyes, my extremities. Every muscle and tendon in my body stood at attention and I was in danger of splitting the seams on yet another pair of scrubs.

I knew what time it was because Lexi was alerted by chimes every hour to take my vitals, take my blood, and our food was brought in at regular intervals. But since my standoff with Hicks, I'd grown more and more agitated. I couldn't sit. I paced, I worked out, but I couldn't calm my mind, nor could I get rid of enough of the excess energy flowing through me to make it bearable.

"Creed, he could be back at any time. What are you going to do?"

I shook out my hands and felt shocks traveling between my fingers. It stung, but it kept me centered.

"I don't know. I'm so... it's too much. I'm too full. I feel like I'm going to explode."

"Hey, why don't you try to sit down?" She approached and laid a hand on my arm, then immediately pulled it back with a yelp. "Holy shit, Creed. You've built up static electricity." She looked around. "It's like you've been rubbing your feet on carpet. How can you get rid of it?"

"I need to get outside. I need to get grounded."

I was not an anxious person, but I was about to have a full-blown panic attack if I couldn't let some of this go. I moved around Lexi and went into the bathroom and went to turn on the metal sink.

An arc appeared between my skin and the metal before I made contact.

It gave me an idea.

I hurried to her side and spoke low next to her ear, hiding the movement of my lips from the camera. "Lexi, I want you to get on the bed."

She blanched and stared up at me, wide-eyed. "Excuse me?"

"Not... no. It's the only thing that's not metal in the room. Get up on the bed and make sure your feet are off the floor, okay? I'm going to try something, and I don't want to hurt you."

She looked skeptical but she followed my orders. She sat in the middle of my bed with her knees up to her chest.

I started to pace again, but this time I concentrated on the feeling of fullness, on the current running through me. I let it go, stopped trying to keep a lid on things. My chest heaved and my teeth ground together, but I kept going. Around and around the small space until I felt like that explosion, implosion, whatever was going to happen, was imminent.

I stalked up to a socket on the wall next to the door and I reached out a finger.

Lexi gasped as an arc shot out and fried the socket with a loud pop. The lights flickered for a moment and then they started to buzz.

"What was that?"

I let out a breath. "Our ticket out. You sure about doing an Exchange?"

She nodded and straightened her posture. "I consent."

"Make it look like you *don't* consent."

She gave me a sly smirk, and though I hated the fact that she was here at all, I was grateful to have her at my side for what could prove to be a disaster… or our freedom.

Lexi proved to be a great actress. She let out a bloodcurdling scream as I grabbed her and pinned her arms to her side with one arm. With the other, I moved her hair to the side and whispered, "It won't hurt but you better make it look excruciating."

"Please don't hurt me," she shouted, and then pleaded, turning on the waterworks in a convincing way.

I released my pheromone, and though I knew I wasn't hurting her, she carried on like I was killing her. I sank my teeth in, making sure my canines were visible, making it look vicious, but I took only the three pulls and healed her tissue. I kept some of her blood in my mouth to coat my lips and let some run down my chin. Like a real prince of darkness.

"I won't take any more from you," I whispered, "but I want you to pretend to faint. Can you do that?"

"Please," she pleaded, letting her body go slack against mine.

I growled and made to bite her again, acting menacing for appearances, and when she let her head fall forward, I lifted my head and shouted, "Hicks! Get your ass in here."

I picked her up and looked around the room for something sharp.

"Hold on, this is going to be loud."

I grabbed her sweater with one hand, wound it around my fist, and punched the mirror above the sink. She flinched but continued to look passed out.

I carefully lifted a large piece of glass.

"Hicks! I'll do it, I swear to the Goddess. You made me do this! I killed her, and I'll kill myself next!" I stared into the camera and held the shard to my throat, nicking myself slightly. It would heal in seconds.

The door flew open and two guards entered first. I grinned at them and used a small amount of energy to depress their carotid enough to make them pass out, but the effect was dramatic. They both slammed to the floor, one of them hitting his head hard. I couldn't worry whether he was okay.

"Okay, which way?" I asked her, and she directed me.

"Out the door, turn right."

I stepped over the guards and into the hallway, adrenaline running through me. We were doing this. We were getting out of here one way or another. Thankfully Lexi weighed next to nothing, so I was able to move quickly with her in my arms.

"End of hallway, turn left."

Alarms sounded loud as sirens and the flashing lights brought footsteps pounding down the hallway behind us.

"I remember going through a door and then down a stairwell. Do you see anything like that?"

The hallway was long with fluorescent lights running down the middle. There were unmarked doors with key card locks on them every ten feet or so, but no markings anywhere. How the hell did anyone know where they were going? Finally, I saw up on the left a door with a small window and stairs beyond it.

"I see the stairs." I had to hope that my plan would work.

"Put me down, now, Creed. We can go up the stairs faster that way."

I set her down and reached for the door as a voice came over a loudspeaker.

"You might as well stop now, Creed. You're not getting out of here."

Hicks's bored voice ramped up my anger, giving me a smidge more energy.

"Oh yeah?" I muttered.

Boots came around the corner, and we caught sight of ten men dressed in some sort of security outfits coming our way.

"Here goes nothing."

I stepped closer to the wall where there was a socket. I bent down, gave them a smile, and put my finger to the outlet.

Immediately, the lights exploded and plastic and glass rained down upon the men. A couple slipped in the mess and went down hard. I smelled blood spilling from more than one of them.

"Creed, the door!"

I turned back to Lexi as some of the men were trying to navigate the darkened hallway, the crunch of glass getting louder.

I reached for the keypad and focused my energy on it in bursts, shorting it out.

"Try it," I told Lexi, as I turned with my piece of glass in hand. I would run interference if it meant she could get out.

She rattled the door a few times and cursed.

"Here, let me."

I yanked that fucking door off the hinges. *Huh*. Why hadn't I tried that earlier?

She hesitated one second before she took off running up the steps.

The security guys were gaining on us, so I threw the door hard in their direction and took off running, catching Lexi at the second landing.

"How many floors?"

"I don't remember, maybe four?"

The door burst open on the landing above us and there was my nemesis, leaning over the metal railing with a sneer.

"Creed, you've broken your oath. You've hurt people."

"Lexi, move away from the handrails."

I rubbed my hands together and touched the rail.

Hicks's body went rigid and spittle flew out of his mouth, his eyes rolled back in his head.

"Come on," I said, not wanting to touch Lexi because the current was running through me now completely unhindered. Sparks flicked off of me the closer I got to the railings. Lexi's hair stood out as if she were touching static electricity. We passed Hicks's body on the floor. He was moaning.

"There," she said, pointing to the next landing. "I can see windows. It's gotta be here."

"Don't touch," I said, and she stepped back with her hands up. I stepped in front of her and yanked the door open. We ran through it—

Into an office space filled with people.

Lexi crashed into my back, and I heard her cry out from getting shocked, but I couldn't lose focus.

"Let us out and none of you will get hurt." My body was vibrating and my voice boomed out across the open space. Anger coursed through me, keeping the current flowing. Little did Hicks—or even me—know just what his little experiment would unleash. I was so furious, I wanted to lash out. How dare they keep us held hostage? How *dare* these people do their petty tasks while Hicks played with people's lives?

No one spoke. Those in cubicles sat there staring at us wide-eyed, as if they had no idea who I was. The few people who were standing simply looked at us as if we'd crashed their garden party, not that we were running for our lives.

"Creed," Lexi squeaked. "Behind you."

A security team was coming through the doorway, so I backed away with her toward the middle of the room. The men spread out on either side of the rows of cubicles and stood at the ready.

Then Hicks staggered through the door we'd come from.

"Subdue them. Tase him, tranq him, I don't care—*just get him!*"

"Do you know what he's doing? Do you care that he's holding hostages below? That he kidnapped this woman, kidnapped *me*? Do you care that he's making me hurt people?"

No one spoke. No one moved. And then I was hit with the prongs from a taser.

Lexi screamed, and then gasped.

The taser voltage only joined the current already running through me. It didn't slow me down.

I laughed. "So you'll sit there and do nothing? You'll let innocent people be hurt on your watch!"

None of the workers moved except one—who picked up a phone and punched in three numbers. *Good. Call 9-1-1.*

"Hit him again!" Hicks was screaming now. He reached for a security guard's taser and pointed it at me.

They wanted to play.

Let them see what they've created.

Two more sets of prongs hit me. I barely registered the sting.

"So mote it be."

I closed my fist over the wires and sent the measly spark right back to the tasers they'd come from. The men screamed and thrashed before hitting cubicle walls and falling to the floor, taking out a few desks. Hicks managed to drop his taser.

They had no idea what they'd created.

"Go after them!"

"Lexi, run!"

The first two men who touched me were instantly electrocuted. Sparks shot from their bodies and caught a stack of paper on fire, which quickly spread. Once they dropped, I reached down and touched an outlet on the floor between cubicles. The overhead lights all popped and went out as before. Computer monitors blinked off and the smell of burnt wires filled the room.

Finally, the workers started to move, shrieking as they ran toward the front of the building, which was all glass. The sickness that was festering in me wanted to stop them, wanted them all to pay.

Sprinklers kicked on but the water merely served as a balm for me. My skin felt as if it were on fire, but the pain only fueled my rage.

I stalked toward Hicks, who hid behind four guards.

"Hand him over," I ordered, but they stood their ground. "He is not worth your lives."

Two of them hesitated before stepping slightly away.

Hicks reached into one of the men's side holster and brought out a gun. It appeared he was ready to take out his cash cow.

"I swear I'll kill you, Creed! Lexi too. You will not step outside those doors!"

"You are finished, Hicks. End this now, or I will burn this fucking place to the ground."

His eyes widened and he took a step back.

He raised the gun and fired.

I absorbed the impact to my chest and the pain sent me over the edge. I threw my head back and screamed.

Glass shattered.

Fire crackled.

The walls shook and the ground cracked beneath my feet.

The floor opened below Timothy, and he and his men fell into the crevice. His cries were silenced by a sickening crack, and when I looked down, I could see him arched over the railing that had caught his fall. He was alive, his eyes were wide and darting all over, looking for help, but he was paralyzed. And terrified. For the first time, I sensed the immense power gained through another's fear. I inhaled the stench of it.

"You brought this on yourself."

He moved his mouth as if to speak.

Concrete chunks dropped onto the level below and one landed on Timothy's chest. He was still then. I should have felt relief, but I was too far gone. His was an anticlimactic ending for someone who had caused so much devastation.

But there were others, and they would not be allowed to flee unscathed. The people in this building had to know they were a part of something evil, and yet they made whatever excuses they needed to believe that what they were doing was acceptable.

Multiple voices begged for mercy.

That time is over.

I gave up trying to hold on to the power and let... it... go...

Twenty-Three

R oman

I'd never flown in a helicopter before, and I wasn't sure I ever wanted to again, but I was grateful when I began to recognize the Bay Area landmarks that let me know we were close.

"We're ten minutes out," the pilot called over the radio.

I leaned in closer to my uncle, not because I needed his support anymore, but because I was scared to death of what we'd find when we arrived, and he was the only person grounding me.

Amergin sat on the other side of me, and I watched them wringing their hands as their eyes darted around.

"Your first time in a helicopter?" Mr. Hart asked.

"Yes—"

"Yes."

Amergin and I answered at the same time, and they smiled at me. I took their hand and immediately I felt their power prickle over my skin. They smiled.

"I have learned much since the first time I took to the skies in an airplane. The pilot had to land the plane after my essence caused a power surge to the electrical system." They giggled and it made them sound young, not like an ages-old being. I hoped they had that particular issue under control this time.

Mr. Hart leaned forward. "I didn't particularly enjoy the sensation my first time either," he said. "I've since become accustomed to air travel. It's necessary in my line of work."

"And what *is* your line of work?" Rey asked, raising his voice above the noise of the rotors. The helmets had coms, or else conversation would have been impossible.

Mr. Hart smiled, and I shivered at the effect. He had such a benevolent way about him, but he possessed an underlying power that reminded me of the feeling I'd gotten from Stephen Adams, only it wasn't slimy. Creepy maybe, but not nefarious.

"My line of work runs in many directions and sometimes even parallels the likes of Stephen Adams and Timothy Hicks. From time to time, I cross paths with individuals such as these gentlemen, and I assure you, I am not one to suffer fools, nor do I overlook bad behavior. I, too, have a way of acquiring the desired outcome from any endeavor. I do not, however, use the talents I possess to operate in an untoward manner. My desire is to make the world safer for all, but in particular, for individuals with enhanced abilities, and to keep those who would use those gifts to hurt others from taking advantage of the innocent."

"That sounds... nebulous," I answered, feeling Rey stiffen beside me.

"I would imagine after what you all have experienced that it would." He folded his hands over his bended knee. "I will let you in on a few details that may make you feel a bit more at ease. I met our mutual friend Agent Barringer recently while Captain Howe was on a rescue mission. Todd has become an invaluable asset, and since I have some associates who possess quite a bit of influence with the US government, I was able to... *borrow* him. The task force and security teams are just two of the programs I currently oversee. My sole purpose in this life is the protection of those who are extraordinarily gifted. I use my vast resources to see to the needs of children, to aid those in mortal danger such as Creed Lowell, and I oversee a vast legal network that works to protect the most vulnerable in our society. I also dabble in diplomatic matters and financial consulting."

Was this guy for real? He'd explained everything in such a way that gave us the minimum amount of details and didn't leave room to ask him to elaborate on much.

"Are you a member of the nobility? You describe your livelihood as similar to that of a nobleman." Amergin gazed at Mr. Hart with excitement. I wondered if they could tell more about the man than he was letting on.

"I forget you have experienced many different eras of leadership. My family was well-situated financially, and I have been fortunate enough to grow our economic influence immensely throughout my adulthood. In the United Kingdom, which is not far from where you originated, my family does hold titles—however, I left there as a young man. In this country, there is no official nobility, only the wealthy, who use their wealth to gain influence with those in power." He chuckled and it was nearly sinister. "I do not require wealth to influence whomever I choose, but it helps fund my many pursuits."

Amergin laughed and covered their mouth with both hands. "I knew I detected something very special about you. Your strength comes not from the Earth, but from elsewhere."

"Fueled by human contact and interconnectivity. If I had to assign a celestial body from which I gathered the source of my influence, I believe it would be the moon. Its pull is irresistible." He winked at Amergin, and they clapped their hands together.

"I like you, Nigel. I believe we could learn much from each other."

Nigel? *Interesting*. Rey and I exchanged a look. I hoped we didn't have to worry what would happen if he turned out to be *not* so benevolent.

"I would very much appreciate that," Mr. Hart said, taking one of Amergin's hands and kissing the back of it. He showed no fear or hesitation as most people did around them, and based on the flush that crept up Amergin's cheeks, I don't believe they were expecting it either.

"Sir, we're nearly there. Prepare for landing."

"Thank you, Captain, however, Joanna has let me know that we are about to hit a rough patch. Please hold on."

We all turned to look out the windows—in time for a flash of brilliant light to illuminate the sky from below us.

Amergin jerked in their seat. "Oh no," they breathed.

"What is it? What's happening?"

An alarm began blaring from the cockpit.

"Sir, we've been hit with a power surge. We're losing power."

Rey cursed. My heart pounded. Mr. Hart frowned and then leaned forward. "You can fix this," he said to Amergin.

"But I'm not... I cannot access the ley lines from here."

He smiled kindly at Amergin. "You have the power within you. Go on. Reach for it and stabilize these engines."

He made it sound so simple, like, "Of course. Just make the helicopter fly. No biggie."

But fuck me, Amergin reached their hand up and touched the ceiling of the helicopter and closed their eyes. The helicopter dropped two or three feet, making us rise from our benches and slam back down, but then the engines began to sound as they had on the flight here. Normal.

"Holy shit," Rey breathed, putting a hand to his heart. "I know I ain't old yet, but I don't think *my* heart can take much more of this shit."

I turned to find that the other helicopter was still trying to get control, and it went down—the one with Todd in it.

"No!" I shouted, pressing my hands to the window as I watched.

"Do not fret, Dr. San Angelo. They will be unharmed. Joanna let me know they would be making an emergency landing and then meet us at the complex."

How he could be so calm?

"Because, good sir, I have faith in my people. Joanna is a Seer, and though she is still a student at my academy, she is quite stubborn and would not be left behind once she'd Seen Creed's dilemma. I'm not at liberty to tell you much about her, but I have a feeling she will want to speak with you herself when the coast is clear."

"I... fine. Sure."

My head was spinning. Was he talking ESP? Psychic? And he ran an academy? What, was he like some real-life Professor Xavier?

"I've heard there are similarities," Mr. Hart said with a laugh. He really was a goddamned mind reader! "Though I've no need for machinery, and as you can see, I've still got my follicles as well as faculties." He chuckled heartily, which made Amergin laugh once more. Those two certainly hit it off. I wondered if that meant Mr. Hart could help us with Amergin. As much as I wanted to teach them, I was limited in my knowledge of life as well. I'd been through a lot, but I was twenty-five years old, and if they truly needed to be accompanied twenty-four-seven, that was too much for Creed.

The helicopter set down a moment later in a large parking lot across an access road from the complex, and as we stepped out of the aircraft, we were surrounded by fire trucks and cops all responding to the fact that the complex was on fire.

"Creed," I breathed. I started to run, but was cut off by a dude dressed in SWAT gear. I threw up my hands as Rey yelled my name.

"You cannot approach." The officer carried an AR-15 and didn't look as if he was ready to converse.

"He's with me," Todd shouted as he ran toward us, his FBI windbreaker flowing behind him. He was gasping for air. "I'm Agent Barringer," he said, yanking his badge out of his back pocket as he approached with his other hand up. "Call your supervisor. We're expected."

The cop spoke into his shoulder piece and a moment later, he nodded for us to follow him.

An explosion at the rear of the facility sent out a ball of heat so strong, my cheeks felt scalded.

"He's ascended," Amergin murmured beside me, their eyes bright.

"What do you mean, ascended?"

They turned and placed a hand on my arm. "It's been so long, I'm not sure how to adequately describe it, but it is a tenuous time for beings who practice The Way. I've not seen it for millennia, but if it were to happen to anyone in this current world, Creed would be the most likely."

"What does that mean?"

They smiled sadly. "When our powers grow, especially at a rapid rate, there may come a time for some when they can no longer contain the level of energy within their bodies. It must be released. It can also occur if the being becomes... unstable."

"Which could happen when threatened," Rey said.

Amergin nodded and reached for Todd's arm.

"You must allow me to approach. If Creed has ascended, he may not have control over the distribution of his power. I know it would trouble him deeply if anyone were injured."

Todd opened his mouth to speak, looked around, and huffed. "I don't know that I can. They're not going to let us go in while there's a structure fire."

Another explosion rippled through the complex.

"Todd, you saw what happened at Loch Lomond," Amergin said slowly.

Todd's eyes widened. "I did."

"That is nothing compared to a being's ascension. He could... level this entire area."

"How do we stop it?"

Amergin let out a slow breath. "It must be siphoned. Absorbed. Redirected in a positive way. I can help him to do that."

Todd only nodded and took Amergin by the arm.

"Wait," I said... but what could I do? I was healed, but I wasn't extraordinary like Creed.

Amergin turned and gave me that kind smile, sending a ripple of energy my way, the way Creed used to. "Fear not, Roman. I shall do this. He was there for me when I needed him to bring my powers to heel. I shall do the same for him."

Rey put an arm around me, probably because he knew my fool self was ready to run into the fire after my lover.

I nodded, and Todd led Amergin away. I watched helplessly as they wove their way through emergency personnel who were trying to determine how to attack the fire.

I glanced over to see Mr. Hart standing with Captain Howe and Joanna. The three of them were in a tense conversation.

The glass along the front of the building shattered and everyone ducked to avoid getting pelted. We were at least a hundred yards from the front of the building and moving as close as we could.

Rey held on to my arm when I would have charged in.

"They've got to get that fire managed before—oh shit, look!"

A flood of people came running out the front of the building, screaming, and the cops sprang into action, trying to figure out who was a threat and who were victims.

Rey guided me closer to the blockade of police cars.

"Stay behind this truck, Junior. If there's another blast—"

His words cut off as we saw another bright flash of light from inside. A piercing scream ripped through the air, and we all covered our ears in pain.

"*What the fuck was that?*" Rey yelled.

Shouts of alarm filled the space around us while howls of pain and anguish came from inside the building, growing in intensity along with the light. We squinted against the brightness. Some of the cops pulled on their sunglasses, others covering their eyes in hopes of protecting their retinas from damage, it was that bright.

But I could only stare.

"*Oh God.*"

A being engulfed in white flames walked out of the building slowly, and when the police began shouting commands, the being threw out his arms and shrieked, the sound shattering the windows of every car.

"Creed."

I peered through my fingers to see Amergin standing in front of the police barricade while Todd held the others back.

That couldn't be. This person, this being inside the flames had no hair and they were massive, more bodybuilder than my beloved, but then the skin, the clothes, the person wasn't burning. It was like some special effect from a movie. How—

"Rey, is that—"

"Yeah, honey. That's him."

Pain ripped through my chest and tears burned my eyes. *Not my Creed.*

"*No.*"

He'd become what he most feared.

"All will be well, Creed. I can help you—"

"*Noooooooooooo!*"

His voice was otherworldly, like Amergin's had been at Loch Lomond. It reverberated through my bones, shaking me to my core.

Was Creed lost? Could he come back from this?

All I could do was watch in absolute terror as Amergin continued to approach him slowly, speaking in low tones with that melodic voice of theirs that had done wonders to me during my healing.

"Stay back!" Creed finally shouted in a voice that sounded like his. "I can't... I can't make it stop."

He was hoarse, his throat thick with tears.

"Together, we can make it stop. We can do this. You are so strong, Creed."

Amergin began to walk toward Creed as arcs of energy shot out from the aura of flames surrounding him, catching the dry grass on fire and shorting out the parking lot lights.

"Stay back," a cop shouted. He lifted his weapon, causing the others assembled to do the same. There were at least forty guns pointed at my beloved. I tried to run for him, but Rey and James held me back.

"Hold your fire!" Todd shouted, jumping out in front of the officers with his hands raised. "Stop. Let them tend to him," he pleaded. An officer in SWAT gear and two more FBI agents yelled at Todd to fall back, but he continued to stand before them, his arms outstretched, his back to Amergin. He backed up slowly, trying to keep Amergin protected.

"He's going to get himself killed," Rey muttered. "Fuck, Todd, *don't.*"

"Let me go. I can get Creed's attention. I can—"

"No way," Rey said. "Don't ask me that, Junior."

Tears spilled down my face, and I hated that Rey was once again terrified for me.

Amergin raised their arms to their sides and lifted their face to the heavens, speaking in another language. Thunder rumbled across the sky and wind whipped through the palm trees surrounding the complex.

"Down on the ground, now!"

More cops moved forward with weapons drawn, shouting orders at Amergin as Todd pleaded with them.

Creed looked up toward the sky and then back at Amergin, and he let his shoulders drop, his head bowed. He took a knee before the now-glowing Amergin, and it appeared he was surrendering to Amergin's influence. He reached for them—

And a shot rang out.

Twenty-Four

Creed

Amergin's words were a soothing balm. I was so tired, every nerve ending in my body screamed for relief, and yet the energy inside me continued to build and build, now siphoning off the stress of the multitude of police officers and first responders.

Aggro.

That word came to the front of my mind, bringing Roman into my consciousness.

My beloved.

I'd fought so hard to be by his side and now…

I couldn't contain the maelstrom any longer. My limbs were going to be pulled from my body, my skin would split open at any moment. I was filled with rage, and it was excruciating.

Roman.

"Creed, let me take your burden," The Source murmured, moving closer, and I yearned for that to be possible. Despite all we'd been through, I wanted to believe they could help carry this load, that they were truly good despite all that had happened. I wanted their comfort.

I fell to a knee and reached out a hand.

A loud crack pierced the haze around me, and my breath caught in my chest.

The Source's eyes widened and their body jerked once, then fell forward.

I caught their weight, confused, until I felt a warm wetness.

Blood pooled between us.

"Amergin," I whispered, clutching them close to me. Their glow flickered before my eyes, which were hazy from the energy surrounding me like a forcefield.

"I would take your burden." Their voice was so weak.

"How can I help you? Don't go. Don't leave me!"

Their mouth turned up at the corners as their eyes fluttered closed. "You know what to do."

Was it that simple?

"I have your consent?"

The weakest nod.

I pulled their small body against mine and sank to the ground, curling myself around their body to protect them from the overeager police, and I did something I never thought I would ever do again.

I prayed.

And as I called to the Goddess and asked for guidance, I unleashed the energy I'd amassed, finally having a positive place for it to go. This is what I'd been trained to do, what I'd been *made* to do.

The air around us grew super-charged, the energy snapping and crackling as I fed it to my Teacher, my maker, and focused on drawing out the bullet, healing the tissue, and sealing the wound. I gave and gave, and it felt like I could give forever, but then there was movement around us and I went back into protector mode.

"Creed, it's Todd. You have to let me approach."

"Stay back, Todd. I don't know if I can control it." I had never possessed this much energy before, and the more the cops tensed up, the more it fed me. "Those cops are making it worse. Their stress. I can't stop it... it's growing, surging. Amergin can only take so much from me."

"Let the first responders look at Amergin. They can—"

"*Todd, stay back—*"

"Agent Barringer, he's healed me. We are fine, aren't we, Creed?"

I looked down to see their eyes open, their fathomless gaze fixed on me, and everything else fell away.

"That's it. It's just the two of us. Together. We shall take this energy and send it where it is needed."

"Show me how."

Amergin moved from my lap and sat before me, our legs crossed, mirroring each other. We held hands and I listened to them speak, but not from their lips.

"This is good," they spoke in my mind. "This is how it was in the early days of The Way. Together we harnessed our energy and used it to heal the Earth. Come with me, Creed. Use your inside eye. Where do you feel we are needed?"

I opened my inner eye as I'd been instructed all those years ago and continued to focus on Amergin's words. My consciousness traveled through space until I felt the pain, sensed the waves of discomfort.

"Heal the wounded, Creed. Send the current into the ground beneath us. Let it travel where it's meant. The Goddess will guide."

Amergin's touch grounded me enough that I was able to ignore the movement around us and focus. I didn't hesitate to send healing energy to those I'd wounded as we'd attempted to escape. Of course, they'd been wrong to be a part of Hicks's plan, but I'd taken a vow never to harm and I needed to make restitution. Flashes of injuries—from glass cuts to electrocutions—came to me, and I sent energy to each and every one of them. Amergin talked me through the whole process as the images sped up, the energy flowing freely—

"Lexi," I cried, losing my focus. "Lexi's trapped in there!"

Amergin exerted force on my hands, and it was enough to pull me back.

"Find her with your mind. Is she conscious?"

"No." She'd convinced me to leave, but I'd sworn to protect her, and

I let her get hurt in the process. After everything she'd been through, I couldn't believe I'd lost control and—

"Creed, focus. You can save her. Talk me through it. Show me."

I was panting now, the flow of energy now leaving my body unfettered. I couldn't slow it down or direct it. I tried to focus on where she was and pull back so I could describe it.

"She's... she's near the front windows, she's trapped, a cubicle wall fell against the desk she was hiding under. Her..." I exhaled. Her leg was broken.

Even from this distance, my energy was drawn to the wound and I focused all of my attention on knitting the bone back together and healing the skin from which it had protruded. I sent a flow of energy to kickstart her breathing to a normal rhythm, set her pulse back to a sinus rhythm. I worked on weaving the tissues together to heal the cut on her forehead. She began to moan as if she were coming around, and I sighed with relief.

Amergin had pulled away from our link, and I heard their voice as though they were outside the bubble we'd both been in.

"I can't... I can't." I felt as though I'd been hit with the worst vertigo. Everything was spinning and I couldn't orient myself. My limbs grew heavy and the ground was pulling at me, tugging me down.

"Creed!"

My beloved. Roman. I gazed up at the dark sky and the moon... It seemed so close, as if I could reach out and touch it. It was more beautiful than ever, and then it was his face, and it was pulling me down... down...

Twenty-Five

R oman

"This can't be happening." Rey lost his grip on me and I ran for Todd, but a cop grabbed me and pulled me back.

"Agent Barringer!" I shouted. "Tell them to let me through!"

It was a ball of confusion around me. Cops wondering what the fuck they were seeing, Todd arguing with command staff to back off and let him take control.

Then the fire seemed to... go out. On its own. And the cops lowered their weapons and started talking and laughing with each other, packing up their gear and climbing into their cars.

What the actual fuck?

"Junior." Rey trotted over toward me and he lifted his chin. "Look."

More of Mr. Hart's men had arrived and they were forming a perimeter. The cops didn't even seem to see them. They moved into formation and entered the building right under their noses. The cops just kept on gabbing like it was end of shift.

The command staff Todd was arguing with suddenly stopped speaking, shook his hand, and got back into their cars. Within minutes they were all gone. Even the firefighters. The employees who'd been huddled by the side of the building had been allowed to return to their cars, and they drove away as if it were the end of their workday.

Mr. Hart leaned back against a light pole and sighed, removing his glasses and rubbing his eyes. The young girl reached for his arm and they spoke softly to each other.

"We need to clear out of here," the blond guy, Captain Howe, said. "Nigel can convince them all they've got better places to be, but if dispatch gets any more reports, they'll send more cops. Gather your people. We need to get you all out of here."

Rey opened his mouth and then closed it, a perplexed expression on his face.

"Officer Cabral, Mr. Hart has experience with this kind of phenomenon. He's aware that law enforcement is 'quite ill-equipped to handle the unexplained,'" he said the last with a strikingly similar English accent. "He's made arrangements to have Timothy Hicks and any of his co-conspirators taken to his secure location to be dealt with. This is what he does. We've had experience with criminals who possess gifts, ones who use them to do evil and will never see the inside of a prison... or if they do, won't remain there."

Howe looked at the young girl and frowned. "They're powerful people." He shrugged with a smirk, his expression turning more mischievous. "Mr. Hart is *more* powerful. Let us deal with Hicks. You get your people to safety. You're free to go home, to Santa Cruz, if you like. We've had the place staked out and updated with an advanced security system. You'll be safe there. Get back to your lives." He handed Rey a key fob. "We'll be in touch. Stay safe."

Rey held the fob in his outstretched hand, his mouth opening and closing.

"You did *what* now? Go home? Just like that?" How was that even possible? This wasn't the downfall of EVE. They were still out there. They could be out there right now—

Howe chuckled. "I get it. I do. You've been through a lot, or at least that's what I heard from my daughter. Mr. Hart will do everything in his power to eliminate the threat against you and yours. I've known the man for years, and he still leaves me doing the fish-out-of-water thing sometimes."

"But," I said. *But what?* "How?"

"He'd like to spend some time with you, Dr. San Angelo. So would my daughter. She's had experience with cults, and we understand you're an expert."

"I... yes?"

Captain Howe smiled. "Take some time. Go get your man. Go home. Take it easy." He winked at me, and then trotted over to Mr. Hart and the young woman. The bald soldier with the goatee joined them, and the group headed back to the helicopter.

"Weird. Motherfucking. Shit. Just when I think it can't get weirder..."

"Probably you should stop thinking."

"Right."

We approached Creed and Amergin slowly, and it appeared Amergin had Creed somewhat subdued, but as we got closer, I saw that his face was screwed up in pain, and he was panting. They were both covered in blood.

"Creed?"

His eyes were unfocused, and he was swaying. Amergin turned to face me.

"I can't bring him out of it. He's losing too much energy. I can't get through to him."

"Creed? Baby?"

I thought maybe he'd heard me, but his gaze seemed to go past me to the sky.

"The moon. So beautiful. So beautiful, Roman. So Roman."

I crouched and caught him before he smacked his face on the ground, and got a major shock in the process, enough to rattle my teeth. I pulled him into my lap and held him, rocking him, tears blurring my vision.

"We've got to move," Todd said, his gaze darting around the lot as if he couldn't believe what had happened either. "Rey, you've got the key? The Lincoln is over here."

Rey frowned at me. "You got him?"

"We're about to find out." I got my feet under me and cradled Creed in my arms, lifting him as if he weighed nothing.

"You are so strong, Roman. He will need you."

Amergin tried to stand, but they staggered. Rey caught them and scooped them up.

"You were shot," he said. "How are you—"

"Creed. Before he... before I lost him, he was able to heal me and restore me, but I'm afraid the Exchange between us was not without difficulties. I will need... rest."

"What about Creed?" I looked down at my poor man. He looked battered, as he'd looked the night he returned to me the first time he'd gone away. He was so big though. Way bigger than he'd been before.

"Rey!"

We all turned toward the building, where the commandos were leading a group of people out. A group that included—

"Lexi!"

We were headed in the same direction and caught up to her. She was limping and had blood on her clothes, but otherwise she was in one piece.

"Oh my God, Roman, you would not believe what happened! They kept feeding him and making him—"

"Ma'am, it's important that you relax now. You've had quite a shock."

I recognized Larsson's voice. Man, that guy could put a screaming baby to sleep with that voice.

"Can I come with you? I... is he okay? They shot him." She ran her fingers over Creed's shaved head, and her eyes filled with tears. "He saved my life, Roman. He protected me. It was... awful."

"Yes, Lexi," Rey said. "Please, come with us. We're cleared to return to Santa Cruz."

Home. My heart sang at the thought of being back in my house, the place I'd felt safest in my life.

The rest of the dozen or so commandos guided several men away from the building—they'd been detained with zip-ties—and escorted them to a van with no windows. They were loaded inside. Half the commandos went toward the third helicopter, and the others climbed in the van and sped off.

We didn't have time to ask questions. Todd urged us to hurry. Rey, Amergin, Creed, myself, Larsson, Lexi, and Todd reached a black Navigator, and Rey hit the fob to open the locks.

A bark sounded from inside.

"Rhonda?"

Larsson smiled as he opened the door. "We cleared out of the compound. Gordon and Craig took Mr. Jenkins back to Puesta Del Sol for the time being." Larsson petted Rhonda's head and her tongue lolled out. *Huh.* His charm worked on dogs, too. "She did so good in the helicopter ride. She's a tough little soldier, aren't you, girl?"

Rhonda started licking Creed's face as I climbed in and somehow managed to scoot us to the middle seat. Rey and Amergin sat beside us, Lexi climbed in the back, and Larsson and Todd took the front, with Larsson behind the wheel. Todd was visibly shaken. Once the doors were shut, Larsson put on some soothing music.

"All right, friends. We've got about an hour drive. I would suggest you spend this time replenishing your energy. There will be plenty of time to debrief when we arrive at Casa San Angelo, all right? All right. That's it."

He pulled out of the lot and the sway of the car, his voice, the music, the adrenaline crash, and the man breathing deeply in my arms had me so drowsy. I pulled Creed against my chest as best I could in the cramped space and held him tight, my cheek against the top of his head.

"Good night, friends," Larsson breathed, and that was the last I remembered of Milpitas.

I woke up confused. I was in my bed alone, though I was pretty sure I'd brought Creed home with me. Unless it was all a dream. I didn't remember how I got to my house. It was dark when I looked outside my window, and it was chilly in my room, as though the heater hadn't been on. The neighborhood was shrouded in fog with the moon shining through breaks in the clouds above. I threw on lounge pants and a hoodie and left my room, worried about what I'd find. Would I be alone? Was this all a dream?

The scene in the living room answered some questions.

Two of the soldiers, Gordon and Craig, were asleep in bedrolls on the floor. A glance out the front window showed me the SUV we'd traveled in, as well as two more parked in front of my house. One of them had two men sitting in the front that I recognized from the EVE complex. The passenger must have caught my movement. He nodded at me, and then turned to speak with his partner.

Okay, so we weren't sitting ducks. Hurray for small miracles.

I crept up the stairs, avoiding the creaky ones, and managed not to wake the others. I peeped in Rey's room and found Lexi in his bed. Rey was on the floor with a blanket and pillow. I walked past Lola's room. The door was opened and showed that it had been untouched since she'd left. I was pleased to find no one in there, but I was assaulted by memories of her, of the nights I'd crawled into bed with her, even as a teenager, when the nightmares got to be too much. How was she faring without Nurse Creed? How much ground had she lost?

The spare room door was open a crack, and I peered in to find Todd asleep in the bed, a frown marring his handsome face even as he slumbered. He'd been given a seemingly insurmountable task, and yet he'd persisted. But at what cost? This was the first time I'd seen him sleep since we lost Creed. I know he felt personally responsible for Creed's abduction, and I'd been incredibly hard on him. Would he be able to forgive himself now that we had him back?

Or *did* we have Creed back?

My chest tightened. Where *was* he? Had he awakened in the night and left again? And if not, why wasn't he in my bed?

I heard a soft humming sound above and frowned. The attic? There was a bed of sorts in there, sure, but it was mostly a space we used for storage. We'd only used it for guests in the days before my parents died. If Lola had family visiting from the Philippines, the kids would get sent up there to sleep. It was a cool space, with large windows at either end and smaller ones along the bottoms of the eaves on the sides, and sloped ceilings, and as kids, we loved hanging out up there. Me, my cousin Ronnie and his two older brothers, Tita Phyllis's daughter Regina and her son Rogelio... My life before middle school had been so innocent. We'd played kid games like hide and go seek, board games, we'd have water gun fights. We were a big happy family. Then high school came and we all went our separate ways. The attic was like a time capsule, and I couldn't decide if the contents brought up good memories, or reminders of the hell I went through—hell I caused—after my parents died.

I climbed the narrow staircase that went up to the attic and paused outside the door. I heard the faintest voice... singing? There was light coming from under the door. I wondered if I should knock. *In my own fucking house?*

I hated every second I stood there wondering what move to make.

The door opened a crack.

"Roman."

Amergin smiled at me, but they were different. They weren't in their red robes, the only clothes I'd ever seen them in. They were wearing a pair of... sweatpants? An SCPD sweatshirt? Rey had stored clothes up there—perhaps they'd found them?

"I'm... are you okay? Is...?"

They smiled and opened the door to reveal Creed sitting before the window shirtless, in a meditation position.

"I felt your presence," they whispered. "Creed is... processing. He must find a way to achieve balance after what he's endured. He's conflicted over all that occurred and... worried. I attempted to help him as best I can, the only way I know how."

I exhaled but my chest still felt tight. Not like when I'd been at the rehab facility. No, this was the feeling I'd had when Creed had left before. Left *me*.

Rhonda pushed herself to standing and came over to lean against me.

"She is a wonderful companion. She helps ground him."

I petted Rhonda while I tried to figure what to even say, what I could even do. Amergin was the right person to care for Creed, considering the circumstances, but dammit, I wanted it to be me.

"What about... you were both shot. Do you need medical attention?"

They shook their head. "He healed me and as for his wound, he possessed so much energy the bullet disintegrated on impact. There's no entry wound and the bruise is already nearly gone."

I peeked around Amergin, but they made no move to give me passage. I was helpless to comfort my lover and I hated it.

"He will come back to us," Amergin said with a sad smile. "I have faith. But for now... he needs your patience, Roman. Something that I know is not easy for you."

I coughed out a laugh, but tears burned my eyes.

"Guess it's time to do some more growing up."

Amergin reached for my hand and gave it a squeeze, sending a little buzz through my arm. They were trying to comfort me. It didn't feel as awkward as when I'd first met them and they assumed consent because of who they were. Who would turn them down? But I had, and it took some time for them to understand where I was coming from. This prickle was just innate to them. They couldn't help but desire to make others feel comfortable. It was in their very nature, in their DNA likely.

"Can I do anything for you?" I asked. "Are you hungry?"

Amergin smiled. "I am not in need of nourishment, thank you. But I think Rhonda is. Perhaps you can see to her needs?"

"Of course," I said, tugging gently on Rhonda's collar. She looked back at Creed, gave a sigh, and took off down the stairs.

I swallowed, not sure I wanted to ask this question. "Is he... has he spoken to you at all?"

Amergin tilted their head, taking a moment before speaking. "You want to know if he wishes to be here." They inhaled and exhaled. "I don't believe it's as simple as that for him now. His consciousness, his awareness, is elsewhere. He is here, but not. His body is attempting to protect his mind by shutting down. It will take him some time to recover. All we can do is wait and see."

Trauma response I could understand. Catatonia was something I could fathom. If I looked at this from a clinical standpoint, perhaps I could be patient.

But this wasn't clinical. This was my lover, my soulmate, my fucking Moonwish. It was killing me to not be able to go to him, take his hand, hold him against me, share my body with him. My blood.

"Would it help him to do an Exchange?"

Amergin shook their head. "Creed still has an excess of energy within his body, and he's been unable to release it like he did when he healed others. At the moment, he's not *able* to heal others. He is... stuck, I think you'd call it. I'm sorry, Roman. I wish I had something more positive to share with you."

I stepped back and held up a hand, reluctant to leave, but knowing I could do nothing here. The best thing I could do for Creed right now was to take care of his girl.

"I get it. Let me go take Rhonda out and feed her. I'll bring her back in a bit, if you think it helps him to have her here."

"It does," they said. "The companionship of an animal is good for the soul, don't you think?"

I smiled. Rhonda had helped to heal my heartbreak once before. "It is. I'll come back to check on you."

"You are kind, Roman. Thank you."

I started toward the stairs, but I stopped at the top. For a fleeting moment, I had a terrible thought. What if Amergin was keeping me away from Creed on purpose? For their own gain? What if they were attempting to manipulate him?

I turned back and was about to enter the room when I heard the humming start up again. Pushing the door slightly ajar, I watched as Amergin took a seat beside Creed and hummed a tune that I'd heard somewhere before. They watched him with a pained expression, and a moment later, they took a shuddering breath and tears spilled from their eyes as a gentle rain began to fall on the house.

This went on for a week. I took care of Rhonda, I listened to the law enforcement folks debrief. I took turns cooking with Rey and Larsson. I watched Creed when Amergin needed fresh air and some recharging of their own in the sunshine. There was no change. He sat staring out the window without moving, around the clock. He hadn't eaten or drank. Amergin said it was not necessary. Rhonda sat beside him, pressed up against his thigh, and made her old lady noises, but he didn't move to pet her.

The garden had become a favorite place for all of our houseguests. Mark and Cross had shown up and at night they played music around the firepit. They'd returned to town briefly and planned to move on to play gigs elsewhere. They wanted to make sure Creed was all right before they left, and when he wasn't, I think they felt a duty to stay.

Rey provided folks with booze and the guys told stories around the fire. I think it helped him to be around other men who were in law enforcement. Even though his future as a sworn officer was unclear, it was such an ingrained part of him that I didn't know how he'd do with any other sort of occupation.

It didn't help that he and Vanessa weren't speaking. Turned out my auntie was livid not only that he'd let me get healed by "that person," but that he'd allowed me to go after Creed when it put us all in danger again. She knew what had happened when Creed was taken, what he'd said, and she had believed his words.

"Why are you still putting your lives at risk for this reckless man when he obviously doesn't care enough to make better choices?"

Rey told her she didn't know shit, she told him to fuck off, and it was a Cabral feud of epic proportions. I hated that Rey was getting the heat for looking out for me, but he waved me off anytime I tried to apologize.

Todd didn't socialize. He worked on reports, he researched more of the financials on EVE, and he was downright despondent. I worried about him almost as much as I did Creed. Gone was the confident man who'd held us all together. I got the sense that he hadn't failed before, and he considered this a failure even though, with his work, Timothy Hicks had been located, and with his death, a huge portion of EVE's operation ground to a halt. Todd learned from his informant that the facility where Creed had been held was where they were putting the finishing touches on this serum, which had been about to go into circulation. Longevity Health was being investigated not only for their role in the abduction of Creed and Lexi, but for detaining the fifty test subjects they'd kept under false pretenses. Some of the people they found at the scene were missing persons. Several folks in the California operation were going to prison for a long time.

It wasn't enough to soothe Todd. Nor me, for that matter. For all of us gathered, however, the thing that mattered most was Creed's recovery. It did help to know that we were all united in that hope.

In the evenings, I often sat on the back porch and listened as the soldiers and Rey talked about everything other than what was going on in the attic. They were all good men and I was grateful to have their protection, but I didn't know what to even say. I couldn't carry on like normal when my heart was upstairs, catatonic and in pain.

After Rhonda's last bio break of the night on the eighth day, I brought her into the attic and she plopped down next to Creed with a sigh. Amergin had gone with Larsson and Gordon to the beach to commune with the tides in the moonlight for the full moon, leaving me in charge of my beloved.

My notoriously limited patience had grown thin. I entered the room and sat on the other side of him, not touching but close. I poured out my heart to him in my awkward, petulant way.

"We had such a short time together before all of this, but I know you, Creed. I know your heart. You told me after Loch Lomond that you thought I had strong intuition, that it had grown since we'd met. You could be right about that. Mr. Hart certainly thinks so. If it's true, then I'm going to tell you what I know to be true.

"I know you didn't go with the men from EVE on your own volition. There wasn't even a fleeting moment when I allowed myself to doubt you. I knew in my heart the whole time that you said those things to try to *make* me believe you. I knew you didn't mean them, even if you might have thought them.

"I can also tell that you're in there, and that you're doubting yourself. Maybe even doubting me. But I'm not doubting *us*. We've been tested so many times. You got the worst of it this time. And now all I can do is wait to hear your words, to hear what's in your heart. It's killing me, but I've been through tough times before and I survived. Technically I've died twice, if you think about it. Makes me realize, anyway, that I know some shit. Maybe not as much as you, oh wise one, Nurse Creed. But I know *you*. I know your soul—and I want it back.

"I know what I said, that if you walked away from me again, that was it, but until you tell me you meant what you said outside that damn

Dairy Queen, I'm going with the theory that you felt you had no choice."

I huffed out a breath and waited a few moments to see if he made any response. I had no idea what the right thing to say was, so I continued making my plea, even if I was blurting random nonsense.

"Lexi said you were so brave. She's okay, by the way. I don't know if Amergin has told you anything, or if you're even aware of what's going on around you. I don't know if you can tell that I'm better." This sucked, making confessions like this, but maybe it would get a response out of him. "I wish I could take you downstairs to my bed and hold you. I'm tempted to pick you up again and do it, regardless of what Amergin says about not touching you. I can do that now, carry you. You'd be surprised at how strong I am. You might even be pissed at me."

Maybe that was what it would take to wake him, to make him angry. He could turn that power on me, but I knew he wouldn't.

"I know I promised I'd never be alone with The Source, but I broke that promise, and you can be mad at me all you want. They healed me. There was no Exchange, although I thought about doing it, to be perfectly honest with you. I was ready to do whatever it took to save you, whether you wanted me to or not. Who knows if you even wanted to be saved. *I* don't know. Maybe you meant it, that you don't want this life anymore. You never asked for any of this. You never wanted to be anything other than a healer and to stop Stephen." My throat grew tight and it grew difficult to speak. "Maybe at one point you wanted to belong to me, but maybe that isn't what you want anymore. I would understand. If you don't want to come back, if you want this all to be over, I wouldn't blame you."

I knew those were all the right things to say, but I couldn't put the weight behind them.

I wanted him back.

I wanted a chance to make him happy. To give him the love he deserved after all the years he'd taken care of everyone else. After everything he'd done for my family.

"You also might disagree with this, but I'm a selfish bastard. I'm not going to back down and let you go off into the aether or wherever without a fight. We've come too far for that." I leaned so close to him that I was practically kissing his ear. I was careful not to touch him, though.

"I hope that somewhere in there you remember how it felt when we were together. Not only when we touched or when we kissed, but when we talked for hours. When we got competitive over stupid shit. When you talked me down from giving up in the rehab center. When you gave me your healing energy. When you fucking cared enough to take my negative energy from me, and I know you'd say that was *you* being selfish because it fed you." A tear ran down my nose and fell onto his shoulder and I sniffled. Not the most romantic sound when you're trying to convince your lover to stay.

"I'm the one that's selfish, because I hope you realize before you drift off that if you give up, if you leave, you'll be giving up on a once-in-a-millennia special thing." I wasn't above a little manipulation myself, it seemed. "Amergin called me your Moonwish. I don't know if *you* know what that means, but they described it to me and, well... it was spot-on. Two halves being stronger together and all that. I never felt like I could handle all the shit in my life, no matter what I used to say to my uncle. Not until you came along. I had to grow up really fucking quick, and you believing in me went a long way in helping me do that.

"Now I want to be strong for both of us. You and me, we're powerful together, and I don't know if you know this, but we still have a lot of work to do to put a stop to the evil shit your buddy Stephen started. So wake up, goddammit. Come back to me." I was snotty-crying by this point and I didn't care. "I swear I'll never eat another goddamned Blizzard again if you'll just come back to me."

A sob broke loose from my chest and I sat back from him, wiping my eyes and nose with my sweatshirt. I sniffled once more... twice more.

I smell cookies.

I held my breath several long moments, and then I inhaled. Probably it had been wishful thinking. My mind could have been playing tricks on me, but I thought I saw movement in his eyes. I heard nothing, though, not even the persistent ringing in my ear that I'd had for the past ten years. I hadn't even wondered whether Amergin's healing would fix my brain. I probably would have been more excited about that if my heart wasn't breaking yet again.

I sat there for ten more minutes, unable to quit with the stupid tears, but whatever I'd thought I'd smelled or seen had to have been a figment of my imagination.

I heard the front door close and Larsson's voice drifted up the stairs. I didn't want to hear it from Amergin for disturbing Creed. I stood from the floor in one move, amazed at the ease of a task that would have required a cane or even two strong men to help me with just weeks ago, and I exhaled once more.

"I'll wait for you. I will," I whispered. "Till I'm the actual old man in this scenario, if that's what it takes. If you can hear me... if you can see the moon, know that you're *my* wish, and that I'm waiting for you."

Rhonda lifted her head as I stepped back from the motionless Creed, and she whined. How long could *she* wait? She hadn't quit eating, but how much longer would she hang on before we had to make decisions? Either Amergin could give her blood, or we'd have to put her down. We couldn't let her suffer. Creed wouldn't want that either.

God, this fucking hurt. How many times could I lose this man and still survive?

I made my way downstairs, and I paused at the landing. Amergin was in the kitchen talking to Larsson.

"You would make an excellent candidate. Your constitution is very strong. It would not take much instruction to educate you in The Way."

I almost snorted. *Back at it, huh?* Would they take this freedom and start another cult? Would that be so bad? From what I'd learned of The Way, at its core, it was a positive movement. More healers in the world could be good, but look at how out of control things had gotten.

"Perhaps instead of teaching me *your* way, you could take this time to learn a thing or two about the importance of self-restraint and humility."

Holy... did this guy have a death wish? Was he unaware that this being could level a city block if they were angry?

But they hadn't. We'd all challenged them at one point. I'd heard that Creed had done it quite a few times at the compound.

"Perhaps you are right." And then Amergin spoke in a language that sounded Nordic of some sort.

Larsson answered without missing a beat.

Interesting.

I managed to turn the corner and slip down the hall and into my bedroom without being detected. The last thing I needed was Amergin to question me, or Tito Rey to see me destroyed. He'd visibly aged since this shit started as it was.

I cleaned up in the bathroom across the hall and then returned to my room. I stripped down to my trunks, turned on my salt lamp, and somehow managed to dredge up more tears and snot. I didn't have the strength to do more than let them flow onto my pillow. I tried to close my eyes, but my usual dungeon-dark bedroom was brighter than normal. I rolled over to find the drapes open a crack. *Shit.* I'd looked out there earlier and must not have pulled them all the way.

And then I saw the moon.

Full and majestic in the dark, the moon sat in the crystal-clear sky, surrounded by pinpricks of light from stars not usually seen here. Too much light pollution, too much fog, but tonight? The sky was breathtaking. I fully understood why Amergin had wished to commune with the tides on the full moon. I'd enjoyed that once upon a time. My hooligan friends and I loved to go night surfing. Until someone we knew got attacked by a great white. Nearly lost his leg. That was the last time we went.

I'd been such a fool, but then that had been my developmental stage. Self-centered, prone to impulsivity, and self-destructive. I'd wised up, but that anger, that chip on my shoulder, drove me through undergrad and my master's program. It wasn't until I was faced with living alone, meeting Creed, and then nearly losing my life for the second time that I'd really felt something click.

Self-aware, prone to contemplation, and self-reflective. I was getting there. Life was a journey, and I'd been so looking forward to taking that journey with Creed.

What the fuck was I supposed to do now?

Twenty-Six

C reed

I'd lost the ability to tell the difference between waking and sleeping as the nightmares never left me. Images of fifty years ago, of fifty minutes prior, they flowed together. Violence, death, nothingness. Pain, terror, quiet.

A voice interrupted the terror every so often, reminding me to breathe, to focus... to come back when I was ready. But the more I strained to grasp the lifeline they were offering, the further I slipped away, until the terrors branched out to refresh pain I hadn't allowed to surface in decades.

The year or so I'd spent working at the hospice facility for AIDS patients in the Castro was one of the hardest memories to relive, and yet it was right there, so vivid I could smell death and antiseptic all around me. Some of the men were aware enough to have conversations, but most were in their final days by the time they reached us. Realizing that I could have been one of them if I hadn't been taught The Way made me determined to pass on as much comfort as I could. My heart broke with the admission of every new patient, and with the cleansing of the rooms after every passing.

Losing the first patient I grew emotionally attached to, Alice Foreman, at the first convalescent home I worked at tore at my insides. She'd been such a love. We'd talked late into the nights many times about her long-term partner Rebecca, and how much she wished Rebecca would come see her. Another nurse let me know that Rebecca had passed away, but the management felt it was kinder to let Alice believe that Rebecca would be coming soon.

Alice never remembered anything longer than a few hours, even with my healing, but she helped me come to terms with my queerness and showed me that it was possible to find a lasting love, as she and Rebecca had been companions for over fifty years.

Alice's brother Robert was also a patient at the Kansas City facility, and he became one of my longest companions for nourishment. I'd been so devastated when they passed days apart that I'd left after my shift and never returned, the only time I'd abandoned a job.

The night Muse and I were attacked on the street in San Francisco played out in my mind like a bad movie, both of us beaten and robbed... her robbed of control of her body as I lay crumpled nearby, unable to move. That event had been the last straw for us. A few days later, we heard about Gateway of the Sun and hopped in the van, glad we'd have a safe place to sleep and food in our bellies.

As if the others hadn't been painful enough, the memory of the night I'd told my parents I was leaving home for good was dredged up and added to the reel of my worst moments. My father's disappointment, my mother's resignation. It had been so easy for them to let me go. My sister's tears when I told her. We'd been as close as we could be in our family, but she was never above using my parents' irritation with their "less-than-masculine" son to get what she needed. It came down to emotional survival for her, and I didn't blame her.

But then the memories became confusing. Faces I didn't recognize passed through my consciousness like flickering TV images, places I was sure I'd never been sprawled before me, and languages I didn't recognize filled my ears as I strained to make out the words...

Flashes of red gauzy material draped over my skin.

The Source.

These were Amergin's memories.

They led worship in the grove at our compound on the solstice before the mutiny, when I was still in wonder about all we were experiencing, eager to learn more, but I saw the tableaus from their perspective, not my own. I'd had no inkling of what was to come. Neither had they.

I witnessed Amergin imparting wisdom to acolytes in small sessions in a different setting, more remote than the place where we'd met. They were surrounded by older people who had been their companions for many years, since the early twentieth century.

I began to wonder, how much more would they have been able to teach me if the mutiny hadn't happened? Would I have learned incredible things, or become as strong as I was now if I hadn't had to exist on my own?

But then, The Source had been on their own for centuries.

I was taken back further in time to when The Source lived as one with nature as their only companion. Memories of lying in the grass, staring at the sky, feeling the vibrations from the earth and the river nearby, closing their eyes as they sent their energy flowing toward disturbances, feeling at peace. Then there came the influx of folks who needed healing. Women having pregnancy struggles, villages beset with plague, injuries from accidents... an endless supply of energy derived from those most vulnerable, and Amergin accumulated that knowledge, that experience, and wondered how they could use it to improve humanity's quest for understanding and continue to keep the balance with nature.

I tried to take it all in, the development of The Way in reverse, until the images slowed down and there appeared eight beings dressed like Amergin. They shared the same appearance, the same energy signatures, the same purpose.

Eight. One for each of the cycles, the ceremonies, and each led one of the rituals. This was the origin I was witnessing. The beginning of The Way. How did these eight beings come together? Where did they find each other?

As the scene settled in around me, I watched as they drank blood of humans and animals, and they praised the Goddess for the gifts. They fornicated, and laughed and sang under the stars. They were at peace as the world began to wake up around them. The visions became hazy then, fractured, until the others were gone and time stopped. Amergin was alone in the darkness, terrified.

Alone. The beginning.

There was no memory of their birth, no family unit. How had they come into being? What had happened to the other seven? What had separated them, and what happened to the others? Were any of them still alive? Practicing The Way some place? Or had they long ago given up the practice and taken the easy way out to survive by consuming blood? Easy, but not as effective, and not likely to keep them strong for long.

Amergin mourned their loss. Like me, they carried on because they felt it their duty. Through pleasure and peril, they never stopped providing for others and sacrificing of themselves, no matter the personal cost.

Then time began to move forward once more, and I saw the seven with them again. There was joy, and then they were alone once more, but no longer afraid.

There were moments in which Amergin had to flee an area because of threats: a volcano eruption, floods, a forest fire, an earthquake, and they met each challenge with strength and grace.

And then they came in contact with men.

The scenes of brutality that played out before them were devastating. So many near-death experiences, and yet they rose from the literal ashes, took what they needed to heal and survive, and they carried on. Burnt at the stake, raped, stoned, thrown into the water weighted down... They were called witch, heretic, heathen, and yet they continued to help others who needed them desperately, science long ago thrown out in the name of religion.

They'd endured through all of it to continue teaching The Way and healing those who needed them.

I was ashamed. I'd criticized them, blamed them for what I'd been through, after they'd experienced so much hardship. When Stephen stole them away, they grew tired, despondent. They were utterly alone like they'd been in the very beginning of their existence. None of their modern companions could fathom what they'd been through, who they were, and so they isolated amongst those who'd gathered to learn from them. The world had changed drastically and they were afraid of the modern technology they'd been exposed to.

"I will protect you with my life," Stephen told them. *"I will ensure The Way continues on and provide everything you need to make that happen. You must come with me. There are those who would destroy you and all you have done."*

The Source took the leap in that moment, surrounded by fire and devastation. What choice did they have?

Taking that leap took them from terror to despair quickly. They knew they were being mistreated and felt helpless to stop it, helpless to try to exist in this modern world.

This time, when faced with a choice, they trusted me, and they'd done nothing but try to be helpful and repair the damage they'd done. They'd become brave and bold in their desire to understand the modern world.

They came to my rescue and were nearly destroyed.

They stayed by my side while I was lost.

Now it was my turn to decide whether to be brave, to be bold.

I had a decision to make. Either accept their help and pull myself back from the brink of nonexistence, or let go.

A calm settled over me at that possibility. No more suffering. No more pain. No more responsibility.

No more joy.

No more love.

And as I floated, unmoored in a blank space, an absence of energy, everything around me buzzed and hummed. Zingers of pain traveled through my body, like hitting my funny bone over and over, and I was beyond the capacity to stop them. I didn't know how to let go of what little awareness I had, nor did I sense a tether, something to grab hold of. There was someone who needed me, someone I'd... wanted. Someone I'd been so desperate to fight for, someone I'd hurt deeply.

The moon.

His face.

Roman.

"I'm the one that's selfish because I hope you realize before you drift off that if you give up, if you leave, you'll be giving up on a once-in-a-millennia thing."

A new sensation, this one not unpleasant, woke in my chest. A warmth that eased my breathing, eased the numbness, brought back feeling gently...

"Amergin called me your Moonwish. I don't know if you know what that means, but they described it to me and, well... it was spot-on. Two halves being stronger together and all that."

A light pierced the darkness, and I winced. The light before had been bad, it had been pain, panting, pulling, tearing, burning. This light was... warm, like the feeling taking over my chest. It wasn't the fire; it was the embers of something that had meant everything to me, something I'd been willing to sacrifice it all for. *Someone* I'd sacrificed it all for.

"I never felt like I could handle all the shit in my life, no matter what I said to my uncle. Not until you came along. Now I want to be strong for both of us. You and me, we're powerful together, and I don't know if you know this, but we still have a lot of work to do."

Purpose. That was important, having something to do, I had something important to do, somewhere important to be, someone important...

"So wake up, goddammit. Come back to me."

A warm ocean breeze tickled my nose, and I inhaled the scent, instantly feeling a jolt. My mind flickered like a computer screen coming to life and my body rebooted, systems coming back online. Breathing. Hearing.

Sniffles. Shaky breaths. Someone was crying.

A wet droplet hit my shoulder, sending a ripple through my body, penetrating the buzz and hum with warmth and purpose and—

Love.

Roman.

Longing overpowered me, and I reached out with my mind for something, some link, some way to reach him and let him know I was here, I was trying...

"I swear I'll never eat another goddamned Blizzard again if you'll just come back to me."

His words slammed me back into my body. The Dairy Queen. The man from Longevity Health whom I mistook for Todd's benefactor. The gun in my back. Roman's face when I spoke those horrible words.

"Make him believe it or he'll never have peace."

I gasped and my fingers twitched. Feeling returned to my legs, and I uncrossed them.

A weight pushed against my leg, and I reached for it. A cold nose pressed into my hand.

Rhonda.

My most loyal companion. The best friend I'd ever had. I'd felt her presence but couldn't make myself reach out for her. Now I wrapped my arms around her and she popped up, tiny whines coming from her nose as she licked my face and pawed at me. I collapsed onto the floor next to her as she wiggled and nudged me as if to say, "It's about damn time you woke up."

I squeezed my eyes shut and when I opened them, instead of vast nothingness before me, I found myself in an unfamiliar room in front of a window. I felt the energy signatures of several others nearby, including some I recognized. Amergin, Todd, Rey—

Roman was here.

I wanted to shout his name, scream for help, but my body was only slightly cooperating with me and my vocal cords weren't functioning at all.

I knew at one point I'd possessed ample self-discipline and self-control. I'd meditated, and I'd been able to achieve the ultimate focus needed to carry out my duty as a healer. That didn't seem to be the case now. My legs flailed when I tried to sit up once more. I tried to get my hands underneath me to push myself up and found myself slammed down onto my chest, narrowly avoiding crushing my nose. I wasn't injured, I knew that. There was no inflammation or wounds on my body, but it just didn't want to work right.

But the sparks had ceased. That was a blessing. I was on a wood floor that could have easily erupted into flames.

Fire. Lexi. The complex. I hurt people.

"Blessed be. You've returned."

Amergin. Their scent filled the room as they approached but I had trouble understanding this new stimulus. I held onto Rhonda tighter, and she remained still.

"Creed? Can you hear me?"

I squeezed my eyes shut and opened them but I was getting so much stimulation I couldn't tell whether this was real or another memory.

"Be at peace. I am here. I'm going to take your hand."

Yes, please. Help me find myself.

"You are in the attic of Roman's house. We brought you here from the place where you'd been imprisoned."

A shudder ran through my body, and I swallowed. I tried to speak but no sound came out.

"Those who harmed you have been detained. Lexi is safe, she's gone to stay with family, but she comes to see you. Todd is here with the men from his team. Rey is here. And Roman. He comes to you each day. He waits for you."

"Roman."

My mouth was dry, and I yearned for him. I needed to be near him, to have an Exchange with him, to be as close to him as humanly possible, skin to skin, breath to breath. I needed to know he was alive, that he'd forgiven me.

Amergin smiled and brushed my hair back from my face. "You have been through so much."

"I'm... apologize. I need... I was awful to you. You went through horrors..."

Their eyes widened and tears collected in the corners. "I wondered what you would see," they whispered. "You will have questions."

I clutched at their hands, trying to make my fingers work. My muscles and joints were fatigued from being frozen in place for—

"It's been eight days, Creed. Roman has tried to be patient—"

"Does he... forgive... will he... have me?"

"Go to him. He is waiting for you."

As my senses continued to come online, my brain began running diagnostics. My skin was sore and grimy, my hair—oh Goddess, my hair was gone—and I didn't even want to think of what eight days without brushing my teeth smelled like.

"You smell fine," Amergin said with a laugh. "But let me help you to the bathroom so you can freshen up. Then I'll help you to Roman's room."

"I appreciate you." I didn't know how else to express how I was feeling. I'd been so angry, shown them such disrespect. I had a lot to atone for.

They smiled. "And I appreciate you. I'd like to think we have a better understanding of each other now. Perhaps it will help us move forward as... friends."

"I would... yes, please."

They helped me to my feet, and I leaned on them as I tried to remember how to put one foot in front of the other. My muscles were so tight, every step took so much effort, but then I was in the shower and the warm water helped loosen things up.

I thought of the last time I'd been in this house.

I'd come crawling back to Roman then too, damaged from a motorcycle accident, my body as close to the end of its existence as I'd ever been. He'd forgiven me then. He'd held me in his arms, given me his blood, and used my body for his pleasure, the act grounding me and putting me on my way to being whole.

Since then, he'd been nearly drained of blood, he'd died and been brought back, spent weeks in painful recovery. We'd had a brief reunion full of promise... and then I'd walked away from him again, only this time I became a monster. I'd hurt people. My body had been stuffed full of food and blood until I was disgusted with myself, with the gluttony. I lost control and I destroyed a building, nearly killing Lexi in the process. And then I'd almost given up. I wasn't sure I *hadn't* given up.

Somehow I was here, however, which either indicated I was needed for something more, or I was meant to continue on this journey.

Meant for something more.

Would Roman accept me as I was, after all I'd done?

I stepped out of the shower and dried off, realizing I had no clothes.

It was almost enough to make me laugh. Just like last time, I'd be going to him in a towel.

Rhonda sat outside the bathroom door waiting for me, her expression giving me no quarter.

"I know, girl. It's time."

I followed her down the stairs, my girl leading me to my heart.

Twenty-Seven

R oman

I don't know how long I lay there ruminating before a weight settled in next to me on the bed. Rhonda hadn't spent the night with me since we'd been back, as she hadn't wanted to be away from Creed. Poor dog was just as confused as I was. I rolled over to pet her—and sat up with a gasp when I saw a shadow in the doorway.

I couldn't speak. My heart pounded in my chest, my fight-or-flight reflex trying to ascertain the threat level.

A car went by the front of the house and the headlights illuminated Creed's face.

"Baby," I murmured. I went to pull the covers off but he stepped back, his gaze unfocused. I sat still, afraid to spook him.

Rhonda turned her head toward him and whimpered. It was enough to spur him forward. He dragged his feet a bit, his shoulders slumped rather than his usual starkly upright posture. He reached for her on the bed and she stood, moved to the other side of me and then sat down, letting out a whine. Had she led him down here?

Creed stood at the edge of the bed, looking down for several beats, so I took a chance. I pulled back the covers slowly and scooted over, giving him a wide berth.

Eventually he lowered himself to the bed. He lay on his side with his back to me and let out a long sigh. I waited until he was settled, and then I covered him with the blankets. I wanted to wrap myself around him, but I didn't know if it would spook him. Instead, I lay down and prayed once more, and Rhonda rested her head on my hip, watching him with me.

It wasn't like me to hold my tongue, but he seemed... frightened. Unsettled. I fought the urge to touch him for fear I'd send him skittering away. I inhaled and let out a slow, steady breath.

"However long it takes," I said softly. "I'll be here for you."

There was no response.

I exhaled a shaky breath and tucked into my pillow. *I can do this.* At least he was here, in my bed. That was a start.

I was just about to close my eyes when he rolled over, took my hand in his, and drew it over his body, clutching it to his chest as he curled up into a fetal position.

"Baby," I whispered. I pulled him against my body, and he shuddered, holding tight to my hand. I kissed the back of his head and realized I was about to be tested yet again.

Creed had returned to me after experiencing profound trauma. He'd been kidnapped, tortured, and forced to betray the values he'd lived by for fifty years.

It would not be easy, but I would not fail him this time.

I would hold him up until he got his bearings.

March

Creed's recovery took weeks. He spent his days with Amergin and his nights with me. He barely spoke, he spooked easily, and at times, his frustration would boil over and he'd shut himself up in the attic with Rhonda for hours, only to come downstairs and apologize profusely once he'd managed to release his negative energy. All of us present worried about him, and we were all determined to give him a safe place to land, however long it took.

When we were alone, we lay in my bed with the salt lamp on, listening to music and just breathing. It was good for both of us. It allowed me to let my overactive brain settle and it was peaceful. I held him tight to me as he breathed me in, and whenever he needed—I'd learned to recognize the signs—I encouraged him to initiate an Exchange.

It was... different. He took my blood from my wrist. It was very chaste, just like he'd done for decades before meeting me. No longer were we ripping each other's clothes off, but our closeness felt even more intimate than those frantic lovemaking sessions that seemed so long ago. He asked me to talk to him, he wanted to know about my classes, everything going on in the house—wanted to hear my voice—but he struggled to concentrate. He would apologize and I would shush him.

"I need to hear your voice, Roman. It heals me."

I assured him he could have whatever of me he wanted or needed. I belonged to him.

Amergin and I spoke often, and they bade me to be patient.

"He will come back to you."

But I was beginning to wonder if the charismatic, charming Nurse Creed was even still in there somewhere. It didn't matter, he would always be mine, but I missed that part of him and wondered often whether it could be jumpstarted.

During those weeks, I resumed teaching online at the university and working on my dissertation, preparing to defend it in May. The university bent over backward to accommodate me, and my frequent messages from Nigel Hart had me wondering if he'd had anything to do with the ease in which I was accepted back. I knew it would be up to me to put all of the information we'd gathered together into a coherent document, but not having to fight to be heard by men who'd previously questioned my legitimacy was a relief.

Todd continued building the case against EVE, working diligently out of the bedroom upstairs in my house. We spent hours rehashing everything that had happened. He'd been so shaken by this op going sideways that he asked Nigel for time to regroup and rethink strategies for the team before they took on another case. Nigel was patient, thank goodness, because I worried whether Todd would be able to continue on with his special assignment, or even return to the FBI. We'd all been wounded by this confrontation with EVE, and we needed each other.

Larsson stayed on and acted as head of security, chef, and all-around relaxing presence. His gift was different than Amergin's, or even Creed's, but it could be just as potent. If conversations got heated, he'd lay on the Larsson treatment and we'd all start nodding off in our chairs, or getting up to go to bed without realizing we were tired. He and Amergin spent hours together in what started off as a devil's advocate scenario, but the more time they spent together, the more common ground they found.

Between the time spent with Larsson and me, Amergin was growing more confident in their ability to operate in the modern world. They'd continued wearing clothes they found in the attic. They even went downtown with Larsson from time to time to shop, have meals, and observe the tourists. I was so grateful for him. Without Larsson's unique talents, I didn't think I'd be able to keep Casa San Angelo afloat on my own.

Gordon and Craig eventually returned to their family's property in Northern California, with the understanding they would be on-call if needed. They encouraged us to consider coming up to visit when Creed was well, or at least better. I couldn't think that far ahead, but I appreciated the offer. Maybe Creed *would* benefit from a change of scenery. It might be good for him. But the idea of leaving this safe space felt reckless.

Rey flirted with the idea of joining Todd's merry band of mercenaries. He and Vanessa had epic battles about his indecision over rejoining the PD. She wanted him to smooth things over with Rojas and return to duty. Rey dug his heels in and refused. Vanessa was also furious about the goings-on at Lola's house. She refused to allow Bernadette or Emmanuel over with Amergin present, "and I can't believe you're allowing Junior to be around them, either, after everything that happened." I understood her anger, but I couldn't explain to her our situation in a way she'd understand. She didn't like weird any more than Rey did.

He had no choice, though. He'd experienced it firsthand. He still grumbled about his normal life being upheaved, but the more time he spent with Larsson and Todd, the more he seemed to embrace his new normal. It killed me to be at odds with my aunties, but Creed had to be my priority. I went to see Lola as often as I could, and that was all I could do until Vanessa was ready to parlay.

We ate dinner as a peculiar family each night, with Rey, Larsson, and I taking turns cooking. Having a full house filled a part of my soul that had been grieving since the loss of my parents, and even more, since Lola moved to Puesta Del Sol. Creed joined us when he felt up to it. The other nights, I brought him food on a tray and sat with him as he ate. He struggled with food after being force-fed. Lexi shared with me in detail everything that happened during their captivity, when she felt ready to talk about it. I hurt for both of them. Creed couldn't stand to feel full, couldn't tolerate any tight clothing on him. Yeah, that massive body he'd emerged from the compound with shrank back to his normal size within a few weeks, but he was terrified of ever being in that state again. It was a challenge to get him to consume enough nutrition.

The clinical side of me knew he needed professional therapy, but who would be in a position to work with him? Anyone not in our circle would immediately have him committed if he shared his truth. But without some way of putting things in perspective, he was... stuck. He didn't even have the benefit of negative energy to help him. I knew that was the key to helping him, but he was afraid to leave the house.

One late afternoon in mid-March, I managed to get him outside during the day to get some Vitamin D. It was just the two of us at the house, with the exception of our guards out front. Todd had to travel to meet with his agent in charge about the case against EVE and would be gone for at least another day or so. Gordon and Craig had returned in his absence, but they remained on the perimeter of the property, trading off with our other security, unless they were sleeping. The day had been peaceful, and it had felt good to get my hands dirty. Lola's garden had been neglected long enough.

Creed was watching me quietly and throwing the ball to Rhonda when Rey came outside, just as the sun was setting.

"Junior, your presence is required."

Creed glanced at Rey before returning to his task. Rhonda was persistent, which I appreciated, because it was good for Creed. He'd do anything for her, if not for himself.

"Where and when?"

He raised his eyebrows. "You seriously don't know what today is?"

I'd been pulling weeds in the last sunny spot in the yard with my shirt off, and I was covered in hard-earned dirt and sweat. I sat back on my haunches and tried to think. Time had kind of become arbitrary. I kept my schedule with teaching, but there were a lot of days I didn't leave the property so they began to run together. I wasn't unhappy, but things had grown... stagnant.

"Instead of standing there with your dick in your hand, you could tell me. And bring me that bag of mulch while you're at it, would you?"

Rey kicked a hip out and planted his hands on his hips. "It's Tita Frances's birthday, dumbass. Did you really forget?"

I dropped my head. Yeah, I'd forgotten just about everything but what was right in front of me. It had been easier to take a little emotional distance from Puesta Del Sol because it hurt too much to have Creed out of reach and Lola slipping away.

"I'm sorry." I pushed myself up to standing. "I... fuck, I'm sorry."

Rey nodded once, glanced at Creed, and spoke in a low voice. "We're bringing her cake at six. Do what you gotta do, clean yourself up, and be ready to go shortly."

"Right. Thank you. I can't believe I forgot."

Rey put a hand on my shoulder, pulled it away with a grimace, and wiped it on his pants. "Gross."

"Fuck off." I bent over to wipe my forehead on his shoulder and he dodged contact, cursing me all the way.

Good to know Dicknaldo was still around.

I wiped off my forehead with my shirt that was hanging out of my jeans.

"I can feed myself and Rhonda dinner. You should go."

I turned to look at Creed. "It's okay. I have time. I want to do it." I moved closer to him and petted Rhonda's head.

He shook his head and looked down at his feet. "You're doing too much for me. I'm taking up too much of your time."

I reached for his hand. I was still leery of touching him the way I wanted to. "I'm not. *You're* not. Everything's okay, baby. I've just been—"

"Distracted. By me. I'm sorry, Roman. I... I don't know what to do."

I took his hand and he grabbed on tight. "Are you open to suggestions?"

Creed exhaled through his nose and looked off into space. "I don't know," he whispered. "But I can't keep living like a leech off of you—"

"God, please don't ever say that again," I said, bringing a hand up to his cheek. "It's me and you. We do this together. I was only going to suggest you come with me."

"What if I can't?" He looked up at me, and the pain in his gaze was so like those times he threatened to pull away from me. "What if I can't *ever*?"

This was a test of my restraint. Old Roman would have become angry, would have lashed out, gotten frustrated, and given up. But I took a deep breath, gave him a small smile, and let go of his hand.

"I'll fix you two dinner before I take a shower. You can think about whether or not you want to join us."

He opened his mouth to speak, but nothing came out. He took Rhonda by the collar and they went inside.

I let out a breath. It was difficult to know how hard to push. I followed them into the house but let him go alone up the stairs, where I assumed he would go to the attic. I sighed. It wasn't helping him, all that time he spent up there alone.

"Roman!" Amergin burst in the front door with a bright smile. "We went for a drive today and Larsson showed me your university! Such beautiful grounds. Your learners are lucky to have such a special place. The ley lines are close to the surface there—"

"Which is true," Larsson interjected. The guy had balls, seeing how often he interrupted and corrected Amergin, but they never got upset with him. "It's also surrounded by a large nature preserve, and that much nature makes all learning more conducive." Larsson winked at Amergin, and they sighed.

"You are right. Nature makes learning conducive. Ley lines do not always play a role in matters of human interaction."

Larsson leaned close to them. "And that makes how many times I've been correct today?"

Amergin made a frustrated sound, but they were smiling. "You are an infuriating man. You have been correct four times today—"

"Five. Don't forget the hawk I correctly identified."

Amergin laughed loudly, and the sound rattled the glass cabinets. "Since you insist on keeping score, I will give you five victories today, Larsson. Now, can we be finished competing for the evening? I would like to watch the television performance we discussed."

"*The Lost Boys*? I'm not sure you're ready for The Santa Cruz Vampire movie."

I had a thought. "Amergin? What is your understanding of a vampire?"

They blinked at me with large eyes. "I know there are some modern practitioners of The Way who refer to themselves in that manner. Mark and Cross use that term. I believe there was a book over a century ago that told a story about a mythological member of the nobility who stalked humans as their prey and lived off of their blood. I can't guarantee that none of my acolytes were responsible for that myth being spread, but I highly doubt that any of them would have lived in a castle alone in a place called Transylvania. I do not know where the myths originated, but they were not my doing."

I had so many questions. If there was a true source for the vampire mythology, and it wasn't Amergin or anyone they knew, was it a being like them? This line of thinking had me recalling the conversation I'd had with Alistair, and the similarities and differences in vampire lore from around the world. Maybe there was something there? Perhaps I'd found my next area of research... modern-day vampiric practices. I knew of cases of vampiric serial killers. What if there was a connection with EVE? What if—

"You about ready, Junior?"

Rey was waiting for me by the stairs dressed in slacks and a dress shirt.

"Sorry. Give me ten minutes. I'm just going to feed Rhonda and make a plate up for Creed."

"I'm happy to take care of that," Larsson said. "I understand it's your grandmother's birthday. Gratulerer med dagen. Blessings on her special day."

"That is wonderful," Amergin said, staring up at Larsson. "The day of one's birth is to be celebrated. How will you celebrate with her?"

"My sister is bringing a cake and we'll sing to her. She's not getting around as well anymore." Rey cleared his throat and gave me a pointed look.

Time was running out.

"Thanks, Larsson." I stepped closer to him. "Listen, Creed is having a difficult afternoon. I'm concerned about leaving him alone."

Larsson didn't even wait for me to finish. He lay a hand on my shoulder. "I'll look after your beloved. He will not be alone."

"Thank you." I rushed into the bathroom, took the quickest shower ever, and slicked my hair back in a low ponytail. I dressed in a turtleneck and slacks, and I put on my lolo's watch and a gold chain that belonged to my father. I needed the armor of the San Angelo men who went before me if I was going to face the women of the San Angelo family.

I came out of my room and stopped at the foot of the stairs. I wanted to go up and ask Creed once more to come with me, but I wasn't sure that the new, mature Roman would be able to take more rejection. It would do Creed good to get out, and there, he'd be around people who cared for him, but it would also be a lot to contend with when he hadn't been out of the house in months.

Lexi had visited with him a few times and left in tears when he wasn't really responsive, but she swore she understood. She'd mentioned to him that Yvonne asked her to pass along word that his job was there whenever—if ever—he was ready to come back. He thanked her, but then gave me a heartbroken look that I took to mean he feared he'd never be ready.

"Junior! Let's go!"

"Coming, Dicknaldo," I sang to him, and he punched me in my left shoulder as I passed. I waved to Larsson and Amergin, who were still deep in conversation in the kitchen. They waved back and continued arguing about whether Amergin was ready to watch the cult classic movie.

As I got to the passenger side of Rey's truck, I looked up to the attic window.

Creed stood there with a hand on the glass. I waved to him and said that prayer once more, the one I'd said for the first time when Amergin explained the Moonwish... the one I'd said every night since.

Please let him be free.

"You're doing so good for him, pamangkin. Hang in there. He'll come around."

I sighed as he backed away from the house.

"That's all I can do."

Twenty-Eight

C reed

How Roman could keep smiling at me, and being kind to me, when I continued to flounder made no logical sense to me.

I made my mind up right then: this would be the last time I denied Roman. I'd faced worse than leaving the house. I'd fought hard to escape my imprisonment for what? To remain a prisoner of my own making in this attic? A captive of my troubled mind, my traumatic experience, kept from my beloved when all I wanted was to give myself to him, to be with him the way we'd only just begun to experience. He was the promise of a future I wanted desperately.

I'd never been so afraid, not in my life before The Way, and not since. This was worse than being away from him and thinking I'd never see him again. Now I was terrified I'd lose him because I wasn't strong enough to take the necessary steps to free myself from this prison.

Amergin cried out from downstairs, and it was so loud that I felt it as much as heard it. I made my way down the stairs, worried they were in distress.

I was not prepared for the scene before me.

Sometime after we'd returned to Roman's house, I'd noticed that Amergin no longer wore the traditional red garments. They wore clothes that likely belonged to Rey or Roman, but also, they wore some polyester pantsuits and dresses that might have belonged to Frances. They seemed to delight in trying on different outfits, perhaps to find their comfort zone in their new normal, but I never asked them about the change. I'd been selfish. Tonight, they wore a pair of jeans and a t-shirt with the movie poster from *The Lost Boys* on it as they sat on the couch beside Larsson, and they seemed happy, more than at any time I'd ever witnessed. They had a bowl of popcorn between them and Amergin was drinking... a beer?

"Creed! Have you watched this performance on the television? It is outrageous! Hanging upside down while they sleep by their feet like some sort of bats. Whoever thought of such a thing?"

I balled my hands into fists. I could do this. Roman had been so brave for me. I could do this for him.

"I'm going to Puesta Del Sol. I want to... I need to go."

Larsson sat up and set down his glass of water. "Let me grab my keys. I can take you."

"No, thank you. I would like to... run. It's been too long."

Amergin used the remote to pause the movie and they stood from the couch. "This is good, Creed. We cannot allow you to go alone, however, for your safety. Let us run with you."

I hadn't forgotten that we were still under protection. EVE remained underground, whatever was left of the organization, and Todd was handing over the investigation to the FBI for the time being, with the understanding that he would continue to hunt down the serum and anyone involved in its manufacture or distribution. I hated the idea that my blood was out there somewhere, being used for their nefarious plans, but I couldn't do anything about it now.

What I *could* do was run the two miles to Puesta Del Sol and be strong for my beloved. I prayed it was enough.

Larsson grabbed Rhonda's leash, and he and Amergin agreed to stay behind me, which I appreciated. I needed the time it would take me to get there to bolster myself. Returning to Puesta Del Sol meant answering questions that I wasn't quite sure how to address. It meant seeing the patients I'd come to know and love, and knowing that my absence meant they had likely lost ground. It meant seeing Roman's aunt, who was furious that Amergin and I were still around, and angry with Roman and Rey for sheltering us.

I was afraid, but it was a step I needed to take for my own healing.

I was winded by the time I reached the facility. I hadn't run in way too long. Larsson and Amergin waited in the shadows with Rhonda as I approached the entrance. I reached for the door and looked down at myself. I should have at the very least worn something nicer than sweat-pants and a t-shirt, but I didn't have anything of my own. Roman had said more than once that we could go shopping, but I hadn't been ready.

"You'll just have to accept that you are as ready as you're gonna get," I whispered, as I pushed the door open.

Lexi looked up from the front desk, and her shock immediately melted into relief. She stepped out from behind the desk and waited...

I held my arms open, and she dove in for a hug, squeezing me so tight I huffed out a breath.

"I'm sorry, I ran here," I said, to explain the sweat.

"You're just in time. We wheeled Frances into the library for the cake. It's just the family in there—the rest of the patients are watching a movie in the cafeteria. Go on in."

"Creed? Is that you?"

I turned to see Yvonne coming out of her office. She had the kind of smile on her face that let me know someone had told her I'd been through a terrible experience. She gave me the biggest mom hug I'd had in the longest time, and I relaxed into her hold—

And then I felt it.

Little tickles of energy licking at my skin, like voices begging for relief.

"I am so glad you're here," Yvonne said. "Roman said you've been recovering at his home. I'm... I'm so glad to see you, Creed. We've missed you."

I smiled at her, so overcome with emotion I couldn't speak, but then the tickles grew stronger, more insistent. This was the missing piece of my recovery.

I hadn't had negative energy since we'd seen Stephen in prison. No sexual energy since the last time Roman and I were intimate on the island. No sundowning. And it was prime time for it.

"Do you mind," I asked Yvonne, "if Lexi takes me for a walk around? I'd like to see everyone before I interrupt the San Angelos."

Yvonne seemed surprised but she held out her hand. "I'll watch the front. No problem."

Lexi took my arm, and we went down the hall in the opposite direction from my usual patient floor.

"How do you feel?" she whispered. "Are you okay?"

I blew out a breath, but the energy in the building was knocking on my psychic door. All I had to do was let it in. I stopped walking for a moment, closed my eyes, and took in a deep breath.

And it was as if everything in the world made sense once more.

This was what I'd needed but had been unable to seek. It wasn't about me anymore, or my recovery; it was about bringing peace to the seniors in this facility. They'd experienced life, love, and now their existence was full of so much pain, fear, and confusion. I called it all to me, maybe a little too quickly as it flooded my system, but then it began righting everything that had felt wrong.

"Blessed be." Their pain and resulting relief washed away my guilt, cleansed me of the filth I'd accumulated in that horrible place. How could I have forgotten the release? Or the joy I felt at being able to give peace back to those who suffered needlessly? Why had I waited so long to do what I knew would make me whole?

"Whoa, Creed!" Lexi laughed as her hair stood out from her head. "This doesn't feel like last time."

"No. This is how it's supposed to be. Although," I said with a laugh. I spun around in a circle, feeling more energized than I had in a long time. "This is a lot all at once. Have things been extra stressful lately?"

She nodded, and her lips turned down on the corners. "We've got more end-stage patients than ever. We get calls for help all evening, every day. The staff is tired. Jamal has been out with a back injury, Carter hurt his neck, and even Yvonne has had to help us some nights." She gave me a questioning smile. "Do you think you're ready to come back? Do you think you'd want to?"

I looked down at my hands, at the hair standing up on my arms, at the healthier tone to my skin. "I think I *have* to work if I want to stay well. I might need time. This is a lot, and I don't have total control yet—"

A lightbulb popped next to us, and Lexi shrieked, but then we both laughed. It wasn't at all like last time. I was able to breathe and focus on the output of good energy I released. This was right. I belonged here.

"Let's go call maintenance to take care of that. Do you feel ready to see Frances?"

I nodded, my eyes filled with tears. Happy tears. It was as if the light at the end of the tunnel had flicked on and I was closer than I'd thought to reaching it. The sorrow and despondent cloud hanging over me was lifting. The pressure against my body lessened as I took in the negative energy and sent back out positive with every breath, the act as natural to me as breathing in this place.

Lexi took my hand, and we stopped at the front desk so she could call the maintenance man to clean up my mess. I heard the singing in the library, and my breath caught. I knew Roman wanted me to come, but would the others? Could Vanessa forgive me? Would Frances recognize me?

"Ready?"

I took Lexi's hand and let her lead me as I sent up a silent prayer to the Goddess and followed her into the library.

My heart thudded at seeing Roman smiling at his beloved grandmother and holding the cake for her to blow out the candles. She struggled the slightest bit getting them all out, but then she smiled up at him from her wheelchair with so much love. Her mental acuity and physical health had definitely deteriorated in the time I'd been away. I would have to ask Roman what he wanted me to do for her, if anything.

Rey saw me first, and his frown relaxed the slightest bit, which was probably the most welcome he'd made me feel in a long time. I hated that I'd caused him so much stress, so much worry for his nephew.

Stella and Phyllis came over and hugged me first, and their whoops of delight caught Roman's attention from where he was serving cake onto small plates. His already joyous expression lit up even more, and he pressed a hand to his heart.

"Nurse Creed, we've missed you so much."

The two women kissed my cheeks, likely leaving lipstick behind. I turned to greet Vanessa, and she nodded my way without a smile, but also without a scowl. I didn't know whether now was the time to apologize profusely to her, but that was in my future, if she'd let me. Bernadette and Emmanuel still didn't remember what had happened at Loch Lomond, and I assumed the family decided it was better not to tell them anything else because they greeted me as if no time had passed.

Then I got to Frances's chair. I knelt beside her, and she smiled.

"Lola," Roman said. "Do you remember Nurse Creed?"

She gave me that flirtatious smile like she had the very first time I'd met her.

"I would remember such a handsome man."

The eyerolls and groans from Roman and Rey made me chuckle.

I took her hand and kissed the back of it. "It's a pleasure," I said. I took a quick moment to scan her and sensed that she was on the verge of congestive heart failure, and her blood sugar hadn't been regulated while I was gone. I kept a hold of her hand and sent enough healing energy to put those two encroaching nightmares at bay. Her smile lit up.

"Have you met my grandson, Roman?"

I stood and smiled at my beloved. I held out a hand to him. "Hi. Creed."

He sucked in a breath and blinked back tears. "Roman."

It took everything in my power not to grab him in a bone-crushing hug and never let go. Now that I was coming out of my fog, I saw just how much he'd been affected by my state. I wanted to be strong for him once more. He'd tried so hard to help me out of my darkness, but I'd needed this place and the special people here. Now that I could think—and feel—clearly, I intended to show him how much I loved him, how vital he was to me, and I prayed that it would be enough.

"Why don't you play a song for Mrs. San Angelo, Creed?" Lexi smiled from her perch in the doorway. "She loves the classics."

I remembered the perfect song.

I sat at the piano, gave Roman a wink, and stretched out my hands. Thank goodness playing was etched deep in my muscle memory.

I played the opening notes to the Dionne Warwick classic "I Say A Little Prayer." Stella and Phyllis stood next to Frances's chair and the three of them sang along with me. The sisters did a little dance step while Frances bounced happily, clapping her hands. Vanessa stood next to Bernadette with her arm around her wife. Rey leaned in and whispered something to Roman, who wiped at his eyes and laughed.

I had said a little prayer for Roman so often. I would love him forever if he'd let me.

Cheers from the doorway had us all laughing. Several of the other night staff members were dancing together and singing along. They waved to me, and I smiled. I'd felt more welcome here than anyplace else in my long existence. It made sense that it would be the place for me to take the next step in my recovery.

"All right, party's over," Lexi said. "Frances, I need to get you your medicine."

She pouted. "But it's my birthday. I want to dance."

Roman wheeled her next to the piano bench, and I put my hand out for hers.

"Lovely lady, next time we'll dance. Happy birthday."

She leaned over and kissed my cheek, whispering conspiratorially, "You're a good one, Creed. You know, my grandson is single. He can't make hospital corners to save his life, but he's a good boy. I'll give you his phone number." She patted my hand and then turned to Rey. "You take me to my room, Reynaldo. I want you to help me with my picture frame. It's not playing all the pictures. I need my pictures."

Rey took the wheelchair from Roman and gave me a chin lift. "Be right back."

Roman did the chin lift back to his uncle, then looked down at me. He ran his fingers through the stubble on my head and smiled so softly. "You came."

"You waited for me."

"Roman." Vanessa stood beside him with her arms crossed over her chest.

He spoke to her in Tagalog. She raised an eyebrow in defiance, and then seemed to deflate, like she'd resigned herself to the fact that Roman would choose me if pushed. I hated to come between them.

"Detective Cabral—"

She huffed out a breath and held up a hand to me. "Call me Vanessa, Creed. We're family, after all."

She didn't look happy about it, but I grinned all the same.

"Thank you." I'd make all of this up to her, somehow.

"Creed, it's nice to see you," Bernadette said, shooting Vanessa a funny look. "It's been a while. Are you coming back to work here? The aunties miss you."

"I'm not sure, but it sure is good to see you too." I smiled at her, then shook hands with Emmanuel. They wished us good night and went to walk Stella and Phyllis back to their rooms.

I stood from the piano bench and turned to face Roman. My hand shook as I reached for his. "I hope it was okay that I crashed the party."

"More than okay." His eyes searched mine, as if he wasn't sure what all this meant.

I squeezed his hand. "Will you let me walk you home?"

"I would love that more than anything."

But we weren't able to make a clean getaway.

Yvonne stopped us and gave me a big hug. "Think about it, please, Creed. We miss you."

I assured her I would.

Lexi gave me a hug and made me promise we'd go catch a show soon. "You have the best taste in music."

I promised to call her.

"Junior, you've got bingo duty this week." Rey took one look at our clasped hands and looked pleased. He was tired of weird. Perhaps we were closer to things being right with the world. He could have one less thing to stress about.

Roman gave him a smart-assed retort. They punched each other but neither of them put much effort behind it. Rey flipped us off as he walked to his truck, not even asking if we wanted a ride, which was odd for him.

And then we got outside and found a potential disaster.

I'd totally forgotten Larsson and Amergin were waiting for me. The two of them were sitting on the grass, and Amergin was laughing their head off. Rhonda lay between them looking totally put out. To anyone not in the know, they would look like drunk twenty-somethings who'd stumbled and fallen on the grass and now thought the world was hilarious.

"You guys can't be carrying on like this out here," Roman scolded, but even he had a hard time keeping a straight face.

"You're feeling it, aren't you?" I asked Amergin.

They grinned up at me with rosy cheeks. "Why does it feel so good here?"

"It's a particularly potent form of energy."

They nodded. "This is why. This explains everything. Creed, I want to know more. I want to meet these people."

I opened my mouth to tell them to slow down, but Roman touched my arm.

"Actually, that might not be a bad idea. Does Puesta have a volunteer program?"

I frowned. "They do."

"And if *you* were working here..." Roman began.

I saw where this was going. I placed a hand on his chest. "Before we decide if Nurse Creed is ready to rejoin the world, can we walk, please?"

Roman must have seen the stress behind my smile, because he put his arm around me and nodded. "A walk sounds perfect."

Larsson stood and pulled Amergin up off the ground. "We'll be behind you," he said, a reminder that though I'd come out of my fog and Amergin was acclimating to modern life better than we'd anticipated, there were still threats out there and we couldn't afford to be complacent again. We weren't totally in the clear, but for tonight, we could walk.

We didn't speak for a few blocks. We entered the boisterous downtown area on Pacific Avenue, ducked around college kids and folks coming out of the clubs, turned down Cathcart Street, and cut through the parking lot where we'd had our first near-kiss all those months ago. I could feel Roman's tension. He had questions. I did too. I wanted to answer them all; I wanted to give him the world. I wanted to be well enough to do that, and I was on my way.

"You know that song is one of Lola's favorites," he said finally. "I always used to think it was corny, but hearing you sing it was pretty amazing."

I laughed. "Lexi said it best. I have great taste in music."

Roman shook his head, but he was smiling. "You are insufferable about it, too." His smile slipped. "Creed... I've been praying—"

"Me too," I said quietly. "Every day. Asking for answers, how to get well. I don't know if this is just a hiccup or if I'm really on the mend, but—"

"I asked every night for you to be set free," he said. He'd stopped walking and turned to face me, his dark eyes wide. "Whatever that means. Even after we freed you from the facility, I still prayed for your freedom. I don't want you shackled to this life. I want you to choose what happens next, even if it means I'm not a part of your future. I'm okay with that. I mean, I will be. I want—"

I pulled him so close that we stood chest to chest. "I want *you*, Roman. I want *this*, you and me. I *fought* to be with you, and I'm going to keep fighting. You've been so patient. You've grown so much since I met you. I want to deserve you. If you'll have me."

Roman's touch was tentative as he put his hands on my waist. The streetlight flickered above us and then went out, though I wasn't sure if it was my doing or just bad maintenance. It remained bright around us, though, so I looked up.

The moon was so damned close, like I could reach out and touch it. I knew it was an optical illusion, but it took me back to the night Roman rescued me. The moon had been close that night, too. He'd rescued me so many nights, even that night we had our almost kiss, before I lost control and my pheromones caused him to have a bout of vertigo.

"I smell you," he murmured. "Warm cookies. You're doing it again."

"I was remembering that night we stood right here."

Roman licked his lips and pulled me closer. When he spoke, his lips brushed mine.

"I won't get dizzy this time."

I cradled his jaw in my hands and searched his gaze. "I love you so much, Roman. You were always my choice. My wish."

Roman's eyes flared, and he kissed me. Hard. As if he'd been holding back for too long and the dam finally broke.

"You were always *mine*."

He kissed me breathless, there in the moonlight, and time was finally on our side. All we had before us was time to discover more about each other, time to find answers, and time to love each other.

And at that moment, I wanted nothing more than to take him into my body and be completely his.

I heard the scrabble of claws on the ground a second before Rhonda barreled into us, nearly knocking both of us on our asses.

"I'm sorry," Larsson said, running toward us. "The minute you two started that lip-lock, she yanked her leash right out of my hands. Either she's pleased with this development, or she wants treats."

Roman laughed and rested his forehead on my shoulder as he caught his breath.

I reached down for her leash. "I know, girl. I've got a lot of making up to do with you, too."

"Let's go home, baby." Roman's soft plea was exactly what I needed to hear.

He took my hand, and Rhonda led us back to Roman's house, our home, where hopefully we could start the rest of our lives. Together.

Epilogue

R oman

June

I never thought I'd be the type to enjoy sitting on a wooden porch, staring out at the sunset over the high desert, but there were a lot of things I'd learned to enjoy since Creed Lowell came into my life.

Rocking chairs.

Hippie music.

Sharing my blood...

Okay, the last one sounds weird, I'll give you that, but participating in the ritual of the Exchange with Creed was the closest thing to heaven I'd ever experienced, though Heaven was a place I didn't want to visit for a long time. I'd been close too many times. I wanted to focus on living in the now, with Creed.

After successfully defending my dissertation and receiving my doctorate degree, Creed and I were whisked away to Northern California for a rendezvous with some associates of the mysterious Nigel

Hart. Our security team members Gordon and Craig made good on their offer to loan us their cabin, which was one of four they'd built on their property since joining Nigel's band of merry mercenaries. They really needed to come up with a better name or I'd keep calling them that.

Rey lived up here now in a trailer he bought with his signing bonus, having taken Todd up on his offer to join his team. I missed having him around, but as a member of the team, he didn't have to deal with bureaucracy, nor did he have to have a filter. Todd and the other guys appreciated his experience and his opinions. I was happy for him. Vanessa, not so much, but they'd come to an understanding. She and I had as well. She even invited Creed and I over for dinner on a regular basis. My auntie wasn't ready to meet The Source yet, but she agreed to consider it. That was progress.

Todd had a cabin of his own, which was currently the team's head-quarters. Gordon and Craig lived in their family home on the other side of the property, and the fourth cabin was now occupied by a couple visiting from Nigel's other passion project, Havenhart Academy. In addition to stopping folks from harming those with exceptional gifts, Nigel also believed in educating the gifted. The guy really spoke my love languages. Education and protection.

The night of Lola's birthday proved to be a turning point for the better for all of us. Creed and I finally broke down that wall between us and we were closer than ever. He was completely open with me, no more Mr. Mysterious, and he talked to me about his life like I'd always dreamed he would someday. Having him in my bed every night was as wonderful as I thought it would be. I still feared he'd be taken from me, or me from him, but each passing day made it a little easier to breathe.

And the sex? Even more mind-blowing than before.

I couldn't keep him naked and in my bed all the time, apparently, so he decided he wanted to start taking his life back. He and Amergin began volunteering at Puesta Del Sol a few nights a week, getting a feel for being back in the mix, and when we returned from this getaway, he'd go back to working there full-time. Yvonne and Lexi were thrilled.

The purpose for this trip? To get him some much-needed therapy. Nigel, it turned out, was truly a benefactor in possession of many valuable resources, including a counselor who relied on a special brand of emotional healing to do her work, and who treated differently-abled folks for a living. Delaney Preston was a gifted practitioner who was not shocked by anything, not even the whole drinking-blood thing.

"I've had a student tell me when and where I was getting married. I had one who could literally stop a person's heart with her touch. And, well, you've met Joanna."

We *had* met Joanna. Nigel had brought her and her guardian-slash-adopted father Jackson back to see us shortly after Lola's birthday, and she'd assured me that I didn't need to worry, my dissertation would be a huge success and I'd be receiving an offer for a professorship at UC, though she said I might want to hold out for other offers. I assured her I wasn't interested in leaving home, not yet.

She'd also told me all about the cult her father founded—the one that he'd used her psychic abilities to build. Todd had been working on that case before coming to Santa Cruz, where he'd discovered a franchise of health clinics with some shady and unethical business practices, which is how we'd become part of this bizarre group of acquaintances. Joanna was a powerful psychic, and she asked me to help her with her research into her biological father's affairs after she graduated from Nigel's academy in a few months. She wanted to undo some of the evil he'd done, and from the little bit she'd shared, I knew this girl had been through hell. I was looking forward to getting to know her better and assured her I'd help however I could.

Delaney offered to work with Creed via Zoom, but he still struggled a little with power surges, especially when he was emotional. He'd already fried more than one laptop, so this trip seemed like the best option. At first, he'd been hesitant, but then he met her British husband, Dr. Damien Preston MD, who was another of Nigel's talented employees. Damien, it turned out, was also an incredibly gifted healer. Though he hadn't heard of The Way, he possessed innate skills that allowed him to heal the sick and wounded. Creed had been ecstatic to meet someone with similar gifts, and he'd agreed that talking to Delaney could be helpful.

We'd driven up here for a week so they could have daily intensive sessions, leaving Larsson, Mark, and Cross with Amergin. This way I could meet with Damien as well as Joanna so she and I could discuss her situation. Damien was also able to give me a thorough medical exam, which showed without a doubt that Amergin's healing ceremony had completely reversed not only the injuries I'd sustained at Loch Lomond, but also the lingering effects from my brain injury. I was instantly smitten with him, and we got along famously. He wanted to know all about my research and asked about meeting with Dr. Santos.

"If this nonsense is going on in any part of the world, we've got a duty to put a stop to it."

Creed had teased me when I excitedly told him about our conversations at the end of the first day.

"You just have the hots for any guy with an accent, huh?"

I'd rolled my eyes. "Yours is the only one that gets me hot, baby. Want me to show you?"

Sitting there on the porch as the sun set over the distant mountain range, I got hard thinking of what we'd gotten up to the night before—and how much I couldn't wait for Creed and Delaney to finish so we could get back to our own intensive sessions. I was insatiable, and Creed was more than willing and able to match my sex drive. Nearly dying, spending months wondering if I'd ever have a normal physical life again meant that I took every day as a gift, and every moment spent with Creed as a blessing. Especially when I got all up inside his beautiful body.

Having the cabin to ourselves after living with our little peculiar family for months was a welcome reprieve. We still had a protection detail at the house made up of four guys that were a part of Todd's team. They brought a trailer and parked it in the side entrance to the backyard of Lola's house and they rotated shifts. We invited them to eat with us occasionally, but they mostly kept to themselves. Larssen asked to be assigned permanently to us. He'd gotten quite close with Amergin and having him there made things much easier on Creed. Their friendship continued to be competitive, but good-natured, and his unique ability to calm any environment was exactly the energy we needed to keep the place functioning. Larsson stayed in the spare room and I moved Amergin into Lola's room. They understood what a big step it was for me, and we had a good cry about it together, though they almost flooded the neighborhood.

Mark and Cross were in and out. They'd taken over the attic room and turned it into a living and recording space so they could work on a new Bloody Brilliant album. They traveled for gigs occasionally, but they mostly wanted to stick close. The events of the past few months had shaken all of us, and they agreed we should stick together for the time being. Their music certainly made the place feel festive. It took me back to my childhood when the house was full of love and shenanigans.

"Thanks, Delaney," I heard Creed say, bringing me out of my thoughts. "But I think Roman and I are going to stay in tonight. Let's plan on dinner together tomorrow, since it's the last night for all of us."

The two of them came out onto the porch, and he gave her a hug.

"Sounds great. Ugh, man, I don't want to go back to gross Arkansas summer weather. I miss California weather so bad."

I stood from my chair, where I'd been holding a book but not actually reading it. "You're welcome to visit anytime," I told her. "We're only a few minutes from the beach and we've got plenty of room."

She groaned, and Creed and I laughed. "I'd love that. Seriously. Help me work on Damien tomorrow, would you? We've got time before we have to be back to campus and the bugs."

She gave me a hug as well and waved as she descended the steps. Damien had been out riding motorcycles with Gordon and Craig, getting the tour of their off-roading paradise. We'd been invited to join a nighttime airsoft match, but Creed politely declined. He truly was a lover and not a fighter.

"You sure you don't want to go? I bet all that aggro they got going on would get you a nice buzz."

He slid his hand insinde the back of my pants and squeezed my ass. "I can think of plenty of other ways you can give me a better buzz right inside this cabin."

"Fuck, baby." My semi was now at full mast, and the thoughts I'd had of Creed all day had me raring to go, but I needed to check in with my lover. "You sure you're up for it? We went kinda hard last night."

Creed licked his lips and grinned at me. "The harder the better. I'm still high from you going down on me this morning."

I pulled him in front of me and pressed my erection against his ass.

"You keep talking like that and I'm gonna use that mouth of yours." I ran my tongue up the side of his neck, and he leaned a hand against the railing to remain upright. "You've got me so worked up, I'm ready to go all night. Think you can handle that?"

Creed moaned and reached back, stroking my cock through my sweatpants. "Are we still talking? Why are we talking? I thought you were going to use my mouth—*ohhhhh*."

I licked my fingers, slid my hand down the back of his pants, and inserted a finger into his hole, which seemed to call his bluff. He gasped, and then he pushed back against me.

"Now," I said into his ear, as I moved that finger in and out slowly. "If you're going to continue to sass me, I'm going to take this ass right here on the porch, and you'll have to explain to our friends why you were screaming." Another finger, and his legs started to shake. "If you'd like to be civilized, we can take this inside, where I'll still make you scream, but at least you can do it into a pillow. The sound will carry quite far out here, you know. I'm fine either way." A third finger. He groaned, and as I continued to stroke inside of him, his whole body trembled. "But decide, baby, because you sound so fucking hot right now, I want this ass."

"Smart-mouthed grad student," he grumbled, but then he gasped as I found his prostate and gave it a little nudge.

"That's *Doctor* San Angelo," I said with another nudge. "Tenure-track University Professor of Criminal Psychology to you, Nurse Creed." I removed my fingers, and he whimpered.

"Please, Roman. I need you."

I bit down on the side of his neck, and he shuddered. "I love it when you beg. Get those clothes off and get in bed. On your knees. Ass in the air. Wait for me."

Creed turned and gave me a wicked smile. "Yes, Professor." He stepped quickly toward the door, pulling off his shirt as he went inside. I watched him move, the light silhouetting his incredible body, and I sighed happily. We'd been through hell, but dammit, he was mine, and I was going to savor every moment I had with him.

My phone buzzed on the table next to the rocking chair. I'd almost forgotten it was there. By the time I picked it up, the call had gone to voicemail. I went inside the cabin and locked the door. I could see Creed struggling with his socks and shoes in the bedroom, so I went to the kitchen to grab us some waters from the fridge. When I closed the door, the phone dinged with a voicemail. I wanted Creed to have ample time to get ready for me so I listened to the message.

"Hello, Roman, it's Alistair Gardener. I confess that I've gotten this number by illicit methods, but it's very important that I speak to you. I have some information to share and another confession to make. I hope that once I make that confession, you'll still be willing to speak with me, because I need your help. It's not an emergency... yet, but... Please. Call me when you return to town. I'll look forward to speaking with you."

What a strange message. I was still frowning at the phone as I re-read the transcript when I walked into the bedroom.

"Presented as requested," Creed said, and I looked up from my phone.

He'd done exactly as I asked.

Alistair had said it wasn't an emergency, and I had a boyfriend to savor.

I dropped the phone on the nightstand with a clunk, and yanked off my shirt and sweatpants. "Are you comfortable, baby? Because I'm going to be here for a while." I knelt on the bed and spread his glutes.

Creed dropped his head onto his forearms and pushed his hips back. "I'm all yours, Professor."

Goddess, he was beautiful. And he was all mine.

Everything else could wait.

Stay Tuned for More...

If you enjoyed *Sundowners* and *Moonwish,* meet the Gifted...

The Gifted Series follows the students and staff of Havenhart Academy who are all victims of trauma who have developed a little something...extra. Explore a world where psychic powers are used to protect the vulnerable and battle evil.

Healer
Connection
Protector
More coming soon...

And if you want more queer paranormal romance, check out the Carnival of Mysteries series.
You Can Do Magic
You Can Save Me
Book Three coming September 2025

About the Author

Award-winning author and Bay Area native R.L. "Ro" Merrill (she/her) is an advocate for social justice, a sucker for rescue pets, and a spinner of compelling stories. A veteran public school educator, parent of two brilliant young adults, and wife of a patient collector and fellow bookworm, she was raised on a steady diet of eclectic music and campy horror. She writes quirky and relatable queer and heterosexual characters that know how to use their words and are willing to work hard for their happily ever afters. Readers who dig swoony contemporary romance or shivery supernatural suspense will find themselves right at home in her extensive catalog. Her books contain killer soundtracks, generous amounts of spice, and enough laughs to get readers out of their heads and into their feels. When she's not writing, you can find her cruising in her Bronco, adding to her vinyl and skull collections, or head-banging at a rock show. ***Stay Tuned for More...***

facebook.com/rlmerrillauthor

instagram.com/rlmerrillauthor

amazon.com/stores/R.L.-Merrill/author/B00PI6Q1LI

bsky.app/profile/Rlmerrillauthor.bsky.social

goodreads.com/rlmerrillauthor

bookbub.com/profile/r-l-merrill

Also by R.L. Merrill

Haunted Series: (Contemporary Romance)

Haunted

Fated

Bated

Jaded – (Coming Soon)

Minded Series: (Paranormal Spinoff of Haunted Series)

Minded

Blossomed

Father F'in' Christmas

A Peculiar Prom Night

Magic and Mayhem Universe: (Funny Paranormal Romance in the universe created by Robyn Peterman)

Shifted

Ghoul Me Once

Gator Me Twice

Magic and Mayhem/Shifted Collection

Fang Me Three Times

Fangtastic Four

Five Fanger Witch Punch

Hollywood Rock 'n' Romance Trilogy: (Contemporary Romance)

Teacher

Teacher: Act Two

Teacher: The Final Act

Contemporary Romance Series:

The Rock Season

Road Trip

You Fell First

The Heart Knows (Re-Releasing Spring 2025)

A Match Made in Spain

LGBTQ Romance

Pinups and Puppies (Originally in Love Is All Vol. 2)

I Want, More – Bolder Breed Studios #1 (Originally in Love Is All Vol. 3)

Love and Pride – Bolder Breed Studios #2 (Originally in Love Is All Vol. 4)

Everything's Better With You: An MM Sports Romance

All I Wanna Do — Bolder Breed Studios #3 (Email Ro for your copy)

Under His Sheets: Accidentally Undercover – Out April 9, 2024

Feuds and Interludes: Road To Rocktoberfest 2024 - November 2024

The Banes of Lake's Crossing (Historical Horror Romance)

The Fourth Man (The Banes of Lake's Crossing) (Historical Horror Romance)

The Redemption of Nathaniel Bane

<u>The Absolution of Jonah Bane</u>

The Gifted Series: (Supernatural Suspense/Paranormal Romance)

Healer

Connection

<u>Protector</u>

Sundowners (M/M Paranormal Romance

<u>Sundowners Book One</u>

Sundowners Book Two (February 13, 2025)

Forces of Nature Series: (Gay Contemporary Romance)

Hurricane Reese

Typhoon Toby

<u>Earthquake Ethan</u>

Summer of Hush Series: (Gay Contemporary Romance)

Summer of Hush

Brains and Brawn

Carnival of Mysteries: (Gay Paranormal Romance, connected to Summer of Hush series)

<u>You Can Do Magic: Carnival Of Mysteries </u>(Season One, Book One)

You Can Save Me: Carnival of Mysteries (Season Two, Book Two)

You Can Make Me: Carnival of Mysteries (Season Three, Book Three Out September 13, 2025)

Anthologies:

Thanksgiving Day Parade From Hell (Worst Holiday Ever) (Gay Contemporary Romance

Valentine's Day From Hell (Worst Valentine's Day Ever) (Gay Contemporary Romance)

Salty and Sweet (Summer Fair) (Lesbian Contemporary Romance)

The Fourth Man (The Banes of Lake's Crossing) (Historical Horror Romance)

A Piece of Him (Gone With The Dead) (Horror)

<u>Breaking Bread</u>—Dark Divinations from HorrorAddicts.net Press (Horror)

Exchange (Renewal) (Science Fiction)

Tap-Tap-Tap (Impact) (Horror)

Human Sacrifice (Innovation) (Horror)

The Sitter (Clarity) (Horror)

Joy Is A Phone Call Away – A More Perfect Union (Lesbian Contemporary Romance)

The House Must Fall – Haunts and Hellions from HorrorAddicts.net Press – May 2021 (Horror)

A Kept Woman – BAQWA Presents: Horror Show 2021(Lesbian Horror Romance)

Gods of Rock 'n' Roll (Free on Wattpad)

How Bittersweet is Karma? (Free on Wattpad)

Let Me Stand Next To Your Fire (Queer Cheer)

Midnight in the Renaissance Elevator

Holiday Romance

A Peace Offering (Re-release)

Love and Pride – Bolder Breed Studios #2

Once Upon A Goth Dog Solstice

Audiobooks

The Rock Season (Kiss App)

Brains and Brawn (Kiss App)

Teacher (Kiss App)

Hurricane Reese (Kiss App)

A Match Made in Spain (Audible)

Healer: Gifted Book One (Audible)

You Can Do Magic: Carnival of Mysteries (Audible)

You Can Save Me: Carnival of Mysteries (Coming to Audible Spring 2025)

Road Trip: A Rock ’n’ Romance Story (Audible)

You Fell First: A Rock ’n’ Romance Story (Coming Soon to Audible)

Under His Sheets (Audible Coming Soon)

Non-Fiction

Horror Addicts Guide To Life Volume 2 - Edited by Emerian Rich

Death’s Garden Revisited - Edited by Loren Rhoads (Out Fall 2022)

9 781953 433237